Driver

A golf novel

Tim Southgate

High Tee Press

Driver
A golf novel

First published in Great Britain 2002
by High Tee Press
83b Bath Road, Cheltenham GL53 7LH
www.highteepress.com

A CIP record for this title is available
from the British Library

ISBN 0 9543210 0 6

Printed and bound in Great Britain
by Biddles Ltd, Guildford, Surrey

To Lynda,
(who nagged me into it)

Acknowledgements
Many thanks to Peter, Robin, Claudine, Rosemarie
and John for reading the manuscript and for their
constructive suggestions and encouragement.
Thanks, too, to Robin for technical support
and to Claudine for lending a hand!

Driver

This book has eighteen chapters, each of which has three, four or five sections. The structure of the book therefore reflects the golf course described in the story. The names of the holes at Branfield Park, as shown on the back cover, serve also as chapter headings for the book.

Driver is a work of fiction. The characters and the locations described within it are entirely fictional.

The author

Tim Southgate is a former special school head teacher and administrator. He is also a keen (some might say compulsive) golfer. However, any resemblance to the leading character in this story is purely wishful thinking. Apart from playing golf, he and his wife now run a guest house.

Hole	Name	Yards	Par	Score
1	Hopeful	377	4	

1

The door closed and David sat back in his chair.

Well, there's nothing more I can do now, Tess, he said, to himself. Just have to wait and see. I hope I said all the right things. What they wanted to hear. They seemed happy enough but, I don't know, I'm not sure I really want the job, even if they decide they want me.

David looked across the room at the two other candidates. He wasn't too worried about the smartly dressed man with the patent shoes, strong after-shave and a selection of gold rings. Far too sharp and slick for this situation, David thought. More suited to an estate agency or, perhaps, as the thrusting manager of a doctors' practice.

The other chap, though, might be more the sort they'd go for. Tall and upright, David knew from talking to him over coffee that he was a retired military man.

If that Brigadier has his way, he'll get the job, all right, David thought. On the other hand, he is only a younger version of what they've had already. The retiring Secretary is ex-RAF and look at the mess he's landed them in.

The depressing thing is, how middle-aged they look. Yet, they're both about my age. Do I look as tired and worn-out as that, Tess? Some days, I admit I do feel pretty weary. Do I really want to take on the Club's problems? I'm not sure I've got the energy or the drive any more to sort out other people's messes. Yes, I can do the admin, no problem. But, it's all the other stuff. Dealing with people and all the conflicts between them. It's clear that most of that lot in there don't see eye-to-eye with that Brigadier and that he expects to have his say over almost everything.

Oh, Tess, if only you were here, to tell me what to do.

David longed for Tess so much, he ached.

1

But then, he thought, if Tess were here, he wouldn't be sitting here.

If Tess were here, his life would be so different. No, if Tess were here, his life would still be the same. But, because she was no longer part of his life, things were so different. If she were here, he wouldn't have had to give up his job as a headmaster. He wouldn't be feeling so lost. And, he wouldn't be sitting waiting to hear if he'd got the job of secretary of an almost insolvent golf club. He wouldn't be living celibate and alone, with hardly a soul to talk to all day. If Tess were still here, he would be busy, surrounded by colleagues, working hard and then going home to Tess in the evenings – and playing golf at the weekends.

Playing golf at the weekends.

It always hurt when he thought about it.

If only he hadn't spent so much time playing golf at the weekends. And during the week, too, whenever he could. Then, maybe he would have noticed how unwell Tess was looking; realised how tired she was feeling; would have got her to go to the doctors earlier. Then, maybe, Tess would still be here.

"I understand you no longer play golf, Mr Crowley?" the chairman of the interview panel had asked. "Too busy being a headmaster, I suppose!"

David had nodded and smiled.

But, he hadn't been too busy to play when he was a headmaster, had he? In fact, he'd been only too happy to play whenever anyone asked him. He'd worked so hard and played so much, he'd been too busy to notice that his wife was becoming seriously ill.

And, when the diagnosis came, he hadn't been too busy to play then, had he? During that last year or eighteen months, he had gone on playing golf. What was he hoping? That, if he just went on behaving as if everything was normal, everything would be normal? Or, was he just being

2

selfish, enjoying himself while his wife needed him? A bit of both, if he was honest.

But, he could hardly say that, could he?

"No, actually, I don't play golf any more because I played so much, I neglected my wife when she was dying of cancer."

Great conversation stopper that would be! He'd be sure to get the job, then, all right.

"Let's have Mr Crowley. He can cheer us all up telling us why he no longer plays golf!"

Oh, Tess. If only you were here, things would be so different.

David had uttered those sentiments so many times over the past three years.

He looked again at the other two men and knew that, if anything, he looked older than they did. He was only forty-eight but, living alone and without company, he'd become middle-aged almost without realising it.

He knew he had to change something. He didn't really need to work. He had his pension and the house was paid off when Tess died. But, he did need to do something to change his life before he became too old to do anything about it. He was a capable administrator, good with figures and accounts. And, he was computer-literate, although things changed so quickly that, when he talked computers with Ben, he already felt out-of-touch.

And, in spite of everything, he still loved golf. Not playing, perhaps, but he enjoyed talking golf, watching golf and reading about golf.

So, David thought, when he saw the advert in the local paper, why not become a golf club secretary?

Now, he was not so sure. He had vaguely thought that being a golf club secretary would be like being a headmaster, but without the children around and with lots of golfers, instead. Keeping accounts, taking minutes at meetings, chatting about golf to members over coffee. He

3

almost laughed out loud when he recalled the rosy picture he'd conjured up in his mind.

True, some of the job might be like being a headmaster. But, a lot of it would be precisely those bits of being a headmaster that he'd come to hate – the long hours and the conflicting demands. In school, he'd spent so much of his time trying to balance the wishes of teachers, parents, governors, the local authority and the government's inspectors, that he'd had no time left for the children.

Here, at Branfield Park, there were the old members, cocooned in their exclusive club. There were the new members he was supposed to recruit, and then there was 'the Bank', which was threatening to close the club down. And, of course, there was the Brigadier – Brigadier Tufnell – who was obviously used to having things all his own way. He'd had the retiring Secretary completely under his thumb and David could see problems ahead with him.

He could always withdraw.

Yes, he would withdraw.

He would explain that, following the interview, he'd realised that the job wasn't right for him and that he wasn't the right person for them. Thank you and goodbye.

Then, what?

Jobs he could actually do weren't exactly plastered all over the local paper, were they? Most of the adverts were asking for young dynamic types with experience he didn't have. Those jobs that weren't, could often be pretty boring. This was only the third job he had been for in three years, and he'd withdrawn from the other two following the interviews.

David knew he couldn't pull out of this one. There might never be another.

He considered the panel that had just interviewed him. They reminded David of his school governors. Indeed, several of them probably were school governors; well-meaning and more than a little out of their depth. The chairman had come across as very pleasant and earnest. Three of the other men were out of the same mould and were clearly not at one with the Brigadier, who'd tried to dominate the entire proceedings. The only woman on the panel, the Ladies Captain, did seem rather nice. Very attractive, actually. Well-dressed, with lovely, relaxed hair, David noticed, and a very warm way about her, too.

"Oh, I'm pretty used to working with women," he'd replied to her question. "Most of my staff in school were women – teachers, secretaries and dinner ladies. We men just had to learn to cope with them, I'm afraid."

He'd joked and she'd smiled warmly at his joke. She wore a wedding ring and David felt a twinge of envy for her husband, whoever he might be.

In the end, that was the most taxing question David had faced. No one had asked anything that would reveal whether he could actually do the job. He suspected that they would much rather have been out on the golf course and had all been 'volunteered' for the task of finding a new Secretary.

Collectively, they just want someone to come along and get them out of the mess they're in, thought David. And, that led to the real question to arise from the interview; the one he was asking himself.

Do I want it to be me?

2

The chairman closed the door and sat down. He took a sip of tea before he spoke.

'So, gentlemen and, er, lady,' he smiled at the Ladies Captain. 'Those are our three candidates. Now, we have to make a decision.'

'Not a lot to choose from, is there?' Bill Ellery called out. Bill was a local architect who had been a member of the Club Committee for several years.

There was a general murmur of agreement from the others on the panel.

'We had only four applicants, and one of those withdrew before we could even invite him for interview,' the chairman explained.

Giles Southern was clearly not enjoying his role. Until recently, when he'd been elected Captain of the Club, his only involvement had been playing golf and enjoying a drink in the bar afterwards. Now, he and his colleagues were faced with some painful realities. As senior partner in a local firm of accountants, the other members had pressed him to help them save their club.

'Well, we may not have many to choose from, but I think the choice is obvious.'

When Brigadier Henry Tufnell spoke, the muttering ceased immediately.

'It is clear to me that Major Savage is the most, indeed the only, suitable candidate. I propose we vote on the matter without further delay.'

The chairman had fully expected the Brigadier to try to steamroller through his own choice for Secretary and he therefore played for time.

'I think we should discuss each candidate more fully before we attempt to arrive at a decision. After all, each has his merits.'

'The others have their merits, I'm sure,' the Brigadier replied. 'But, only Major Savage has the necessary experience and the right background for this position. I took the liberty of having a chat with his Commanding Officer. He told me that Savage is an absolutely first rate chap who will understand the needs of the members here; the way we think.'

'Forgive me, Brigadier,' Giles said. 'I'm sure the Major is a very agreeable person, but it isn't only the present members that we have to think about. We have had the situation explained to us very clearly. The Club's finances

6

are in a parlous state. The income from members' subscriptions is nowhere near sufficient to meet the running costs. We are near the limit of our overdraft and we have a number of outstanding bills that we shall only be able to pay with the indulgence of our bank manager.'

'Thank God the bank manager's a member!' Frank Partridge joked.

The others laughed to ease the tension.

'Yes. Thank God,' the chairman continued, wearily. 'Unfortunately, while God may have given us the game of golf, He is not known to be a golfer and we can only guess at the extent of His understanding. In short, the auditors tell us that, unless we recruit more members – and a lot more members – the Club will become insolvent within a year.'

'Yes, I quite understand all that,' the Brigadier interrupted. 'I accept that we need some increase in the membership. But, that's precisely why we need someone like Savage, to ensure that we get only the right sort of people.'

'We may not have that luxury, Brigadier,' the chairman went on. 'At least six new golf clubs have opened within a ten mile radius, and most of the 'right sort' of people have already joined those. They might have joined Branfield, had they not been left sitting on the waiting list for so long.'

'We have to very careful who we admit,' the Brigadier responded. 'This club has an excellent reputation and the members need to feel comfortable with whom they are playing or drinking in the bar.'

The discussion was getting nowhere and the chairman decided to move it on.

'Well, I suggest we consider each candidate in turn and see if we arrive at the same conclusion as the Brigadier. What did people think of Mr Bushnell, first of all?'

'Very capable,' said Peter Wilshire. 'Had all the right qualifications on paper.'

'Very sharp,' Frank Partridge agreed. 'But, a bit too sharp, if you ask me. I think he might find our little club rather small for his ambitions.'

'Yes, I don't think he would stay with us long.'

'Well, I think he's got a bit of black in him,' the Brigadier chimed in.

The others fell silent.

'Well, really, Henry! That's a dreadful thing to say.'

Kate Earnshaw had not, thus far, expressed an opinion. However, the racism implied by the Brigadier's comment had clearly angered the Ladies Captain.

'It may or may not be the case that Mr Bushnell has some foreign blood in his veins. Personally, I don't care as long as he's the right person for this job. That sort of prejudice is precisely the reason the Club is in such a mess.'

'I'm sorry, Kathryn.' The Brigadier was suddenly on the defensive. 'I merely meant that someone from a different background might not have the sort of understanding of our culture... I mean, they might not feel as at home in our company...'

The chairman let the Brigadier dig himself into his hole for a few moments more. The old boy's credibility was damaged and Giles Southern seized the initiative.

'And, then there is Mr Crowley. A former headmaster. Very experienced. Excellent admin background. He's clearly had a lot of practice dealing with people and he even knows how to operate a computer. The auditor tells me that Branfield Park is the only club he has come across that doesn't have a computer!'

'I thought he was very sound, if a little nervous,' Frank Partridge chimed in.

'He's probably more used to interviewing than being interviewed,' Giles said. 'I was most impressed with the quiet way he dealt with questions. He's clearly a very good listener.'

'Well, I liked him very much,' Kate said.

'So did I,' said Bill Ellery. 'If we're going to attract new members, a lot of them won't have experienced the sort of behaviour expected on a golf course. His headmaster skills might come in very handy!'

'Especially, if we attract a lot of young players and juniors,' Simon Cornwell suggested. 'They're the ones we really need if the Club is going to thrive in the longer term.'

The old doctor had hardly uttered a word until now and he spoke slowly and quietly.

'I think Mr Crowley is a very suitable person for this position. What's more, I think he needs the job as much as we need him. I'm not sure that's true of the other two candidates.'

'What do you mean, Simon?' the chairman asked.

'Well,' the old man replied. 'He retired from his post as a headmaster at a very young age. That suggests he took retirement on grounds of ill health, probably because of stress. We all know the sorts of stresses teachers are under these days. He has probably not found the adjustment easy. True, he has a pension, but he is young and he needs to work for his own self-esteem, if nothing else. I don't suppose there are many jobs suitable for retired headmasters. This position could make use of all his skills, both technical and personal, and also offer the sort of responsibility he is used to. I believe that Mr Crowley can help us out of the undoubted mess in which we find ourselves. At the same time, we can help Mr Crowley find his feet again.'

'That's very perceptive, Simon,' Kate said, and she smiled at the old man. 'You're quite a softy really, aren't you.'

Simon smiled back and blushed slightly.

'Well, I must say, I am not at all convinced he's the right man for the job.'

The Brigadier was not yet ready to surrender.

'While it may be the case that Mr Crowley has some of the skills required, his background is rather different from that of most of the members here. Had he been a headmaster in the private sector, perhaps he would be more suitable. However, dealing with the staff and pupils in a comprehensive school hardly qualifies one for the management of an exclusive golf club. After all, a comprehensive school, as I understand it, admits anyone who wishes to attend. We would certainly not wish him to admit anyone who applied to become a member here!'

'As I said, Brigadier, we may not have that luxury.'

The chairman was determined not to lose the initiative.

'It is because our present Secretary has exercised such poor control over the finances, and such tight control over who can become a member that we find ourselves in our present situation.'

'Flight Lieutenant Oakley has always kept very clear books and he can hardly be blamed if we are not attracting enough members.'

The Brigadier knew that criticism of the retiring Secretary was an implied attack on him.

'Of course, he couldn't,' said the chairman.

Of course he couldn't, the old lap dog, thought Giles. The Flight Lieutenant had always been most courteous. He'd shown prospective members round the clubhouse, introduced them to existing members and even arranged introductory rounds of golf. He had provided application forms and, when these were completed and returned, he had discussed them with the Brigadier. And, it was the Brigadier who indicated those who should be consigned to a long and discouraging period on the waiting list.

As time went by, so his criteria for 'the sort of people the Club needs' became increasingly stringent. Many more people had been sidelined on to the waiting list and, as waiting times increased, the Club had gained a reputation for inaccessibility. People began applying elsewhere and, in recent years, applications for membership had dwindled almost to nothing.

Brigadier Henry Tufnell had been a member himself since he was a boy. His father, 'the old General', had introduced his sons to the game while they were still at prep school and all three had become excellent golfers. Moreover, they had become excellent members, serving on various committees, holding different offices and representing the Club in competitions.

As they had grown older, they'd developed an almost proprietorial interest in Branfield Park and had become used to exercising considerable control over its affairs. Guy and Robert were both now dead, but Henry – the Brigadier – had consolidated his hold in recent years. Only the shock-horror conclusions of the auditor's report had finally persuaded the other members of the Committee to stand together and demand that changes be made.

Branfield Park was not a privately owned golf club, run to provide a profit for its shareholders and little say for its members. Rather, it was a members' club, owned and operated, in theory, by the members for the members' benefit. Some older members' clubs have Masonic roots and many are still controlled by a coterie of influential members. At Branfield, this inner core comprised Brigadier Henry Tufnell and a few of his cronies.

'And, another thing,' the Brigadier went on. 'Mr Crowley isn't married. I believe that to be a great disadvantage in a Secretary. He would, for instance, have no one to accompany him to Club functions.'

'Were we interviewing for the position of Conservative member of parliament,' the chairman interrupted, 'I can see we might be interested in his marital situation. I understand that he was married at one time but I don't see what business it is of ours.'

The Brigadier was not to be deflected.

'Well, he might be something of a distraction to the lady members.'

'Oh, for God's sake, Henry!' Kate laughed. 'You're not really suggesting that our ladies wouldn't feel safe if we appointed an unmarried man as Secretary? You're surely not serious?'

'Perhaps not, Kathryn, but I believe it is a factor we must consider. I understand that Mr Crowley is also a very fine golfer,' the Brigadier continued. 'That too can be a great disadvantage, in my experience. A golf club Secretary's role is to serve the members, not to be out playing with them all the time.'

'I hardly think we can hold it against Mr Crowley that he is good at the very sport we all enjoy so much.'

The chairman was becoming irritated with the Brigadier's seemingly endless list of objections. This was how the old blighter worked. When he couldn't win by frontal assault, he lay siege until the opposition faded away.

'Anyway, I gather he no longer plays,' Bill Ellery came to the rescue. 'He told me so over lunch, so it's not really an issue.'

'Right!' the chairman exclaimed. 'If no-one else has any objections, I really think we should try to come to a decision.'

The panel went on discussing the merits or otherwise of the three men for a further half an hour. The Brigadier fought valiantly for his favoured candidate, but support for the Major fell away sharply when someone noticed on his application form that he was "willing to attend a course to learn how to use a computer."

There never was much support for poor Mr Bushnell; he was rather too sharp and slick for their tastes.

And, that left David. That isn't to say they thought him the least unsuitable candidate. All, except the Brigadier, liked him and felt he was right for the post. It was simply that there was a little bit of the unknown about him. Why

12

had he retired so young? Why did he live alone? Why had he given up playing golf? They all liked David Crowley, but there was something about him that left questions hanging in the air. Perhaps, they would find the answers. Perhaps, the answers didn't matter. Clearly, they had no choice but to take a chance. The vote, when they took it, was five in favour and one, the Brigadier, against.

'Let's get him in and offer him the job, then,' the chairman said, moving to the door.

3

'Thank you very much,' David replied.

The Brigadier had gone outside and closed the door. Probably, the others had asked him to break the bad news to the unsuccessful candidates. More likely, they wanted him out of the room.

'So, you will take it on?' Frank Partridge almost pleaded.

David was about to explain that, while grateful for their offer, he should like time to think it over. That way, he thought, when he got home he could always withdraw on the telephone. It was easier to do that. However, when he surveyed the five eager faces, his resolution began to fail.

'Well, I, er, I honestly hadn't expected to be your first choice,' David lied. 'But, if you really feel that I can help take the Club forward.' He stopped, realising he was lapsing into 'local-authority-speak'.

'We all, the five of us, feel that you have just the experience and expertise we need, at this moment,' the chairman said.

The others chimed in with similar words of encouragement.

'Please, do say you'll take it on, Mr Crowley.' Kate's plea was decisive. The others, David might have resisted.

But, when the Ladies Captain's hazel eyes looked straight into his own, his defences collapsed.

'Well, er, yes, I should be pleased to accept your offer. Thank you very much for your confidence.'

'Excellent! When will you be able to start?' The chairman beamed and looked around at the others. 'You've heard about our rather difficult situation, Mr Crowley. I think I can safely say that time is of the essence.'

'I do have a few things to attend to,' David lied again. In reality, he was playing for time. However, he was pretty sure he was going to need a few days to adjust to the idea of getting up and going to work each morning.

'It's the fifteenth, today. Can I suggest that I start on the first of September?'

The chairman looked momentarily disappointed before he agreed to David's suggested date. He stood and shook David's hand and the others did the same.

'We're very pleased, Mr Crowley,' Bill Ellery said.

'And, very relieved, too,' Kate said, smiling warmly and shaking his hand. 'I'm sure it's going to work out very well.'

4

David drove away from the Club and home through winding country lanes. It was late afternoon and a bright, August day was drawing to a close.

After about five miles, when he felt he'd travelled far enough to be sure no one from the Club would pass by, he pulled the Renault into a field gateway and turned off the engine.

David climbed out and leaned against the five barred gate. Quite suddenly, he felt his stomach begin to heave and he recognised the warning. During his final years at the school, he'd suffered continuous nausea and headaches brought on by tension and stress. When the stress had become too much, perhaps after a staff meeting or a particularly tense encounter with a parent, he would often be physically sick. Usually, the sensation he now felt had been the precursor; an early warning. He closed his eyes and leaned back against the gate, breathing slowly until, gradually, the feeling subsided. He opened his eyes and returned to the car.

His shirt was soaked with sweat. Opening the door, David removed his jacket and threw it on to the back seat. Then, he smiled. If he did take the job, he'd have to resurrect all his old work clothes – suits, jackets, trousers and shoes. He'd become so used to casual clothes over the past few years and he wondered if they would still fit.

'Well, we've done it now, Tess.'

He spoke the words aloud. If he looked out of the driver's window and talked to Tess, he could almost feel her sitting next to him in the passenger seat. Sometimes, he half expected her to reply. It was one reason why he'd resisted when Ben had pressed him to change the car.

Ben. He'd intended to drive home and then tell Ben about the interview. Give himself time to think before he told anyone else. Once he told someone else, he knew he would feel committed. David wasn't sure he was ready yet to be committed.

On impulse, though, he took out his mobile phone and punched in Ben's number.

'They've offered me the job, Ben.'

'Which one, Dad?'

There was only one! How could Ben forget which one? The young are always so busy with their own lives. Things that seem so important to the older generation pass them by with hardly a thought.

'The golf club Secretary at Branfield Park. You remember, the club that's almost broke.'

'Oh, yeah. That's great, Dad! It'll be really good for you to get out; do something useful. Use your skills, as they say.'

'I don't know if I really want it, Ben.'

'Well, turn it down then.'

'But, I've already accepted.'

'No turning back then, Dad. Well, you can always leave if you don't like it. It'll be good for you to get out of the house and play some golf again.'

'I'm not going to play golf, Ben. Just run a golf club.'

'Whatever. It'll be fine, Dad. Mum would be pleased.'

'You think so.'

'Yeah. She wouldn't want you sitting around doing nothing all day. Anyway, Dad, great news! Gotta go now. Speak to you soon.'

The car was quiet again.

Of course, Ben was right,

It was no big deal if he got a new job. So, why did it feel like such a big deal?

David had to admit that part of him, if not actually scared was, well, nervous. He hadn't worked for three years. During that time, he'd taken responsibility for nothing more complicated than getting the car serviced or mowing the lawn.

Now, because he'd applied for this job, he was going to have to take on responsibility again. He would have to get up and go to work each morning. That, he thought he could manage, with a little practice! Once again, however, he would be the focus of other people's hopes and expectations. And, perhaps, the butt of their anger.

David had wanted time to think; to decide if he really wanted all that again. But, now he'd told Ben. Now, he couldn't back out, not without having to explain to Ben.

David recalled a recent conversation with his son.

"You see, Ben, in life, there are foot soldiers and officers. Foot soldiers are happy to leave decisions to other

16

people. They might complain about decisions, once they are taken. They might ridicule the decision-makers. But, in truth, they really don't want the responsibility for taking decisions. Basically, they don't want responsibility *per se*. Sensibly, some might say, they prefer to be part of the team; to leave work behind when they go home; to enjoy the remainder of their lives."

"Yeah, yeah, Dad." Ben had laughed at his father's notion.

"Officers take responsibility," David had persisted. "They seek responsibility. They enjoy responsibility. Some see it as their duty. They don't particularly like the long hours or the isolation, but they accept it in return for the buzz that comes with being responsible."

"Jesus, Dad! That's the most reactionary, elitist rubbish I've ever heard." Ben never minced his words but, in spite of what he'd said, David had always seen his son as, potentially, an officer.

He had always seen himself as an officer, too. He would never acknowledge it, of course, but David's view of the world and of his own place in it was not a million miles from that of Brigadier Henry Tufnell.

It's a responsibility, he thought. A lot of problems, but someone has to do it.

So, he would have to do it.

Hole	Name	Yards	Par	Score
2	A Head Start	**498**	**5**	

1

David spent the next couple of weeks sorting through his wardrobe; trying on suits, jackets, trousers and shirts he hadn't worn for several years. He'd put on a bit of flab but fortunately not enough to require any major alterations. Ben was home from university and offered his opinion when David asked if his jacket was too tight.

'It is a bit small for you, Dad. But it's not just the fit, it's the style. The jacket, and those ties, they make you look so, so middle-aged!'

'Thanks, Ben. You really know how to build up a person's confidence, don't you?'

'Only trying to help, Dad,' Ben said, grinning. 'You wouldn't want to turn up looking like a seedy old teacher, would you?'

'Perhaps, I am a seedy old teacher.'

They'd laughed at this and Ben had suggested they go into town to choose a new blazer and some ties. It was the first time they had been shopping together since Ben was a little boy and, on the way home, they stopped at a pub for supper.

Improved nutrition was one of the many changes in David's life since he had taken early retirement. As a headmaster, he'd never had time for breakfast, rarely stopped for lunch and was often too tired to eat supper. Like many managers, he apparently survived, even thrived, on adrenaline and an intravenous supply of caffeine. Now that he had more time, he would eat his breakfast slowly over the morning paper, enjoy a snack lunch listening to the mid-day news and usually consume supper in front of the television. True, his waistline had expanded but this he could accommodate, having always been on the thin side of slim. More depressing, though, was the fact that he almost always ate alone.

During one of his dressing-up sessions, David tried on the dark suit he had worn at Tess's funeral. In the inside pocket he found the *Order of Service*, a discovery that left him in a crumpled heap for the rest of the day. Partly, it was the memories flooding back that caused him so much distress. But, it was also the guilt and sense of loss he felt when he realised that, during all his preparations, Tess had slipped unnoticed to the back of his mind. He'd wanted to talk to Ben about it but somehow it hadn't seemed the right time.

The first day in a new job is always a nervous affair. A good initial impression is crucial, but creating the right image is as important for the new boss as it is for the new clerical assistant. David wore his new blue blazer and a crisp white shirt. In the mirror, he surveyed the bright colours of his silk tie, bought with Ben's encouragement. He had to admit it made him look very smart, although he wasn't sure it was quite 'him'. "It certainly makes a Statement!" Tess would have said.

Giles Southern beamed as he greeted David in the entrance hall.

'Good morning, Mr Crowley,' said Giles, extending his hand.

'David, please.'

Their small talk about the weather and the state of the roads continued for some minutes before Giles led David into the Secretary's office.

'Good morning, Margaret. This is Mr Crowley, our new Secretary. David, let me introduce your assistant, Margaret Kearney, a tower of strength and the soul of discretion.' Giles was a gentle, polite man who clearly took great pains to treat everyone the same.

Margaret stood up and smiled modestly at the Club Captain. A shy, slim woman in her early forties, she spoke softly.

'It's very nice to meet you, Mr Crowley. If there's anything you need to know, I'll try to help all I can.'

'I'm sure I shall need all the help I can get,' David replied.

'Margaret has been with us for, how long is it, Margaret?'

'Seven years,' Margaret smiled, straight dark hair framing her bespectacled face. 'Seven long years.'

'Phil couldn't have managed without her, I know that,' Giles continued.

'Oh, I don't know,' Margaret blushed. 'We helped each other, really. Would you like a cup of coffee, before you start?'

Giles hesitated. 'No, I think, if you don't mind, David, we'll take a quick tour of the place first. I'll introduce you to everybody then bring you back here for coffee. After that, I shall have to dash, I'm afraid. Something's come up at the office, my office that is, and I have to be away by eleven o'clock.'

They left Margaret and climbed the stairs to the bar. The steward, John Hall, a jovial, portly man with a large moustache, was polishing glasses. Hearing voices, his wife, Sarah, an equally large, round and red-faced woman in her fifties, emerged from the kitchen.

'Sarah creates the most wonderful meals,' Giles explained. 'Sunday lunch, especially, is not to be missed.'

'Thank you, Mr Southern. We aim to please.' She smiled and led the way through into the kitchen. Over the range a plaque read, "NEVER TRUST A SKINNY COOK." On that basis alone, David thought, Mrs Hall seemed to qualify as trustworthy.

They walked through into the dining room where the tables enjoyed a panoramic view over the course.

20

'Will you be taking lunch in here, Mr Crowley?' asked Mrs Hall. 'Flight Lieutenant Oakley always liked his lunch.'

'I hadn't thought about it,' David replied, although now he did think about it, it seemed a rather attractive idea. He wouldn't have to cook in the evenings and, with luck, he might even find people with whom he could share his lunch.

'The members would appreciate it, I'm sure,' Giles said. 'But, be careful, you do need some time to yourself.'

After a brief chat with John Hall, the pair toured the rest of the building – the bar, the ladies' lounge, the committee rooms, the changing rooms and the stores – before crossing the yard to the greenkeeper's barn. An array of mowers, tractors, trailers and other equipment was visible and David could tell immediately that not one of the items was the current model.

'Pretty antiquated gear, isn't it?' Bob Morgan, the head greenkeeper, was standing in a doorway. A big man, with the tan of one who spends his time working in the open air, he smiled as they approached.

'It still does the job, but I won't say life wouldn't be easier with something a bit more modern,' Bob explained in a broad Welsh voice.

'Why haven't you replaced some of it?' asked David. 'Surely, it would be more efficient?'

'Course it would,' Bob agreed. 'Trouble is, old Oakley always said the Club didn't have the money.'

'He was probably right, there,' Giles broke in. 'David, let me introduce Bob Morgan, our head greenkeeper. Believe me, Bob does wonders with what equipment he does have here.'

Bob explained the various items of machinery and promised to keep pestering David about replacements. The Captain and the Secretary left the barn and walked back across the yard to the professional's shop.

David had been in plenty of golf professional's shops in his time. Usually, they were packed with equipment – golf clubs, trolleys, umbrellas, shoes and clothing. This shop, however, looked decidedly run down.

Behind the counter, a buxom young woman was serving a customer. As the man walked away, she closed the till and looked up.

'Hello, Mr Southern. Jack's out on the range giving a lesson at the moment.' She spoke with a soft West Midlands accent and, David thought, looked rather sullen.

'Well, in that case, we won't disturb him. David, this is Alison, Jack's shop assistant. Alison, this is Mr Crowley, our new Secretary.'

Giles was clearly not sure how to respond to her.

'Tell Jack we called in, would you, Alison?'

'You can catch up with Jack yourself later,' Giles explained, as he led the way out of the shop and back towards the office. 'He's a first rate chap but it's very difficult for him here. With so few members, he doesn't sell much in the way of clothing or equipment. Not that many people take lessons, either, so he finds it hard to make ends meet.'

It's the same story everywhere you turn, David thought.

The two men said 'hello' again to Margaret, and passed through into the Secretary's office. A few minutes later, while Margaret served them coffee, they sat in easy chairs either side of the gas fire.

'Well, David, as you can see, things are in a pretty sorry state. The greenkeeper is using equipment out of the ark, the professional has nothing to sell and no-one to teach and you don't even have a computer to work on. Have you changed your mind, yet?' Giles was smiling, but it was a rather nervous smile.

'Let's just say, I can see it will be a challenge,' David smiled in reply. 'But, as long as everyone wants to see things improve, I'm sure we can work together to take the Club forward…'

David was becoming aware that he was sounding like the thrusting young manager he'd once been when Giles interrupted him.

'Yes, well, we're all are behind you. Everyone wants to see things improve and you can be assured of our full support. There's only one person who might not, er, shall we say, embrace change as enthusiastically as the rest of us.'

'The Brigadier?' David asked.

'Ah! You noticed he wasn't quite, as they say, on board?'

'It wasn't difficult,' David smiled. 'I've met a few Brigadiers in my time.'

'Oh, once Brigadier Tufnell understands the position and you explain to him what has to be done to get the Club back on its feet, I'm certain he will support you in whatever you have to do.'

Giles had never sounded less certain about anything.

'As long as I have the support of the Committee,' David said, with more than a hint of a question in his voice.

'Oh, you do! You really do! We're all on your side.'

Giles stood up hurriedly.

'Well, I must be going. I'll leave you in Margaret's capable hands. We'll talk later in the week.' He shook David's hand, turned and walked through into the outer office, said goodbye to Margaret and was gone.

2

The Secretary's office was larger than David had expected and quite a bit larger than the office he had occupied as headmaster of a large comprehensive school. Public sector puritanism ensures that managers rarely enjoy comfortable or spacious surroundings. It is as if anything

23

more than the bare necessities might go to the manager's head and, at the same time, offend the sensibilities of the managed.

First, the desk. Not here the familiar teak veneer and steel legs job so beloved of office furniture suppliers. No, the desk behind which successive Branfield Secretaries had sat was huge, solid mahogany and topped with an ingrained leather writing surface. True, it had seen better days but, as David leaned back in his leather swivel chair, he had to admit, he hadn't seen much better.

Although large, the desk did not seem out of place in this huge room. His school office had had barely enough space for a desk and two small Ercol easy chairs. Here, there was an old leather Chesterfield settee and two matching armchairs, set around a coffee table before a fireplace with a gas fire. Against the far wall was a large refectory table, suitable for laying out paperwork.

David smiled to himself. If you had to fall from grace, here was as comfortable a place to land as any.

A gentle knock on the door disturbed his contemplation.

'Coffee?' Margaret asked, as she placed the streaming mug on the desk. 'Finding your way around? If there's anything you need, just ask.'

'I was just thinking what a grand office it is,' David replied.

'The furniture all belonged to old General Tufnell, the Brigadier's father, so Phil reckoned. He gave it to the Club years ago when the Brigadier was a boy.'

'It must be worth a good deal, now. Are you drinking coffee?' David asked.

'Yes, mine's outside.'

'Like to bring it in, then we can have a chat,' David smiled.

Margaret returned warily. David motioned her to sit alongside the desk and she did so, shorthand pad at the ready.

24

'Don't worry. I'm not about to start dictating letters. I thought we should have a chat about the work. I'm the new boy here, so why don't you start by telling me about your job.'

Margaret put down her pad and took a sip of coffee.

'My job? Well, I just do whatever I'm given, really. I type letters; I answer the phone; I keep the books; I work out the wages. And,' she smiled, 'I make the coffee.'

'Good Lord!' David exclaimed. 'That sounds a lot. So, what do I do?'

Margaret laughed.

'Oh, there are letters to dictate, cheques to sign, people to see. You'll find there are plenty of problems here for you to handle. The members always like the Secretary to sort things out for them. Just keeping the Brigadier happy will take up enough of your time. Which reminds me, he'll be here in a few minutes.'

'The Brigadier? He's coming to see me?' David was puzzled.

'Oh yes. He comes in every Monday morning at eleven o'clock. He and Phil had a regular meeting.'

'They did? What did they talk about?'

'Well, I wasn't there, of course. But, I gather Phil would tell the Brigadier everything that was going on and the Brigadier would give him his orders for the week. I know they would go through the applications for membership – Phil always asked me to get them ready. He would give them back to me after the meeting marked 'OK' or 'NO', and I would type out letters telling people they could or could not become members.'

'And, are there any applications today?' David enquired.

'Oh no. Haven't been any for months. I think people have got the message. It's harder to get in here than the Bank of England, if you ask me. Anyway, since that new course opened near Bourton, they've all gone there.'

'But, why did the Brigadier come in every week. After all, he hasn't been the Club Captain for several years, as I understand it.'

David thought he already knew the answer.

'No, but that doesn't mean anything. The Brigadier thinks he still runs the Club. The others – Mr Southern and the rest of the Committee – they don't like it but they won't stand up to him. That's why they've got you in, I reckon.'

'I see,' David said slowly.

'So, you see,' Margaret smiled brightly as she got to her feet. 'There's plenty for you to do.'

She picked up the mugs and went out. She certainly wasn't a pretty woman, David thought. Her dress was very plain and did nothing for her. Nevertheless, she had a warm, open smile and a soft voice and he knew immediately that he was going to enjoy working with Margaret.

David sat back and breathed deeply. During the interview, of course, he'd been aware of differences between the Brigadier and the Committee. What he hadn't recognised before was the extent of the discord between them. Nor had he appreciated that both camps expected him to side with them. He was already beginning to feel as if he were back in school. It was being in the middle of just this sort of conflict that he always found most stressful.

3

'The Brigadier's here to see you, Mr Crowley,' Margaret announced over the telephone.

'Oh, right. Send him in, will you please, Margaret.'

David stood up and approached the door but, before he could reach it, the Brigadier strode into the room. He was bigger than David remembered and his voice was strong. So, too, was his grasp of David's outstretched hand.

'Morning, Crowley. Settled in? Good! Soon get the hang of things. Any problems, ask Margaret. Knows the place backwards, she does. Marvellous woman!'

David pointed to a chair, but the Brigadier was already heading for it anyway. In his green cord trousers, check shirt and cravat, he looked every inch the retired military officer he was.

'Won't keep you too long. First day, and all that. Need to find your way around, I expect.'

David dived in.

'What can I do for you, Brigadier?'

'It's what I can do for you, dear boy,' the Brigadier replied. 'I'm here to support you.'

'Support me, Brigadier?'

'Yes, of course, dear boy.' The Brigadier leaned forward with a conspiratorial smile. 'Look, those blighters on the Committee – Southern and the rest – they're a well-meaning bunch, of course, but they don't understand the Club the way I do. Been here man and boy. My father set the first course record back in 'fifty-three. Took me years before I could better it. My sixty-eight still stands today. Peters has done a sixty-seven, but then, he's a professional, of course.'

'Sixty-eight? That's very impressive, Brigadier,' David smiled, thinking it best to get the old boy on his side.

'Couldn't do it now, of course. Still play off five, mind you. I gather you have a single figure handicap, Crowley?'

'Did, Brigadier. I no longer play, I'm afraid.'

'Pity. Still, at least you understand the game. Damned important that. Lot of tradition to uphold. Can't let people muck around with tradition. Don't you agree?'

David was beginning to feel like he was under fire as the Brigadier launched into another salvo of short, sharp sentences.

27

'Tradition is important, Brigadier, of course. But, it's important to move with the times; to adapt. I know the Committee feel…'

'That's where you need my support, m'boy. I'm not against change, far from it. But, there's change and there's change. Some of the ideas the Committee have been talking about recently could wreck this Club. Change it beyond recognition. Then, where would we be? No, that's where you and I have to work together to ensure that only the right changes are made. D'you see what I mean?'

'I think so, Brigadier.' David could see what he meant, all right. 'Just how do you see that working? I mean, if the Committee ask me to do something, I must obviously carry out their instructions.'

'Of course, dear boy, of course! It's how you carry them out, that's what's important. And, that's where I come in. Oakley and I had a meeting every Monday morning. You and I will do the same. We'll talk over any proposals the Committee may have made, any 'matters arising' as it were, and decide how best they should be dealt with.'

'Every Monday, Brigadier?' David groaned inside at the very thought.

'To start with, anyway, until you find your feet. There are important matters in the air and we need to be ready to deal with them. This notion of letting in a lot of new members, for instance. Very dangerous, that. Could ruin the Club. Got to be ready to outflank them on that one.'

'How do you propose we go about that, Brigadier?' David asked.

'Same as we always have, laddie. Same as we always have. You collect up the applications and we go through them together on a Monday morning. You won't know any of the applicants, of course, so I'll have to let you know who is or isn't suitable.'

'I see, Brigadier.'

David spoke slowly to give himself time to phrase his next point.

'But, as I understand it, the Club has to recruit new members, and a substantial number of new members, in order to remain viable.'

'Stuff and nonsense!' the Brigadier snorted. 'Accountants' jargon, that's all that is. This club has been here since I was a boy and it will be here long after I'm gone. It may be that we need to admit a few new people, carefully selected, of course. On the other hand, there is no possibility of me agreeing to some wholesale recruiting drive among the populace. That would alter the Club completely. It would be an absolute disaster and I will not allow it!'

David realised that there was little point arguing with the old boy. You don't stop a tank by standing up in front of it. Nor do you lie down and let it run over you. The sensible course is to step to the side and let it pass, deal with it from the side or the rear. That's how he would handle the Brigadier.

'I'm sure we can avoid a disaster, Brigadier, if we all work together. I suggest we look at any proposals once the Committee has come up with them. Wait and see, I think that's the best approach.'

'That might work in a school, my boy, but you can't wait and see when you're fighting a war. You need intelligence. I've got my spies. They keep me informed, don't you worry. Then, you need to plan your strategy and carry it out ruthlessly, if you intend to win.'

'We're hardly fighting a war, Brigadier.' The older man's language worried David. He didn't like the feeling that he'd been dropped behind enemy lines.

'Maybe not a war, but certainly a battle,' the Brigadier replied. 'A battle for the soul of this golf club, Crowley, nothing less. I don't want to fight with anybody, but if I have to do so, I shall. And, I shall fight to win!'

29

The Brigadier got to his feet and towered over David. Then, suddenly, he smiled and ran his hand along the top of the desk.

'This was my grandfather's desk, y'know. All this furniture came from his house when he died back in sixty-eight. Beautiful old desk.'

'It's a very attractive office,' David agreed, standing to show the Brigadier out. 'I'm beginning to feel at home already.'

'Good. Good! Well, must be off. Got a fourball to play this afternoon. We'll meet again next Monday, all right? In the meantime, I'll keep my ear to the ground and you do the same. The better we're prepared, the better we can deal with whatever ideas they come up with. Good day, Crowley.'

And, with that, the Brigadier opened the door and departed. David heard him speaking to Margaret for a moment, then the office became quiet again.

'Coffee?' Margaret smiled round the door.

'Oh, yes please, Margaret,' David said. 'Better make it a strong one.'

He sat down and stared at the chair the Brigadier had vacated.

'Well, Tess. What do you think of him? He's a tough nut, all right, if ever there was one. I really think the old Brigadier is relishing the thought of a last ditch battle to save golf club civilisation as he knows it.'

He wasn't in the car and he didn't any more expect Tess to reply. Over the past few weeks, as he'd geared himself up once more for work, David had begun to feel more and more disengaged from Tess. She was daily becoming more a treasured memory rather than a felt presence.

He breathed in deeply. The daily battles in school had eventually brought him down. David had hated them at the time. But, now it was different. Maybe, there would be battles ahead. This time, however, they weren't his battles.

30

He smiled. This time, at least, he wasn't going to let them bring him down.

4

For the next hour, David explored his new office. The desk drawers alone were a golf archaeologist's paradise. Old scorecards, trophies, photographs, minute books, tees, golf balls, pitch mark repairers filled every corner.

'Keeping a tidy desk obviously wasn't Flight Lieutenant Oakley's strong point,' David joked.

'No, he isn't the tidiest of men,' Margaret laughed. Then, as if she had been disloyal. 'But, he is a lovely man. Always very kind and polite.'

David noticed that she used the present tense.

'You clearly enjoyed working with him?'

'He's a lovely man, like I say. He let me do things the way I thought best; gave me a lot of responsibility. I enjoyed that. Made it a pleasure to come to work. That's something my Tom will never understand.'

'Tom?'

'My husband. He can't see why I want to come to work at all. Says he can buy all the things I need. And, maybe he can. But, there's more to life than buying things. I like coming to work because, doing my job here, talking to all these people, it makes me feel like I'm a real person.'

'And, you wouldn't feel that at home?' David enquired, although he didn't mean to pry.

'Not if I had to stay there all day, I wouldn't!'

'What does your husband do?' asked David.

'He's a manager, at the car factory in Birmingham. At least, he is at the moment.'

'Why? Is he looking for another job?'

'No! He's much older than me. He'll be sixty-five next year. God knows what he's going to do when he retires. I

31

just hope he doesn't want me to pack up working when he does.'

Margaret suddenly turned away. She pulled a box file down from a shelf as if conscious of talking too much about personal matters.

'These boxes,' she pointed to the shelf. 'These boxes hold all the accounts. This one is full of invoices for the year, most of which haven't been paid as yet.'

When she opened the box, David could see that all the invoices were simply piled loosely inside. They appeared to be in no particular order and a timely gust of wind would have removed most of the Club's financial obligations in an instant.

One by one, Margaret showed him the contents of the battered old boxes. One contained a ledger, its pages filled with hand written entries that would be legible only to the person who had made them. Another contained what looked like letters, each of which had hand-written markings.

'These are the membership records,' Margaret explained, aware of David's puzzled stare. 'We send out a letter, telling the members how much they owe for the year, then I write on here when they've paid. Sometimes, they don't pay it all at once, which is why some of them have several amounts.'

'So, you can't tell at a glance who has paid and who hasn't?' David was appalled by the casual nature of the book-keeping.

'We don't really need to,' Margaret said. 'At least, not very often. I keep them in alphabetical order and, if a member needs to know how much he's paid, I can pull out his letter and tell him.'

'But, what if *you* need to know? How can you tell who hasn't paid?'

'Oh, every now and then I'll go through the letters and make a list of those who haven't paid their subscriptions.'

32

'Then?'

'Well, then Phil would have a quiet word and get them to pay at least some of it.'

David made a gesture as if to tear his hair out.

'It looks completely chaotic to me,' he said. 'No wonder the Club is in the red!'

Turning, he realised that Margaret was upset.

'Well, it seems to work all right.' She closed the box she was holding and put it back on the shelf. Her face was red and, for a moment, David thought she was about to cry. 'At least, Phil never complained.'

David touched her arm. He tried to look into her face but she turned away.

'I'm sorry, Margaret. I didn't mean to criticise. Really, I didn't. It's obvious to me that you've been doing your best here. It's just that the Club is in financial difficulties and we shall have to start keeping much more detailed accounts, on a computer, probably. Have you ever used a computer? If not, I shall have to teach you.'

David felt her relax beneath his hand.

Margaret turned towards him.

'So, you're not going to get rid of me, then?'

'No, of course not,' David said, relieved. 'For one thing, you're the only one around here who knows where everything is!'

'I would like to learn to use a computer,' Margaret smiled. 'We've got one at home, but my boys think I'm too stupid to understand it.'

'I'm sure you're not,' David declared. 'The Committee has told me to get a computer installed as soon as possible. In fact, I'm going to order two computers, one for me and one for you. When they arrive, I shall teach you how to use yours to write letters and, eventually, we'll use it to keep the accounts. OK?'

'OK,' Margaret smiled. 'Now, I'd better get down to the bank and you'd better go to lunch.'

33

'Lunch?' David looked puzzled.

'Yes. Sarah Hall came down just now and asked me to remind you that your lunch will be ready in the dining room at one o'clock.'

'Then, I'd better not be late,' David smiled, looking at his watch.

5

It was a long time since David had eaten such a lunch. In fact, he couldn't actually remember the last occasion. He'd rarely had time for lunch at school. On the rare occasions when he had, it would be a hurried affair, a school dinner on a melamine plate. And, at home, lunch had always been a snack, even when Tess was alive.

He'd followed the roast lamb, roast potatoes, vegetables and trimmings with apple pie and cream. And, as he ate, John Hall poured him a large glass of a very agreeable Bordeaux. David wondered if they were trying to impress him, keep him sweet, perhaps. Part of him hoped that was the case. He shuddered to think of the consequences of eating a lunch like that every day. He would soon need to replace most of his wardrobe, he thought, feeling his waistband pressing hard against his abdomen.

'Would you like to take your coffee in the bar, Mr Crowley?' Mrs Hall had been hovering nearby, waiting for him to finish his last mouthful of apple pie.

I could get used to this! David thought, as he sat back in an easy chair in the bar and gently pressed down the filter of the cafetière. I don't think I shall be up to doing much work this afternoon, though, Tess.

'Hello, Mr Crowley!'

As David looked up, Kate Earnshaw came across the bar towards him, a broad smile on her face. He struggled to his feet and took her outstretched hand.

'I've just finished my first morning in the office, and the first of Mrs Hall's lunches.' He tapped his stomach, smiling.

'Yes, she's a great cook, isn't she? But, she does tend to pile it on,' Kate laughed. 'She probably thinks you need fattening up.'

'Probably,' David grinned.

'Anyway, it's good to see you. We're all so pleased you decided to take the job. I'm sure you've discovered by now just what a dreadful state the Club's finances are in. It will need some really good management if we're going to get out of this mess.'

'I'm not sure everyone recognises the need for change,' David said.

'You mean, the Brigadier? He hasn't been in to see you already?'

David nodded.

'Well, don't you worry about old Henry too much. Everybody else on the Committee is behind you. We'll certainly back you all the way.'

'Are you here to play?' David changed the subject. The Ladies Captain was wearing dark blue trousers and a light blue jumper. He wasn't sure what the ladies at Branfield Park wore when playing golf.

'No, I have too much work to do, I'm afraid. I just came in to see how you were settling in.' She looked down at the coffee tray and smiled. 'I can see that you're finding your way around.'

David was flustered.

'I'm so sorry! Would you care to join me for some coffee?'

No, thank you, I really can't stop,' Kate smiled. 'Another time, perhaps?'

She took his hand again.

'It's been very nice meeting you again, Mr Crowley. Good luck with the job.'

35

'Call me David, please.'

'In that case, you must call me Kate,' she laughed. 'We'll have that cup of coffee another time.'

Kate went to go and then turned back. She smiled at David and her warmth was apparent from across the room. Her dark hair tumbled to her shoulders and splashed on to the pale blue of her jumper. And, David felt himself smile as he hadn't smiled in quite some time.

Hole	Name	Yards	Par	Score
3	The Balance	368	4	

1

"Wear something different today, Dad," Ben had advised that morning. "Most of the teachers at our school wore the same things every day."

It was true. As a teacher, even when he was a headmaster, David had been too busy to think much about his clothes. He was clean, of course, but his wardrobe, along with that of most of his colleagues, had always been pretty monotonous.

So, today, it was to be the dark suit, a blue shirt and another of the new silk ties; a red patterned one. Standing before the mirror, David felt as if two observers were giving him the once over. At his left shoulder stood the puritan teacher, head of the 'buttons are proud' brigade, staring disdainfully at the sharpness of his outfit. To his right, however, stood another figure, smiling approvingly at the newly emerging, confident self reflected in the glass.

David was beginning to quite like this second observer. He felt taller, smarter and more significant than he had for some time. He'd been boosted by Kate's smile the day before and he enjoyed Margaret's face as she gave him an approving look when he passed through her office.

'I want to spend the morning looking at the accounts, Margaret. Can you make sure I'm left in peace for a couple of hours?'

'I doubt if it'll take you that long,' she smiled. 'The accounts aren't very detailed. Do you want me to get them down for you?'

'No, that's OK,' David replied. 'I can find them for myself. I'll give you a call if I have any queries.'

He closed the door of his office and sat down at the refectory table. The cleaner had only just finished and room smelt pleasantly of lavender polish. It was only his second day, but already David was beginning to think of this room as a haven of peace. The only sound was the gentle ticking of the large clock above the fireplace.

The door opened quietly and Margaret came in carrying a mug of coffee and the day's post.

'Not a lot, today,' she explained. 'Some bills for chemicals, and a welcome letter from the bank manager. He suggests you call him to arrange a meeting as soon as you've had a chance to settle in.'

David looked up at her and smiled. Margaret was standing alongside the desk, holding a shorthand pad and pencil, as if waiting for him to commence dictation. Her straight dark hair contained more grey than he'd noticed the day before and he thought she looked rather old fashioned in her navy blue dress and round glasses.

'Oh, er, I don't think I've anything to dictate, this morning, Margaret, thank you. Did Flight Lieutenant Oakley dictate a lot of letters?'

'All the time. Letters, notes, memos, notices. I think he'd forgotten how to write, to be honest,' she laughed.

'Well, I'm not one for dictating much, so I'll probably draft things out by hand before I give them to you to type, OK?'

'All right,' she said. 'Give me a call if you need any help with the accounts.'

When Margaret had closed the door, David sat back for a moment and sipped his coffee. So, this was it, he thought. This was what it was like to have thinking time. Time to contemplate your work and to devise a strategy for the day. Thinking time is something teachers rarely have. And, even when they do find themselves with a few spare moments, their minds are always so full of what else needs to be done that real rest and relaxation are almost impossible.

The ring of the telephone broke the peace and David smiled as his illusion was shattered.

'I've got Mr Essam, the bank manager, on the line for you,' Margaret announced. 'He obviously thinks you've had quite long enough to settle in now!'

'OK, put him on,' David laughed.

'Good morning, Mr Crowley. Mark Essam here. Very sorry to ring you so soon after writing. I really wanted to give you more time to find your feet, as it were. The thing is, one of my assistants has been in to see me this morning, showing me some figures. He handles the Club's account and his numbers make pretty depressing reading, I'm afraid.'

'I see,' David said. 'Can you post them out to me so that I can have a look at them, too?'

'Yes, of course. But, I do think we need to get together and have a chat about it as soon as possible. I was wondering if you were free on Thursday morning?'

'Thursday's fine,' David replied, trying to imagine familiarising himself with the Club's financial position within the next thirty-six hours. 'Would you like to come out here for lunch?'

Essam hesitated.

'I think it might be better if you came in to the bank, to be honest. More businesslike, if you get my meaning. Shall we say eleven o'clock on Thursday?'

David sat back again. The feeling of relaxed, well-being had drained away. The bank manager's parting words had deflated his spirits. He had known, of course, that the Club was in some difficulty. They had made that clear at his interview. But, the seriousness of Mark Essam's tone, the urgency with which he had arranged their meeting, and his wish to meet at the bank to ensure matters remained businesslike all combined to make it clear that the situation was more serious than he had imagined.

'I'd better have a look through those accounts,' David said to himself. He pulled down the first three boxes from the shelf and began to spread their contents over the refectory table.

For the next hour, he quietly sifted through the papers, attempting to get an accurate picture of the Club's position.

First, he looked through the box containing the invoices. True, they were in date order and Margaret had written "PAID" on some of them in large red letters. But, there were no references to enable him to relate invoices to entries in the ledger. Nor were there any cheque numbers which might have allowed him to reconcile invoices with chequebook stubs.

The ledger had entries such as "AUGUST SALARIES" alongside a total, but it took another ten minutes of searching to find the calculations relating to that figure.

'This is crazy,' David muttered to himself. 'Ben manages his finances better than this and he's always in the red. No wonder Branfield is in such a mess!'

It was clear that Margaret had had no book-keeping training and that the old Flight Lieutenant had been equally ignorant when it came to financial management. Between them, they had tried hard to keep the ship afloat. However, they had focused so much on the day-to-day receipts and payments just off the bows that they had failed to spot the rocks on the horizon. If he were to avoid them, David urgently needed to get a clearer picture of the Club's present position. He put his head round the office door.

'Margaret, I'm afraid I need your help in here.'

Margaret stopped typing and came quietly into the room. She surveyed the contents of the boxes, strewn across the table.

'You've made a real mess of that lot, haven't you?' she laughed.

'Yes, I'm sorry,' David agreed, although he had the impression it had been in quite a mess before he'd started. 'Can you help sort it out for me.'

'What were you looking for? Anything in particular?' Margaret asked.

'I just need to get a broad picture of our income and expenditure over the year. And, our current assets.'

'I don't think there are many of those left,' Margaret smiled. 'You just need the Income and Expenditure Statement and the Balance Sheet. That should tell you all you need to know.'

David sensed his face redden and he suddenly felt very out of touch. He'd spent more than two hours on this paper chase and, all the time, the information he needed was already available.

'Yes, that's right. You've already done those, have you?'

'Not me! The auditor does them every year. He only finished the accounts a couple of months ago, so they ought to be fairly up-to-date.'

Margaret reached up and took down a battered green box.

'Here we are,' she said, passing David a bound copy of the Club's accounts. 'I should think you're ready for another cup of coffee, aren't you?'

2

A few years before he'd retired, the reports would have meant little to David. In those far off days, head teachers worried about children and the local education authority handled almost all the money for schools. Maintenance, salaries, heating, lighting, all those were matters out of his hands. His had been a large comprehensive school with over a thousand children on roll but, even so, the amount of money he'd had to deal with was relatively small.

Then, quite suddenly, everything changed. Schools were given responsibility for their own budgets. Before long, headteachers became more familiar with balance sheets and income and expenditure reports than they were with reports of children's progress.

So now he was on familiar ground. David took the accounts over to his desk and switched on the green banker's lamp.

He was immediately surprised by the small amounts involved. Compared with his school budget, Branfield's turnover was peanuts. The five hundred or so members had paid a total of two hundred and five thousand pounds in subscriptions. In addition, visiting golfers had paid about another four thousand.

That's not very much, David thought. Then, he remembered what Giles Southern had told him about Oakley and the Brigadier discouraging visiting societies and 'the wrong sort of people'.

Sales of drink in the bar brought in just over sixty thousand pounds and Mrs Hall's catering, another ten thousand. So, the Club had a total income of about two hundred and eighty thousand pounds.

'Crikey!' David exclaimed, when he looked at the outgoings. The food and drink sold in the bar and restaurant cost about forty five thousand pounds. Clubhouse running costs and administration accounted for another one hundred and forty six thousand pounds, while expenditure on greenkeeping wages and materials absorbed one hundred and sixteen thousand. David smiled when he saw that, under this section, the auditor had included twelve thousand pounds for 'depreciation'.

'That stuff is so old, it can't be depreciating,' he muttered. If anything, one or two pieces were probably becoming collector's items.

Relatively small as these various costs were, the bottom line was by no means small change. During the past year,

42

the Club had made a net loss of about thirty thousand pounds. What's more, it had had a similar deficit during the previous twelve months and, David didn't doubt, the year before that. But, it was the balance sheet that told the really bad news. The Club was in the red to the tune of one hundred and seventy thousand pounds and was paying interest to the bank of about twelve thousand every year.

This was a haemorrhage that, unless stopped, would soon lead to the Club's demise. Indeed, David thought, the bank manager's ominous tone suggested that the day might have finally arrived.

'I might be out of work by the end of the week,' David laughed as he looked down at his bright silk tie. 'Perhaps, I can take you back to the shop and get a refund.'

'I didn't know the accounts were so funny!'

David looked up. Margaret had entered quietly with a fresh cup of coffee and a sandwich elicited from Mrs Hall.

'It's just my black sense of humour,' David smiled. 'There's nothing very amusing about them is there?'

'Well, I don't really get involved with the details, to be honest. Old Phil always kept them to himself, as if they were a state secret.'

Margaret sat down next to the desk with a smile.

'But, of course, I open the post. So I did have a look at the bank statements. From what I could see, the Club isn't doing very well.'

'It's been making quite a loss, actually,' David replied. 'The funny thing is, it doesn't look as if it should be. Making a loss, that is. I know it's only back-of-envelope stuff but, if we have five hundred members...'

'Four hundred and ninety seven,' Margaret interrupted. 'We had three of the seniors pass away this year and none has been replaced, yet.'

'Well, let's just say, we have five hundred members,' David continued. 'Each member pays an annual subscription of five hundred pounds, then the total income

43

ought to be about two hundred and fifty thousand. If it were, we should be making a profit. Not a big one, but at least, not a loss. But, our income from members' subs is only two hundred and five thousand. I don't understand that. I must be missing something.'

'That's because a lot of the members don't pay five hundred pounds. I know that because I pay in the cheques. Some of them only pay a hundred pounds and a lot of others pay two hundred and fifty.'

'Wait a minute. You mean some of the members are getting their golf for only a hundred pounds a year? And, others are only paying half the normal subscription? But, why?'

'Because they're vicars, or army officers or policemen,' Margaret explained. 'The diocese has fifty special memberships for the clergy. We only charge them a hundred pounds each. They're not supposed to play on Sundays, although I know for a fact some of them do. I've seen them dressed in civvies on a Sunday afternoon...'

'And, the army and the police?' David interrupted.

'They get a special rate, too. Army officers, and air force officers, pay half price. And, policemen pay the same.'

'How many of these, er, officers are there?' David was trying not to let his incredulity show.

'About a hundred, altogether. To begin with it was just the top brass but, over the years, those have retired and kept their memberships. More and more have come along, and then other officers have heard about it and it just seems to have snowballed.'

'How did it get started?' David asked.

'I'm not sure,' Margaret said. 'It was brought in long before I arrived. Probably, it was something the Brigadier's father thought up when the Club started. As I say, it was just a few in those days. Even when I first came, there weren't more than ten or fifteen army and air force officers altogether. And, about twenty vicars. Then, more kept asking and the Brigadier just told Phil to let them in. After all, we weren't getting any other new members.'

'That's because Phil and the Brigadier were turning them away, from what I hear.'

'It wasn't really poor Phil's fault,' Margaret said, sounding protective. 'He just asked the Brigadier, and then did as he was told.'

'Well, it doesn't really matter who had the idea in the first place,' David said. 'What matters is that it's left the Club nearly broke now. Do the other members know about this? Did the rest of the Committee agree to it?'

'I don't suppose so,' Margaret replied. 'It's been going on since long before any of them joined the Committee, so I don't expect it's ever came up at a meeting. I type up the committee minutes and I can't remember anything ever being mentioned. Anyway, the Brigadier always told Phil and me to tell them as little as possible. He called it a "need to know" basis. Like they were still in the army.'

'Well, I think they need to know, now,' David said. 'If it's not too late, that is.'

3

'Morning, Boss!' David turned to find a big cheerful-looking man in his mid-twenties smiling across his car roof. He had just parked his Peugeot Estate alongside David's Laguna in the car park.

'Jack Peters.' The young man held out his hand. 'I'm the golf professional here. Sorry, we haven't met up before now. How are you settling in? Have you got time for a chat? There are a few things I wanted to go over when you've got a minute.'

'Oh, fine, thanks,' David said, shaking the younger man's hand. 'It's always a bit daunting when you start a new job, but everyone has been very helpful. As a matter of fact, I wanted to have a talk with you myself, but I've got

45

something to deal with first. Can we get together later in the morning?'

'No problem,' Jack said. 'I've got lessons until eleven. I can come over to the office about quarter past eleven, if you like?'

'What if I come over to the professional's shop?' David suggested. 'You can show me round and then we can have a talk.'

The two men parted and, as David swept past Margaret into his office, she had time only to notice his new sports jacket and yet another silk tie.

'I've put a copy of the membership list on your desk,' Margaret explained as she brought David's coffee along with the morning post.

'It's broken down into the different categories: full members; ladies; juniors and all the others who don't pay the full subscription – the clergy, the army officers and the policemen. There are quite a lot of them. In fact, there aren't that many who are paying the full amount!'

David sipped his coffee. Although this was only his third day, he was already enjoying the small luxury of being presented with a hot drink immediately he sat at his desk. He scanned the list. Margaret might have exaggerated a little. About three hundred and fifty members had paid the full subscription. But, that still left about a hundred and fifty who hadn't. Their discounts, added together, were the main reason for the Club's shortage of cash.

The telephone rang. It was Giles Southern.

'Ah, David. Good morning. I thought I'd give you a couple of days to find your way around before taking up any of your time. I was wondering if we could get together for a chat later in the week?'

'Of course,' David said. 'I've been having a look at the finances and there are some figures I wanted you to see. And, I'm seeing the bank manager tomorrow. I'm sure he'll have plenty to say.'

'Good. Why don't we have lunch together on Friday? I'll come over at about one if that's all right with you.'

Giles Southern's perfect diction and smooth tones suggested a quiet but firm authority. It was not surprising, David thought, that the other members had turned to him as their Captain at this difficult time.

Twenty minutes later, he drained his coffee mug and slid the membership list into the top drawer of his desk.

'I'm going across to the professional's shop, Margaret,' David announced.

It was earlier than he and Jack had agreed, but he wanted to have a quiet look round the shop first. As Secretary, he needed to familiarise himself with the situation, he would have explained to anyone who asked. To the more perceptive observer, David would have confessed a desire to have a close look at the latest golfing equipment.

The shop occupied a single storey extension to the clubhouse; built as an afterthought some years after the original farmhouse was converted. There was no access from the clubhouse and David walked through the car park to the entrance. As he did so, a number of members were unloading golf clubs and trolleys from the boots of their cars. They greeted him with smiles and one or two came up and shook his hand.

'Good to meet you,' said one elderly gentleman who introduced himself as Rex. He, in turn, introduced his equally elderly but hearty companion, whose name David didn't quite catch.

'Welcome to Branfield Park,' the second golfer smiled. 'How are you settling in? You've got your work cut out, so I hear.'

They exchanged a few more pleasantries before David smiled, extracted himself and entered the professional's shop.

Alison, the shop assistant was occupied with a couple of lady members and so David quietly explored the stock. He soon realised that his first impression had been correct. The limited range of equipment and clothing available was displayed much as it must have been when the Club opened. The general impression was depressing and suggested terminal decline.

The ladies left, apparently satisfied, and Alison disappeared into the small workshop behind the counter. If she had spotted David as he walked among the stock, she gave no indication of it. She probably felt, he thought, that if she didn't acknowledge him, he wouldn't create any work for her.

The stock might be limited but one or two items caught David's eye. He noticed a putter with an insert in its face. Such clubs hadn't existed, had even been illegal, when he had last played.

Then, he took down a driver from a display and gripped it in both hands as if to address a ball.

The driver. The biggest golf club in the bag and the club that strikes the ball the furthest. A good drive makes all subsequent shots easier and a good driver makes for a good drive, or so many golfers hope.

The head of the driver David now held was made, not of wood like his own driver gathering dust in the garage at home. Rather, it was fashioned from titanium alloy and various other hi-tech materials. And, instead of steel, this driver had a shaft of black graphite material. David smiled as he recognised the same feeling he had whenever Ben started explaining the latest developments in computers.

He looked at the tag on the shaft and whistled under his breath at the price. This was obviously a serious piece of kit, as Ben might say. To a golfer, holding such a driver is like sitting at the wheel of a Formula One racing car. Part of him itched to take the club over to the range and put it through its paces. Slowly, almost reluctantly, he returned it to its place on the display rack.

After examining a few other items, David approached the door of the workshop intending to ask how much longer Jack's lesson might take.

Alison was dressed in tight trousers and a low-cut tee-shirt that revealed her ample cleavage. She was sitting on a tall stool alongside the work-bench. The metal shaft of a golf club was held in a vice and the young woman was using a knife to cut away the worn rubber grip. Through the doorway, David watched quietly as Alison cleaned the newly exposed shaft with a spirit-soaked rag. She wound adhesive tape tightly around the shaft and carefully peeled off the backing paper. After spraying the tape with spirit, she grasped the shaft and slowly slid her right hand up and down a few times.

Then, the young woman picked up the new rubber grip from the bench and aligned it carefully before sliding the ten inches of black rubber slowly on to the shaft. As she did so, Alison closed her eyes and made a long sighing sound. She lifted her eyes, looked up at David and ran her tongue across her lips.

'About the only pleasure I gets around here,' she said, with a wicked grin.

David realised that his mouth was wide open and he felt his face flush. He smiled and turned away, relieved to hear Jack approaching through the shop.

'Alison keeping you entertained, is she?' Jack laughed.

'I'd not spotted the, er, more erotic side of re-gripping a golf club until Alison took it on,' Jack explained after he had sent Alison to fetch some cups of coffee. 'Actually, it's quite good for business. You'd be surprised how many more men are having their clubs re-gripped these days. For some reason, they prefer her while-you-wait service!'

David looked across at Jack and saw that he had a mischievous glint in his eye.

'To be honest, she's pretty bored, I think. There isn't much to do in here all day.'

'No. I'd noticed that stock levels are rather low,' David said.

'To put it mildly,' Jack laughed. 'The problem is, most of the members have been here for years. They don't change their equipment very often. And, usually, when they do, they go down the high street or to an out-of-town, where they can get a better price.'

'So, how do you keep going?' David asked.

'Only just, is the answer,' Jack said. 'It's only because I don't pay anything for the premises and the Club pay me a retainer, that I manage to make ends meet. And, there are the lessons, of course.'

'You spend a lot of your time teaching?'

'Yeah, quite a lot. Youngsters, mostly. The children of members. And, the ladies, of course.'

'Not men?'

'Surprisingly few,' said Jack. 'It's amazing, the difference between men and women golfers!'

'In what way?' David asked.

'When women take up golf, most of them start by taking lessons. In fact, a lot of them won't even go out on the course until they're pretty sure they can hit the ball in the right general direction. Same with the kids. Parents who want their children to take up golf nearly always sign 'em up for a course of lessons. But, the men? Most of them will get themselves a set of clubs and then spend the next twenty years hacking their way round the course. They only come to me when they're really desperate. Even then, they don't normally want lessons. They'll come and buy a new set of clubs and think nothing of it. Spend a fortune they will. Then, they'll go out and play just as badly.'

'Why do you think that is?' David asked, although, as a man, he thought he knew the answer.

'I reckon it's all to do with pride. To suggest to a man that he could do with golf lessons, well, it's like saying he's hopeless at driving a car or worse, hopeless in bed!'

50

Jack laughed. 'To a lot of these guys, the game is all about cocks – if you'll pardon the expression. The further they can hit the ball, the more of a man they think they are.'

'Really?' David joined in the laughter.

'It's true!' Jack said. 'And, it's the same with practice. There are some guys who'll turn up half an hour before a game to practice. Then, they get ribbed rotten by their mates for taking it all too seriously.'

'That's a bit like boys and their schoolwork,' David said. 'If a boy starts taking his lessons seriously, he can get terrible stick from his classmates. Even some dads don't like to see their sons becoming too studious. They're afraid they might become soft, or something.'

'Yeah? Well, a lot of them never grow up,' Jack declared. 'You can tell 'em till the cows come home that Nick Faldo has endless lessons, or that Tiger Woods practises for hours with his coach, but it makes no difference. The next day, I find them in here splashing out a hundred quid on a new putter just because one of their mates suggested it!'

'At least it helps keep you in business,' David smiled.

'That's true,' Jack agreed. 'But, if they took lessons, I might improve their game, then they'd want new clubs so they could play even better.'

'You enjoy teaching?' David asked,

'Yeah, I do,' said Jack. 'Don't get me wrong, I like playing golf. But, I was never a great player. I was always experimenting too much when I played, always trying something new. I think I got bored. I never get bored teaching. You were a teacher, weren't you?'

'Yes, a head teacher, for many years. I retired when it became too stressful, I'm afraid.'

'I don't know how anybody teaches in schools, these days, without becoming stressed,' Jack said. 'You were a pretty good golfer, too, so they tell me.'

David flushed.

51

'I played off four at one time. But, I stopped playing – after my wife died,' David explained.

'I'm sorry,' Jack said. He turned as Alison came in and she handed them their coffee. The two men sat side-by-side on two old chairs provided for customers to use when trying on golf shoes.

'So, the ladies keep you busy, at least?' asked David.

'Yeah! Fortunately,' Jack agreed. Then, he laughed again. 'It's funny, really. The husbands spend their money in the shop and I get to spend time with their wives. It's a tough job, but somebody has to do it!'

David was thinking that Jack was hardly the Brigadier's idea of a member of staff. Not subordinate enough, at all. Far too self-confident, he imagined the Brigadier saying. Jack might be young – he was twenty-six it emerged – but he was a big man, rather good looking and he had all the confidence of a natural athlete.

'How did you come to be professional at Branfield, Jack?' David asked.

'You mean because I'm so young?' Jack replied. 'I came here straight from school as assistant to old Graham Trubshaw. He'd been here since the General's day, since the Club started, I think. Then, about four years ago, he began to forget things. After a few months, they said he had Alzheimer's. He went into a home and he died about six months ago. They advertised for a new professional but nobody else would take it on, so they asked me to take over. I don't know how long I'll be able to keep going, though, not unless we get a lot of new members, and pretty soon.'

'That's my job,' David explained.

'So I was told. Well, I just hope old Brigadier Tufnell doesn't stand in your way,' Jack said.

The two men chatted for a while longer before Jack's next student arrived. David liked Jack. They both liked golf, of course, but it was more than that. David could see something of himself as he once was in this young, enthusiastic teacher who loved his subject.

4

'*Six months!*'

'I'm sorry, Mr Crowley, but that's the best I can do.' Mark Essam, the bank manager, sat behind his desk. A teak veneer and steel legs affair, David observed, not to be compared with his desk at the Club.

'But, you know that six months is quite unreasonable. It's just not possible to turn the Club round in that time.'

'We don't expect you to be operating at a profit in six months. That, as you say, would be unreasonable. However, the present outflow of cash shows no sign of being reduced and the bank must safeguard its own interests. There must be clear evidence within a six month period that the Club has taken measures to restore its viability. Otherwise...'

'Otherwise?' David thought he already knew the otherwise.

'Otherwise, we shall have no alternative but to apply for the Club to be wound up and its assets realised.'

'In other words, sold to the highest bidder.'

'The bank is not a charity, Mr Crowley. No bank is. Banks have shareholders and it's my job to protect their interests.'

'I must say I was expecting a little more understanding.'

In truth, David had long since grown out of expecting understanding from bank managers.

'Look, Mr Crowley... May I call you David? Listen, David, you've only just arrived. As I said the other day, I had hoped to give you a little more time to sort things out. After all, I am a member myself and I love the place...'

'Yes, so I gather,' David said. And, he thought, at least you pay the full subscription.

'But, the people at Area Office have been on my back. They wanted me to call in the overdraft right away. The feeling is that there have been enough warnings and last chances. I explained the change of management and argued very hard with them. But, six months is the best I can do, I'm sorry. Even then, they want to see some definite signs soon that you're doing something to put the situation right.'

'You say there have been final warnings and last chances before?'

'Plenty of them. Old Oakley has sat where you're sitting many times. He understood the problem. At least, I think he did. The trouble was, his hands were tied. Every time he went back to the Club to try to sort things out, Brigadier Tufnell over-ruled him.'

'I can imagine,' David smiled. 'He's already made it clear that he expects me to work with him to thwart any changes the Committee might propose.'

'Well, if you don't stand up to the old bastard, he'll face changes even he won't be able to resist,' Essam said. 'And, sooner than he could ever imagine.'

'Look, David.' Mark Essam moved round from behind his desk and sat against the front edge. 'I know it's very early days, but have you had time yet to get a picture of the situation for yourself?'

'I've been looking at the accounts,' David said. 'The situation is pretty desperate. The members' subscriptions don't anywhere near cover the annual running costs.'

'I know. I've examined the accounts, too. As a member, and as a bank manager. It's crazy, isn't it,' Essam went on. 'Any other organisation looks at its annual running costs and sets its subscriptions to bring in enough to meet them. With a bit to spare, preferably. Branfield Park has been operating in cloud-cuckoo-land for years. The old Brigadier and his chums decide what they think members would like to pay. Then, the poor old Secretary is expected to run the place on whatever that brings in. Like I say, it's crazy.'

'Daft,' David agreed. 'Of course, the Club needs to get in more from subscriptions. The problem is, if we increase the subscriptions, a lot of people may leave. Or, a lot of others may not join. Result – no more money in the coffers. Or, rather, the bank.'

'Quite,' said Essam. 'There's only one solution as far as I can see, and it's one I put to Phil Oakley many times. Somehow, the Club has to attract a lot of new members. Trouble is, he said, the Brigadier just wouldn't hear of it.'

'Oh, he's already made it clear what he thinks of that idea,' David said. 'Well, he'll just have to take it on board, this time. Anyway, I'll explain the situation to the Committee. They're intelligent people. They should be able to understand.'

'Oh, they'll understand all right. The trouble is, they're also very nice people, and they're not used to open warfare. The Brigadier enjoys a fight and they don't. That's why they've brought you in. Or, didn't you realise that, David?'

'I'm beginning to. And, I'm not sure I really want to fight somebody else's battles. I retired because I was under too much stress and I don't know that I want to take on any more.'

'Well, if there is anything I can do to help, just give me a call,' said Mark Essam, getting to his feet. 'Even if it's only to let off steam. Just keep me posted, that's all I ask.'

He led the way to the door. David was surprised how the tone of the conversation had changed. All of a sudden, Mark Essam was a listening bank. Might as well take advantage of it, he thought.

'One thing I will need, if I'm going to keep track of things, is a decent computer system,' David explained. 'I know the overdraft's horrendous already, but is it OK with you if I spend a couple of thousand on some hardware?'

'I'm sure that won't be a problem,' Essam grinned. 'After all, we can always sell it if things don't work out!'

David hated bank managers' jokes. He never knew whether he was supposed to laugh or cry.

'And, if you do succeed,' said Essam, more serious now. 'The Committee will back you, I'm quite sure.' He held out his hand. 'All you have to do is handle the Brigadier.'

David smiled and shook the bank manager's hand.

'When you put it like that, it all sounds very easy.'

Hole	Name	Yards	Par	Score
4	Meander	149	3	

1

Mrs Hall had taken a lot of trouble, laying a corner table. Silver cutlery glinted on a white linen ground. White china waited expectantly.

'You won't be disturbed there,' she'd suggested to David when he explained that he and the Club Captain would be lunching together.

In fact, few of the members had a formal lunch on weekdays, preferring snacks they could eat in the bar. Today, there were only two elderly ladies – sisters, David understood – as well as the usual complement of vicars. Otherwise, they were alone apart from Mozart playing quietly over the loudspeakers.

'Well, how has your first week gone?' Giles asked, smiling. He tilted the bottle and red wine gushed into David's glass.

'Quite well, I think,' David said. 'I've been getting to know everyone and finding my way around.'

'You've met Jack Peters – the professional – I assume?'

'Yes, we had a long chat on Wednesday. I think he's finding it quite a struggle to keep going here.'

'Yes, it must be difficult. He's very young, but he's a great chap. I hope we don't lose him. My wife thinks he's a marvellous teacher.'

'He was telling me that he spends much of his time with the ladies,' David smiled.

'Yes, I'm afraid most of us men learned the game years ago and don't really have the time, or the inclination, to do much about improving ourselves. Actually, our Jack is a bit of a ladies man. In the nicest sense, of course.'

'Of course,' David smiled.

'Be careful; they're very hot,' Mrs Hall announced as she placed the plates, each laden with roast lamb, before the two men. They paused while she added roast potatoes, parsnips, cauliflower, carrots, mint sauce and, finally, a rich gravy.

'I surrender!' David said, holding up his hand and smiling. 'Please, Mrs Hall, we both have to work this afternoon.'

'You can't work on an empty stomach. Let me know when you're ready for your dessert,' she said, as swept away to the kitchen.

'She is incredible,' Giles laughed. 'She doesn't listen to a word you say. I've been eating here for years and I've never yet managed to persuade Mrs Hall to serve me a small portion!'

They ate in silence for a few minutes before Giles again spoke.

'You said on the telephone that you'd been looking at the finances. Have you arrived at any conclusions?'

'Only the rather obvious one that the Club isn't getting in nearly enough money to cover its costs, I'm afraid.'

'That's more or less what the auditor said in his report,' Giles said.

'What he didn't say was why.' David let his enigmatic remark sink in while he took a sip from his glass.

'I would have thought that was fairly obvious,' Giles said. 'There just aren't enough members.'

'Oh, there are enough members, all right. The problem is they aren't paying enough in subscriptions.'

'I thought you might be about to say that.' Giles, too, took a sip of Bordeaux. 'I suppose that means we're all going to have to pay a lot more for our golf?'

'Not necessarily,' David replied. He put down his glass and went on. 'Look, Giles, this club – any club – has certain outgoings and it also has an income. In our case, it's the balance between the two that is wrong. Our running

58

costs are about three hundred and ten thousand pounds – very low for a club of this size. Unfortunately, our income is even lower, only about two hundred and eighty thousand pounds. So, we're operating on our overdraft. And, it's been getting worse for some years.'

'That, I understand,' Giles said, grimly. 'What I don't understand is why our income is so much lower than our expenditure. I've spoken to members of other clubs and our subscriptions are roughly comparable with theirs.' He looked down at his plate and smiled. 'I'm sure it can't all be down to Mrs Hall's extra large helpings.'

'It's not, although I admit a little portion control wouldn't go amiss. For the sake of my waistline, if nothing else.'

'What, then, David? You've obviously discovered something the auditor didn't notice.'

'Only because it's not part of his job. He's only concerned with profit and loss; the balance sheet; the bottom line. He doesn't advise on policy.'

'Policy?' Giles was curious.

'Yes. Apparently, the Club has long operated a policy of giving substantial discounts on certain members' subscriptions. From what I can see, in recent years, this policy has got out of hand. It's now costing about forty thousand pounds a year and is, basically, the reason we are in the red.'

'And, who are the members who get these discounts?'

'The clergy,' David nodded his head towards the quartet of priests enjoying a joke in the far corner. 'The armed forces. That is to say, army and air force officers. Not other ranks, as far as I'm aware. And, police officers, although in their case, the discount appears to apply to everyone from beat copper to Chief Constable.'

'Good God! And all these people are paying reduced subs? How much less?'

'Quite a bit less, I'm afraid,' David explained. 'The clergymen over there play here for only a hundred pounds a year.'

'Good God!' Giles said, again. 'No wonder they can all afford to fill up on Mrs Hall's lunches. A couple of good Sunday collections and they've paid their golf subs for the year, I should think.'

'Shame on you!' David grinned. 'Actually, they don't need to raid the poor box or anything like that. Most of them pay in instalments or by standing order.'

'It gets worse,' Giles groaned. 'And, the army, the air force and the constabulary; are they all paying the same?'

'No, fortunately. Otherwise, we wouldn't even be sitting here. The Club would long since have gone under. No, they pay half price; two hundred and fifty pounds each instead of five hundred.'

'That's something at least. But, it still means the Chief Constable gets his golf for a fiver a week.'

'If he played, he would,' David agreed. 'But, a lot of his men do, and so do the squadron leaders and the wing commanders at the air base. But mostly, it's all the lieutenants, captains and majors from the army camp.'

'The captains and the majors? The Brigadier! Don't tell me. Old Henry is behind all this, somehow, isn't he?'

'I don't know if he thought up the policy,' said David. 'It probably goes back to his father's day. Let's just say he's been operating it a bit too enthusiastically of late.'

'He's been operating it? I don't understand. Henry hasn't held an official position in the Club for some years. I don't see how he operated a policy – enthusiastically or otherwise – that none of us on the Committee even knew existed.'

'It seems he and my predecessor had a weekly meeting at which they discussed, among other things, applications for membership. The Brigadier seems to have okayed those from any of the preferred groups and, at the same time, put

60

up the shutters as far as most of the others were concerned. People eventually got the message. Margaret tells me there hasn't been an application from a civilian in months.'

'So, while ours debts have been mounting, the Brigadier has been letting in people at half price or less? It's crazy!'

'Funny. That's what our bank manager said.'

'Far be it for me ever to agree with a bank manager but, on this occasion, I have to admit he's right. What else did Essam have to say?'

'He's given me – us – six months to get ourselves back into the black, otherwise…' David slid his forefinger across his throat.

'Six months? Then, we've no chance. It just isn't possible for us to be trading at a profit and to clear our overdraft in six months.'

'I don't think he expects that,' David said. 'But, I do think he will want to see us taking some quite big steps in the right direction.'

'Well, if what you say is correct,' Giles said. 'If it is these discounts that are causing our deficit, then surely we can get back into profit simply by abolishing them; asking people to pay the full amount?'

'We could try,' David replied. 'It might bring in some extra money. More likely, a lot of those people would simply leave and we would be back to square one. And, even if we got back into profit, our overdraft is huge. We'll need to bring in a lot more money if we're to start paying that off.'

'No, you're probably right,' Giles agreed. Then, he laughed. 'I, for one, wouldn't want to be standing in the doorway when those holy men over there learned that they were going to have to pay five times as much. So, what's the solution, David? I'm sure you've thought of one.'

'There's only one solution, I'm afraid, and it's one the Brigadier won't like. The Club simply has to open its doors. Recruit as many people as it can, as quickly as possible.'

Giles emptied his wine glass.

'I'm sure you're right, David. Both about the solution and the Brigadier's likely opposition. But, it's not just him. I'm sure a lot of his friends will oppose it, too.'

'Well, if they succeed,' David said. 'Then, the Club will go under.'

'Of that, there is little doubt,' Giles agreed. Looking at his watch as he stood up. 'But, we must bite the bullet and get on with it, otherwise there will soon be nowhere around here where one can enjoy a lunch like this.'

The two men laughed and, together, they resisted Mrs Hall's offer of a dessert and coffee.

'I'll talk to the others before the committee meeting,' Giles promised as they left the dining room. 'Make sure they're on our side.'

'I think they'll need to be,' David said, as they parted. 'I have a feeling the Brigadier isn't going to like this at all.'

2

'I don't like it. I don't like it at all!'

He's nothing if not predictable, David thought.

The Brigadier had come in for his 'regular' Monday morning meeting. David had almost forgotten all about it. Indeed, he'd hoped that the Brigadier had, too. But, Brigadier Henry Tufnell had no intention of letting slip his grip on the Club's affairs. He had walked in unannounced, Margaret at his heels, while David was on the telephone and sat down heavily next to the desk.

'Margaret tells me there are no applications for us to worry about, Crowley, so I suggest we get ourselves prepared for next week's committee meeting,' said the Brigadier.

'Surely, the fact that there aren't any applications is something for us to worry about, Brigadier?'

'What are you talking about, man?' The Brigadier looked perplexed. He wasn't used to subordinates questioning his line of thought. 'This is an exclusive club. Got all the members we want or need. You haven't played the course yet, I take it? No, of course, you don't play any more, do you? Pity, that. Damned pity. Anyway, if you had played the course, you would soon have realised the benefit of not having too many members. Never have to wait on the tee, don't you see? Very important, that.'

At another time, in another place, David might have been happy to admit that not having to wait on the tee was an important factor in the enjoyment of the game. But, this was neither the time, nor the place.

'Forgive me, Brigadier. The point I was trying to make is that members pay subscriptions, subscriptions which pay most of the running costs of the Club. As you know, the auditors, in their report...'

'Auditors! Damn pen pushers and clerks! What do they know about the game of golf? Most of them know nothing at all about waiting on the tee, and everything there is to know about waiting for their tea. I hope you are not going to suggest that we pay much attention to people like that; people who have no understanding of the game?'

'With respect, Brigadier,' David replied. 'It's not their job to understand the game. The auditors simply prepare the Club's annual accounts to which they normally attach a report. In this year's report, they expressed their concern about the Club's financial position.'

'As if it were any of their concern,' the Brigadier chuntered, but before he could continue, David went on.

'They expressed their concern about the Club's financial position and, as a result, the Committee appointed a new Secretary – me. I was asked by the Committee to advise them how the Club can best be put back on to a sound financial basis.'

'Look,' the Brigadier said. 'I'm prepared to admit that the Club's finances may be in a bit of a mess. But, that was all Oakley's responsibility. Now he's gone, competent accounting should put the matter right, surely? Your appointment in itself will result in any improvement necessary.'

'If only that were true, Brigadier, I would have little to do and the Committee would have little to worry about. Unfortunately, the situation is, if anything, worse than the auditor suggested. The Club has made a loss for the past five years and its overdraft has grown to over one hundred and seventy thousand pounds. The bank manager has insisted that we must put matters right...'

'Essam? Is he giving you problems? Don't you lose any sleep over him, my boy. I'll ask him out for a game at the weekend; get him to see the situation from our point of view. Chap's a keen golfer. He'll understand, once he's had the problem explained to him.'

'He *is* one of the problems, Brigadier,' David said, raising his voice very slightly. 'As I say, Mr Essam is insisting that the Club starts trading in the black within six months, or else...'

'Trading! Trading? What the hell are you talking about, laddie? This is a golf club, not a bloody grocer's shop. I've never heard such nonsense.'

'It's merely an accounting term, Brigadier. If you prefer, the bank manager is insisting that, within six months, we begin to operate our finances in such a way that we achieve a surplus at the end of the year.'

'Well, if, as you say, he's one of the problems, maybe I should have a word with one of his superiors. As it happens, I do know someone in the area office. Perhaps, if I invite him over for a game...'

64

'That won't alter the situation, I'm afraid, Brigadier,' David said. 'Indeed, it might only serve to reinforce the bank's view that we are not taking the problem seriously. Now, if you will allow me to explain my proposals…'

'Oh, very well,' the Brigadier sighed. 'But, I'm not agreeing to anything at this stage.'

'Of course not,' David replied, his fingers firmly crossed. 'Look, why don't I get Margaret to bring us a cup of coffee and then we can get down to business.'

For the moment, the storm subsided. David could feel that the back of his shirt was soaked with sweat but, gradually, his pulse and his breathing returned to something approaching their normal levels.

He'd been there many times, of course, and, in the past he'd enjoyed the buzz. Indeed, some of his staff reckoned he deliberately provoked conflict, with the local authority or with his governors, simply because he liked the heat of battle. It wasn't true, of course, or at least he didn't think it was. But, if he ever had enjoyed it, he certainly didn't any more. Now, he just found it stressful and he felt that stress in his stomach, in his lungs, in his heart and in his head. And, he didn't like it at all.

While they waited for Margaret, David drew the older man to the easy chairs in front of the fire.

'So, Brigadier,' he said. 'You've been associated with Branfield Park almost since the Club started?'

'Even before that. The farm belonged to a family friend. After the war, father persuaded a number of his friends in the regiment to chip in and buy the land. They paid a local farmer to use his men and machinery to put in drainage and to build some greens and tees. It took only eighteen months from the initial idea to driving the first ball. This clubhouse was the original farmhouse. And, the furniture in this room came from my grandfather's study.'

'Amazing,' David said. 'So it was a privately owned club? To begin with, at least?'

'No, it was always a members' club,' the Brigadier explained. 'The members paid subscriptions and gradually, over the years, the original loans were repaid.'

So, the place hasn't always been run at a loss, David smiled to himself.

He poured the coffee and passed the Brigadier a cup.

'And, did everyone pay the same subscription?'

'No. Those who lent money for the land paid only half the full amount, in lieu of interest on their loans.'

Ah! Now, I'm beginning to understand, David smiled.

'Presumably, those who lent the startup money have long since passed away?'

'Yes, sadly the last survivor – General Sir Michael Hornby – died about seven years ago. Why do you ask?'

'It's simply that, when I was going through the accounts the other day, I happened to notice that quite a number of the members pay a reduced subscription.'

'There are a few, I think,' the Brigadier agreed. 'In the early days, it was necessary to build up the membership quite quickly. A special arrangement was made to allow serving army officers to join at a reduced rate. Chaps serving in the armed services weren't paid what they are today, you know. And, many of them were only stationed here for a year, perhaps even less.'

'But times have changed, Brigadier, so why are so many of them still allowed such a large discount.'

'Oh, I think the C.O. would often ring up and ask if this or that young officer could be a member for a while. Of course, they tend to stay in the area for longer periods, nowadays. But, there are not that many of them.'

'And, the Royal Air Force officers?'

'The RAF? Oh, a few years ago, some of the officers from the regiment went over to the air station for sports day. They started talking in the mess and, the next thing, the wing commander was on the telephone, twisting my arm. I did let in one or two of his young men but, again, I think you'll find the numbers are not significant.'

'The numbers have grown to fifty, Brigadier. And the effect on the Club's income is certainly significant.'

'I'm not sure of the exact number, but I should be very surprised if it were fifty,' the Brigadier replied, more defensively now.

'And, the police? How did they too come to qualify for such a discount?'

'I'm not sure. I'd have to check the records, but I think we were approached by the Chief Constable. I believe only a few senior officers are involved.'

'Again, Brigadier, a sizeable number are involved,' David explained, quietly. 'Fifty police officers, varying in rank from constable all the way up to chief superintendent, are paying only half the normal subscription.'

David thought that the Brigadier was looking decidedly sheepish, now.

'And, another group – the clergy – pay even less for their golf. How did that come about?'

'Damn it, man!' the Brigadier snapped. 'I don't know all the ins and outs of it. You would have to ask Oakley. I believe the local parson was given a sort of honorary membership, right at the beginning. He introduced one of his clergyman friends, a Scottish fellow and a fine golfer, I recall. I know we did let him join for a much reduced subscription. I think there may have been one or two others. But, these chaps don't earn very much you know.'

'Brigadier, there are nearly fifty clergymen on the books at present. And all of them pay only twenty per cent – that's a hundred pounds a year – for the privilege. Surely, you must have noticed the large number of dog collars around the place?'

'I confess, I had no idea that there were quite that many. But, I don't see how it can be having an adverse effect on the Club. They are still paying something, after all.'

'They are, of course,' David said. 'And the loss of income would not be significant if the Club were recruiting sufficient members paying the full amount. Unfortunately, very few other people have applied for membership and those that have, have generally found that their applications were unsuccessful.'

'Well, a lot of them were quite unsuitable, I'm afraid,' the Brigadier said. 'Quite unsuitable.'

'In what way, Brigadier?'

'They were tradesmen, a lot of them. One fellar owned a lorry firm. Tenant farmers; people like that. What you must understand, Crowley, is that golf is very much a social game. People have to be able to mix comfortably on the course, in the bar and in the restaurant. I can assure you that many of the older members would not have been comfortable with some of those who applied in recent years. And, many of the applicants would have been like fishes out of water here. Quite unsuited, I'm afraid.'

I see, David thought. So you were saving them from embarrassment. How kind.

'Well, be that as it may, Brigadier, the time has now arrived when a different strategy is being forced upon us. The bank has given the Club six months to bring about a change. We could, of course, ask all these army officers, policemen and clergymen to pay the full amount overnight. That would improve things substantially.'

'That's quite impossible! Those arrangements have been in place for many years. We certainly cannot go cap in hand to those fellows.'

'The other members of the Committee may have other ideas on that subject. Well, in that case, Brigadier, there is only one course open to us.'

'I'm still not sure that I agree with your analysis of our financial problems. But, tell me, what is your solution?' The Brigadier had recovered his composure now and he had some idea of what was coming.

'The Club must open its doors to a much wider range of people. Recruit as many new members as possible, as quickly as possible.'

'I don't think we need go that far at this stage,' the Brigadier said.

'If we don't go that far, and perhaps further, very soon, Brigadier, there will not be a Club for anyone to belong to. The bank is threatening to cancel our overdraft. If they do so, the receivers will be called in and the course, the clubhouse, everything will be sold.'

'You say, perhaps further,' the Brigadier asked. What could be worse?

'Branfield's other income, from societies and general visitors, is very low in comparison with other clubs.'

'Ah!' the Brigadier said. 'There is a very good reason for that. The members have not wished to find themselves waiting behind groups of villagers and others who might feel like playing. And, I do know there was considerable resentment when visiting societies were able to book the first tee for perhaps two hours at a time.'

'Nevertheless,' David said. 'Encouraging visitors is one way the Club could generate additional income very quickly.'

'Yes, but at what cost. Damn it, man! There must be other ways in which these little problems can be overcome. Oakley obviously mismanaged the finances and left us in a mess. Now, it's surely your job to get us out of it. Managing the finances effectively is, after all, what you are paid to do, for God's sake!'

For a moment, David felt himself rising to the bait, but he managed to calm down without the Brigadier noticing.

'One can only manage the finances if there is sufficient money there to manage, Brigadier. I'm sorry, but I have looked at the accounts and I've spoken to the bank manager. The only course of action open to the Club in the circumstances is to open its doors.'

'Well, we'll see what the Committee has to say about that. And, the rest of the membership,' the Brigadier said, menacingly. 'I doubt if they'll like the idea any more than I do. And, I'll tell you now. I don't like it. *I don't like it all!*'

3

'He's just an animal, that man,' Margaret said as she put David's coffee on his desk.

'Oh, I'm sure he means well,' David replied, sounding unconvinced.

The battle with the Brigadier had made him weary. At the time, he'd quite enjoyed the verbal sparring; it had been almost like old times. But, the mental energy it had consumed, together with the implication in the Brigadier's parting words of further battles ahead, had left him drained. Perhaps, this was the penalty he had to pay; the downside following the buzz. If so, it wasn't worth it. Not any more.

'I don't think he means well, at all,' Margaret went on. 'All he means is to get his own way. It was the same with poor Phil. He hated the Brigadier for the way he treated him.'

'I had the impression that Flight Lieutenant Oakley worked very closely with the Brigadier?'

'Oh, he always did what the Brigadier told him, all right. But, that was just his military training, I think. Never question a superior officer, that sort of thing. And, the fact that Phil is such a nice man. He hates arguments.'

Margaret sat down next to the desk.

'What he hated was being in the middle of the fight all the time. The Committee would ask him to do one thing and, sure as eggs is eggs, the Brigadier would be in here the next day telling him to ignore whatever it was they'd said. Then, when he did what the Brigadier wanted, poor Phil would have to tell lies to the Committee. What they'd asked for couldn't be done, something like that.'

'It must have been very difficult for him. I've only been here a week and I'm beginning to know how he felt.'

'The thing is, for all the times Phil did the things he wanted, the Brigadier never thought well of him. I think he thought Phil was weak, which I suppose, in a way, he was.'

'I think he must have been stronger than you think to put up with that for, how long was it, ten years?'

'Yes, ten years he was here.'

'Well, the way I feel right now, I'm not sure I shall be here ten days,' David said, rubbing his forehead. 'I think they should have advertised for a masochist.'

'Are you all right, Mr Crowley?' Margaret leaned forward, looking concerned.

'Yes, I've just got a bit of a headache, that's all. I don't cope very well with stressful situations any more, I'm afraid.'

'You shouldn't have to,' Margaret said. Suddenly, she stood up and took hold of David's arm. 'Look, you come and sit down over here by the fire.'

Taken by surprise by the gentleness of Margaret's touch, David allowed himself to be led to the armchair.

'That's it,' Margaret said, softly. She took David's coffee from the desk and placed it on the coffee table beside him. 'Now, you just sit there quietly until you feel better. I'll make sure you're not disturbed.'

She closed the door gently and David was left alone in the office, the ticking of the old wall clock, the only sound.

The coffee was hot and he sat back in front of the gas fire and relaxed. He thought about the Brigadier and his bullying disregard for the opinions of others. He thought about poor old Phil Oakley, spending years being battered into submission.

David took a sip of coffee and considered the Brigadier again and what he might do to get his own way this time. He had no doubt that the old boy would spend the coming week working on members of the Committee. In spite of

71

what Giles Southern had said, would they really back him against the Brigadier? He thought about Tess and how much he missed her guidance in difficult times. She was always so much more objective than he was. He thought about Margaret and her kindliness towards him. The dark green dress she was wearing had the same old-fashioned look about it as most of her wardrobe. She was slim and her straight dark hair, streaked with grey, was cut very simply. It was clear that she not a woman who spent a lot of time concerned with her own appearance. Yet, she had a warmth of touch and her face had revealed a concern for his welfare. He hadn't realised how much he'd missed the feel of another human being until she'd touched him. He thought about the Brigadier again...

'How are you feeling, now?'

David awoke suddenly to find Margaret sitting on the edge of the chair opposite.

'I'm sorry, I must have nodded off,' he replied. His mouth was dry and he felt rather foolish.

'That's all right,' Margaret said, smiling. 'You obviously needed the rest. I only came in because Bob Morgan has been asking for you. He's got a problem with one of his machines and he wondered if you'd come and look at it with him.'

'Yes, of course,' David said, half rising.

'There's no rush,' Margaret said, holding up her hand. 'I said you'd come out about one o'clock, if that's all right?'

David looked up at the old clock. It was just before noon. He must have been asleep for almost an hour.

'Yes, that's fine. Tell him I'll see him at one.'

'OK,' Margaret said, standing up. 'In the meantime, why don't you just take it easy? There's some fresh coffee there,' she smiled. 'You must have dropped off before you'd had time to drink the last one.'

Hole	Name	Yards	Par	Score
5	Encounter	344	4	

1

The afternoon was bright and warm. A glorious September day. It was a Monday and not many people were out on the course.

David was enjoying himself. Bob Morgan had wanted him to look at a spiking machine which, he maintained, was on its last legs.

'We're not going to need it until the spring,' he explained. 'But, I don't think it's going to last another year.'

'How old is it?' David asked. 'And, er, what does it do?' His ignorance of greenkeeping matters, especially of greenkeeping machinery, was clear.

'I think it's mentioned somewhere in the Bible!' Bob laughed. 'It makes holes in the greens. The spikes are hollow and when you pull it over the grass it punches out little holes into which we brush peat and sand. Putting it simply, it improves drainage and lets the air in.'

'And, that's obviously important?'

'Very. If you want healthy grass and good greens, that is. And, these are not just good greens; they're great greens.'

'What's wrong with it?'

'The technical term for it is buggered. It's been mended so many times, it screams "Oh no, not again!" whenever any of us goes near it with a spanner. This year, we wasted more time mending it than we spent using it.'

'Well, Bob, if the Club survives the winter, then I'll ask the Committee to buy you a new one in the spring. How's that?'

'That's as near as I've ever got to a promise,' Bob laughed. 'You in a hurry?'

'Why? Are you going to show me more broken-down machinery?'

'No. Although, I could if you're really interested! No, I was going to suggest we took a drive round the course; have a look at the place.'

David thought for a minute. There was nothing waiting for him back in the office. One of the advantages of having no money to spend was that there was rarely anything on his desk that wouldn't wait.

'I'd love to,' he said. 'Do you know, I came for my interview and I've been here a week as Secretary and I haven't actually seen the course, yet!'

The head greenkeeper pulled a battered red Subaru pickup out of the barn and David climbed into the passenger seat.

'Just push that stuff out of the way,' Bob said, indicating the rags, tools, crisp packets and empty soft drink cans on the floor; the detritus of a hundred lunch breaks.

'This old girl is on her last legs, too,' Bob cursed as second gear crunched noisily.

'Is there anything in your shed that isn't on its last legs?' David asked, pretty sure he already knew the answer.

'Well, we do have some very nice rakes!' Bob grinned. Beneath, the bonnet, the cold diesel engine rattled.

The two men laughed and the pickup rolled gently across the grass towards the first tee. As they drove down the fairway, Bob pointed out features of the course, the surrounding woodland and the wildlife. It was clear to David that this was a man who had a passion for his surroundings.

The first and the eighteenth fairways were the only parts of the course visible from the clubhouse. Relatively flat and open, there was nothing about them to suggest that over the horizon lurked a golf course of exceptional beauty.

Yet, as they drove on past the first green, set in a clearing among tall beeches, this is what began to unfold around them. A gravel path through the trees led down to the second tee, standing high on the side of a wooded valley. A long par five hole, the drive from the tee was to a small, sloping arc of plateau along one slope of the valley. The second shot had then to be hit down over a gorge with its narrow trout stream, to a tight landing area on the far side. Miss the plateau from the tee and getting across the gorge with the second shot was almost out of the question. The third shot, from the valley floor to an elevated green perched on the opposite side of the gorge required even greater accuracy.

'Make you want to get your clubs out?' Bob asked.

'I haven't played for a few years,' David smiled. As they drove down the valley, however, his hands and arms almost twitched as he played imaginary shots through this golfing paradise. It was only as they crossed the river over the old stone bridge that it occurred to David that he hadn't said, in reply to Bob's question, "I don't play any more."

The fourth hole was a par three. Only a hundred and fifty yards from tee to green, yet, within this short distance, the gurgling stream wound back and forth twice before encircling the far side of the sloping green. This short hole alone was enough to test the skill and nerve of any golfer.

'You can see why the farmer sold the land,' Bob shouted as the Subaru pulled its way slowly up through the beech woods towards the fifth tee. 'It definitely isn't suitable for growing crops!'

'But, it certainly seems ideal for a golf course,' David replied. 'It's not at all muddy like most parkland courses.'

'Partly, that's because it doesn't get the wear and tear that many courses get,' Bob explained. 'But, it's also the work they did putting in drainage all those years ago. Whoever did that, made a terrific job of it. Somebody once said that this stretch of land was always intended by God to be a golf course.'

75

'That's been said about many courses,' David smiled. 'But, I can believe it in this case. Perhaps, that's why there are so many priests about!'

The two men laughed as they emerged on to a plateau. Ahead of them, David could see that three holes formed a broad triangle around a large man-made lake and an area of beech wood. The term, 'area of outstanding natural beauty' might have been coined for such a place. Geese and ducks scurried across the lake, while pheasants strutted the fairways. Yet, no golfers were to be seen.

'Monday's always a quiet day,' Bob explained, as if reading his mind. 'The ladies have a competition tomorrow, so they'll be a few more up here then.'

'It's so peaceful,' David said.

'If it's peace you want, you've come to the wrong place, from what I hear,' Bob grinned.

'Oh, you mean my little battle with the Brigadier? Margaret told you about that, did she?'

'She did mention it. Giving you a hard time, is he, the old boy?'

'I think he sees it as his job to defend the Club against any change,' David replied, holding back from saying what he really thought of 'the old boy'.

'He's not too bad, really,' said Bob. 'He and his wife were very kind to me and the missus, when we first moved up here from Wales. She's a typical officer's wife. A tremendously strong woman, but also very kind. I think she's the only person who can really handle the Brigadier.'

'I'd like to meet her,' David laughed. 'Perhaps she could give me a few tips!'

'There's only one thing you need to know about the Brigadier,' Bob confided. 'He loves this club. It's his whole life, really. He stood alongside the tractors as they built the tees and greens. And, he watched as his father drove the first ball down the first fairway. He and his brothers grew up playing here and apparently couldn't wait to get back whenever they got any leave.'

'It's certainly a special place,' David agreed.

'You haven't seen the back nine, yet,' Bob smiled. 'Some of the holes out there will take your breath away.'

'Do you know who designed the course?' David asked.

'I think the basic layout was worked out by old General Tufnell and a couple of his army friends. After that, it was refined gradually over the years as people found new ways to play it.' Bob grinned, 'Mind you, if God intended the land to be used as a golf course, I reckon the Devil had a hand in designing some of the greens.'

'Why do you say that?' David asked.

'Because it's so easy to three-putt them!' Bob laughed, and he pointed to the seventh green.

David could see what he meant. There was almost no level area anywhere on the velvet sward. Two large steps ran across the green which, itself, sloped steeply from one side to the other. Smaller undulations made the whole a putting challenge of the highest order.

'Want to try a putt?' asked Bob. 'There are some clubs in the back.'

'Another time, perhaps,' David smiled. "Well, perhaps just one putt," murmured a little inner voice. But then, another whispered, "Get thee behind me, Satan!" Those same two characters who stood behind David as he looked at his reflection in the mirror each morning, had somehow insinuated themselves within the cab of this dilapidated Subaru.

'Do you play much?' David asked.

'As much as I'm allowed,' Bob replied.

'By the Club? But, surely…'

'By the missus!' Bob laughed. 'I grew up in Wales near the Rolls of Monmouth. That's where I learnt to play. And to keep greens. This is the only place I know that's better.'

More temptation was on offer at the eighth tee where the golfer was offered two options. The average player could hit his ball about one hundred and fifty yards, over some low bushes to a flat area far below, just short of the water. From there, it was a shortish iron shot to the green, which was almost encircled by the meandering trout stream. Two putts across the sloping green would yield a par four. The more ambitious player, however, could try to drive his ball over the bushes and across the water. If successful, this would leave him only a short chip and a putt for a birdie three.

'What a challenge!' David whistled.

'Yes, almost every shot on this course offers the same sort of options, and the same sort of challenges,' Bob agreed. 'That's why the Brigadier loves it, I think. A round to him is like a military campaign, full of risks, dangers and rewards.'

'You make it sound very poetic,' David laughed, although he could see what the greenkeeper was getting at.

'Perhaps, that's the Welsh in me,' Bob smiled. 'But, I've spent enough time with the old man to know how he thinks when he looks at the course. It's been developed and refined over the years until, now, he sees it as almost perfect.'

'Which is why he doesn't like the idea of any changes?'

'I think so,' Bob nodded.

'Well, he'll have to get used to some of them, I'm afraid. I'm sure it's no secret the Club has money worries, to put it mildly. If the Brigadier won't accept any change, he could lose it altogether.'

The Subaru had crossed back over the river and was winding alongside the ninth fairway towards the clubhouse.

'It's none of my business, of course,' said Bob. 'But, if you want to get the Brigadier on your side, you'll have to let him know that you love the game, and the place, almost as much as he does. If he thinks you're just a pen pusher or a money man, he'll never trust you.'

'Thanks for the advice – and the guided tour,' David said, smiling. He climbed out of the cab and turned away.

'Let me know when you want to see the back nine,' Bob called after him. 'Or, better still, when you'd like to play it!'

2

'Can I say something, Mr Crowley?' Margaret spoke quietly as she placed David's coffee on his desk.

David had just arrived on Thursday morning. It was the day before the committee meeting and he wanted to spend the morning preparing all the necessary papers.

Margaret sat down next to his desk.

'You ought to go up into the bar and restaurant more.'

David was surprised by her suggestion.

'But, I do, Margaret. I had lunch on Tuesday, and I went up for coffee yesterday.'

'No, I mean just go up there and sit around for a while. There's a lot of talk going on. Sarah Hall's picked it up and so has John. People are complaining, saying that you're going to ruin the Club, that the Club's going to go bust, that you're going to let all and sundry join, things like that. The Brigadier and his friends are spreading a lot of it around, so Sarah reckons.'

'And, you think if I go and sit up there, they'll stop saying all those things?' David asked.

'Well, they wouldn't say stuff like that if you were there.'

'Perhaps not. But, they could just as easily say it out on the course, or in the changing rooms, or over the telephone.'

'I suppose so. I just thought that, well, it's not fair, when you've only just arrived and are trying to do your best to put things right.'

David was moved by Margaret's concern. He leaned forward and smiled.

'Look, Margaret, there was a time – when I was a headmaster – when that sort of talk would have upset me quite a lot. But, not any more. I'm here – you and I are here – to do a job. We'll do it as well as we can and I hope we succeed. But, if they don't like it, well, that's just too bad, I'm afraid.'

As he leaned forward, David noticed a large bruise on the side of Margaret's face.

'What on earth have you been up to?' he asked.

Margaret went red and turned away so that the bruise was no longer visible.

'Oh, nothing. I just banged myself. I'm always doing things like that. Daft, I am!' She smiled and stood up.

'I'll go and get on with the photocopying,' she said, and her full skirt brushed against David's arm as she swept by.

David picked up the steaming white mug and took a sip. Margaret had learned quickly exactly how he liked his coffee. He closed his eyes and relished the taste for a moment.

In truth, David was not quite as unconcerned about the members' gossip as he had let on to Margaret. Such talk still had the capacity to wound. But, he was becoming stronger. Of more concern to him, at the moment, was that the bruise on Margaret's face had clearly been made by a human hand.

3

'And so, ladies and gentlemen, if we could move on now to item eight on the agenda.'

Giles Southern's precise tones brought the muttered conversations around the room to a halt.

David had sat quietly alongside him for a full hour and a half. Inside, he felt a mixture of impatience and amusement. Here was a club in the most dire financial straits imaginable. Nevertheless, its chairman – the Club Captain – and indeed all the ten men and one woman present, had decided that they must work through their agenda in the usual order.

Finance had always come near the end of committee meetings at Branfield Park. A tradition had evolved to allow those who had something pressing to contribute on matters such as catering, the condition of the course or the provision of towels in the changing rooms, to have their say first. They would then be free to leave to attend to more pressing personal business before the tedious subject of money was discussed.

No wonder they're in the state they are! David thought. *Talk about rearranging the deck chairs on the Titanic!*

It was Friday evening. Committee meetings were always held on Friday evenings.

During his latter years as a headmaster, David had fought a rearguard action against a proliferation of meetings. The quiet tradition of weekly staff meetings and termly governors' meetings had changed, almost overnight. Suddenly, gatherings were called to discuss virtually every aspect of school business. There were departmental meetings, curriculum meetings, financial meetings and sub-committees for each and every this and that. Eventually, when senior staff wanted to ensure that they had their way at a forthcoming meeting, they would even hold a 'pre-meeting' meeting to ensure they presented a united front at the meeting proper.

David had found himself in demand at most of these meetings since meaningful discussion required information that was often only to be found inside his head. For some time, he'd managed to keep Friday evenings meetings-free. His chairman of governors, an intense and humourless woman in her sixties, had supported him because her evening classes were normally held on Fridays. However, when these were changed, the school's entire meetings schedule had also to be rearranged.

This evening, the Branfield Park Committee had spent some time considering the report of the catering sub-committee before moving on to address the important matter of the format for the Winter League foursomes competition. The possibility that the Club might not actually exist before the winter was over was not, apparently, sufficient reason to advance finance up the agenda.

The arrangements for the autumn dinner dance had at last been finalised. It was the afterglow of this animated discussion that Giles now interrupted as he called those present to order.

'As you know, David was asked to take an urgent look at our financial position following the auditor's rather adverse report. He has, of course, been busy finding his way around, but I know that he has now had time to look at the accounts. I understand he has some suggestions for us to consider as to the best way forward, so I shall now hand the meeting over to him.'

An alarm bell sounded faintly in David's head. *Some suggestions?* Where was the biting of bullets and the iron resolve with which he and Giles had ended their pre-meeting meeting over lunch the previous Friday? David looked at the faces around the large table. Suddenly, the warm smiles had evaporated. They were not hostile, perhaps, but wary and suspicious.

Something had changed.

'Thank you, Giles,' David said, looking around with a smile. 'I for one am really looking forward to the autumn dinner dance.'

The assembled faces stared back impassively. His smile, finding no reflection in their surface, quickly evaporated.

Certainly, something had changed.

'Well, as you all know,' David began. 'The auditor's report left little doubt about the Club's financial situation. It didn't take a great deal of financial expertise on my part to appreciate that we are in serious difficulties. Following my meeting, last week, with the bank manager, Mr Essam, it is clear that we have very little room to manoeuvre. We must decide on some urgent changes if the Club is to survive in its present form...'

'Surely, that is for the Committee to decide?'

David stopped. The interruption had come from Toby Kelham, across the table, to the Brigadier's right.

'I'm sorry, I'm not sure I understand? I thought we were all agreed...'

'Nothing has been agreed, Mr Crowley. *We* have agreed nothing. Your job is simply to provide any information that the Committee may require and, when asked for it, advice. It is then for the Committee to arrive at any decisions.'

A large man, Toby Kelham owned much of the land surrounding the Club. Indeed, he still retained the fishing rights to the trout stream that flowed through the course. He sat now with his arms folded across his immense chest, staring at David with hostile eyes set beneath huge, upswept eyebrows and a large, balding pate.

For a moment, David was knocked off his stride. Nods of agreement from others around the table made it clear that the brooding landowner was not alone in his view.

David was perplexed. He hadn't expected the Committee to embrace the changes he was about to propose with open arms. Nevertheless, following his lunch with Giles, neither had he anticipated open hostility. Yet, here he was, being put in his place before he'd even had an opportunity to propose anything.

Then, he looked at the Brigadier and, from his identical implacable pose, he gleaned the truth.

They've been got at! David thought. *The bloody Brigadier has got at them!*

'Of course. It is, of course, for the Committee to decide what actions, if any, it wishes to take…'

David's struggle to regain his composure and to get the meeting back on track was suddenly interrupted. The door opened and everyone turned as Kate Earnshaw bustled into the room.

'So sorry to be late, Giles. Sorry, everyone. Couldn't get away from work until now.' She turned to David and smiled warmly as she passed him on the way to her seat. Kate was wearing a simple beige linen dress. From her elegant hair and make-up, however, David deduced that she had certainly not rushed straight from work.

'Do hope I haven't missed anything important,' Kate whispered, as she passed him.

'Not at all.' David smiled. He felt as if the cavalry might have arrived in the nick of time. He had no idea how Kate stood on the matters they were about to discuss. However, he suspected from her knowing smile that, if the Brigadier had been trying to get her on his side, he hadn't succeeded.

'David was about to give us his analysis of our financial difficulties, Kate,' Giles explained. 'And, his suggestions for resolving them.'

Kate sat down next to Pat Taylor, her vice-captain, and Giles nodded to David to continue.

4

For the next half hour or so, David talked quietly to the men and women around the table about what he now knew about the Club's financial position. He explained the extent of the cash flow problem and the crippling overdraft this had produced. He reported on his conversation with the

84

bank manager and the ultimatum that had stemmed from it. Then, he spent some time on a detailed assessment of the Club's immediate spending needs: several new items of greenkeeping equipment, a replacement refrigerator for the kitchen and a computer, preferably two, for the office.

Of course, none of this was, or at least should have been, new to any of those present. Most of what he told them had been in the auditor's report, although every now and then a Committee member would throw out a question that revealed how little of the report he or she had digested. David fielded these questions politely and with patience so that, soon, he was beginning to feel the confidence flowing back into his system. This was the old David, he thought at one point, holding forth before a group and carrying them with him towards some eventual goal.

By nine-fifteen, the car park outside the committee room windows was in darkness. Inside, David was beginning to believe that light might finally be dawning around the table. No member of the Committee had left, which suggested that they knew how important the situation was. Either that, he thought, or the Brigadier had asked them to stay and support him. It was difficult to tell which from their faces or their questions. Now, it was time to find out.

'So, I hope you will agree with my assessment that the only possible course of action is for the Club to increase its membership. Only by opening its doors to a large number of new members, and by welcoming a considerable increase in visitors, can the Club hope to pay its way out of this crisis.'

It was an assured performance. The conclusion was delivered with all the confidence of a speaker who knew his facts and was used to guiding others towards a consensus.

There was a pause, then Giles spoke.

'Thank you, David, for that most sobering assessment of the Club's position. I'm sure the Committee will wish to take on board all that you have said.'

There were a few nods from around the table.

'Now,' Giles continued. 'If we can move on to Item Nine on the Agenda: The construction of a new bunker alongside the fifth green.'

David was stunned. He knew he'd given a good performance. And, while he hadn't expected them to swallow the medicine he was prescribing without complaint, he hadn't been prepared for them simply to ignore his proposals altogether; just to move on to the next item, almost as if he'd said something quite interesting about the weather!

'Excuse me, Mr Chairman,' he interjected. 'I was wondering if anyone had any more questions they would like to ask regarding the Club's financial situation. Before we move on to the next item, that is?'

'I was under the impression that people had asked all the questions they wanted,' Giles replied, clearly rather irritated by the interruption. 'Now, as I was about to say, the Club has at last obtained planning permission for the construction of a bunker to the right of the fifth green...'

'Am I to understand, then, that my proposals for the Club's survival are accepted by the Committee?'

David could feel himself becoming very hot and his heart was thumping hard beneath his bright silk tie.

'I don't think you can infer that at all,' Giles responded sharply. 'The members of the Committee have listened to your presentation with great patience, David. It is not normal for the Secretary to speak at such length at a committee meeting. However, this is clearly a matter of some importance and the members felt it only right that they should hear what you have to say.'

One or two Committee members nodded or murmured agreement.

'Having done so,' Giles continued, 'they will no doubt wish to consider your proposals, along with others, at some future date. Now, time is pressing and I must insist that we move on...'

'Well, clearly, the gravity of the Club's position has not registered sufficiently if the Committee is happy to leave the matter to a future meeting,' David persisted. 'Unless the actions I have proposed are taken, and taken urgently, there may not be many future meetings.'

'*What nonsense!*' the Brigadier exclaimed.

'Damned nonsense,' echoed Toby Kelham, pushing his immense frame back in his chair and looking up at the ceiling. He bent forward and glared at David.

'Listen here, Mr Crowley, this club has been around for longer than I care to remember. Its not about to disappear just because you say it is. So, I suggest you keep quiet and let the chairman run this meeting. Then, we can get through the agenda and all go home.'

'Yes, well, as I was saying...' Giles began again, but David was becoming angry now.

'I'm sorry, Mr Chairman, but I'm afraid I'm going to have to interrupt you again.'

Toby Kelham sighed with exasperation.

Alongside him, the Brigadier muttered, 'Damned cheek.'

Two or three similar mutterings echoed around the table.

'No, I'm sorry, Mr Crowley,' Giles replied, his voice shaking slightly. 'I really must insist that there are no further interruptions. As I said, it isn't usual for us to have spent so long on financial matters, as it is.'

'Perhaps that is why the Club is in the mess it is!' David retorted, emboldened by the discomfort he had detected in the chairman's voice.

Toby and the Brigadier hissed a sigh in unison.

'Look,' David said, trying not to reveal the tension he was feeling. 'When I was interviewed a few weeks ago, the panel made the state of the Club's finances very clear. And, it was made equally apparent that they wanted me to do something about it.'

For the moment, David's assertiveness had worked and the Committee fell silent. From their glares, however, he guessed that they were not quiet because they agreed with him.

'I have presented the situation to you this evening, as best I could,' David went on. 'It really is as grave as I have indicated and I am not sure that even the measures I've proposed will be enough to turn things around in the time available. Clearly, you all love this club very much. I can only suggest very strongly that, if you really do, you agree to take at least some action this evening. Otherwise...'

'Otherwise what, laddie?' Kelham interrupted. 'Otherwise the big, bad bank manager will come and eat us up! Come on, Mr Chairman. I suggest you bring this meeting to order. Then, perhaps, we can finish our business and adjourn to the bar.'

Giles opened his mouth to speak.

'Otherwise, I'm afraid you will have to find another Secretary,' David declared.

David looked around the table. Now, they were quiet. Now, he had their attention.

'As some of you will know,' he went on. 'I retired early from my post as a headmaster because I was finding the situation rather too stressful. Well, I have my pension and I no longer need that sort of stress in my life. What I certainly do not need is to be treated as if I was an office boy; as if I should speak only when spoken to. I thought at interview that you were serious about getting the Club back on an even keel. However, it is clear to me now that you have no intention of changing the way you operate. In those circumstances, Mr Chairman, I feel that it would perhaps be better if I were to leave now. Certainly, I should prefer not to spend the remaining few months of the Club's life fighting stressful battles with yourselves. So...'

'Remaining few months!' Toby Kelham almost exploded.

'Never heard such gibberish,' the Brigadier added.

'If you can't stand the heat, laddie!' Kelham smirked.

'Get out of the kitchen, eh?' the Brigadier completed. 'Mr Chairman, I think the time has come for you to take control here. Can't have this feller laying down the law to the Committee, what? If he doesn't want to operate in the way we want him to work, accept his resignation and let's get the meeting over with.'

'Well, I, er,' Giles began. 'I'm not really sure about that, Brigadier.'

Then, he turned to David.

'If you really feel that you wish to resign, David, obviously the Committee wouldn't wish to stand in your way. However…'

'*I don't believe it!*'

The interruption came from the opposite side of the room. From Kate Earnshaw.

'I cannot believe what I am hearing here,' Kate went on. 'You are seriously considering accepting David's – Mr Crowley's – resignation rather than face up to the issues he has raised?'

'Steady on, now, Kathryn,' the Brigadier said. 'It's not a question of facing up to anything.'

To the Brigadier, it was a major innovation for women to be on the Committee at all. However, if they were going to be there, he would prefer that, like the Secretary, they should speak only when spoken to.

'Yes it is! Not facing up to reality is exactly what it is,' Kate retorted. 'This club is in a real mess. And, it's in a mess precisely because you, Henry, and your chums,' she looked straight at Toby Kelham, 'have behaved for years as if Branfield were your own private kingdom. Every time anyone has dared to raise the question of money in the past, they've been shouted down; told it's none of their affair.'

'Absolute poppycock,' Kelham muttered.

The Brigadier sat red-faced beside him. Kate was one of the few people in the Club who addressed him to his face by his first name. It always disarmed him.

'Sorry?' Kate glared at Kelham. 'I'm afraid a lot of what I've heard here this evening is poppycock. And, none of it has come from Mr Crowley.'

She looked around the room. Then, she turned and smiled gently at the chairman.

'Listen, Giles, you know that what David has been saying to us makes sense. We all know it.'

She looked directly across at Kelham and the Brigadier.

'We also know that certain people have spent the past week trying to lean on the rest of us; telling us to keep quiet tonight. I didn't think they would have got to you though, Giles.'

Giles looked at Kate rather sheepishly.

'Look here, Kate, it was put to me, and to some others around this table, that the future of the Club is at stake. That what is being suggested could destroy...'

'What is being suggested is not going to destroy the Club,' Kate interrupted. 'Sure, it will change it and some of those changes might not be to everyone's liking.'

Again, Kate looked across at the two colossi.

'But, unless we agree to take the sort of action David has described, and quickly, there won't be a club for any of us to fight over. That may not bother some people but I for one have a lot to thank the members of this Club for. And, I don't want to be on a committee that allows it be destroyed. So, if you're willing to accept David's resignation, then you'd better accept mine, too.'

'Now, Kate,' said Giles. 'I'm sure no-one here wants you to stand down.'

'Absolutely not!' Pat Taylor agreed, anxiously. 'I'm certainly willing to support Mr Crowley's proposals.'

'And, I shall second them,' Simon Cornwell added his support. The old doctor hadn't uttered a word throughout the meeting. Now, he spoke slowly and quietly.

'I'm sorry, Giles. And, I'm sorry to you, Mr Crowley. I should have spoken up earlier. I must confess that I am one of those who has been 'leaned upon' over the past few days. And, I'm sorry that I didn't have the sense to see it for what it was. People who are so short-sighted that they would rather see the Club destroyed than contemplate any change.'

He turned towards Kelham and the Brigadier.

'People – I'm sorry, Toby, and I'm sorry, Brigadier – who are behaving like ostriches; who think that if they keep saying everything is fine, it always will be. Well, life isn't like that. When my dear wife was ill, I thought like that. I was sure that, if I just behaved as if nothing was wrong, everything would be fine. Well, it wasn't, and it isn't. When things are going wrong, you have to face up to them and do something about it or they get worse. That is why I shall second the proposal.'

Kate reached across and grasped the old man's arm. Simon smiled at her.

Emboldened, Giles broke the silence.

'Ladies and gentlemen, I confess that I, too, was misled into keeping silent on this matter. For that I wish to apologise. We now have a motion; one which I intend to support. Pat has proposed that we support Mr Crowley's plans to increase the membership and encourage more visitors. Simon has seconded the motion. May I suggest that, as it is getting late, we now take a vote on the proposal so that we can get on with the rest of the meeting. All those in favour?'

He looked around the room. Slowly, one by one, the members of the Committee raised their hands.

'Ten in favour,' Giles announced, matter-of-factly. 'All those against?'

'Can we assume that applications for membership will be monitored very carefully?' the Brigadier interrupted. 'We're surely not being asked to accept that anyone who turns up will be allowed to join the Club?'

'From what I hear, Brigadier, no-one is actually turning up at present,' Giles replied.

'Maybe not, Chairman, but if, as you are suggesting, the new Secretary initiates some sort of recruitment drive, people may well start to show interest. All I wish to be sure of is that, if and when that happens, every application will be properly scrutinised.'

Giles was becoming irritated.

'Look, Brigadier, ten members of the Committee have voted in favour of increasing the membership. I am quite sure that, if we are fortunate enough to attract applications, then those applications will be properly considered as they have always been. Now, are there any votes against the proposal?'

David felt a slight alarm. What Giles had said left open the question of exactly who would 'look at' any applications. He was about to interrupt, but hesitated when he saw the annoyance on the chairman's face.

'All those against?' Giles repeated.

The Brigadier and Kelham looked at each other as if satisfied. Neither moved.

'Abstentions, two,' Giles said, sounding relieved. 'Now, can we please get on with the business of this blessed bunker?'

HOLE	NAME	YARDS	PAR	SCORE
6	THE VIEW	387	4	

1

'For God's sake, Ben! Couldn't you have got a room on the ground floor?'

'No way, Dad! These are the best rooms in college. Only final year students get to live up here. Great view and, best of all, nobody to disturb you.'

David had just carried Ben's computer monitor three flights up the old winding staircase. He had been up and down the stairs at least six times already and he could feel his heart thumping. He dumped the monitor on the bed and made his usual mental note to start visiting the gym again.

'That's about the lot, I think,' Ben said. 'Ready for a cup of tea?'

David nodded and sank into the only available armchair to get his breath back.

Ben was right about the view, at least. Set high on a hill overlooking the Thames Valley, the main college hall had originally been a Victorian mansion. From Ben's loft room, on a clear day, it was possible to see for many miles.

'It's amazing,' David said, as Ben returned from the kitchen with two mugs of boiling water. 'Years ago, when I went off to college, I took everything I needed in a rucksack. Now, it's like moving house every term. I mean, I know you have to have a computer, son, but do you really need your hi-fi, a television and a video? I mean, if you're working as hard as you say, how do you get time to watch anything?'

'Gotta keep up with the culture, Dad,' Ben grinned, scooping the tea bags from the steaming mugs and adding UHT milk from a carton. He passed one mug to David and sat on the edge of the bed.

93

'So, you got your own way with the old duffers then, Dad?'

'I think most of them saw sense in the end, even if reluctantly. I don't think the Brigadier and his chums will give up just yet, though.'

'But even the old Colonel Blimps must see that the Club has got to bring in more money than it's spending, surely?'

'I must say, that's rich, coming from you!' David laughed. 'No, Ben, their concept of financial management is similar to your own. Don't worry about money and money won't worry about you.'

'OK!' Ben grinned. 'This year, I promise, I'll be more careful.'

'You certainly have your mother's optimism, I will say that,' David smiled. 'I wish she could have seen you here. She would have been very proud of you, Ben.'

'I know, Dad.' Ben took a sip from his mug and looked out of the window. 'Fancy a game before you go?'

'A game?'

'Yeah! We've got a nice little nine-hole course here, remember. I've got my clubs and I could borrow some for you if you'd like to play a few holes.'

David had forgotten that Ben's college enjoyed the luxury of its own golf course. He'd introduced his son to the game when he was only nine years old and the boy had quickly proved to be a natural. They had enjoyed many a close match together, before Tess's death.

'Thanks for the offer, Ben. But, you know, I haven't played for a while,' David said.

'I know. You haven't played since Mum died,' Ben said. 'Don't you think it's time you started again?'

'I'm just not ready yet, Ben. Sorry. I have my reasons.'

'I know your reasons, Dad. You think you neglected mum when she was ill. And I've told you before, that's total crap. You did all anybody could have done. Look, I miss Mum all the time, Dad, just like you do. But, she

94

would be the last person to want to see you sitting around doing nothing. She knew how much you enjoyed your golf. Mum wouldn't have wanted you to give it up.'

'Maybe,' David said. It was the first time they had spoken about Tess for some time. The first time, too, that Ben had admitted missing his mother. 'I'll think about it, I promise.'

David got to his feet and the two went down the spiral staircase and out into the sunshine.

'She sounds quite a woman,' Ben remarked.

'Who?'

'The Ladies Captain. Nice looker is she?' asked Ben.

David reddened.

'Well, yes, actually she is rather attractive,' David said.

'Actually, she is rather attractive,' Ben mimicked. Then, he grinned. 'Are you going to ask her out, then?'

'God, Ben, you're nothing if not blunt! No, is the answer. Look, I'm the Secretary and she's the Ladies Captain. As far as I know, she's married and, even if she isn't, I can't start asking the members out. Anyway, I'm not ready for that, yet, either.'

'Pity,' Ben said. 'I'm sure mum wouldn't want…'

'Me to be sitting around on my own,' David completed. 'I know. Anyway, how come you're such an expert on what your mother would want. As I recall, you became pretty expert at doing what she didn't want!'

They laughed together and then hugged briefly before David climbed into the Laguna and drove away down the winding drive.

2

'Brigadier Tufnell rang to say he may be a little late,' Margaret reported as she placed David's coffee on his desk. The morning's post had been opened and arranged in a neat pile on the blotter.

'Late?' David queried. 'Oh, God, I'd forgotten. Of course, it's Monday, isn't it?'

In truth, David had forgotten neither the Monday nor the Brigadier. What he had hoped, as he had driven through the lanes that sunny morning, was that Friday's meeting had convinced Brigadier Tufnell that their Monday get-togethers were no longer necessary. He imagined the Brigadier quietly conceding that the balance of power in the Club had shifted and that decision-making was now to be more democratic.

He sat back and hugged his coffee mug. Remembering the small concession the Brigadier had wrung from Giles over the scrutiny of any new membership applications, David smiled at his own naïve optimism.

The old bugger isn't going to give up, he thought.

David reflected again how alike they were in some ways, he and the Brigadier. How many times in his career had he pressed on with some project or proposal, despite opposition; almost encouraged by opposition? He had been so determined to prevail over those who stood in the way of what he thought was right for his school. He was certain he was right because he cared so much about his school and its children. But, were the others always so wrong? Usually, he had got his way but at what cost? His colleagues had been stressed and his own health had suffered.

Now, he suspected, the Brigadier was determined not to give ground on something that he cared so deeply about. And, this time, David was on the other side.

He looked quickly through the post. That, at least, was an easy task. In school, he had eventually become depressed and suffocated by the avalanche of paper that daily buried his desk. Sometimes, he would work all through Sunday to clear it, only to find that a fresh load had been deposited by the middle of Monday morning. Now, after scanning a few statements from suppliers, the latest bank statement and a catalogue from a computer equipment supplier, David sat back again, to think.

To think.

What a luxury, he thought. *Time to think*!

In a world in which speed and work-rate are worshipped, time to think, the space to consider and to reflect, have been largely sacrificed. So much so, that those who still have some time to think are often thought by others to be under-employed. And, the lucky ones who are able to snatch a little thinking time are rarely able to enjoy it without feeling at least a twinge of guilt.

As he planned the day ahead in his mind, the pleasure of being able to do so was combined with a restlessness that was tainted by this guilt. Thus, when the door opened and Margaret suddenly came in to the office, David lurched forward and quickly assumed a pose as if reading the papers on his desk.

'Another letter, just came in by hand,' she explained, smiling. 'Believe it or not, a membership application.'

'Oh,' David looked up. 'Who's that from?'

Margaret dropped the letter on his desk.

'Mr Spiros Makrides. At least, I think that's how you pronounce it. He's filled in a form and everything, although I can't ever remember sending one out to him.'

'Spiros Makrides? Who is he? Should I know him?'

'If you lived around here you probably would. Actually, he's quite well known, locally. Runs a nightclub in town. And, he's a bit of a property developer, I think. My Tom reckons he runs the local mafia, too,' Margaret laughed. 'But, I think that's only because he's a foreigner.'

'A foreigner?'

'Yes, he's a Greek. From Cyprus, I think. I've only seen him a couple of times, when he came here for lunch with the Brigadier and Mr Kelham. I do remember he wears lovely suits, and nice ties. Just like you do,' Margaret said, smiling.

97

David flushed and looked down at the papers on his desk.

'He came here with the Brigadier and Toby Kelham, you say? He doesn't sound as if he's the Brigadier's sort. A nightclub owner and property developer? Hardly a pillar of the local establishment, is he?'

'No,' Margaret agreed. 'Although, he did marry a local lass, but, she's not exactly a society girl. In fact, she worked in one of his nightclubs, so I heard. He's got a reputation for being pretty tough, I think. In business, I mean. Actually, he seemed to be more friends with Mr Kelham than with the Brigadier.'

'Well, no doubt the dear Brigadier will tell me all about it when he arrives,' David said, glancing again at the letter on his desk.

'How did your meeting go on Friday?' Margaret asked.

'Oh, I expect he'll want to talk about that, too. The Committee did eventually agree to let me try and recruit some new members. But, let's just say that the Brigadier and Mr Kelham weren't very keen.'

'I wouldn't trust him, if I were you,' Margaret said, leaning over and brushing David's arm as she picked up his empty coffee mug.

'The Brigadier? Oh, I think he's honest enough,' David said. 'He's made it pretty clear where he stands from the day I arrived. So, there's not much to mistrust really.'

'No. I don't mean Brigadier Tufnell,' Margaret said. 'I can't say I like him; not after the way he treated poor old Phil. But, he's straight enough and I know he loves the Club. No, it's that Mr Kelham I don't care for. He's a smarmy one all right. Butter wouldn't melt when he talks to the ladies. But, he's only looking out for himself and, round here, he's got a reputation as a pretty hard man.'

'I'll bear that in mind,' David smiled. 'Now, before the Brigadier comes, I want to make a start on the job of recruiting some new members. What's the local newspaper for this area?'

'The *Herald* is the one most people read, I think,' Margaret replied. 'Then, there's the *Post* and the *Chronicle*; they're the free newspapers.'

'Well, let's start with the *Herald*, shall we?' David suggested. 'If we pay for a nice big advert, we might be able to get them to write some editorial about the Club as well. Tell everyone how keen we are to welcome new members and visitors. That sort of thing. They want the advertising revenue and they're often looking for something to fill an empty space.'

'Would you like me to find their number for you?'

'Yes, please. In fact, would you like to have a chat with them about it? Find out who we have to talk to if we want them to do a big splash about us.'

'OK,' Margaret smiled. As she walked to the door, she looked out of the window. 'The Brigadier's just arrived, so I'll bring you a fresh cup of coffee, shall I?'

3

'An advertisement? In the local newspaper? No, no, laddie. I don't think much of that idea, at all!' The Brigadier dismissed David's proposal out-of-hand.

David had just spent a patient half-hour taking coffee with the Brigadier. The old boy had clearly not had a good weekend, following Friday's committee meeting. He was obviously not happy with the way the vote had gone. However, by Monday morning, he appeared to have acquired a new determination. The electoral setback was dismissed as a minor insurrection; a mere skirmish, one that could largely be ignored or circumvented with David's co-operation. His recollection of the outcome of the meeting differed markedly from that of the new Secretary.

99

'No, I think what we need to do is put out a few feelers,' the Brigadier confided. 'What is it they say? Put the word around? That's it. Put the word around in the right places. Let a few people know that we might be more receptive if they'd be interested in joining. That should do the trick.'

David suppressed a sigh.

'With respect, Brigadier, I don't think that would do the trick at all. We need to attract a lot of new members, and quickly. Putting out a few feelers isn't likely to yield the sort of numbers the Club needs to survive.'

'There you go again. It was all that talk about surviving that got the people on the Committee so worried. Quite unnecessary. Lot of damned defeatist nonsense, if you ask me,' the Brigadier said.

'With respect, Brigadier,' David began again, rather less respectfully, this time. 'The members of the Committee were quite right to be worried about the Club's survival.'

He picked up the bank statement from the pile of post on his desk and held it out so that Brigadier Tufnell could see it.

'The real situation is quite desperate, I'm afraid,' David explained. 'Our income does not anywhere near match our expenditure. And, look at the extent of the overdraft.'

David pointed to the bottom line of the statement. Then he picked up the other items from the morning's mail.

'And, we're getting demands for payment from our suppliers every day. One or two of them are becoming quite aggressive in tone. If we don't pay up pretty soon, they could go to court. They could ask for us to be wound up. Then, there really would be a question of survival.'

The Brigadier looked at the correspondence and then sat quietly for a few moments before replying. David took the opportunity to take a sip of coffee.

'I must say, you paint a pretty bleak picture, Crowley.'

At last, David thought, I'm finally getting through to the old bastard.

100

'Yes, a very bleak picture,' the Brigadier repeated, soberly. 'Damn it, man, I'm not a fool. I can recognise a difficult position when I see one. Can't say I share your assessment entirely, though, and, I certainly don't agree with your alarmist talk. And, most certainly not to those people on the Committee. Never been in action, d'you see? Don't react well under fire. Likely to make hasty decisions.'

The Brigadier sat back.

'The position may well be difficult but I will certainly not accept that it is hopeless. You and I must now do something to retrieve matters,' the Brigadier said. 'God knows what Flight Lieutenant Oakley was doing all those years to get the Club into this position. No head for figures, I suppose.'

David bit his lip.

The Brigadier suddenly brightened.

'What we need to do is a bit of tactical manoeuvring. Keep the enemy at bay until we can call up reinforcements, what?'

'What did you have in mind, Brigadier?' David thought he might as well hear the old boy out.

'Oh, you know, the usual things. Hold off paying any bills until you have to; cut down on non-essentials. That sort of thing. You're supposed to be the financial wizard. I'm sure you can come up with some ideas. What's our biggest item on the debit side?'

'Salaries, of course. But, you're surely not suggesting that we don't pay our workforce, Brigadier?' David asked.

'No, of course not. But, I'm sure we could cut back, somewhat. There always seem to be too many of those young girls standing around behind the bar, if you ask me. And, maybe Mrs Hall could make do with a little less help in the kitchen.'

'Maybe she could,' David conceded, becoming impatient. 'But, Brigadier, that is mere tinkering. Those

101

people earn very little. If we got rid of one of the barmaids and lost a kitchen assistant, it would still take us over ten years to pay off the overdraft from any saving we made. If you really want to make savings, it would be better to cut down on the greenkeeping staff.'

The Brigadier looked alarmed.

'Most certainly not! There must be no economies in that area, Crowley. We must preserve the quality of the course, whatever we do. I will accept no compromises in that quarter,' the Brigadier exclaimed. 'I am merely suggesting that consideration could be given to a reduction of non-essential personnel.'

'And, as I have explained, Brigadier, it would do little to help. Apart from the fact that any saving would be minimal, it hardly seems fair to discuss sacking the lowest paid workers in the Club, when some of the members, who earn far more than they do, are paying greatly reduced subscriptions.'

'Now, listen here, Crowley. As I've said before, those discounts are long-standing arrangements that cannot be changed. I should be grateful if you would not raise the matter again. And, certainly not with members of the Committee.'

'Then, what steps do you propose we take, Brigadier?' David asked.

'As I said, m'boy, as I said. We keep an eye on expenditure until reinforcements arrive.'

'Reinforcements, Brigadier?' David was getting really irritated at being addressed as if he were the office boy.

'Reinforcements. Exactly. You persuaded the Committee to let us recruit some extra members. Didn't agree with you at the time, but now I've had the weekend to think things over. I'm pretty sure that if you ask the right people, discreetly of course, we can get one or two new members...'

David had heard enough.

'I'm sorry Brigadier, but we've already been through this. Recruiting one or two new members isn't going to help the situation in any way. I really thought for a moment that you were serious about addressing the Club's problems...'

'Now, look here, laddie...'

'And, please don't keep calling me 'laddie', Brigadier!'

He picked up the papers from the desk.

'This paperwork tells us only one thing, Brigadier. It tells us that the Club is broke. In fact, it tells us that the Club is so broke that it probably can't be fixed...'

The Brigadier tried to interrupt, but David was in full flow.

'As I say, it probably can't be fixed. But, if it is going to be fixed, it isn't going to be by tinkering and a little tactical manoeuvring. This club's problems aren't going to be solved by laying off a couple of hired hands or by a few discreet phone calls to the 'right people'.'

The Brigadier was not accustomed to insubordination and tried to speak again.

'No,' David continued. 'This club's problems are so serious that they will only be solved by taking radical measures...'

At the word 'radical', the Brigadier bristled. But, David pressed on.

'... by taking radical steps to increase the income. And, that can only be achieved by recruiting a large number of new members and by accepting a big increase in paying visitors. That is what I proposed to the Committee and, if you recall Brigadier, that is what they agreed.'

'I do not recall any numbers being mentioned at the meeting,' the Brigadier replied. 'Some expansion of the membership was certainly approved, yes. But, I am certain that none of those present had in mind a large increase.'

'Oh, come on, Brigadier!' David exclaimed. 'It's true that no actual numbers were mentioned but everyone present knew we were talking about a significant growth in the membership.'

'I'm not sure I would agree there. Certainly, Mr Kelham and I abstained on the understanding that a small rise, carefully monitored, was being approved.'

'Well, until the next meeting, Brigadier, we must agree to differ on what the Committee intended when it voted by ten votes to none in favour of a membership increase. In the meantime, I intend to take steps to recruit as many people as possible.'

'And, just how do you propose to do that?' the Brigadier asked, warily.

David explained that, as a headmaster, he had found the local press very helpful in promoting school activities. If he took out an advertisement for, say, a concert, the newspaper concerned would often be willing to augment this with an article about the school. In this way, the profile of the school was raised and a better response to the advertisement would be achieved.

Predictably, the Brigadier didn't like the idea.

'You're surely not serious? Look here, Crowley, this is a very exclusive golf club. Membership has always been by invitation only. We do not accept applications from people who have not been invited. We most certainly do not go around touting for members in the local newspaper. The idea is quite preposterous!'

'Nevertheless, Brigadier, that is what I propose to do.'

David began to feel very hot. He wasn't enjoying this stand off with the Brigadier at all and he wished the old man would just go away and leave him in peace.

'The Committee resolved that I should get on and recruit new members,' he continued. 'In the absence of any of your 'reinforcements', I believe that the only way I can let people know that we want them to join the Club is to advertise.'

The Brigadier rose to his feet.

'Now, listen here, Crowley. I came in here this morning prepared to be reasonable in spite of your behaviour in front of the Committee the other evening. But, my patience has its limits. Must I remind you that you are an employee here...'

'Indeed, Brigadier, and I am employed by the Committee. I am trying my best to carry out their instructions and, if you have a problem with that, I would suggest you raise it at the next meeting.'

The Brigadier was perplexed. He had little experience of subordinates standing up to him or speaking out of turn. If anyone had had the effrontery to do so, they had usually been cajoled or bullied back into line without delay. He tried another tack.

'Come now, Crowley.' The Brigadier sat down again next to David's desk and adopted a more conciliatory tone. 'Now look here, old chap. There's no need for us to fight over this matter. You and I have got to work together for the good of the Club. We're both reasonable fellows. I want only what is best for Branfield Park and I'm sure your intentions are sound, even if I don't agree with your methods. What do you say we start again, work together on this one, what?'

'What did you have in mind, Brigadier,' David tried not to sound as suspicious as he was.

'Well, lets say I agree to you placing your advertisement in the local press. No harm done, there. I'm sure there are some perfectly acceptable people around; people none of us have thought of inviting to join the Club. You go ahead and place the advertisement. Then, I'll look through any applications we receive and see if we have anyone suitable. How does that sound?'

David had to admit that, to anyone else, the Brigadier's suggestion might sound perfectly reasonable. However, he knew that it was anything but. The Brigadier was simply proposing to move his gatekeeping activity one stage further down the recruitment process. The end result would be the same: few new members and little new money.

'I don't think that was the Committee's intention, Brigadier. They did, after all,' David argued, 'agree by ten votes to nil to support my plan to increase the membership. I don't recall they accepted a regulatory role for you.'

'Don't you, Crowley? Well, I distinctly remember the chairman agreeing that any applications would be properly looked at "in the same way that they were in the past". The vote was taken on that basis. And, I suggest, laddie, that if you have a problem with that, you raise it at the next meeting.'

You sly old bastard! David thought. He had been outwitted and he knew it. He was dealing with an experienced campaigner who had no intention of losing any battle for control of the Club. There was no arguing with the Brigadier. David decided to make a tactical withdrawal. He would fight another day.

'Very well, Brigadier. I'll place the advertisement and we'll see what response we get. But, I hope I'm not wasting my time. Remember, the Committee's intention was that I should work to increase the membership.'

'Of course, dear boy. Of course!' The Brigadier felt he could afford to appear magnanimous in victory. 'Now, is there anything else for us to look at this morning?'

At that moment, David wanted nothing more than to get the Brigadier out of his office. However, he was curious about the remaining item of mail on his desk.

'Only this, Brigadier,' he replied, rather wearily. 'An application for membership, from a Mr Makrides. Do you know anything about him? One of your reinforcements, perhaps?'

The Brigadier took the letter and scanned it briefly.

'No. I didn't invite him. I don't really know him, although I have met him a couple of times. He's a local

106

businessman, I believe. Greek chap, I think. Seemed a smart enough fellow.'

'Well, if you didn't invite him, Brigadier…'

'Toby proposed him. Toby Kelham. They're business associates, apparently. Toby seems rather keen to get him involved in the Club. Can't quite see why. Chap's hardly ever played golf, as I understand it.'

'So, what do you want me to do about it, Brigadier?' David was annoyed with himself even as he asked the question. Almost without resistance, he was going along with the Brigadier's role as membership decision-maker.

'Better write and say he can join, I suppose,' the Brigadier replied. 'He's not the sort we really want to recruit, but Toby's invited him, so I suppose we'd better agree.'

David was curious. At the committee meeting, he had assumed that the Brigadier and Kelham were close allies. It was now apparent that their relationship was not as intimate as it had appeared. Irritating as the Brigadier was, David knew that his first and only concern was his golf and his golf club. However, Kelham, he suspected, had quite a different agenda and he recalled what Margaret had said about not trusting him.

'If you're sure, Brigadier,' David said. He was torn between his irritation at again conceding to the old man and his recognition that he and the Brigadier shared a common concern about the proposal before them.

'I'm not sure, Crowley. Not sure at all!' the Brigadier retorted. 'I may appear a stubborn old duffer to you, but I can assure you that I am as concerned for the future of this club as anyone else on that blessed committee.'

'No one doubts that, Brigadier,' David said quietly.

'No? Well, I have always set my face against these sort of memberships. What I call 'memberships of convenience'. A chap wants to impress a business colleague and so he tries to get him into the Club. Don't hold with it. This is a golf club, Crowley, not a damned social club! First and foremost, we want golfers here. People who understand the real meaning of golf. People who appreciate the spirit of the game.'

'So, Brigadier, what do you want me to do about Mr Makrides?'

'I don't know. Toby Kelham is very keen to get him in and, God knows, we may need Toby's help before the next few months are out.'

The Brigadier looked grave.

'His help, Brigadier? What kind of help?'

'Financial help, of course,' the Brigadier explained. 'Toby Kelham is a wealthy man, Crowley, a very wealthy man, indeed. He's one of the biggest landowners in the county, you know.'

'So I understand, Brigadier. But, how can he help us financially?' David was intrigued.

The Brigadier looked towards the door and leaned forward. He lowered his voice.

'Look here, Crowley. This is a very hush-hush matter. It must go no further, d'you understand? What I can tell you is that Toby Kelham is as aware of our predicament as everyone else on the Committee. He has privately assured me that, if the Club is not able to extricate itself from its present financial difficulties, he would be willing to assist us.'

'Assist us, Brigadier? In what way, exactly?'

'A loan, dear boy. Toby would lend us the money we need to keep the bank manager happy.' The Brigadier sat back, relieved to have shared his secret. 'Very generous, don't you agree? Not a word to the others, now, remember.'

'But, how would we repay him, Brigadier?'

'That's for you to work out, of course, Crowley,' the Brigadier said, getting to his feet. 'The Committee has every confidence in your abilities.'

'And, Mr Makrides?' David asked.

'Better write and tell him he can join, I suppose. Don't want to upset Toby at this juncture. Don't suppose the damned fellow will play much, anyway.'

The Brigadier walked to the door and turned.

'Glad we've reached an understanding, Crowley. Got to work together for the good of the Club, what? You get on with placing your advertisement and keep me informed. OK?'

He opened the door and went out.

4

'That's great, Margaret. That is really great!'

'Hope you don't mind me getting on with it. I know you said you wanted to talk to them yourself.'

David thought she looked very pleased with herself. While he had been locking horns with the Brigadier, Margaret had been on the telephone to the local newspaper. She had found someone she knew – an old friend from school – and had explained what David wanted. Through a chain of transferred calls, Margaret had spoken in turn to the advertising department, to a local reporter, to the sports editor, then to another reporter and, finally, to the editor himself. She was flushed with triumph.

'They say that, if we place an eighth-of-a-page advert with them, they'll write an article about us, with photographs, and the sports editor says he will even mention us on the back page, too. Their reporter – Mr McKay is his name – wants to come over with a photographer on Friday.'

'That's absolutely brilliant, Margaret,' David declared.

'I really enjoyed doing it, actually,' Margaret beamed. 'I've only ever done the typing and the book-keeping here. It was really great to use my head for a change, take some responsibility, if you know what I mean.'

David knew what she meant. And, he was moved. After all those stressful years as a headmaster, responsibility had to him often seemed a burden, long since stripped of its excitement. Yet here was Margaret, clearly able and enthusiastic, leading a working life so limited in scope that she got a real buzz from using her own initiative for half an hour on the telephone.

'I do know what you mean, Margaret,' David smiled. 'And, you've done a great job. Now, all we have to hope is that, if this advert does bring in any new applicants, the Brigadier will let them join.'

'You didn't have such a good morning, then?' Margaret asked.

'Oh, the Brigadier agreed to us placing the advertisement, at least. But, I think there is still some way to go before he'll accept the idea of any appreciable increase in the membership.'

'But, surely he understands about the money situation?' Margaret asked.

'He does, but he has his own solution. One I can't tell you about, I'm afraid,' David explained, and he shook his head. 'I don't know, Margaret. Is all this stress worth it, I ask?'

Margaret put the papers she had been holding down on the desk and stood up. She moved behind David and placed her hands on his shoulders.

'There, there,' she said softly. 'Don't you let old Brigadier Tufnell get you down.'

David made to rise and protest, but she pushed him gently but firmly back down into his seat.

'After an hour with that old devil, you need something to help you relax.' Margaret spoke quietly. 'Look at you, your shoulders are up round your ears.'

With her thumbs and fingers, Margaret carefully kneaded away at David's shoulders and neck.

110

'That's better,' she whispered as she felt him relax. 'That's what you needed. Just you close your eyes and let go.'

David did as he was told. Margaret worked the sides of his neck with her hands. As she did so, she gently pressed his shoulders back against her warm belly. After some minutes, David began to feel a pleasant sensation, not only in his shoulders but also in his loins.

As if recognising the impact her moving fingers were having, Margaret slowly removed her hands.

'There, does that feel better?' she asked.

'Yes, er, thank you,' David replied. 'That felt very good, Margaret. I must say, you're quite an expert.'

'We aim to please!' Margaret looked down at David and smiled. Then, she picked up her papers and left the room.

Hole	Name	Yards	Par	Score
7	Press On	376	4	

1

On Tuesday morning, David sat sipping coffee at a corner table in the club bar. Margaret brought him coffee whenever he asked for it, and often when he didn't. However, he had decided that he would try, as often as possible, to take his morning break in the bar. He told himself that it was a good way of making contact with the members; that it would help him keep his ear to the ground. After all, he might hear things in passing over a cup of coffee that would never be said formally to him or by anyone on the Committee. The truth, however, was that he was starting to find it depressing to sit alone, drinking coffee in the clock-ticking silence of his huge office. He needed to escape. He was beginning to need people again.

David sat at a table near the large windows overlooking the ninth green and began to pour a second cup. The sun was streaming in and the course was looking very green and inviting.

As he stared into his coffee, his mind filled with anticipation at the thought of the press coverage to come and the hoped-for applications to follow. There was an obstacle, in the shape of Brigadier Tufnell of course, but obstacles are there to be overcome. He thought, too, of Margaret's massage and the resurgence of physical needs it had evoked.

'Mind if I join you, David?'

David started. He hadn't noticed Kate in the bar. She was smiling down at him now, coffee cup in hand.

'Not at all,' he half stood and indicated an empty chair. 'Do join me. Are you playing today?'

112

'I was,' Kate explained, sitting down. 'But Jane Howland has just rung to say she can't make it after all. Some problem with her mother, apparently. So, I thought I'd have a cup of coffee and then call it a day. Unless you fancy coming out for a few holes?'

Kate smiled warmly. David thought how slim and attractive she looked in her light trousers and pink polo shirt, and how tempting her suggestion was.

'Thank you, but no. My playing days are in the past, I'm afraid.'

Kate poured some milk from the jug on David's tray into her coffee.

'You were quite a golfer once, I hear,' she remarked.

'Oh, I don't know about that. I did play a lot at one time. Rather too much, in fact. I got my handicap down to four at one point, when it seemed important to do so. But, as I say, those days are over.'

'That's a pity,' Kate said. 'If you don't mind me saying so, you do seem awfully fit and healthy to give up playing. Did you just lose interest? Or, weren't you enjoying it any more?'

'Oh no. I loved playing and I still love golf. It's just that, for my own reasons, I decided that I should hang up my clubs.'

Kate was becoming curious and David could sense she was about to ask more questions.

'What about you? How often do you get to play?' he asked.

Kate realised that she was being deflected and decided to hold on to her questions, for now, at least. But, her curiosity was aroused and she was determined to find out more about the new Secretary.

'Only once a week, I'm afraid. I'd like to play more often in the summer but that's usually a busy time for me, so it's not always possible.'

'Forgive me, Kate,' David said. He was sure someone had told him what the Ladies Captain did for a living. 'But what is it that you do that keeps you away from the golf course?'

'I run my own business,' Kate explained. '*Potty about Plants* its called. Pot plants for offices. Hanging baskets for shops and pubs, that sort of thing.'

'So, it's your little van I've seen scooting around the town? Well, it sounds as if you're doing very well if it's keeping you that busy.'

'Oh, I'm busy enough, but it certainly won't make me rich! I'm glad I'm not totally dependent on it.'

'How did you come to be running you own plant business?' David asked.

'Well, I had to do something when I was left on my own and I didn't know much about anything else. I started very small. My solicitor is an old friend. I happened to say that his offices looked rather cheerless and would appear much more welcoming if he had a few pot plants around the place. I suppose I wasn't feeling very cheerful myself, at the time. But, he was very kind and he asked me to help by choosing some plants for him.'

Kate took a sip of coffee.

'Of course, then I discovered why he didn't have any plants already. He never touched them! I ended up going in every week and watering the poor things. You know, feeding them and generally keeping them tidy. I was right, though. It did make his offices feel more attractive. Other people in the same block saw them and asked me to find some plants for them. So, before long, I became 'The Plant Lady'.'

'And, a very attractive plant lady, too,' David smiled.

'Thank you, kind sir! You should see me when I'm up to my elbows in compost.'

'I should like to,' David said. 'I'm afraid I'm not much of a gardener, myself. Tess always did most of it. I just

114

mowed the lawn, dug the beds when needed. That kind of thing.'

'Tess?' Kate tried not to appear too inquisitive.

'My wife. She was an artist and she really loved the garden.'

'Was?'

'She died,' David said, as he got to his feet. 'Four years ago.'

'Oh, I am sorry. Forgive me. I didn't mean to pry.'

'That's quite all right. You weren't to know. I don't go around broadcasting it.' David looked at his watch. 'Now, if you'll excuse me, I'd better get back to the office. Margaret is sorting out some papers for me.'

'How are you getting on with our Margaret?' Kate asked, suddenly anxious to prolong their conversation.

'She's certainly helped me a great deal. I'd have struggled without her, these past few weeks.'

'She always seems so quietly competent,' Kate said.

'Oh, she's very good at her job,' David agreed. 'Yesterday, she persuaded the editor of the local paper to do a feature about the Club, to go alongside our advert for new members.'

'Gosh!' Kate said. 'You've certainly wasted no time getting started on your recruitment drive.'

'There's no time to waste, I'm afraid,' David replied. 'I only wish the Brigadier would appreciate the urgency.'

'Henry? But, surely you're not still having trouble with him, are you? After all, the Committee vote was pretty emphatic.'

'Yes, but – I don't know if you noticed – he cleverly slipped in the bit about new applications being scrutinised as they were in the past. To him, that means he retains the right to say yea or nay.'

'The crafty old fox!' Kate laughed. 'That wasn't what we agreed at all. Look, David, talk to Giles if you have any more trouble from Henry.'

'Thank you, I will. Let's hope it won't be necessary.'

'Maybe, but I think I might have a word with Giles myself.' Kate hesitated, then she said, 'I am sorry if I seemed inquisitive earlier.'

'Not at all,' David replied. 'After all, it was four years ago.'

He smiled, turned and walked away.

2

David was in his element. It was almost like being back at school. As a headmaster, that is. He was helping the *Herald's* photographer orchestrate the pictures that would accompany the editorial about the Club.

They had begun with the usual shots of the Club sign and followed that with the clubhouse main entrance, complete with a couple of accommodating golfers. Another pair of smiling members had held up their glasses to the camera in the bar and, in the restaurant, Mrs Hall had poured a glass of wine for a diner at the table with the best view over the course. Hopefully, the fact that it was only ten o'clock in the morning would not be apparent to the *Herald's* readers.

Downstairs again, David had posed behind his desk, first alone and looking earnest with his pen poised over some important-looking document. Then, he had sat smiling as he received some equally vital looking paperwork from Margaret.

They had visited the professional's shop before moving outside to the driving range. Here, Jack had set up a demonstration lesson with one of the lady members. The photographer soon became quite agitated, taking pictures from all angles and varying his shutter speed to get the best action shot. The poor lady became quite nervous and Jack had to offer her a couple of free lessons to persuade her not to walk off the 'set'.

'Don't get much chance to snap anything really interesting,' explained Gareth, the young photographer, kneeling down and trying to compose his picture. The camera was close to the ball, which would appear huge in the foreground while, behind it, the club's shaft tapered away into the distance to where it was gripped anxiously by the lady pupil with Jack peering over her shoulder.

Standing up again, Gareth turned to David.

'I'd like to get some shots of the course. It looks great out there. One look at that should get the punters flocking in.'

David was rather relieved that the Brigadier wasn't around to hear about the possibility of the 'punters' flocking in. However, he explained that, attractive as golf courses might appear to the observer, particularly the keen golfing observer, attempts to record them on film can often be disappointing. In the end, Gareth settled for a picture of Jack teeing off over the valley from the second tee. Jack's shot was so graceful and the result so perfect – the ball travelling a tremendous distance and curving slightly from right to left to finish at the very end of the plateau – that David was lost in admiration. He ached to try to match Jack's shot and he could feel the edifice of his resolve beginning to crumble.

'Let's finish with someone putting out on the eighteenth green,' David suggested quickly, anxious to steer the photographer away from the tee. They climbed aboard the buggy and Jack drove them back down the course towards the clubhouse. When the final photographs had been taken, David returned to his office to meet the sports editor, Iverach McKay, whose arrival had been delayed

McKay, it emerged, had been trying to get a proper look at Branfield Park for years. He'd hoped at one time that he might be able to become a member. However, his letter of application had not even been acknowledged.

'You could say they're getting what they deserve,' he said, when David had finished explaining the Club's need to attract new members.

'Perhaps,' David replied. 'But, what's past is past. Let's just say we're now under new management.'

'Well, you're not going to find it easy,' McKay said.

'You don't think so?'

'No. At one time, golf was a rich man's game. When I first moved down here from Edinburgh, there were only four courses in the County. The clubs could take their pick. A man sometimes had to wait years to be invited to join, if indeed,' he smiled, 'he ever was invited.'

'And, you think things have changed?' David asked, although he thought he already knew the answer.

'Aye, beyond recognition. So many new golf courses have been built, you see. There are a least sixteen clubs within twenty miles now. Not all of them are as beautiful as Branfield Park, of course. Not many of them, if I'm honest. Nevertheless, there are now so many clubs that it's become a buyer's market. You can walk into most of those hereabouts and join on the spot or, at most, wait a few months.'

'So you think we might struggle to bring in new members?'

'In the short term, yes I do. Eventually, of course, you will find new people but, around here, anyone who wants to be a member of a golf club, will probably already have joined one.'

David found McKay's analysis depressing, although he had already suspected as much himself. He had, of course, been the very picture of confidence and enthusiasm when he addressed the Committee. And, they had shared his assumption, at least most of them had, that all that was necessary to increase the membership was to open the gates a little wider.

Stop turning them away, start to be welcoming and they will flood in, he had naïvely thought.

The Brigadier, he had seen as the only likely obstacle. He would, no doubt, resist the admission of anyone he deemed not to be the 'right sort'. But, there would be no shortage of applications and, ultimately, even the Brigadier would bow gracefully to reality and accept their admission.

It was only after several weeks that doubts began to creep in. Each day, as the post was neatly deposited on his desk, David looked eagerly through the pile for any applications for membership. There were bank statements as well as bills from companies and the usual trade literature. Increasingly, there were final demands and threatening letters. However, Makrides' letter remained in splendid isolation.

'Somebody's done an excellent job of turning people away,' David remarked one morning to Margaret.

'So many of the farmers around here have turned their land over to make golf courses,' she had replied. 'If my Jimmy and his mates want to play, they just pay on the day. That way, he reckons, they get to play on different courses, not the same one all the time.'

'Perhaps the answer in the short term is to attract a lot more visitors,' David suggested to Iverach McKay.

'I think you may be right,' McKay replied. 'Even if you do persuade people to leave their present clubs, they aren't going to want to do so until the end of the year.'

'And, if they've paid a year's subscription as a fee to join their clubs, they won't want to waste that,' David conceded.

'Absolutely!' the old Scotsman agreed. 'If, on the other hand, you can persuade a few societies to book up lots of golf days, you could bring in some fresh money quite quickly.'

'So,' McKay said, 'we're agreed that the emphasis of my copy ought to be on the welcome awaiting visitors at Branfield Park?'

'Yes, and also the excellent lunches and suppers they can get in the restaurant,' David suggested. The two men had just enjoyed one of Mrs Hall's meat and potato pies. Now, they were relaxing over their coffees in the bar.

'Mind you, it may not be so easy to attract visitors, with the winter coming on,' David added.

'Yes, you're right,' McKay laughed. 'Probably better if I give up now and don't waste all those column inches.'

'I'm not ready to give up just yet,' David smiled.

'I'm pleased to hear it,' McKay said, with a twinkle in his eye. 'I say that because, not only is this the best golf course for miles around, but also because I want to get to play it myself before I'm too old to carry my clubs.'

'I'm sure we could arrange something, if you're really keen.'

'I might take you up on that,' McKay replied, downing his coffee. He looked at his watch. 'But, for now, I'll just have to be content with a quick look.'

3

David didn't need much persuading to desert his desk. He went in to the professional's shop to get the keys to a buggy from Alison and was surprised to find her sitting on the counter, holding a golf club and posing provocatively for Gareth.

'You should have some pictures of me in the paper, Mr Crowley,' Alison smiled and ran her tongue across the top of the golf club grip.

David laughed.

'Thanks, Alison, but I think I'd like us both to keep our jobs for a little longer!'

'I've only seen the first nine holes, so far,' David explained, as the buggy trundled out across the car park. 'So, if you haven't that much time, we'll start at the tenth.'

'Fine by me,' McKay said. 'I'm always happy to look round a golf course. As long as my editor understands that it's in the line of duty, of course.'

David followed the buggy path alongside the tenth fairway. He drove on past the green, set on the top of a hill and surrounded by deep ditches and dykes. Long ago, the site had been the centre of an iron-age camp.

The track took them down a wooded hillside and out on to the eleventh tee. When David had stopped the engine, both men gasped at the tranquil beauty of the spot. From the tee, tucked into the hillside, the golfer was required to hit his shot across the valley, over the trout stream to a sloping green on the far side. Stray to the left and you would find the water. Be too short or hit your ball too long and you risked the same fate. Slice your ball to the right and you could go down in the woods. Seldom had David seen a par three hole that was at once as challenging as it was exquisite.

'You didn't happen to bring a golf club with you, did you,' McKay muttered.

'Don't tempt me!' David laughed, as he steered the buggy past the green and up into the woods on the far side of the valley. Near the top, they emerged into a clearing from which the twelfth hole ran dead straight for five hundred yards along the side of the hill. Along its entire length, the narrow fairway banked from left to right and was bordered on both sides by mature forest.

'That one's not as easy as it looks,' McKay exclaimed.

'No?' David queried, smiling. 'Surely, all that's required is to hit three consecutive shots, dead straight and as long as you can, up the left side of the fairway, without straying into the trees.'

'Exactly!' McKay laughed. 'Once I've learned to do that, I'll come back and play it!'

Passing the thirteenth green, they came out on to the opposite end of a large plateau. Within this open area were the fifth, sixth and seventh holes together with the fourteenth, fifteenth and sixteenth. They followed the course, stopping here are there to admire the view or, more often, to discuss the challenge presented by a particular shot.

The fourteenth fairway lay to the left of the lake. The second shot, of about one hundred and sixty yards, ran alongside the lake to the green. Given that the prevailing wind was from left to right, the smallest amount of slice and a ball would find the water.

'An alternative route might be to drive your tee shot down the right side of the lake and then hit your second over the lake and on to the green,' McKay suggested.

'The only trouble with that,' David pointed out, 'is that the green is very narrow and has bunkers on each side. So, coming in across the lake, approaching the green from the side, you would have to be spot on for length.'

'No problem,' McKay said, smiling. 'We'll have a fiver on it when I come over and give you a game.'

'You're on!' David laughed, quite forgetting to remind the old journalist that he no longer played golf.

As they drove slowly up the fifteenth fairway, they paused and watched two elderly priests hit their shots to the green. Both men missed their target, and they smiled and waved to David as he drove past. As they did so, it occurred to David that these were the only golfers they had seen throughout their tour.

'It's no wonder you've a cash flow problem,' McKay said, as if reading his mind. 'The place is almost deserted.'

'And, those two aren't even paying the full subscription!' David grinned.

122

'Mind you, it must be wonderful never having to wait to play your shot,' said McKay. 'When I started to play, in Edinburgh, you had to get up very early or you could end up waiting ten minutes every time you wanted to hit your ball.'

'Did you play a lot in Scotland?' David asked.

'Oh, never more than three times a week!' the older man laughed. 'There just wasn't time.'

'So, you became a pretty good golfer?'

'Aye. There was a time I played off scratch. But, that was a few years ago. Now, I'm lucky if I go round in under eighty.'

Me too, David thought. Me, too!

They drove alongside the sixteenth fairway and David sensed that they must now be nearing the clubhouse. The second half of the course had lived up to his expectations and was as beautiful as the first. Every hole had been initially well-designed and subsequently developed. The entire course had thus been honed into an unparalleled golfing challenge in a setting which was, both men agreed, without equal.

'It's no wonder your friend, Brigadier Tufnell, wants to keep it to himself,' McKay remarked.

'It's difficult not to sympathise,' David agreed. 'But, unfortunately, even the best golf clubs have to operate in the real world!'

The buggy rounded a bend and they approached the penultimate tee.

David thought that they had seen it all. All golf courses have good holes and bad holes, he thought. Every course has scenic golf holes and others that are uninspiring. But here, every hole, without exception, was as challenging and attractive as any that preceded it. Each was a unique golfing experience. However, the seventeenth was quite exceptional.

The buggy came to a halt alongside the tee, set on the rim of a deep gorge. A hundred feet or more below, the trout stream, the remnant of a river that had, long ago, carved this gorge out of the solid limestone, wound its way around a small circular green. Between the green and the stream, there were bunkers. Beyond the stream were woods. The tee shot had to be hit straight up and out into space. And, when it had exhausted its horizontal flight, it would fall perhaps a hundred and fifty feet down into the bowels of the chasm. It had to hit the green. There was simply nowhere else for a ball to land.

'Wow!' David exclaimed.

'Wow, indeed,' McKay agreed. 'Are you quite sure you didn't bring a club with you?'

The two men stared into the abyss, each mentally assessing how they would get a small, white ball from the ledge alongside them into the hole, barely visible far below.

'That is just fantastic,' said McKay. 'Do you know, on my office wall, I have a calendar with pictures of imaginary, fantasy golf holes. And, not one of them is as fantastic as this one.'

'It certainly is amazing,' David agreed, starting the buggy engine and steering gingerly along the path that ran at a steep angle down the side of the gorge.

'You wouldn't want to walk up and down here too many times in a day,' McKay laughed.

When they had reached the bottom, David pulled up alongside the green and turned off the engine.

Beside them, the green putting surface appeared almost to glow in the afternoon sunshine. The crystal clear waters rippled as the stream approached along the gorge, then turned and ran fully two thirds of the way around the green, before turning again and continuing on its way.

'It's a peaceful spot, all right,' the reporter said, quietly.

'Yes, it is,' David agreed. 'I thought the eleventh was golf heaven, but this is golf paradise.'

Suddenly, and without any warning, a golf ball thudded into the putting surface less than ten feet from where they sat.

Both men were startled. David looked up towards the top of the gorge, but from their position, the tee was not visible. He pushed his foot down on the pedal and the buggy lurched forwards, over the bridge across the stream and out of danger.

They looked back just in time to see a second ball hurtle into the green, only six feet from the flag. High above, the two priests waved, apologetically.

'*Bloody idiots!*' McKay exclaimed, clearly shaken. 'It's a miracle they didn't hit us.'

'Well, I suppose they're in the miracle business, aren't they?' David replied, smiling. 'Actually, from where their balls finished up, it does seem as if those two might be pretty handy players.'

'So would I be if I only worked one day a week!' McKay replied, rediscovering his sense of humour. 'It's a good job I have to get back to the office or I might be tempted to give them both a sermon.'

On any other course, the eighteenth hole would have been considered outstanding. Here, especially after the grandeur of the seventeenth, it appeared almost ordinary. The dog-legged fairway broke around an ancient, spreading oak. The forest ran down the left side all the way to and around behind the green. The undulating putting surface sat between the trees and a small lake and this, together with a sprinkling of strategically-placed bunkers meant that, at Branfield, the golfer could not rest for a moment until his final putt was in the hole.

'Very impressive!' said McKay, as David drove across the car park and deposited him alongside his car. 'Very impressive, indeed. I have to get back to the office now, but I'll get something down on paper and fax a draft over to you sometime tomorrow, if that's OK with you.'

'You could, but unfortunately we don't have a fax machine,' David replied, with a rather embarrassed smile.

McKay raised his eyebrows.

'You really do have your work cut out here, don't you?' he smiled.

'Let's just say it's a challenge,' David grinned.

'Well, the best of luck,' McKay said, as they shook hands. Then, nodding in the direction of the sports car parked alongside his own, he said, 'You might tell that photographer of ours that it would be nice to see him back in the office. When he's ready, that is.'

David parked the buggy and was still laughing at McKay's parting comment when he entered the professional's shop. At first, he thought there was no-one there. Then, he realised that he was mistaken. The grunts and sighs emanating from behind the storeroom door suggested that Alison had yet to say goodbye to the young photographer. Quietly, David placed the buggy key on the counter and returned to his office.

4

'Got a minute, Boss?'

When he saw him in the outer office, sitting alongside Margaret's desk, David wondered if Jack knew what Alison was up to in the shop storeroom. For a moment, he even thought Jack might have come to talk to him about it.

'Come on through, Jack,' David said. 'How can I help you?'

Jack sat down next to the desk.

'How did you get on with old Iverach?' he asked.

'Fine!' David said. 'I really enjoyed chatting to him. I only hope he writes as well as he talks. You already know him, do you?'

'Oh, yes. Iverach's been covering sport in this area for

126

years. He reported on a juniors' match I played in once. Said I had great promise, if I remember,' Jack grinned.

'Well, he was right there,' David smiled.

'Maybe,' Jack said. 'Anyway, it's good to see something being done about getting some more members. Let's hope it does the trick.'

'So, what's the problem, Jack?'

Jack leaned forward, his elbows on his knees. He looked at the floor, then up at David.

'Look, Boss, I really like this place. I enjoy it here. The last thing I want to do is walk away…'

'So? Come on, Jack. Tell me. What's the problem?'

'Well, it's simple really,' Jack went on. 'If business doesn't improve, and improve soon, I shall have to pack up the shop. If we don't get some new members, people who need lessons and who want to buy stuff from the shop… Well, I can't see me lasting here more than another six months.'

'I see.' David had suspected as much.

'Don't get me wrong. I don't want to leave. It's just that, you know, we all have to pay the rent and things.'

'I know, Jack. Don't worry about it. And, thanks for coming and telling me. So, now I have two six-month deadlines, instead of one.'

'Two? How do you mean?' asked Jack.

'Oh, a few weeks ago, the bank manager gave us six months to start turning the Club around,' David explained. 'Now, I know that, if we don't, we won't have a professional's shop, either.'

'I'm sorry to add to your problems then, Boss,' Jack replied.

'You haven't, really,' said David. 'After all, if we don't meet the bank's deadline, we won't need a professional's shop. So, if I don't make the bank manager smile, I shall be the one adding to your problems.'

'Yeah, I suppose you're right,' Jack said, thoughtfully.

'So, all the more reason to hope that we get it right. Right?'

'Right!'

'Anyway, we do have at least one new member on the horizon,' David said.

'Oh, who's that?' Jack asked.

'A guy called Spiros Makrides. Toby Kelham has proposed him.'

'Makrides? So he's applied to join, has he?'

'You know him, too?' David asked.

'Big Mak? Yeah, everybody around here knows him. He runs a nightclub in the town and he's a sort of property developer, among other things. A real hard case, if you ask me. Why does Kelham want him to be a member? I wouldn't have thought he was their idea of the 'right sort'.'

'Yes, it is odd, isn't it? The Brigadier doesn't like him, but Toby Kelham wants us to sign him up.'

'Come to that,' Jack chuckled. 'Why in God's name would Makrides want to join a golf club, anyway?'

'What do you mean? Isn't he any good?'

'Hopeless! Kelham brought him up a few weeks ago. They came for lunch, I think, and afterwards he brought Big Mak over to the driving range. Talk about a Greek tragedy. It was embarrassing!'

'So, why is Kelham so keen to get him in as a member?'

'Don't ask me,' Jack shrugged, getting to his feet. 'One thing's for sure. It won't be out of kindness.'

'You know him well then, Toby Kelham?'

'Yeah, I know him, all right.' Jack went to the door.

'Oh, Jack,' David said. 'I, er, went into the shop just now. To return the buggy keys. I couldn't see Alison around…'

'Don't worry,' said Jack. 'I can guess what she was up to. I'll have a word.' Then, he grinned. 'You just can't get staff these days.'

128

Hole	Name	Yards	Par	Score
8	Temptation	299	4	

1

'I love opening boxes,' Margaret said. 'Don't you?'

'It brings out the child in all of us, doesn't it,' David agreed, smiling. He had been enjoying himself. Suddenly, in trying to squash the huge packaging flat, he caught his foot inside a box and he began to jump around, trying to throw it off.

Margaret looked across at him and laughed.

'Here, let me pull you off,' she said, taking hold of the box. Then, realising what she'd said, she collapsed in giggles at his feet.

'Christmas has come early, I see!'

Giles had entered the office unnoticed; they had been making so much noise.

'Oh, hello Giles,' David smiled. 'In case you were wondering, our computers have arrived.'

'So I can see,' Giles said, joining in the fun. 'You know, last Christmas, my children seemed to get just as much pleasure from playing with the packaging as they did from the toys inside. I can see it doesn't change when you grow up. I assume, that is, we are dealing with grown-ups?'

The two men were still laughing as they stepped over the piles of boxes and chunks of polystyrene and walked through into David's office.

'I've just picked up a copy of the *Herald*,' Giles explained. 'Most impressive, I think. Old McKay has certainly done us proud with his purple prose.'

'I suspect he's hoping we'll make him an honorary member,' David grinned as Giles spread out the newspaper on the refectory table and began turning the pages.

The article was indeed impressive. Rather than a small box, the Club's own advertisement had been stretched into a banner across the top of the page. Beneath an attention-grabbing headline, there was McKay's text, interspersed with photographs of the bar, the restaurant, David at his desk and two of the members putting. Pride of place had been given to Gareth's unusual picture, which was entitled *"A Golf Ball's Eye View of a Golf Lesson!"*

Skimming quickly through the copy, David had to agree with Giles' assessment. Iverach McKay had posted him a draft following his visit, two weeks earlier, but it was nevertheless satisfying to read the finished article.

'It's really good isn't it?' Giles said. 'Driving McKay round the course was obviously a great idea of yours. The way he waxes lyrical about the seventeenth would make anyone long to come and play it.'

'Has anyone else seen this, yet?' David asked.

'I shouldn't think so. The *Herald* only came out this morning. I bought several copies and I was going to suggest you pinned one up on the notice board.'

'I'll do that right away,' David agreed. 'I should think people will be very pleased with this treatment.'

Margaret placed a tray bearing coffee on the table.

'Well, let's hope there's a positive response for you to report at next Friday's meeting,' said Giles.

'I'm sure we'll get some interest. But, while he's been kind enough not to mention it here, McKay himself pointed out the problems.'

'Oh?'

'Yes. For a start, he suggested that most people who might want to be in a golf club will already have joined one.'

'That may be true, but I'm pretty certain they won't be playing on a course as good as this one.'

'No, but, if they've paid a joining fee, they might not be willing to waste it by leaving their present club to join us?'

130

'Well, what about waiving the joining fee for people transferring from other clubs?' Giles suggested.

'It does sound rather like poaching, doesn't it? But, needs must, as they say,' David conceded.

It was while they were laughing at the main photograph that David told Giles about Jack's warning.

'We mustn't let that happen,' Giles said. 'A golf club without a professional's shop would look a very sorry sight.'

He turned back to the newspaper.

'That's why this article has to succeed, David. Let's hope we have some better news before the committee meeting.' Giles drained his coffee cup, went to the door and turned.

'I wonder what the Brigadier will think?'

'I'm sure we'll soon find out,' David said.

'Kate Earnshaw had a word with me about him, the other day. It appears the Brigadier thinks he's still going to be the one to decide who can or cannot join the Club?'

'He always has, it seems,' David said.

'Well, not any more, he doesn't. I've spoken to several of the Committee. We're all determined to prevail this time.'

'I hope you don't think I was complaining to Kate. Behind your back, I mean?'

'Not at all,' Giles replied. 'She's a splendid girl, Kate. Such a pity.'

And, with that, Giles was gone, leaving David puzzling over his coffee cup.

A few minutes later, David had cut the feature from the newspaper and he went out into the hallway to pin it to the notice board. Even before he had finished, several members had gathered around it and David went back into his office feeling quietly satisfied.

He spent the rest of the day installing the two computers that had been delivered earlier in the morning. David had taken some time before deciding which system to buy. Initially, he had been amazed at how much had changed over the four years since his retirement; even in the two years since he'd bought his own computer at home.

However, he quickly realised that the work at Branfield would not demand the latest equipment. Eventually, he'd ordered two end-of-range Pentiums which, while not exactly state-of-the-art, were perfectly adequate for the task.

David set up the computer he would use on a table in the corner of his office. When he went out to find the printer, he found Margaret busy with a screwdriver assembling the computer trolley that would sit alongside her desk. She smiled up at him.

'I can't wait to get started.'

'I don't know if we'll be ready to begin today, Margaret,' David replied. 'I have to install all the software, first. That'll take me a couple of hours, at least.'

'Well, can I at least take the manuals home to look at,' she asked.

With the computers had come word processor software and a spreadsheet. About these, although more advanced versions than he was used to, David was quite confident. However, there was also a book-keeping program and a payroll system together with some golf club management software with which he had been particularly impressed. All this, he knew, he would have to become familiar with himself before he could show anyone else how to use it.

David decided to take the software home, play with it over the weekend and introduce it to Margaret on Monday.

2

'I am simply saying, Crowley, that it would have been better had the article been cleared with me prior to publication.'

The Brigadier had come in for his Monday morning meeting.

'I gather people are rather pleased with it,' David said.

'That is neither here nor there,' the Brigadier replied, testily. 'Put a picture of someone they know in the newspaper and most people appear to go weak at the knees. The fact is, the article gives quite the wrong impression.'

'In what way, Brigadier?'

'Well, for one thing, the very fact that it appeared at all could give people the idea that the Club is in some difficulty.'

David had to admit privately that the Brigadier had a point.

'But, the whole tone suggests that we are only too ready to welcome all-comers. If people act on that assumption, they will certainly be disappointed.'

'Brigadier, the Committee agreed...'

'Never mind what the Committee agreed, laddie. And, never mind what this reporter chappie McKay has written, either.'

The Brigadier picked up the newspaper.

'Did you read his description of Branfield Park as...'

The Brigadier searched the article.

'...one of the county's foremost sporting venues. What on earth does he mean by that? No, my boy, it's business as usual, for us. If this newspaper shindig produces any interest, you just bring it along to our Monday meetings.'

David decided it was time to let the old man know the score.

'The Captain has asked me to report any progress to the Committee, Brigadier. You will have to raise the matter with them if you aren't happy with the way I am handling things.'

'There is no call to take that tone with me, laddie,' the Brigadier snapped. 'I thought I had explained to you the way in which any new members are to be admitted.

However, if you have a problem in that regard, I shall ensure that the Committee clarifies matters for you.'

'I think that would be best, Brigadier. To avoid any misunderstanding.'

'Very well,' said the Brigadier. 'Now, are there any other matters we should discuss.'

'There is one thing, Brigadier,' David said. 'At the last committee meeting, it was agreed that I should ask the greenkeeper to proceed with the construction of a new bunker alongside the fifth green...'

'That's correct,' the Brigadier interrupted. 'Been talked about for years. The Committee agreed to it long ago. But then, Oakley discovered we needed planning permission, for some reason.'

'I understand that planning permission has now been granted, Brigadier.'

David indicated a sheaf of documents on his desk.

'Yes, so now you can get on with it. And, not before time. The shot in to the green from that side of the fairway has become far too easy for the longer hitters.'

'I'll get Bob Morgan to make a start on it as soon as possible then, Brigadier. Now, if there isn't anything else, I'd like to get on with setting up our computers.'

'No, nothing else. Just get Morgan to check with me before he starts work. That bunker needs to be nearer the front of the green. The drawing you have there shows it too far to the side of the green.'

'From what I can see, the planning permission was quite specific on that point, Brigadier. The Council gave permission on condition that the bunker is not visible from the footpath crossing the course. I understand that, were it nearer the front of the green, people would be able to see it as they walked past.'

'Absolute poppycock! What do these rambling types understand about playing a golf shot? Anyway, how many people walk along that path compared with the number of people playing golf?'

'I'm sorry, Brigadier, I can only follow the Council's wishes on this one, I'm afraid. If you don't want Bob to proceed with the bunker, why don't you raise it at the committee meeting on Friday?'

'Good God! Don't want to set that lot talking again. No, no. Just tell Morgan to go ahead as planned.'

The Brigadier left and David felt uneasy. The old boy had given in far too easily. It wasn't like him at all.

Margaret came in carrying a mug of coffee and a sheaf of papers.

'Do you want the bad news or the bad news?' she asked with a grin.

'Oh, give me the bad news first,' David said. 'Then, I'll have something to look forward to.'

'Well, the bad news is that we have another final demand from the chemicals supplier. And, from the brewery. And, from British Gas...'

'And, the bad news?'

'The Brigadier asked me to put next week's meeting in the diary. Just so you won't forget.'

'Is that it?'

'No. We have three letters from people who might be interested in joining the Club. Came in by hand, this morning. And, we had a phone call, just now from a Mr Chidgey. He's secretary of a golf society at that electronics factory in town. They want to book a day here, but not until the spring.'

'Well, that's something, at least,' David said, taking the pile of letters.

'So, can we start work on the computer, when you've finished your coffee?' Margaret asked. 'I read through the *Word* manual and I'd like to have a go at it, if that's OK with you.'

'All right,' David smiled. 'Give me half an hour to look through the mail and then we'll get to work.'

David sipped his coffee. He put the letters from suppliers to one side. They could wait. It was the three membership enquiries that he was interested in.

The first was from a schoolteacher who explained that he'd recently started teaching locally. He had played off a twelve handicap at one time and would like to take up the game again.

The second came from the managing director of an industrial cleaning company. He'd lived in the village for years and played occasionally, though never at Branfield Park.

The third letter was from a local self-employed plumber, who wrote that he'd played a lot of golf when he lived in the north of England but had never joined a club since moving south.

Well, they may not be the Brigadier's cup of tea, but they're a start, David thought.

He wrote a note on each letter asking Margaret to invite them to come in for a chat at their convenience.

'Right,' said Margaret. 'Now, I've switched the phone through so, if you're ready…'

'OK,' David smiled. 'Let's get started.'

David pulled up a second chair and he and Margaret sat side-by-side in front of his computer

'Now, I think it best, to begin with, if you use the computer for word processing, writing letters, committee minutes, things like that. We'll bring in the book-keeping and accounts and the payroll as and when we can.'

'OK,' Margaret nodded. 'Anything will be better than that old typewriter.'

As David had expected, Margaret proved a very quick learner. Of course, she already had very confident keyboard skills and she'd spent the weekend absorbing everything in the manuals. But, as he explained the main features of the

136

word processor programme: deleting; editing; formatting; saving and retrieving files, Margaret seemed almost one step ahead of him. Operations which had, over the years, become second nature to David, Margaret now picked up so quickly that, before many minutes had passed, she was beginning to correct him.

So rapid was her progress that, after an hour or so, David moved on to creating a mailing list of the members and merging them into letters. As the afternoon wore on and the light outside faded, David became aware that, in the darkening office, he and Margaret were very close together. Occasionally, she would playfully grasp his hand and move it aside in order to try something herself. At one point, David noticed that their thighs were in contact. He moved his leg away slightly but, before long, he again felt a gentle pressure on the side of his thigh. Then, as he explained how to print addresses on envelopes, Margaret gently stroked the back of his hand. This time, he noticed that the pressure was inside his trousers.

'I've really enjoyed this afternoon,' Margaret said quietly, still looking at the screen. 'It's been so nice working together, like this.'

'You've picked it up very fast,' David replied.

'I've had a good teacher.'

'And, I've had a good student,' David said, standing up.

'I wonder if there's anything I could teach you, in return?' Margaret looked up into his eyes.

David flushed and turned away.

'I think that's enough new stuff for today,' he said. 'Why don't you carry on for a bit? Practice some of the things we've been learning. I have to see someone up in the bar.'

Margaret smiled and turned back to the computer.

David went through into the outer office and, as he did so, he could feel cold sweat over his back and under his arms. He stopped and breathed deeply several times before he started up the stairs.

3

David sat at his usual table. Mrs Hall had brought him a pot of tea and a large slice of her home-made coffee cake.

Except for the customary brace of parsons in the far corner, the bar was empty and David was relieved to have a moment to think.

He thought about Margaret. He had fled her proximity and he was not really sure what had forced him to his feet and impelled him from the room. Certainly, he had found the contact with her warm body pleasurable. But, the look in her eyes and the touch of her had had produced both arousal and alarm.

Was it that she was a married woman and he was… well, he was her boss? He had to admit such considerations had not really weighed heavily with him. He was, after all, a widower, a free man.

He thought about Tess. Then, he felt guilty because, more and more, he had to make an effort to think about Tess. Previously, she had rarely been absent from his thoughts but, recently, a transition had taken place. Whereas before, he had felt that Tess was still with him, now he knew that she was there no longer. He wondered for a moment if this transition was behind the belief, common in many religions, that after a suitable waiting period, the soul departs for heaven, or wherever else it goes.

In Tess's case, he knew that it would be heaven.

Close together, in the darkening office, he had found Margaret physically attractive, that much was certain. He was less sure of how he felt now. It was so long since he had been in this position. He wondered whether he was

138

expected to respond. Did he want to respond? Could he even respond to what he took to be her advances?

Then, he thought of Kate.

He remembered how attractive Kate had looked when they had sat together in the bar. He thought how warm and encouraging she'd been since he had arrived at the Club. He had assumed that she was married. Now, at least, he knew that she, too, had been left alone. Was she still alone?

David recalled what Ben had said about asking her out. Should he respond to her solicitousness with an invitation to dinner? Would that be a bold step out of loneliness and towards happiness? Or would it prove a calamitous and embarrassing misreading of imagined signals?

He smiled. He hadn't felt this lost since he was a schoolboy.

What should I do, Tess? David thought. Should I, in fact, do anything?

There was no reply. Not from Tess, anyway.

'You look very relaxed sitting there with your pot of tea, David. Mind if I join you?'

David looked up to find Simon Cornwell standing over him.

'Not at all,' David smiled. 'Please, sit here. Let me get you a cup. Have you been out?'

'Only nine holes. I find that's quite enough, these days, I'm afraid.'

The old doctor took the seat across the table and waited as David poured him a cup of tea.

'I was most impressed by the newspaper article,' he said. 'Marvellous publicity, I should have thought.'

'Thank you, Simon. Let's hope it produces the goods,' David replied.

'Well, we all wish you success.'

'Not quite all,' David said, smiling.

'Oh dear. Is old Henry still giving you a difficult time?'

139

'Let's just say he hasn't yet welcomed the idea of change with open arms.'

'But, surely, after the committee meeting, he isn't still trying to stand in your way, is he?' Simon asked. 'Mind you, if it wasn't for Kate, he might have got his own way, even then. She stiffened our resolve just when we were dithering. She's a strong girl, Kate. She's had to be, of course.'

'Why do you say that?' David asked.

'I shouldn't really be talking about her, I suppose. But, it's common knowledge, I think. Kate was married to James Earnshaw. He was Club Captain and a tremendous golfer. Won the Club Championship several times.'

Simon pointed to a polished wooded plaque on the wall, bearing the names of past club champions. The name, James Earnshaw, appeared twice, painted in gold lettering, the last time some seven years earlier.

'Anyway, after the last occasion, James noticed he was dragging his right foot. Came to see me at the surgery. Said it felt numb. I sent him to see a specialist and that's when we discovered the worst. Motor Neurone Disease.'

'How dreadful!' David said.

'Terrible. He got weaker and weaker until he couldn't speak or swallow. Couldn't even blink, poor man. Kate – and her daughter Sarah – nursed him until the end. It was three years before he died.'

'As you say, she's had to be strong. And, she's never remarried?' David asked, trying not to sound too inquisitive.

'No,' Simon replied. 'You see, James dying wasn't even the worst of it. Afterwards, it emerged that he'd been having an affair with one of Kate's best friends. She was completely devastated, of course. I think it's made her very wary of being hurt again. It's a pity. She's such a lovely girl.'

'Yes, she is,' David said, pouring another cup of tea.

The conversation moved on to other topics before returning, as it almost always did at Branfield, to Brigadier Henry Tufnell.

'The problem with Henry,' Simon explained, 'is that he hasn't learned to let go, to relinquish control and grow old gracefully.'

'I don't think he sees himself as old, quite yet,' David smiled.

'No? Well, he and I are about the same age, you know. Although, I confess he's kept himself in much better shape than I have.'

Simon took a sip of tea.

'You see, if we're honest, at our age none of us especially relishes change. The difference is, I accept that it's sometimes a good thing and, even if it's not, that it will probably happen anyway, whatever I say! Henry just can't take that on board.'

'He's certainly very determined,' David agreed.

'Pig-headed is probably a more accurate description. Poor Martha is driven to distraction, sometimes.'

'Martha?'

'His dear wife. A splendid woman. The absolute opposite of Henry. She's calm and kind. How she manages to stay like it, none of us will ever know. Martha's the only one who can handle him, I think. She's quite a good golfer, too.'

'I imagine she'd have to be, to understand him,' David smiled.

'Oh, he certainly loves his golf, does Henry,' said Simon. 'Nothing wrong with that, of course. And, he can still play a good round of golf at a stage when most of us can no longer get our bodies to do what we want them to do. But, there's more to it than that. As you've discovered, Henry still wants to control the Club.'

'I had noticed, now you come to mention it,' David grinned.

141

'Partly, it's because he's afraid of what might happen if he doesn't. But, I think, he's also afraid he won't have anything else to do. It's as if he's lost an empire and is yet to find a new role.'

'You think so?' David asked.

'I do,' said the old doctor. 'You sort out a new responsibility for Henry and you might find him causing you a lot less trouble.'

'I'll give it some thought. That is, if the Club is still here to provide any of us with a job,' David smiled.

4

'It's true, the telephone has hardly stopped ringing all week,' David said.

'That's absolutely marvellous!' Giles replied. 'And, these are mostly people wishing to book rounds of golf?'

'Yes. It seems quite a lot of golfers around the area have been waiting for some time to play a round of golf at Branfield Park. Our advertisement, together with the tone of McKay's article has encouraged them to come along.'

'Encouraged them to crawl out of the woodwork, don't you mean?' Toby Kelham sneered. The others ignored him.

'But, not so many people who want to become members?' asked Bill Ellery.

'Not thus far. We've only had five calls from people asking how they can join. But, it is early days.'

'And, visitors still bring in money, even if they don't wish to join the Club,' Simon Cornwell pointed out.

'Yes, ten visitors each paying a green fee of twenty five pounds every week day would bring in more than we need to break even,' David said. 'We're not getting that many yet, of course. And, even if we do, we shall still need to get some more members if we are ever to pay off our overdraft.'

The Committee had been discussing the newspaper article and David had been explaining the response to date. Most members, it seemed, were very impressed with the way in which the Club had been presented. The Brigadier looked unimpressed but, until now, he had not commented.

'Perhaps, the Secretary would let us know how all these visitors are to be accommodated?'

The Brigadier's intervention brought quiet upon the room.

'Surely, ten visitors each day, playing two balls or four balls, will make very little impact on the course, Brigadier?' Giles suggested.

'And, we don't yet have ten visitors a day,' Bill Ellery added.

'No, nothing like,' said Simon Cornwell.

'Perhaps not, but, to use the Secretary's own words, it is early days. The general tone of this meeting so far has been to congratulate the Secretary on the publicity he has achieved. You all appear anxious to encourage him in his efforts to attract more people on to the course. I simply wish to know how all these visitors and new members are to be fitted in.'

'Surely, you would agree that the course is hardly crowded, Brigadier?' David said.

'No, but it will certainly become very crowded, if all these visitors and new members arrive to play at the same time.'

'Which is why I propose that we introduce a booking system, to enable people to reserve tee times,' David explained.

'Ah!' the Brigadier hissed, looking around. 'As I feared.'

'Members and visitors are expected to reserve tee times at most golf courses, these days, Brigadier,' David explained.

143

'This is not *most* courses, sir! This is Branfield Park Golf Club. Since its inception, members here have never been required to book tee times.'

'But surely, Brigadier, it is no hardship to have to sign your name on a sheet on the notice board?'

'That is not the issue, if I may say so. The point I am making is this. One of the benefits of being a member of an exclusive golf club such as Branfield Park is that one is able to play when one wishes, at a time to suit oneself, and not at a time allocated by the Secretary. Let us say that the Secretary reserves tee times for a visiting party of twelve. An entire block of time is then not available and visitors are thus given precedence over members.'

'Only to a limited extent, Brigadier,' said David.

'But, where will it end? Where will it end? Is one to find that there are so many visitors that the first tee is booked all day?'

'Of course not, Brigadier,' David said, and he explained his proposed booking system which would ensure that every alternate teeing-off time was reserved for members. Everyone, except for the Brigadier and Kelham, expressed their admiration.

'And, who is to decide which of these visitors is suitable?' the Brigadier persisted.

'Oh, that's easy!' Simon exclaimed. 'Surely, visitors are deemed suitable if they are willing to pay.'

'I think we can trust David to ensure that only serious golfers are encouraged,' Kate said.

There were murmurs of agreement.

David was grateful for Kate's support, but he was not at all sure how he would go about ensuring that all the visitors were serious golfers.

'And, then we come to the question of additional members,' the Brigadier continued, as if ignoring the points made by the others on the Committee.

'The Secretary has had several enquiries from people interested in becoming members. No doubt, more will follow. At the last meeting it was agreed that applications would be vetted as before. I have always fulfilled this role and I am sure you will agree that the quality of those admitted to membership has remained consistent with the high standards set in the past...'

'That's because no-one has been admitted to membership, Brigadier,' Simon interrupted.

The Brigadier glared at him.

'Perhaps not as many as some would like, but the maintenance of high standards is essential to the future of the Club.'

'The maintenance of high standards, as you call them Brigadier, is now threatening the very future of the Club,' Simon persisted.

'I do not agree, Doctor, that the future of the Club is under threat. Anyway, as I was saying, I have always vetted applications in the past. This has taken up some time on my part. However, I am perfectly willing to continue to fulfil this role, if that is the Committee's wish.'

'Excellent idea, I should have thought,' Toby Kelham said.

No-one else spoke.

David looked around the table. Most of the members of the Committee were fiddling with their pencils or examining their nails.

They're going to let him do it, David thought. The old bugger's got at them again. Not one of them is going to stand up to him.

But, he was wrong.

'Well, I'm afraid I don't think it's a good idea.' It was Kate.

Everyone turned towards the Ladies Captain.

'I'm sorry, Henry,' Kate continued. 'But, you've made it perfectly clear that you're opposed to any real increase in

145

the membership. We've all heard tonight what an excellent job David has done in publicising the Club's new policy of welcoming visitors and new members. If the vetting procedure applied to future membership applications is the same as in the past, the very procedure that has brought us to our present sorry state, then we all know that nothing will change. I shall therefore vote against accepting your offer.'

'And, so shall I,' said Simon.

'Yes, I'm sorry Brigadier. I do think we need to change the procedure,' Giles agreed.

'I propose that the Secretary and the Captain consider applications together,' Bill Ellery said.

There were murmurs of agreement around the table.

Inwardly, David sighed with relief. He looked across at Kate and she beamed back at him.

'All those in favour?' Giles asked.

Only two hands did not rise.

The Brigadier looked momentarily stunned. He and Kelham looked across at each other. Then, the Brigadier's powerful voice rose above the murmur.

'I must say, I am disappointed. Indeed, I am saddened that so many members of this Committee appear so ready to dispense with the guarantee of high standards that has served this club very well for so many years.'

David looked around the room. Everyone was looking down at the table as if being scolded by an angry parent.

'As I say, I am most disappointed,' the Brigadier went on.

'Here, here!' Kelham chimed in.

The Brigadier smiled at him.

'Ladies and gentlemen, Toby has a proposal to make to you which, we believe, will solve the Club's problems and secure its future. It was not our intention to bring this proposal forward at tonight's meeting. Rather, we had intended to wait and see what action, if any, the bank took at the expiry of its six-month period of grace. However, your decision to throw open the doors to all and sundry, to abandon the safeguards which have served this club so well in the past, forces us now to act.'

The Brigadier was the focus of everyone's attention.

'Toby,' he said, nodding in Kelham's direction.

'Thank you, Henry,' Kelham said, getting to his feet. 'Ladies and gentlemen, as you know, the Club has acquired a substantial overdraft. No doubt, this was the result of poor financial management by past secretaries.'

David wanted to disagree but kept his counsel.

'However, we now have a new Secretary, one who I am sure will keep a much tighter rein on expenditure. If he is successful, and the Club's overdraft were to be paid off, then the drastic changes being considered – more visitors and members – would be unnecessary. Is this not the case?'

A few heads nodded slowly. Most appeared puzzled.

'I am therefore willing, personally, to lend the Club the amount necessary to pay off its overdraft so that the main danger can be removed. This loan would be repayable at commercial rates over a very long period. In this way, the far more significant danger – a large influx of visitors and an unrestrained increase in membership – can be removed.'

Kelham smiled benevolently.

'Fellow members, as some of you will know, I have been fortunate. I am a very wealthy man. But, I am also a sentimental man, and Branfield Park means a great deal to me. I hope it means as much to you all.'

Jaws dropped all around the table.

'Thank you, Toby.' The Brigadier took up the reins. 'I'm sure the silence in this room reflects the fact that everyone is made speechless by your tremendous gesture.'

Toby smiled modestly.

'Ladies and gentlemen, I am sure you will all agree that Toby has made us a most generous offer. It is surely one that no sensible committee would even hesitate to accept.'

147

Suddenly, the Brigadier's tone became more menacing.

'Indeed, were the Committee to decline such an offer, I feel sure the membership would, at its Annual General Meeting, wish to reconsider the make-up of the Committee itself.'

Giles was aware that he had been usurped as chairman of the meeting.

'May I ask what conditions would be attached to this, er, most generous proposal?'

'None,' Toby replied. 'The purpose of my loan is to make it possible for the Club to continue as it always has. I therefore ask only that the safeguards that existed in the past, regarding visitors and new members, should remain in place.'

'In other words, you will pay off our overdraft if the Brigadier can control who plays at the Club?' Simon asked.

'Very crudely speaking,' Kelham agreed. 'Clearly, the maintenance of a high quality club is the best possible guarantee for my loan.'

'And, given the Club's negative cash flow, how do you propose that the loan should be repaid?' David enquired.

'As I have already said, the Club's present problems are due to poor financial management in the past. Now, that we have a new Secretary…'

'I'm sorry, but I don't agree,' David said. 'The Club's financial problems are the result of the very safeguards that you now seek to re-impose.'

'Ladies and gentlemen!' the Brigadier boomed. 'I must say I am amazed that you should allow the Secretary to speak to Mr Kelham in this manner. The offer on the table is a most munificent one. Surely, no lengthy discussion is necessary. I should like to propose that Toby Kelham's offer is accepted forthwith. All those in favour?'

A number of hands begin to rise.

'Just a moment, Brigadier,' Giles interrupted. 'As I recall, I am still the chairman of this meeting.'

148

The Brigadier smiled as if this were merely a procedural delay.

'Before we vote on any proposal, does anyone have anything else to add?' Giles asked.

'Yes, I do.'

Everyone looked at Kate.

Kate stood and walked slowly round the table. When she was directly behind David, she stopped.

'A few weeks ago,' she began, 'this club was in a terrible state. We had had an auditor's report telling us that we were, in effect, broke. We had an ultimatum from the bank manger telling us that we had, at most, six months to put our affairs in order. There seemed no way out.'

Kate paused for a moment.

'Then, this man,' she pointed at David. 'This man began work. At our last meeting he presented us with his analysis of the problem. And, he put forward a solution. We voted by ten votes to nil, if I remember correctly, to support his ideas. Isn't that so?'

One or two heads nodded.

'David arranged an advertisement and the accompanying article in the newspaper. And, people have responded to it. Not as many as we should like, but it is a start. Suddenly, people in the Club are feeling more optimistic. This meeting began in the same vein. There is a feeling that maybe, just maybe, we can get ourselves out of this mess. Yes, it will involve some changes and probably not everyone will like all of those changes.'

'And then, suddenly, Toby and Henry come up with their proposal. And, quite a bombshell it is. And, just as suddenly, everybody appears to have abandoned the course we agreed and to be ready to accept something that hasn't even been discussed properly. Now, I admit that Toby's offer sounds fantastically generous. Perhaps it is. Well, if it is, it will stand close examination. I detect, from his questions, that David has some reservations. OK, then let's

149

examine those, too. After all, what's the hurry? The bank has given us six months. I should therefore like to propose that we take our time. We ask Toby to put his offer in writing together with any conditions attached. And, at the same time, we ask our Secretary to put in writing the pros and cons, as he sees them. I suggest that we look at all aspects carefully and agree to make a final decision in, say, three months' time.'

Kate walked slowly back to her seat.

'Mr Chairman!' the Brigadier began. 'Kathryn has spoken most eloquently. But I really must insist that time is of the essence. The Club's future needs to be secured, now. Let us come to a decision, tonight.'

'I disagree,' said Simon. 'Kate has indeed argued most convincingly and I, for one, am persuaded. I should like to second her proposal.'

'I agree with Simon,' Bill Ellery declared. 'This is far too important a matter to be decided on the spur of the moment.'

Other voices murmured agreement.

'Well,' Giles said. 'First of all, we have a proposal from the Brigadier that we accept Toby's loan forthwith. Do we have a seconder?'

No one moved.

'Very well,' he continued. 'We have a proposal from Kate that we should ask Toby Kelham to put his offer in writing and David to do the same with any reservations he may have. We will then arrive at a decision in three months' time. Simon has seconded that proposal. All those in favour?'

One by one, those around the table, with the exception of Kelham and the Brigadier, raised their hands.

'Those against?'

No-one moved.

'The motion is carried,' Giles announced.

David heaved a sigh of relief.

As usual, finance had been the last item on the agenda and, almost immediately, the meeting began to break up. In the midst of the post-meeting bustle, David was gathering up his papers when he saw that Kate was leaving. He rushed across and caught up with her in the hallway.

'That was a marvellous speech, Kate!' he said.

She smiled.

'It seemed to do the trick, didn't it? I hope I did the right thing.'

'I'm quite sure you did,' David replied. 'Er, are you rushing off?'

'Well, I've got some work to finish at home. Why?'

'Perhaps, I could buy you a drink?' David asked. 'To say, thank you.'

'Oh, that's very kind, David,' Kate smiled. 'But, really there's no need. And, we wouldn't want them to think we're in league, would we? Perhaps, some other time.'

She turned and went out and David returned slowly to the room, feeling very deflated.

Hole	Name	Yards	Par	Score
9	Awakening	**182**	3	

1

'So, Mr Makrides, you want to take up golf?'

'Please, call me Spiros. Yeah, I got a bit more time now. And, Toby says it would be good for business if I could play the golf.'

'You and Mr Kelham are partners, I gather?' David asked.

'Not partners, exactly. We're maybe going to do some business together. So, why not on the golf course?'

'Have you played much?' Giles enquired.

'Never! Me, I'd rather watch the Arsenal play any time. But, I've watched the golf on television. It don't look too hard to me.'

David caught Giles' eye and both men suppressed their smiles. This was their first interview with a prospective member. A trial run, they had agreed, since the Brigadier and Kelham had already informed Makrides that he could join.

'I do agree, the chaps on television can tend to make it look easy. However, do you think it might be a good idea to take a few lessons, before you start? Golf has a way of making us look awfully silly, you know,' Giles explained.

'Lessons? Yeah. Why not?' Makrides agreed. 'A few lessons can't do no harm.'

'Good,' David smiled. 'We'll go and meet Jack, our professional, in a moment and get things organised. Do you have any other questions, before we do that.'

'No, I don't think so. Except, maybe, all those things they talk about on the telly. You know, Handicaps, Pars, Birdies. That kind of stuff. They're always talking about par this and par that. What does it mean? I mean, I don't want to look stupid when I'm playing and somebody starts talking about pars and handicaps and things.'

'Absolutely not,' Giles agreed.

'Well,' David said, looking very serious. 'Every golf hole has a par. Par is the number of shots a good golfer should take, under reasonable conditions, to get his ball from the tee into the hole. Short holes, those measuring up to about two hundred and seventy five yards long, are Par Threes. Par Four holes are those between two hundred and seventy five yards and four hundred and seventy five yards long. Any hole longer than this is a Par Five. Is that clear enough?'

'Yeah. Now, all I got to do is understand what yards are!' Makrides laughed. 'Why can't you British use metres, like everybody else?'

'I think, Mr Makrides, er, Spiros, it would be easier if you think of yards and metres as roughly the same,' Giles suggested. 'For players of our sort of ability, it doesn't really make that much difference.'

'OK. I got that. Now, what about handicaps? I know all about handicaps in horse racing, but I'm pretty sure you golfers aren't running around with lead weights on your backs!' Makrides rocked with laughter at his own joke.

'It can sometimes feel like that,' Giles smiled. 'No, handicaps are an essential part of golf. Their purpose is simple. They allow golfers of widely differing abilities to play together and still have a meaningful competition.'

'Roughly speaking,' David explained, 'a golfer's handicap is the number of shots over par he might expect to take to complete a round of golf. So, if all the pars of the eighteen holes on the golf course add up to seventy-two, and a player has a handicap of ten, then he might be expected to take about eighty-two shots to complete his round. And, if his handicap is, say, twenty-four, his average score will be nearer to ninety-six.'

'I think I got it,' Makrides said, slowly. 'But...'

153

'If the first of these golfers plays the second,' David went on, before Makrides could interrupt, 'the difference in their handicaps will be fourteen. The better player could therefore 'give' the other a fourteen-shot start. They might add up their scores at the end of the round and take fourteen from the poorer player's total. Alternatively, the better player might give his opponent a one shot allowance on the fourteen most difficult holes. The winner is then the player who wins the most holes.'

David saw that Makrides eyes had begun to glaze over.

'In practice,' he continued, 'the scales are tipped in favour of the better player. First, because he is better he will probably be more consistent. And, second, in competitions, the better player only has to give perhaps three-quarters of the difference in handicaps to his opponent. Without such an adjustment, the worst player might win the Club's championship just because he is having a good day!'

Makrides held up his hand.

'Enough, please, I think maybe it would be easier to carry some weights, like a horse! So, anyway, how do you get these handicaps?'

'The Secretary will work that out for you,' Giles explained.

'We'll give you a handicap of twenty-eight to start with,' David added. 'Then, as you get better, we'll gradually reduce it.'

'And birdies? When do I get to meet the birdies?'

'You get a birdie when you score one less than the par for a particular hole,' Giles explained. 'So, if the par for a long hole is five, and you score a four, you have a birdie. And, if you were to score a three, that would be an eagle.'

'I don't think you need worry too much about birdies and eagles at this stage, Mr Makrides,' David said, getting to his feet. 'Let's go and see Jack about those lessons.'

The three men went out across the car park to the driving range. There, with evident relief, David and Giles handed Makrides over to Jack.

'Crikey!' Giles said as they walked back towards the clubhouse. 'I do hope all our new members aren't quite such absolute beginners!'

'Yes,' David agreed. 'But it's strange, isn't it? There's the Brigadier, the staunchest advocate there is of the spirit of golf, fiercely resisting anything that might change 'his' Club...'

'... telling us we have to admit a chap who clearly has no real interest in the game at all,' Giles agreed. 'It is very odd, isn't it?'

'And, there's something else I can't work out,' David went on. 'What sort of business could Kelham and Makrides possibly have in common? One is a wealthy English landowner, a pillar of the local establishment, and the other is a Greek nightclub owner.'

'He's a property developer, too, don't forget,' Giles said. 'But, yes, I agree, it's strange, isn't it?'

The two men sat themselves at a corner table in the bar and Mrs Hall brought them a pot of coffee.

'Do you think he'll ever get his handicap down below twenty-eight?' Giles asked.

'Who? Makrides? I shouldn't think so,' David smiled. ' But, you never know. Golf handicaps are funny things. To some golfers, they are more than just a number, and their purpose and meaning is far greater than how many shots over par they can expect to score. For many people, handicaps have a symbolic as well as a numerical value.'

'I'm not sure I follow you, David,' Giles said.

'What I mean is this,' David went on. 'If a golfer has a low handicap, others may tend to see him – he may see himself – not just as a better golfer, but as a better man. Indeed, more of a man. Like a fast motor car, for some, a low handicap can be a penis substitute. Walking into the club bar as a single figure handicapper has a certain cachet. It allows you to stand tall alongside the also-rans with their handicaps of twenty, twenty-four or even, like Makrides, twenty-eight.'

'I've never thought of it like that,' Giles confessed, with a grin. 'I mean, as I play off fourteen, what sort of member does that leave this member?'

'Perfectly adequate, I should think!' David laughed. 'But, the thing I have noticed is that golfers are divided into two categories. There are those who want to get their handicaps reduced. Most only to reassure themselves that they are getting better, but some to reassure themselves, and to demonstrate to others, that they are real men, *mensch*, able to stand alongside the better players. The 'Holy Grail', for many of these, is a single figure handicap or, even better, to play off 'scratch'.'

David poured out the coffee.

'Then, there are those who like to keep a bigger handicap than they should have because this gives them an unfair advantage and allows them to win competitions and matches.'

'*Bandits!*' Giles hissed.

'That's right,' David agreed. 'The funny thing is, bandits may win, and win often, but no amount of winnings can compensate for the disdain with which they are regarded. Nor can any winnings equal the quiet pleasure of being able to say, "My handicap has been reduced".'

'You're quite a golf philosopher, aren't you?' Giles said.

'I just find most things about golf fascinating, that's all.'

'Everything, except playing, that is?'

'At the moment, yes,' David agreed.

'I don't wish to pry, David. But it does seem odd that someone who is as fit and healthy as you clearly are, who obviously loves the game and who was a good player, by all accounts …'

'...should choose not to play?' David replied. 'It's quite simple, really, Giles. Some years ago, my wife Tess became ill. Breast cancer. We thought she'd beaten it at one time. But, then it came back. And, eventually, it killed her.'

'I'm sorry,' said Giles. 'I didn't mean...'

'No, that's fine. It's just that, during her final illness, during that year when she really needed me, I carried on playing golf as often as I could.'

'We all deal with these things in our own way.'

'We do, indeed. The thing is, I'm not sure whether I was escaping from something I couldn't handle, or just being selfish. At the moment, I tend towards the latter. And, that's why I decided to hang up my clubs.'

'As a penance?'

David nodded. 'Something like that.'

Giles stood up.

'Thank you for telling me that, David,' he said. 'I'm sure it must seem the right thing for you to do at present. Not to play golf, that is. However, we can never be certain why we act in the way we do. So, don't go on punishing yourself for too long. You're too good a man to be lost to the game for ever.'

2

The after-effects of the publicity afforded by the newspaper continued for some weeks and the number of visitors playing at the Club increased steadily. There were some conflicts over tee times, but David and Jack, between them, resolved these as they arose.

David and Giles were kept busy, meanwhile, interviewing a steady stream of applicants for membership. Most of these were already quite accomplished players who were either looking to change clubs or to take up golf again after a period out of the game. It wasn't often necessary, therefore, to repeat the sort of basic explanation they had given to Spiros Makrides.

'It's always difficult deciding what a new member's handicap should be, isn't it?' Giles remarked. 'Especially, when people haven't been playing for a while. Take this schoolteacher chap, Brian Taylor, for instance. He says he played off twelve at one time.'

'Yes, but that was a while ago,' David said. 'If we start him off with too low a handicap, he won't stand a chance. On the other hand, if we pitch it too high, he could run away with all the prizes.'

'Yes, but you can always ask him to submit some scorecards or adjust it according to how he performs in competitions. I know that working out the adjustments in handicaps is a laborious task.'

'And one that usually falls to the Secretary,' David said, smiling. 'Actually, we now have a computer program that will calculate handicap adjustments just as accurately and much more speedily than the old pencil and paper method.'

'Really?'

'Yes,' David explained. 'Nowadays, all I have to do is take people's cards, enter their scores into the computer and it will print out the results and any handicap adjustments.'

'Remarkable!'

'It would be even easier if I could put the computer out in the hall and ask the players to enter their scores themselves.'

'I'm not sure many of the people here could handle that,' Giles laughed.

'It's very easy, actually. I'll bring it along to the next committee meeting. Once the players have entered their scores using a simple keypad, all that's left for me to do is to pin the results sheet to the notice board. Then, I wait for one of the members to offer to buy me a drink!'

And so, a month after installing the computers, David set one up in the committee room to demonstrate the special golf club management software. Having previously fed in all their handicaps, David asked those present to pretend that they had just played in a competition. He handed out scorecards and asked everyone to fill in their imaginary scores.

'Now, I want you all to enter your pretend scores into the computer, please,' he explained.

For many, touching a computer was a new experience.

Some initially sat paralysed over the special keypad, even though this was much simpler to operate than a normal keyboard.

'I've never touched a computer before!'

'What if I press the wrong button?'

After much coaxing, however, all eventually entered their scores. David then pressed a few buttons and produced a results sheet that also showed how the handicaps of those present would have been adjusted if this had been a real competition.

'That's amazing!'

'Fantastic!'

'The computer has one program for calculating men's handicaps and another for the ladies,' David explained.

'That's good!' Simon laughed. 'We wouldn't want them to start mixing too much!'

One or two Committee members took the exercise rather too seriously and actually began to question the changes in their handicaps. Eventually, however, they got the message that it was not for real and everyone agreed that the computer should be put to use in future competitions.

'What about those who don't enter their scores?' Bill Ellery asked.

'Yes,' Kate agreed. 'It's not going to be any use if only half the players bother to put in their scores.'

'Of course, some people may not like computers,' Pat Taylor groaned. 'I'm afraid, I'm one of them.'

'Oh, come on, Pat! This system is no more difficult than programming your video recorder at home,' Frank Partridge declared.

'I haven't yet learnt to do that!' Pat laughed.

'Well, I think it's a splendid system,' Kate went on. 'Quite apart from getting the results and handicap adjustments out much more quickly, David will be available to us to talk to after a match, instead of being locked away in his office with his tables and calculator. I should like to propose we adopt the computer system as soon as possible.'

Although nobody said so, few of the others could really understand why they would want David to be available to talk to after the match. His predecessor, old Oakley, had never been much fun in the bar. Having him closeted away at the end of the day had usually seemed a blessing.

'I'm sure this computer program will save the Secretary a lot of work. So, I can understand why David is in favour of it. But, the main benefit, as far as I'm concerned, is that we will find out the outcome of competitions much more quickly,' Bill Ellery said. 'For that reason, I'm all in favour of it.'

Eventually, everyone agreed that using the computer had such benefits for the Secretary and the Club that it should be brought into use immediately.

'We still haven't decided what to do about those who don't enter their scores into the computer,' David reminded them.

'The only thing you can do is disqualify them,' Frank said.

There were cries of horror at this draconian suggestion.

'But, if someone doesn't put their scorecard in the box, they're disqualified, aren't they?' Frank asked.

'Yes, and, if they sign for an incorrect score, they're also disqualified,' Simon added.

'That's settled then,' Giles said. 'David will put up a notice explaining that everyone must enter their own scores into the computer. And, at the same time, he will point out, in very large letters, that they will be disqualified if they don't. All those in favour?'

Everyone raised their hands. No-one noticed the absence of the Brigadier who was away in London for a few days, attending a regimental dinner. That isn't quite true. They had all observed how the discussion had taken only half as long as usual. And, they'd noticed, too, that decisions had been reached without tension of any kind.

'It's so much more relaxed when the Brigadier isn't here,' Pat remarked to Kate afterwards.

'Yes. If only he would realise that we're all adults and that we're capable of acting in the Club's interests just as much as he is,' Kate agreed.

'Good meeting, David,' she said, as he passed their table in the bar.

'Yes. I think it went well,' David replied, as he sat down. 'I just hope the Brigadier agrees with the rest of you.'

'He only has one vote, you know, David,' Kate smiled. 'So, it doesn't really matter whether he likes it or not.'

'His power lies in the control he exercises over some of the others, remember.' David cautioned. 'He wants to control everything. So, if he doesn't like a decision that's been taken, he'll lobby quietly until he gets it changed.'

'Is he still giving you a hard time?' Kate asked. 'I can talk to the others if you'd like me to; get them to ask the Brigadier to leave you alone to get on with your job.'

David hadn't had an opportunity to speak to Kate for several weeks, not since she had rebuffed his invitation to join him for a drink.

'Thank you, but I'm learning to handle him myself. If he thinks I've been running to the Committee, he'll only see

161

me as weak and there is nothing the Brigadier despises more than weakness. Just look at old Phil Oakley. By the sound of it, he spent most of the last fifteen years scurrying to and fro doing the Brigadier's bidding. And, what did the Brigadier say about him the other day when I mentioned that someone had suggested we should make him a life member? "Oh God! We don't want him here all the time, dreadful little man!"'

'He is terrible, isn't he? The Brigadier, I mean. So, he's not softening his attitude towards the new members, then?' Kate asked.

'Afraid not,' David replied. 'He still keeps asking to see applications for membership, even though Giles and I see the applicants together. Never a week goes by without him asking why we've allowed so-and-so or such-and-such to become a member. The other day, he even demanded to know why we'd allowed in the local butcher!'

'Tradesmen!' Kate laughed. 'What is the world coming to?'

'A sticky end, if you want the Brigadier's opinion.' David laughed too.

'Seriously, though, David,' Kate gently touched his hand. 'The Committee members are all behind what you are doing. If you need our help, we'll support you.'

'Thanks,' David said. 'I hope it won't be too long before the Brigadier gets the message himself.'

David was on the point of repeating his invitation to Kate. Then, thinking better of it, he moved on towards the notice board where he began speaking to a group of new members.

3

'I can't see what the Club would gain. They could just be jumping from the frying pan into the fire.'

162

'That's what I think,' David agreed. 'You try telling them that, though. As far as most of the older members are concerned, the bank is always the villain. Being in debt to one of their own is infinitely preferable to owing money to the bank.'

'I can appreciate that,' Mark Essam laughed. 'But, the Club would be no less vulnerable, can't they see that? This Kelham character could call in his loan just as easily as we could our overdraft.'

'Of course he could,' David agreed. 'Perhaps, I'll get you to come along to the next committee meeting and tell them that.'

'I'll tell them more than that, if you like,' Essam said. 'You're doing all right, I reckon. Visitor income has increased quite a bit, hasn't it. And, you have what, fifteen new members? That's not bad in two months.'

'Yes, but we may be just mopping up a local surplus. The real test will come in January, when people start renewing their subscriptions.'

'It should help allowing people to transfer from other clubs without paying a joining fee,' Essam said. 'If I were playing on one of these newer courses and I had the chance to switch to Branfield at no cost, I'd jump at it.'

'Maybe, but bank managers only ever think about the money, don't they?' David grinned. 'They don't have friends like normal people, so they don't mind moving on.'

'Bloody cheek!' Essam laughed. 'I'll have you know I have lots of friends. It's hardly my fault that none of them want to be seen in my company.'

The two men were sharing a drink in the bar. It was the first Saturday of the month, the day of the Club's monthly competition. During the preceding week, David had entered every member's handicap into the computer.

The computer now sat on a table in the main entrance hall and many players stopped to look at it as they passed on their way to the changing rooms. To a man, they pressed various buttons on the keypad until they found their own name. Having thus reassured themselves that they were 'in the computer' and that the computer had their handicap correctly recorded, they went on into the changing room and prepared to play.

'What time are you teeing off,' David asked.

'Eleven-thirty,' Essam said, looking at his watch. 'But I want to go and hit a few balls before I go out. I must say, Jack's looking a lot more cheerful, these days.'

'Yes, he is,' David agreed. 'Quite a few of these new members are going to him for lessons, to brush up their game. And, sales of balls, new shoes, waterproofs, stuff like that, have increased. It all helps his turnover. He was quite worried a couple of months ago. Even thought he might have to shut up shop. I think his fortunes are improving now along with those of the Club.'

'And, he's such a good teacher,' Essam said. 'He made a tremendous difference to my game, you know. He was telling me the other day that people are even coming to him from other clubs. And this nightclub owner, what's his name?'

'Makrides?'

'Yes, Makrides. He's been having lessons. And now, apparently, he's talking about bringing his wife along to learn as well. I must say, David, this club has really started buzzing since you arrived.'

'Thank you,' David smiled as they descended the stairs. 'Have a good game.'

Play went on all day and those going out earlier had the benefit of the better weather. During the afternoon, steady rain fell and this, together with the cold wind, resulted in higher scores.

As each group of players came in, they sat in front of the computer and entered their scores. Some were nervous but, coached and encouraged by their fellow players, they quickly got the hang of the new system.

164

On the Monday morning, David printed out the results and scanned them quickly before pinning the list to the notice board. The winner was Phil Dryden, who had scored seventy-eight. Phil's handicap was ten, so his net score was sixty-eight, one better than Bill Ellery, who had a net sixty-nine.

David was surprised to see that the Brigadier wasn't one of the leaders and he was even more perplexed, when he looked down the list, to find that the name of Brigadier Henry Tufnell was absent altogether.

'The Brigadier must have missed the competition on Saturday.'

'That's not like him,' Margaret said, as she placed David's coffee on his desk. 'I thought it was his monthly opportunity to assert his superiority over the others.'

'Now, now,' David smiled. 'He must have had something more important to do.'

David didn't feel quite so charitable an hour later when he heard raised voices in the outer office. Opening the door, he found Margaret looking very anxious, barring the Brigadier's path.

'I'm afraid he's rather busy at the moment, Brigadier.'

'It's all right, Margaret,' David said. 'Come in, Brigadier. What can I do for you?'

'You can change that damned score sheet, that's what you can do!' the Brigadier boomed.

'What's wrong with the score sheet, Brigadier?' David asked, although he already had a pretty good idea.

'*I'm not bloody on it, that's what's wrong with it!* I had a gross seventy-four on Saturday. That's a net sixty-nine, the same as Ellery.' (the Brigadier always referred to others by their surnames, even those who counted themselves among his friends). 'So, I came second and you've missed me off all together. Absolute bloody incompetence!'

'But, I didn't miss anybody off, Brigadier. The computer worked out the results and it can't have missed your scores.'

David was trying not to allow his voice to reveal the tension he was feeling.

'The computer! What's it got to do with the bloody computer, man? You're the Secretary. It's your job to work out the results. It's no use blaming a blasted machine!'

'I'm not blaming the computer, Brigadier. The computer isn't to blame if someone's name is missing from the result sheet. Are you sure you entered your scores properly into the computer?'

'Entered my scores into the computer? What the hell are you talking about, man? Do you think I'm a bloody building society clerk? You're the Secretary. Surely, it's you're job to operate the computer? Or, are you suggesting you can't do your job now?'

'Not at all, Brigadier,' David smiled, hoping to calm the older man. 'If you recall, the Committee agreed that everyone entering the monthly competition had to enter his own score into the computer. I was asked to put up a notice to let people know that they would be disqualified if they didn't. Did you not enter your score into the computer?'

'Of course I didn't! I put my scorecard in the box, just as I have for the past thirty years. If the Committee wants to change things around here, it had better get my say-so first.'

'With respect, Brigadier, the Committee voted on this change and it was written up in the minutes. I put up notices to let everyone know about the new procedure, and what would happen if they didn't follow it. You didn't follow it and, I'm afraid, you were disqualified. If it's any consolation, several other people were disqualified because they didn't enter their scores either.'

'It isn't any consolation, laddie, and if you think this is the end of the matter, then you're very much mistaken. If you had been doing your job properly, you would have noticed that my score wasn't recorded in your damned computer. I'm going to get the Committee together to do something about this. And, at the same time, I'm going to raise a lot of other things that you are doing around here to ruin this Club. The riff-raff you're letting in, for one thing. The type of visitors you're allowing to play. I should start to consider your position, if I were you. Good day, sir!'

The Brigadier turned and stormed from the room, slamming the office door as he went. David was shaken and slumped into his chair.

The man's mad! David thought. He's a tyrant and he won't be happy until I'm forced to leave and he's re-established control. He'll go to the Committee and they'll all bow to his pressure.

David could already hear their excuses.

There was a quiet knock. Margaret came in.

'Are you all right, Mr Crowley? You look terrible.'

She picked up his coffee mug.

'This coffee's cold and you haven't even touched it. Sit down there and I'll get you a fresh one.'

'Thanks,' David said. He hadn't the energy to resist.

He was still sitting, staring at the same spot a few minutes later when Margaret returned. She placed his coffee on the desk and asked, 'Are you sure you're all right?'

'Yes. I'm just feeling rather shaky, that's all. The Brigadier can be pretty devastating when he looms over you and fires both barrels.'

'He's a pig, that man! Look, you need to relax, somehow. Not let him get to you.'

'Nice idea,' David smiled thinly. 'I'm not very good at relaxing, though, I'm afraid.'

'Well, let me show you how,' Margaret said, quietly. She went to the door and turned the key. Then, she moved

167

to the window and closed the blind. It was suddenly quite dark and very quiet in the office.

'You've been on your own too long. That's one of your troubles,' she said, almost whispering. 'You need someone to take you in hand, that's what you need.'

Margaret stood behind David and began massaging his shoulders and neck. Under the gentle pressure of her warm hands, he settled back into the chair.

'That's very nice,' he murmured, his eyes closed.

'I can feel your shoulders relaxing already,' she said, quietly.

David could feel Margaret's warmth as she pressed his shoulders back against her belly. Slowly, she slid her hands round and removed his tie.

'You do wear lovely ties,' she whispered.

'You like them, do you?'

'Mmm. I think they're ever so sexy.'

David could feel Margaret unbuttoning his shirt, but he was so relaxed that he felt powerless to resist. She ran her hands over his shoulders, up the sides of his neck and down through the hair on his chest. As she did so, Margaret began softly kissing his neck and shoulders.

'Feeling more relaxed, now?' she whispered.

'Much,' he murmured.

'Good.'

Margaret swivelled David's chair round to the side and dropped to her knees at his feet. She unbuttoned his shirt to the waste and ran her hands over his chest and down his arms. Then, she began to unbuckle his belt.

'Margaret, what if somebody comes.' David whispered. 'I don't think it's a good idea…'

Undeterred, Margaret pulled aside his buckle and unzipped his fly. She opened his trousers and slid her hands beneath his underwear

David protested feebly but she already had him in her hands. He had been in no hands other than his own for over

168

three years and, in spite of his anxiety and confusion at the unexpected turn of events, in Margaret's warm and gentle grasp, he soon began to rise up.

She stroked him gently, running her hands through the thick hair between his thighs. He was very hard now and Margaret looked up at him with a smile.

'Well, somebody down here thinks it's a good idea,' she smiled. 'A really good idea…'

David leaned forward and kissed her. He began to unbutton Margaret's dress but she gently removed his hand.

'This time is for you,' she whispered.

She moved her head forward and caressed him from root to tip. Then, she took him into her mouth and began to stroke him, slowly at first, then more vigorously as his arousal increased. David's stress and anxiety dissolved into a pleasure he hadn't experienced for years. He closed his eyes and surrendered to the sensation in his loins. His hands ran through Margaret's dark hair, stroking her head and pressing her against him. He began to feel his excitement mounting and Margaret sensed it too. She increased her movement until, suddenly, he felt a glorious release.

'There. That's better, isn't it?' she said, after a few minutes.

Gently, she pulled up his pants and trousers, tucking him in and zipping him up.

David said nothing.

'You're not cross with me, are you? I thought you'd like it. My Tom always says I'm his head girl.'

'No, no!' David replied. 'It was very nice.' *Christ*, he thought. *What a stupid thing to say!*

'That's all right then,' Margaret smiled.

'But, what about…'

'Don't you worry about Tom,' said Margaret. 'What he doesn't know about, won't hurt him. Anyway, Tom gets all he wants or needs. Twice a day, sometimes three times, he

169

has what he wants. Only trouble is, I don't get much out of it, myself. The way I see it, if one person is getting all they need and the other isn't, there's no harm in finding pleasure somewhere else; as long as nobody gets hurt, that is. Especially, if somebody else needs it, too.'

She looked up at David.

'And, you think I need it, too?' David sat back on the edge of the desk.

'Course you do! Everybody needs it. It's not good for a fit, healthy man like you to be living without any comfort. It's time you found a nice young lady to share your bed and make you happy.'

'That's not as easy as you make it sound, Margaret.'

'What, with all these women golfers around? There's lots of them looking for a man, believe me. What about that Kate – Mrs Earnshaw? She's a lovely lady and she's been a widow for long enough, if you ask me.'

'Now you're talking silly,' David smiled. 'I'm just the Secretary here and, anyway, I have to be careful to treat everyone the same.'

'I'm not suggesting you give them all one!' Margaret laughed.

She stood up, moved to the door and unlocked it.

'But, I'm sure there's somebody out there who would be good for you. Just think about it. In the meantime, if I can be of service…'

She turned, smiling. 'Drink your coffee.'

Hole	Name	Yards	Par	Score
10	The Camp	**357**	**4**	

1

'Jack, my boy. Let me introduce you to my wife, Karen. Karen this is Jack. Jack is the golf professional here.'

Spiros Makrides looked every inch the medallion man. Tanned and good-looking, the top four buttons of his shirt were left open to reveal powerful pectorals set off by an impressive gold chain. A few paces behind him stood Dinos, his driver and, it was said, his bodyguard; a huge square hulk who also acted as his caddie.

Jack was certainly no weakling. Indeed, he'd always prided himself on being big and athletic. However, he felt almost insignificant alongside Big Mak and Dinos.

'Jack,' Makrides said, putting his arm around Jack's shoulder. 'Jack, I need you to teach Karen here to play golf.'

Next to her husband, Karen Makrides appeared tiny. Slim and blond, her tanned face and arms and her exquisite figure were shown off perfectly by her tight, white trousers and sleeveless blouse.

'Hello, Jack,' Karen said, shaking Jack's hand. 'It's so nice to meet you after all Spiros has told me about you. He says you're a great teacher.'

'I don't know about that,' Jack smiled, modestly. 'It depends a lot on the student, of course.'

'Well, if that's the case, you've no chance!' Karen laughed. 'I've never been any good at sports.'

'So, why the interest in golf?' Jack asked.

'It's Spiros, here,' she said, running her hand down her husband's hairy forearm. 'He says he wants me to be able to play golf like all the other wives.'

'Yeah, that's right,' Makrides said. 'I want her to be able to play in matches with me. I got big plans locally and it's

171

important for a man that his wife can join in with the things he does. Don't you agree, Jack?'

'Well, Mr Makrides. I think it's quite important that Karen should actually want to play golf. She'll need to put in a lot of practice, so she's really got to be committed…'

'Look, Jack, you just do the teaching, OK? I'll see she does the practice. Don't you worry about that.'

They talked for a few minutes about golf clubs. Jack suggested Karen try out a number of different clubs during her lessons.

'Good idea,' Makrides agreed. 'Don't worry about the money, OK Jack? You just decide which clubs are the best and tell me how much.'

'Fine,' Jack smiled. He wasn't used to people presenting him with a blank cheque.

'And shoes and a bag and all the other stuff, OK Jack? Only the best, mind. I want my Karen to look the part.'

'I'll do my best, Mr Makrides,' Jack promised.

'Good boy!' Makrides looked at his watch. 'Now, I gotta go out and play. So, you sort out with Karen when she's gonna come for her lessons. OK? Come on, Dinos.'

Makrides kissed his wife on the cheek.

'See you later, darlin', all right?'

'Yeah, see you, Spiros.'

Makrides stopped and picked up three boxes of the most expensive golf balls.

'Charge these to my account, OK Jack?'

Karen waited until her husband and his heavy friend had left the shop.

'Hello, Jack. Long time no see?'

'Karen!' Jack exclaimed. 'It's good to see you. I had no idea…'

'That I was Mrs Spiros Makrides? No, it is a bit different from the sixth form at school, isn't it? Mind you, I didn't know you'd become a golf teacher, either.'

172

'Yeah. It's my shop, now,' Jack said, proudly. 'I came here eight years ago as assistant professional, straight from school. And, I took over a couple of years back, when the old pro retired.'

'Eight years? Is it really as long as that, Jack? Eight years since that party, do you remember, when you tried to put your hand up my... '

'Yes,' Jack said, smiling at the memory. 'It's a long time. You look absolutely fantastic, Karen!'

'Thanks, Jack. Being the wife of a rich businessman never did a girl any harm. Anyway, you look pretty good yourself. You were always tall, but I don't remember you being so, you know, strong looking.'

Jack grinned.

'Yeah, I have filled out a bit since school. Mind you, your husband and his mate make me look quite puny.'

'What? Spiros? He's just a muscle-bound gorilla, he is. Spends most of the day at the gym, when he's not doing some deal or other.'

'He's obviously doing all right for himself, though. How did you come to...'

'Marry him? I was working in one of his night-clubs and he – and his Rolex – just sort of, swept me off my feet. He can be quite impressive to a young girl, when he wants to be.'

'I can imagine,' Jack smiled. 'So, about these golf lessons...'

'Forget that, for the minute,' Karen said. 'I'm not in any hurry to start bashing golf balls around. It's been such a long time, Jack. Tell me about you, first. Where are you living, now? Are you married? Have you got a girlfriend?'

'Well, I've moved into a flat on this side of the town. And, as a matter of fact, I don't have a girlfriend. Not at the moment, anyway,' Jack said, smiling.

He looked at his watch.

173

'Sorry, Karen, I've got a lesson to take in a minute, so I can't stop and talk now. Let's get your first lesson booked and we can chat a bit more when you come along then, OK?'

Jack took down a large red diary and opened it on the counter. For a moment, Karen looked disappointed. Then, she smiled.

'All right, Jack. But, next time, I want to hear all about what you've been up to during the past eight years.'

'We'd better book a double lesson, then,' Jack said, with a grin.

'You bet. We've a lot of catching up to do, you and me.'

They settled on a time early the following week.

Karen smiled at Alison, who was leaning on the counter, chewing, and the younger girl stared open-mouthed as Karen kissed Jack on the cheek.

Karen began to leave the shop, then she turned.

'It's been really great seeing you again, Jack. I can't wait until next time.'

'I'll look forward to it, Karen.'

2

Word quickly began to spread, among the golfers of the area, that Branfield Park Golf Club was more receptive to visitors. Those who play golf seriously are always looking for different courses against which to pitch their skills. They came to play at Branfield and, as those visitors returned to their home clubs after a day on the course, they began to spread the news that a golfing jewel had been discovered in their midst.

By mid-November, an initial trickle had developed into a small but steady stream of daily visitors. Each morning, the sound of trolleys and bags being unloaded could be heard in the car park. The bays of the driving range echoed to the striking of dozens, sometimes hundreds, of golf balls. In

174

contrast, the putting green, a semi-circular expanse of emerald sward sheltered by high beech hedging, was often populated by a silent army of young men in a state of intense concentration.

'Things are on the up, Boss,' Jack said one morning as he and David shared a pot of coffee in the bar.

David had always been amused at Jack's insistence on addressing him thus. After all, Jack wasn't employed by the Club and David wasn't, therefore, technically his boss. The golf shop was Jack's own business and the Club simply paid him a retainer for services rendered.

'The thing is, Boss,' Jack explained, with a smile. 'I can never really feel comfortable calling my old headmaster by his first name.'

'What? You don't mean...?'

'Yeah. That's right, Boss. You don't remember me at all, do you?'

'I'm sorry, Jack. I don't,' David confessed. 'Mind you, it was a long time ago. What is it, eight years? And, it is much harder for us teachers. The kids all look pretty much the same in their uniform. And, there are far more of them...'

'Yeah, yeah! So, all that stuff you said when we left, about us being unique individuals with our own personalities. That was all a load of bollocks, was it?' Jack grinned, feigning hurt.

'Good Lord! Did I really say that?' David laughed.

'Anyway, if I remember right, most of you teachers wore the same uniform. Sports jackets, grey trousers, boring ties. I must say, Boss, you've obviously discovered a new men's outfitters since you retired. Your smart ties have become quite a talking point among the ladies around here.'

'Thanks,' David smiled, looking down at his tie. 'Anyway, back to business. So, the shop's becoming a little more viable these days is it?'

'Quite a bit, actually. It's nothing fantastic or anything, yet, but all these visitors are bringing in a steady trade. Most of them come in for balls and tees and you'd be surprised how many buy themselves a new glove.'

'Perhaps they think it will help as they're playing a new course.'

'Maybe. Anyway, Alison's not very quick at serving people. I don't know if you've noticed. But, that's actually quite useful because, while they're waiting for their friends to be served, the others have a look at the rest of the stock. I've sold quite a bit of gear, that way.'

'I really think you're exploiting all that young lady's attributes and deficiencies just to drum up trade, Jack,' David laughed.

'You've got to try anything in this business,' Jack grinned. 'It's certainly helped joining up with that golf wholesalers, because now we can match the prices in the high street. Yeah, I think you could say we might have turned the corner.'

'And, what about the teaching?'

'That's keeping me pretty busy, too. I could probably get a mortgage on what I'm earning from Big Mak's lessons alone. Not that he's showing any great improvement. I haven't yet managed to persuade him that the aim isn't to club the ball to death! But, yes, a lot of these new members you're bringing in are signing up for lessons. And, the word must be getting around because I've had a couple of guys in who, I know, are members over at Silhurst.'

'That's really great, Jack,' David said. 'Mrs Hall has certainly noticed a difference in the restaurant. She was rushed off her feet a couple of days last week.'

David poured some more coffee.

'Actually, another ex-pupil from the school came in yesterday morning,' said Jack.

'Oh?'

'Yeah. Karen Makrides, as she is now. Karen Bayley, she was then. I bet you'd remember her.'

'I must say, I don't remember the name. Why, do you think I should?'

'If not the name, certainly the face. And, if not the face, well, the rest of her. Karen was quite a stunner.'

'Oh, you know us teachers never noticed things like that, Jack,' David laughed.

'No? Well, you'd notice her now, all right. Even if you are getting a bit old for it,' Jack grinned.

'Thanks! So, she's married to our new member, is she?'

'Yeah. He brought her in to fix up some lessons. Wants to be able to parade her round the course, I think.'

'He's a funny character, Makrides. He doesn't seem that interested in golf at all, really,' David remarked.

'That's right,' Jack agreed. 'He's had all these lessons, and he's spent loads on his equipment. Yet, he seems more interested in how much profit the shop is making than what we actually sell.'

'Is that so?' David said. 'I must say, he's a very odd choice for Kelham and the Brigadier to introduce as a new member.'

'Speaking of which,' Jack muttered. 'Keep your head down. The Brigadier has just come into the bar.'

It did not, however, take Brigadier Tufnell long to spot them.

'Ah! There you are, Crowley. You too, Peters,' the Brigadier said, looking at Jack.

'Good morning, Brigadier,' David said, cheerily.

'It most certainly is *not* a good morning.'

'Why, what's the problem, Brigadier? It's a beautiful day out there. A little cold, perhaps...'

'I'll grant you, it may be pleasant out, Crowley. Unfortunately, it doesn't look as if I shall be going out this morning. Thanks to your visitors.'

'Visitors, Brigadier? I don't think there are many visitors this morning, are there, Jack?'

'We've a party of twelve; a group from Sedbury, that's all. Three four-balls. Some of them are out on the putting green now, and they're off between ten-thirty and eleven, I think.'

'Precisely,' the Brigadier snapped. 'I had arranged to meet Tony Hockley here this morning for a game. Now, I discover that the tee is reserved for this shower.'

'Well, they won't be long getting off, Brigadier,' Jack explained. 'There are only three groups.'

'Three groups of four, Peters. Have you any idea how long it will take to play a round of golf behind three groups of four players, none of whom has played the course before? And, half of whom have probably never played the game before?'

'I see your point, Brigadier,' David said. 'Well, they won't be teeing off for another twenty minutes, so why don't you and Mr Hockley get off now?'

'Because, Crowley, Mr Hockley is not yet here. He has just telephoned to say that he will not arrive until just before eleven o'clock. As you may or may not know, Tony Hockley is a country member and he has to drive a very long way to get here. For him to be faced with this sort of delay when he arrives… Well, it is quite unacceptable!'

Doesn't mind driving sixty miles to get half-price golf, though, does he? David thought.

'I don't know what to suggest, really, Brigadier. If you had arranged your tee time with Jack, he could have ensured that you didn't clash with…'

'It has never been necessary before,' the Brigadier declared. 'I have always played at this time on a Tuesday morning. You assured the Committee that these visitors of yours would not impinge upon the members. It is clear to me now that we have been misled and that my worst fears will soon be realised.'

'Brigadier,' David said, sounding slightly irritated. 'These people are not *my* visitors. They are the Club's visitors and they are bringing in much-needed income to the Club. What I explained to the Committee was that I had introduced a booking system. Had you reserved a tee-time, this problem could perhaps have been avoided.'

The Brigadier looked explosive.

'Damn it, man...' he began.

'Can I suggest something, Brigadier?' Jack interrupted. 'Why don't I ask our visitors to wait until eleven-fifteen before teeing off.'

He turned to David.

'I'll get them in the bar, give them a cup of coffee and tell them about the course. The best way to play it, and so on. Then, the Brigadier and Mr Hockley can get on their way, first.'

'Thank you, Peters. That's very kind of you. I'm sorry that you, too, have been put to so much trouble by these people.'

The Brigadier turned to David.

'This is not the last you shall hear of this, Crowley. The Committee will be informed about it, be assured sir. Mr Hockley is highly regarded by many in this Club. Highly regarded. When people hear that members have been treated in this manner, I'm sure they will wish to see changes. The sooner the Committee stops dithering and accepts Toby Kelham's kind offer, the quicker things can return to normal around here. All these damned visitors! Changes the whole tone of the place.'

The Brigadier stormed off and Jack rose to follow him.

'Thanks, Jack,' said David. 'Thanks for coming to the rescue.'

'That's wonderful, Mrs Hall. Thank you.'

Having managed, at last, to invite Kate to join him for lunch, David was anxious that they be left alone. He had been getting into his car earlier in the week when Kate had pulled up alongside in her little yellow van. She'd asked if she could talk to him about using the new computer scoring system for the ladies' medal competition later in the month. When he had suggested they talk about it over lunch, he had half-expected another rebuff, but there was no hint of reluctance when she accepted.

Mrs Hall, however, was at her most solicitous. She insisted upon serving all their vegetables herself, even pouring the gravy. Meanwhile, John, her husband, made a great show of pouring two glasses of his house claret.

'They are a marvellous couple, aren't they?' Kate said, smiling. 'James and I often came here for Sunday lunch. It was always delicious, but a disaster for my waistline.'

'James. He was your husband?' David thought it better not to reveal that he had talked with anyone about Kate.

'Yes, sorry,' Kate said, quietly. 'James died almost four years ago. He'd been very ill for a long time. So, in the end it was a release for everyone, I suppose.'

'I'm very sorry,' said David.

'No, it's all right,' Kate replied. 'James was a pretty good golfer. Club Captain. Played for the county, too. Played squash two or three times a week. All that sort of thing. Always the life and soul of the party, was James. Then, he got this terrible disease and... Well, he just wasted away.'

'It must have been dreadful for you.'

'It was. At the time.'

Kate's expression brightened.

'Anyway, come on, tell me about you. You've had a pretty rough time of things, too, haven't you? Your wife died, you said?'

'Yes, about four years ago. Tess had cancer. Breast cancer. She seemed to be cured for a while, but then after a couple of years it returned. And, that time, there was nothing to be done.'

'I am sorry,' said Kate. 'You said she was an artist?'

'Yes, water colours mostly, but Tess could turn her hand to almost anything. She was quite an accomplished potter, and a sculptor. And, she ran a local theatre group. Never seemed to stop, in fact, until...'

'You must miss her terribly,' Kate said.

'It's strange that,' David said. 'I do miss her very much. But, until a few months ago, I always had the feeling that she was still close by; that she could hear me when I talked to her. If I had a problem or something to sort out, I would talk to Tess about it. Then, quite suddenly, the feeling faded and I knew she wasn't there any more. On the one hand, it helped – the depression eased, but, on the other, I was even more aware that she was finally gone.'

'I experienced something similar myself,' Kate smiled. Even though we had known that James' death was inevitable from the moment he was diagnosed, I still found it very difficult when it finally happened. I would talk to him – in the evenings mostly – you know, asking what I should do about this or that. Then, sometimes I would get angry and shout at him for leaving me to sort everything out. I used to imagine him sitting there, laughing at me. Silly really.'

'And, this feeling faded with you, too?'

'It didn't get the chance, really,' Kate said.

'Why was that. I'm sorry, I don't mean to pry.'

'That's all right. You're not. No, something happened, about three months after James died. I was going through a box in his study – he worked from home – when I discovered some letters.'

'What sort of letters?' David asked, although, from what Simon had told him, he could guess.

'Love letters, I'm afraid. Love letters to James. And, from one of my closest friends, or so I thought. Pretty explicit stuff, too. It was clear that they'd had some sort of relationship. And, for quite some time, by the sound of it.'

'How can you be sure they were genuine?' David asked. 'Perhaps, she was obsessed with him. Wrote him letters and James hid them to spare your feelings. These things do happen, you know.'

'You're very kind to suggest it, David,' Kate said, gently placing her hand on his. 'But, no, it didn't take long to confirm the truth, I'm afraid. The letters referred to certain places she said they had visited together. I checked his old desk diaries and, sure enough, James had been away on business to those places. I contacted the hotels and, no surprises, James had checked in with his 'wife'.'

'That must have been pretty devastating,' David said.

'It was. I was so angry. I screamed and cried. I went round to see my friend and had a terrible row. Poor girl, it had all been over for more than three years by the time I found out, of course. I went home and made a big bonfire of all James' clothes. Then, I felt a bit better. I stopped thinking he was there quite quickly after that!'

'I can imagine. It must have been very painful.'

'It was at the time. I decided that that was it for me as far as men were concerned. I don't feel quite so bad about it – or him – now. I mean, I did love James, he was a great father and he clearly went to some lengths to make sure I wasn't hurt.'

'That's very generous,' said David.

'Perhaps. What I can't understand is why he felt the need. I mean, we seemed to have such a good marriage. There didn't seem to be any problem with the physical side

182

or anything like that. That's the hardest thing. Never really knowing why.'

David was silent. He tried to imagine how he would have felt if he had discovered that Tess had been unfaithful. It would, he thought have finished him. Yet, Kate appeared almost stronger as a result of her experience.

After a few moments reflection, Kate suddenly looked up with a broad smile.

'What a pair! We finally get to meet for lunch and all we can talk about is death and disaster. I'm sure it can't be the only thing we have in common. So, tell me, David. Did you and Tess have any children?'

David explained about Ben. How he was in the final year of a science degree. How he was a big, cheerful boy and a very good golfer.

'He must have found his mother's death very hard to take,' Kate said. 'How old was he, seventeen? Young men are still very much boys at that age, aren't they?'

'Yes, I suppose they are,' David said. 'To be honest, we've never really talked much about Tess since she died. Neither of us has found it easy, I think.'

'Well, maybe it's time you did, the two of you, before Ben is so grown up that it's too late. It's none of my business, of course, but I found talking to Sarah very helpful. And, I think she appreciated it, too.'

'Sarah?' David asked.

Kate was right, he was sure. He would try and have a talk with Ben, and soon, but he was glad of an opportunity to turn the focus away from himself.

'My daughter. She's twenty-two now. She helped me nurse James right up to the end. She started at university only a month after he died. We were able to talk a lot while her father was ill, and we've had several long chats since. I haven't told her about the other business, though. I think it would only hurt her.'

'And, what is she doing now?'

183

'She finished at Uni in the summer,' Kate explained. 'Got a 2:1 which I was really pleased about after all she'd been through. Now, she's up the jungle – somewhere in Africa. Working with VSO. I probably shan't see her for another six months. I'm sure it will be good for her, but I do miss her terribly.'

After explaining to a disappointed Mrs Hall that they would skip the dessert, they mollified her somewhat by moving through into the bar where she brought them a pot of coffee.

'So, have you always played golf?' David asked.

'No! In fact, I was never really interested in sports until I met James. I only took it up so that we could do something together. Then, I became quite good at it, even if I do say so myself,' Kate smiled.

'So, you became Ladies Captain?'

'Not because I could play well,' she smiled. 'There are lots of better players here than me. No, after James died, everyone here was so kind and thoughtful. They made sure I wasn't alone when I needed company, and they never intruded when I needed to be alone. Martha Tufnell was an absolute tower of strength. Even old Henry did his best to be kind!'

David said nothing.

'I felt a great debt of gratitude to them all. And so, when they needed a Ladies Captain this year and nobody else would volunteer, I said I would do it.'

'They couldn't have had anyone better at this time of crisis,' David said.

'Thanks,' Kate smiled. 'Although, I do sometimes wish I'd kept my big mouth shut.'

Perhaps not a big mouth, David thought, but certainly one with a wide and generous smile. Kate's jawline was broad and her forehead high. Her dark hair tumbled down the sides of her face in a very gentle and feminine way.

But, her face, and her eyes in particular, suggested great inner strength.

They talked about other things for a while. Kate loved gardening and enjoyed walking. David described how he'd never really had time for such pastimes, but said he hoped to put that right in the future.

'I realised, too late I think, that I had spent far too much time either working or playing golf,' David explained. 'I think both my health and my family suffered, as a result.'

'I don't believe you neglected your family,' Kate said. 'But, I can believe, from what I've seen of you here, that you can rather throw yourself into your work. What happened to make you retire from teaching at such an early age, if you don't mind me asking?'

'Not if you don't mind me telling you,' David laughed. 'After Tess died, I did, as you say, throw myself into my work. I suppose I allowed the stress to accumulate and the paperwork to pile up until, one day, it all became too much. I'll spare you the gruesome details but the governors came to see me late one afternoon and said, either jump or be pushed. So I jumped.'

'It must have been very painful.'

'What, jumping?' David laughed. 'Yes, it was, at the time. But, it was the right thing, both for me and for the school. Actually, starting this job has been a great help to me in recovering my old confidence.'

'It's funny, you should say that,' Kate said, with a smile. 'Simon Cornwell suggested, when we were interviewing, that this job might be good for you.'

'He's a very nice man, isn't he,' David said.

'Simon? He is a very dear man,' Kate agreed. 'He was fantastic when James was ill, even though his own wife was dying and he could do nothing to help her, poor man. I think, if he hadn't been able to escape from all the misery and play golf occasionally, he might even have succumbed, himself.'

'There's a fine line between escape and neglect, I think,' David said.

'And, I'm absolutely sure that neither you nor Simon neglected anyone. Is that why you gave up golf, David? Because you felt you'd neglected Tess in her hour of need?'

'Something like that,' David said, quietly.

'Well, I don't know you that well. Yet,' Kate said. 'But, I'm pretty certain you didn't neglect your family to play golf. If you want practical proof, you have only to look at Ben.'

'I'm sorry, I don't follow?'

'It stands to reason. Any boy who's father teaches him to play golf and who achieves a single-figure handicap before he's sixteen, is not neglected, David. In fact, it sounds to me as if he's bloody lucky to have such a great father!'

'I hadn't thought of it like that,' David said.

'Well, perhaps it's time you did.'

They walked down the stairs together and David accompanied Kate out to her van.

'Thank you for lunch, David,' she said. 'I really enjoyed it.'

'Perhaps, we could do it again some time?'

'Yes. I should like that. Away from the Club next time, though. It must be like a busman's holiday for you,' Kate laughed.

She waved as she drove away. It was as he was walking back towards his office, with a new spring in his step, that David realised that they'd quite forgotten to discuss the computer scoring system for the ladies competition.

4

'They're an assorted bunch, all right,' said Giles. 'Although, I suppose, no more so than the old members.'

186

He and David had been interviewing prospective members and were having a drink in the bar with Jack

'Well, all I can say is thank the Lord for early retirement!' David declared.

Giles asked what he meant.

'What I mean is that more than half of all the applicants thus far have left their work prematurely. Not only do people who've retired early have the time and energy to play, they also had their retirement lump-sum, so they can afford the joining fee.'

Three of the latest batch were teachers who had ended their careers early.

'Seems like a great life to me,' Jack said, with a grin. 'Thirteen weeks holiday a year, then you get to retire while you're still young enough to play golf three times a week. I'm obviously in the wrong branch of teaching!'

'And, while we're on the subject of retirement,' Giles said. 'What about that farmer, Arthur? He's been so successful at diversifying and sub-contracting the work on his farm that he doesn't have anything left to do all day.'

'And, he's got a great swing,' Jack reported. 'I said to him, you've played this game before, haven't you, Arthur?'

'What did he say?' asked David.

'Twas a long time ago, mind,' Jack said, mimicking the farmer's broad accent. 'Thought I might as well take it up, again, now I've got more time on my hands, like. Dunno if I'll still be any good, though.'

The others laughed.

'He's got 'bandit' written all over him!' Jack declared.

The ability level of the new recruits was as mixed as the personalities, although, thankfully, Spiros Makrides was, by far, the least golf-literate of those who had applied to join.

'Talking of farmers,' Jack went on. 'One of those retired teachers has got the most 'agricultural' golf swing I've ever seen. I'm amazed he can still walk upright!'

'Did he come to you for lessons?' David asked.

'No! I suggested it but he said he thought all he needed were some new clubs.'

The Brigadier had objected, sometimes privately, but more often publicly, about almost every new member of this early crop. When Roger, the local butcher; Billy, a self-employed plumber; Trevor, an electrician, and Dave, a painter and decorator, were all accepted for membership, the Brigadier reacted as if his worst nightmares were about to come true.

"I'm not saying they shouldn't play golf, of course," the Brigadier had remarked. "But, they need to be in the right place. Had plenty of chaps like that in my unit. Did a damned fine job, too, given the right leadership. But, you wouldn't have wanted to drink with them in the officers' mess."

The Brigadier recounted each and every misdemeanour committed by these newcomers. Triumphantly, he would stride into the office to report the latest transgression.

'I think he has scouts out everywhere,' Giles joked. 'And, if any of them spot an infringement of the rules, of etiquette or a breach of the dress code, they send a signal back to headquarters immediately.'

'The trouble is, sometimes he's right,' David said. 'But, it doesn't make it any easier for me.'

'What do you mean, David?'

'Well, we've laid down rules of dress that are very difficult to enforce. For instance, we stipulate "No Jeans". Then, somebody comes along wearing expensive moleskin trousers with patch pockets. So I put up a notice saying, "Jeans are defined by style not material." Then, somebody turns up wearing ordinary trousers made of denim cloth!'

'I see your problem,' Giles said.

'Another problem arises because we say, "Golf shoes must be worn. No trainers are allowed".'

'Well, I should have thought that was perfectly reasonable,' said Giles.

'It is,' David agreed. 'Until Jack here started selling golf shoes that, from a distance, look like trainers. I've been fooled several times by those!'

'Sorry about that,' Jack grinned.

'So you should be,' David laughed. 'I've been up and down, out of my chair at least ten times this week!'

'We had the same sort of problem in school over uniforms,' David went on. 'We'd lay down certain rules and half the kids would then spend their time pushing those rules to the limit, just to see what they could get away with.'

'On the whole, though, I think they're a pretty well-behaved lot,' Giles said.

'Yes,' David agreed. 'One or two have turned up in the usual jeans and trainers but, once I've had a quiet words with them, they don't usually re-offend.'

'So, your headmaster skills have come in handy?'

'I haven't really needed them. We've had very few instances of bad behaviour, although Kate came to see me last week about a couple of the ladies who were rather upset.'

'What had offended them?' Giles asked.

'Oh, some guys playing behind thought they were being rather slow. One of them shouted a suggestion that they should, "Hurry up, darlin' or Sainsburys'll be closed!"'

'I can see that wouldn't go down well.'

'No,' David laughed. 'Especially as the lady concerned would never allow her housekeeper to shop at Sainsburys!'

Perhaps, one of the more colourful of the new members was Jimmy McGrath, a former coal-miner from Lanarkshire. After taking redundancy, Jimmy had moved south to live with his daughter and son-in-law. A veteran golfer, he'd played the game for years on Scottish links but, nevertheless, still had a handicap of twenty. Jimmy liked his drink and joked that, not for nothing, was he known as 'James the thirst of Scotland'.

Jimmy was another who's admission to the Club the Brigadier had questioned. However, the Brigadier had been strangely quiet for a few weeks.

'Perhaps, he has finally accepted the situation,' Giles cautiously suggested.

'I don't think so,' said David. 'I expect he's just biding his time until the Committee meets. He seems quite convinced that they'll vote to accept Toby Kelham's loan. And, when that happens, and the old regime is restored, the nightmare will be over and he can wake up to Branfield as it always was.'

'He may well be right, of course,' Giles conceded. 'He's got a lot of people in the Club on his side, you know. So, if the Committee do vote against accepting Kelham's money, the Brigadier could well lobby to get a different committee elected at the annual general meeting in May.'

Hole	Name	Yards	Par	Score
11	The Trap	152	3	

1

Tuesday afternoon, and the rain had been torrential since first light. Both the course and the clubhouse were virtually deserted. With so much standing water around, Bob Morgan had decided to keep his green-keeping staff off the greens to avoid any damage. Instead, he planned to make a start on digging out the new bunker alongside the fifth green.

The approach to this green had, for some time, been considered too easy and especially for the longer hitters in the Club. The proposed solution was to add a new bunker. But, as with almost any change at Branfield, the decision to construct it had not been arrived at without some rancour.

For once, the Brigadier was the person promoting the change. Although one of the straightest hitters in the club, in recent years, he had lost distance on his drives and long irons. Some of the younger players who were able to far out-drive him, could drive with abandon from the fifth tee in the knowledge that, if they strayed to the right, they would be faced with a relatively easy pitch to the green from that side of the fairway.

'The approach to the fifth green needs to be more challenging for the longer hitters,' the Brigadier had explained to the Committee.

A bunker, he had argued to anyone who would listen, would test those who took this approach and encourage them to be more accurate. No-one dared, or cared enough, to point out that he had fiercely resisted such 'tinkering' when he had been able to hit a long drive.

The Brigadier had intended that the new bunker should be sited at the front of the green on the right side. However, the local planning department had taken the view that a large bunker, gouged out in this position would mar the landscape, and spoil the view, particularly for people crossing the fifth fairway along the public footpath.

The Brigadier had pressed Phil Oakley to argue long and hard for his preference, but to no avail. Eventually, planning permission was granted on condition that the new bunker was dug to the side of the green, out of sight of any potential walkers.

After the committee meeting, David asked Bob Morgan to go ahead with the work as time allowed. Bob had hired a digger and, in spite of the rain, he wanted to get some use out of it.

David's telephone rang.

'I've got Bob Morgan on the line for you,' Margaret explained. 'He's on his mobile. Sounds like he's got a problem with the Brigadier.'

David was engrossed in the accounts. At the words, "problem with the Brigadier", he felt his spirits slump.

'Hi, Bob. What's the problem?' David asked.

'Hello, David. Look, we're out at the fifth green. Thought we'd make a start on this bunker while we've got the digger.'

'Good idea,' said David. 'As long as you don't drown!'

'It's not too bad, once you're used to it. Anyway, the thing is, the Brigadier's turned up. He's been trying to persuade us to site the bunker near the front of the green. Says, he's sure once it's finished, everybody will agree that that's the best place.'

'Well, just tell him you've had your instructions and you can't do anything about it,' David replied, sounding impatient.

'Have you ever tried arguing with Brigadier Tufnell?' Bob asked. 'He just keeps going until you finally give in. He's been here for nearly half an hour, already. Me and the lads just want to get on.'

David sighed.

'Oh, all right, Bob. I'll drive out and speak to him myself. See if I can sort it out.'

'Thanks, David. Don't use your own car though. It's so wet out here, you'll probably end up bogged down. The Subaru pick-up is in the shed; use that.'

'OK,' David said. 'I'll be with you in a few minutes.'

David put down the phone. He certainly wasn't in the mood to stand out in the rain arguing with the Brigadier. But, he knew he had to go and give Bob his support. He explained where he was going to Margaret and walked through to the back door of the clubhouse. The vehicle shed was about thirty yards away.

Damn! David thought, when he saw how heavily the rain was falling.

Rather than go back for his coat, however, he set off across the yard at a sprint. By the time he'd reached the shed, his shirt and trousers were already becoming wet. Once inside, David walked across to the Subaru and found the keys under the seat.

After a few tries, the diesel engine roared into life and a belch of black smoke filled the shed. Slowly, David drove out across the yard and on to the first fairway, the windscreen wipers at full speed.

I really need this, this afternoon, said David to himself as he negotiated the second fairway before entering the woods. He was especially grateful for the four-wheel-drive as the track descended steeply through the trees.

Crossing the old stone bridge, David waved at a pair of golfers who had clearly had enough and were trudging back towards the clubhouse. It looked as if Jimmy and Arthur had decided to take refuge in the bar.

Five minutes later, having climbed slowly up through the woods on the far side of the valley, David emerged alongside the fifth tee. Through the driving rain, he could see Bob's digger and the Brigadier's Range Rover parked alongside the green, almost a quarter of a mile away.

'What's up, Brigadier?' David tried to sound cheerful as he climbed from the truck.

'Ah, good of you to come out, Crowley. It's this new bunker, d'you see,' the Brigadier explained. 'Morgan, here, just won't listen to reason. I've been here over half an hour and I've explained to him at least a dozen times that the bunker should be here at the front of the green. He just won't budge, I'm afraid. Insists on digging it over there.'

'That's because he's been told to dig it over there, Brigadier! You know we've been discussing this for months. The members were all consulted about it.'

'I know the members were consulted. Only right to get their opinion, of course. But, in the end we still have to take the decision we think is best, don't we? That's what leadership is about, isn't it?'

The Brigadier's idea of democracy was one man, one vote, all right. As long as he was the man and he had the vote, David thought. His shirt, already damp, was quickly becoming soaked and he wanted to get this discussion over with as quickly as possible.

'I'm afraid that's not how it works, these days, Brigadier. There's no point in consulting people if you then ignore their opinion.'

'Yes, but when their opinion is patently wrong…'

The Brigadier was not about to undergo a conversion.

'Then, they have to live with the consequences,' David cut in. The cold rain running down his neck was making him very irritable.

'Anyway, Brigadier, what you, or even the members for that matter, think is not relevant here. The Club was granted planning permission for a bunker over there, where it can't be seen from the footpath. So, over there it has to be. I'm sorry, but Bob has his instructions and I must ask you to leave him to get on with his job.'

'So, you won't change your mind?'

'I can't, Brigadier. I'm sorry,'

The Brigadier began walking towards his vehicle. Then, he turned and came back to David.

'You may have won this one, laddie, but don't think you're going to go on ruining this club. You let in all these people without any regard for standards, and then you allow them to muck about with the layout of a course that has been here since before most of them were born.'

'This has nothing to do with the new members, Brigadier,' David replied. 'In fact, I believe that you were the one who proposed this new bunker. The Committee discussed it at great length and agreed to apply for planning permission. Now, it's being built, and you still want to change it. Well, I'm sorry, it is just too late for that.'

The Brigadier came up close to David.

'The Committee may back you on this one but committees can be changed, you know, laddie. Just you be careful how you tread from now on. Good day, sir!'

He slid into his Range Rover, slammed the door and drove away, his tyres throwing up plumes of water.

'Any more interventions from the Brigadier, Bob,' David grinned. 'And you have my permission to use that digger on him.'

2

David tried to sound cheerful but inside he was shaken by the Brigadier's parting words. As he sat in the Subaru, the water in his clothes drained down into the seat. He felt himself sitting in a cold puddle as he drove slowly back down the course to the clubhouse, trying to relax and compose himself. He was still feeling depressed at the thought of further battles with the Brigadier and his cronies as he walked through the deserted clubhouse and into the office.

'Everything all right?' Margaret asked. 'Did you sort out the Brigadier?'

'Yes, I think so. At least, for the time being. But, he'll be back, I'm sure.'

David walked through into his office. Before closing the door, he turned, 'Any chance of a cup of tea?'

Margaret looked up from her computer. 'It'll cost you,' she smiled.

David slumped into his chair.

This latest confrontation with the Brigadier had left him feeling completely drained. It wasn't so much what he had said or even his very unpleasant manner. It was the thought that he clearly wasn't going to give up fighting every innovation David tried to introduce. He had hoped that the Brigadier would accept that he wasn't out to change the Club for the worse; that everything he was doing was in the long-term interests of all the members, himself included. But, it was clear that the old boy would never be satisfied until he had regained control of the Club for himself.

And, that meant more battles to come. At that moment, cold and wet, David wasn't sure that he felt like fighting them. It was all too reminiscent of his final days as a headmaster, trying to balance the conflicting demands of teachers, parents and government inspectors. And, all the while, Tess was dying. He just didn't want stress like that any more, he thought. He had his pension. He could do without it.

The door opened quietly and Margaret brought in his tea. She placed it on the desk and stood beside him.

'Look at you,' she said. 'You're soaking wet! Why on earth didn't you take your coat, or an umbrella, or something?'

'I didn't think about it until I was out there,' David replied wearily. 'Once I was, I just wanted to sort out the Brigadier as quickly as I could.'

'Well, you can't stay in those wet clothes,' Margaret insisted. 'You'll have to change out of them or you'll catch your death.'

She turned on the gas fire. Then, she went to the door.

'Hang on here a minute,' she said. 'I'll see what I can find.'

David was still slumped at his desk five minutes later when Margaret returned, carrying a bundle.

'Come on,' she said. 'You get out of those wet clothes. I've brought you some things from the professional's shop. You can put these on.'

'I'll be all right,' David replied. 'Honestly, Margaret, I'll be going home in an hour or so.'

'You're absolutely drenched. In an hour or so, you'll have pneumonia or something. You really must take off those wet clothes.'

When David still did not comply, Margaret walked over to the window and looked out. It was still raining heavily and the late afternoon light was fading fast.

She closed the blind. Then, she shut the door and turned the key. The office was quiet now except for the ticking of the old clock. Almost the only light came from the computer screen in the corner. Margaret walked back to where David was sitting.

'Come on,' she said, quietly. 'Lets get you out of those wet clothes.'

She began to untie David's tie.

'No, really, Margaret, I'll be fine. It's getting nice and warm in here now.'

But, Margaret would not take "No" for an answer, and David's defences were down. His tie removed, she began to undo his buttons. Gently, she pulled him to his feet and, carefully unbuttoned his cuffs. She peeled off his wet shirt and hung it over the back of the chair. Her warm hands ran over his chest and down his arms. He was still damp but his skin was drying in the warmth from the gas fire.

197

'That's a bit better,' she said. 'Now, those wet trousers, beginning to unbuckle David's belt.

'I can't take those off!' David exclaimed. 'What if somebody should come in? It would be just great if one of the members chose this moment to come in for a chat. Or, the Brigadier returned for another battle of the bunker.'

'Nobody will come in, silly,' Margaret said, quietly. 'The place is deserted except for you and me. Anyway, the outer door is locked and so is your office. So, why don't you just relax and take off those wet trousers?'

David wasn't up to a second fight in one afternoon. Besides, Margaret wasn't the Brigadier. She was a warm, caring woman coaxing him in a gentle voice to remove his clothes. He unbuckled his belt and unzipped his trousers. When he had taken them off, Margaret hung them over his chair as well. He looked down at his wet socks and peeled those off, too.

'That's more like it,' Margaret said, smiling. 'Now, at least we shan't have you dying of hypothermia.'

'I don't know about that, Margaret,' David replied. 'It's not all that warm in here. And, I feel pretty stupid standing here in my underwear.'

'Come and sit by the fire, then,' Margaret said, and she gestured towards the hearth rug.

She guided him to the hissing gas fire, and passed him his cup. David sat down on the rug, leaned back against the armchair and slowly sipped the warm tea.

'That's really great.' he said. 'You're very kind, Margaret.'

'Don't be daft,' Margaret smiled. 'Besides, remember I did say it'll cost you.'

David looked puzzled, but Margaret took his cup and placed it on the coffee table. Then, she sat down besides him and kissed him softly on the lips. David felt himself stir and wondered if it was visible. He didn't have long to wonder, however, as Margaret slid her hand down inside his shorts.

'Mmm,' she whispered. 'I can see you're warming up all ready.'

She kissed him again, a long and lingering kiss and then began stroking him all over his body. David lay back and absorbed the pleasure. After a while, Margaret stood up and removed her dress. She bent and took off her knickers. Then, kneeling down, she straddled him and guided David into her. She sat forward, with her eyes closed and her hands on his broad chest and began a slow, rhythmic movement with her hips.

David's sex life had been almost non-existent for over four years and Margaret's motion soon got the better of him. Suddenly, without any warning, he experienced a warm flood of pleasure.

'Did you like that?' Margaret smiled down at him.

'Marvellous,' David said. 'How about you?'

'Oh, I thought it was lovely. But, I don't expect too much myself. Don't you worry, I'll sort myself out later.'

'That seems rather unfair,' David said.

He raised his head so that he could see across his belly to where his diminishing member was still inside her. He slid his hand down and found her with his fingers.

'I told you, you don't have to bother,' Margaret whispered. 'I'll do that myself later. It's all right, really…'

Her eyes closed as David's fingers found their mark. He hadn't been active for some years, but his lack of practice was lost on Margaret. Her breathing increased and her body gently swayed. For a few minutes, David feared he would not achieve his objective but, suddenly, Margaret gasped, let out a little cry and then a sigh. She fell forward on to his chest and kissed him on his neck.

'Well, you've done something my husband never managed to do,' she murmured.

Margaret lay still for some time, stroking David's chest and kissing him softly.

'I always wanted it to be like that,' she said, quietly. 'How about you?'

'Actually, Tess and I had a pretty good sex life although, in the last couple of years...' David stopped. Suddenly, talking about love-making with Tess felt like a betrayal.

'That's OK,' Margaret said, 'Don't talk about it if you don't want to.'

She stood up, retrieved her clothes and sat down on David's chair to put them on.

'That was nice,' she said. She bent to kiss him on the cheek. 'More than nice, in fact.'

Then, she looked at David's wet clothes.

'Well, you certainly can't put those on. Here you are,' she said, picking up the bundle of new golf clothes. 'Put these things on while I'll go and make you a fresh cup of tea.'

Alone again, David suddenly felt rather exposed. He got quickly to his feet, and began to dress in the rather colourful outfit that Margaret had selected. He was putting on his socks when the ring of the telephone broke the silence.

'Hi, David.' It was Kate.

'Hello, Kate,' David replied, trying to sound natural, as if Kate had caught him in the middle of some paperwork. 'What can I do for you?'

'I was just wondering if you'd like to have lunch again sometime next week? I want to talk to you about something.'

'Er, yes. That would be lovely, Kate,' David said.

'How about Tuesday. Would that suit you?'

David was conscious that Margaret had come quietly back into the room. He felt an uncomfortable twinge of guilt towards both women.

'Tuesday is fine, Kate,' he said, catching Margaret's eye. 'Where shall we eat? Here, at the Club?'

'No. I thought it would be nice to try somewhere else. *The Black Horse* does a very good lunch, so I'm told. Why don't we meet there? Say, about one?'

'Absolutely fine,' David said. 'I'll look forward to it.'

He smiled as he put down the phone.

'I see,' Margaret teased. 'I give him my body and, before my back is turned, he's on the phone arranging to meet another woman.'

David looked embarrassed and made a lame attempt to explain. Then he looked up and saw that Margaret was smiling. She crouched down beside him and looked up into his eyes.

'Don't be so daft,' she said quietly. 'I've told you before. All we're doing is giving each other a bit of comfort. Nothing wrong with that, is there? It's very nice – today was more than nice – but, we both know it can't ever be any more than that. I told you, I couldn't ever leave Tom and my boys. You need more in your life. You need a nice young lady of your own. And, she is a very nice lady, that Mrs Earnshaw.'

Margaret stood up and changed the subject.

'Now, you look like a real golfer,' she said, cheerfully. 'Maybe it's time for you get your clubs out again.'

She went into the outer office and David looked at himself in the long mirror on the back of the door. The colours weren't quite what he would have chosen, but the sizes were spot-on.

He picked up his mug of tea and sat by the gas fire relishing the warmth.

He relived the recent pleasure in his mind. And, he had to admit, it had been a pleasure, his first time in more than three years.

Margaret was a remarkable woman, he thought. In the months since his arrival, he had often noticed how controlled she was by her oppressive, ageing husband. Yet, in spite of this, she had worked hard and cheerfully, and had provided him with loyal support. She had recognised his needs, even before he was aware of them himself. And, in trying to satisfy them, she'd taken some small pleasure for herself.

Then, surmounting the pleasure, came the guilt.

In part, he felt guilty about what had just occurred. True, Margaret had given herself to him freely, even initiated their encounter. But, nevertheless, he was her boss. He felt he had used her when he had nothing more than friendly feelings for her.

Then, he thought of Tess, with whom, not many years earlier, he had shared such precious moments in bed. Suddenly, he felt overwhelmed with despondency that he should, so soon, be reduced to momentary couplings on an office floor.

And then, he remembered Kate. When she had telephoned to arrange their meeting, he was still wet with sex. In a strange way, he felt he had been unfaithful, even though he and Kate were, as yet, no more than acquaintances. He really liked Kate. She, too, was a remarkable woman, seemingly strong but at the same time clearly vulnerable. He felt so relaxed with her and, in her company, he'd found it so easy to be open.

Thinking of Kate, he knew that Margaret was right. He did need more in his life; more than just occasional brief episodes of sex, however, pleasurable those might be.

And, yes, Margaret was right again. Kate was nice. Very nice. They were both alone. He knew now that he needed someone else in his life. Perhaps, Kate did, too. He began to look forward to their lunch.

3

'Oh, I don't think I'll ever get it Jack!'

'Yes, you will, Karen, if you concentrate on gripping the club and not on how you look.'

'But, I do look like a wally, standing like this.'

'No, you don't. You look great.'

'Do you think so, Jack? I think you look smashing, too. It's so good to see you again.'

'It's good to see you, too, Karen. Now, please, try to concentrate.'

In truth, Jack was trying hard to concentrate, himself. And, he was finding it very difficult. No, that's not quite true. He was concentrating on Karen, all right. But, it was Karen, her pretty face, her blond hair, her lovely figure, those tremendous legs, that he kept seeing and not her golf swing.

'Now,' Jack said. 'That's right. You've got a good grip, Karen.'

'Everybody's always said I had a good grip, Jack,' Karen said, with a smile.

Don't smile like that, Karen, please! Jack thought.

'Yes, well you have.'

'Do you like a girl to have a good grip, Jack?'

'For God's sake, Karen! Just concentrate on the lesson, will you?'

'Only if you promise we can talk later.'

'What do you want to talk about?'

'Oh, you know. What we've been up to the past eight years. I want to know all about what you've been doing.'

'You don't want to know about that, Karen. You just want to divert my attention away from the lesson.'

'No, I don't. Honest,' Karen said, trying to be serious. 'Right, now, I've got a lovely grip. Sorry, Jack,' she said, pretending to duck, 'a good grip.'

'Not too tight now,' Jack said.

'Oh, for God's sake, Jack! First, you want me to have a good grip. Now, you're complaining it's too tight. You're never satisfied, you aren't.'

'Look, Karen. What you need is to have your hands in the right position.'

'Well, how can I do that if I've got to hold on to this stupid golf club?'

'Once you've got your hands in the right position, you need to grip firmly, but not too tight. Is that clear enough?'

'Firm, but not too tight,' Karen said, with a wicked grin. 'I've got it.'

'Otherwise you won't be able to move your arms freely enough.'

'Yeah, that follows,' said Karen.

'OK. Now, hold the club out in front of you and bend from the hips. Stick your bottom out a little bit and keep your back as straight as you can.'

'You do like to get a girl into some funny positions, don't you Jack?'

Karen tried to do as Jack had told her, but she looked rather awkward.

'Relax, Karen. You're very stiff.'

'That's a funny thing to say, Jack. What sort of girls have you been mixing with these past eight years?'

Jack was beginning to despair of ever getting Karen to concentrate.

'Right, now let's just try a swing. Try to hit the ball.'

Karen turned and swung the club up and back, then down towards the ball. Unfortunately, she missed the ball altogether and the momentum of the club took her flying forwards and she overbalanced.

She threw the club down and started to walk away.

'That's it! I've had enough of this stupid game. Spiros can bloody play around with his balls on his own.'

'Hang on Karen,' Jack said, catching her arm. 'Everybody finds it difficult to begin with. This is only your first lesson, after all. Let's start again, only this time just concentrate on the golf and not on talking to me. OK?'

Karen frowned. Then, she looked up at Jack with a grin.

'OK, I suppose so. You could persuade me to do anything. You know that, don't you, Jack?'

'Well, at the moment, all I want is to persuade you to try and hit the ball.'

Jack handed the club back to Karen.

'Set yourself up, just like before. That's it! Now, let's see you swing the club again, only more smoothly this time.'

Karen swung back more smoothly and this time she hit the ball. Not perfectly. A little low and a bit right, perhaps. But, she hit it. Karen leapt up and down with delight. She threw her arms round Jack.

'I did it, Jack! I did it!' she cried. 'I can play golf. You're a brilliant teacher, Jack. You could get a girl to do anything, I reckon. Can we have our talk, now?'

'No, we can't! You've only hit the ball once. The lesson's only just started. Let's see if you can do it again.'

Reluctantly, Karen set herself up again. With a few pointers from Jack, she adopted a slightly stronger grip and a wider stance. Then, she held the club out and slowly bent at the hips, pushing her bottom back slightly in the process.

Unlike most of the girls Jack knew, and indeed most of the people who came to him for golf lessons, Karen had always had beautiful posture.

God, she is gorgeous, he thought. What a cracking body!

Jack had always fancied Karen. He'd thought she looked smashing from the time they were put in the same class in the third year. But, she'd always had a harem of boys fluttering around her and Jack had never had a look in. The closest he had got was when he put his hand up her dress at the sixth form leaving dance. He and Karen had been drinking. They'd gone outside for some air and she'd come on to him. They were only just starting when that great oaf,

205

Dave Weller, who was supposed to have taken Karen to the dance, came out looking for her. Next thing he knew, Jack was lying on the floor. He hadn't seen Karen again since.

'Now, swing back smoothly and try to hit the ball.'

Karen did so and, once again, the ball was propelled down the range, a little farther this time.

She's already doing better than her husband, Jack thought.

'That's good, Karen. That's really good,' Jack said. 'OK, now, you need to turn your shoulders a little more. So far, you are only using your arms.'

'I don't get what you mean,' Karen said.

'Well, cross your arms over your chest, like this,' he demonstrated.

Karen did as she was asked. Jack took hold of her shoulders and guided them round through ninety degrees. Karen's head moved round as well so that she ended up looking to the side.

'No, Karen, keep looking forward at me, as I turn your shoulders.'

'I could look at you all day long, Jack.'

'Well, just do it while I turn your shoulders. OK?'

'You've got lovely warm hands, Jack,' Karen said, looking up into his eyes.

Blond hair framed her blue eyes and, as she tilted her face, Jack felt himself suddenly go quite weak.

'And, they're so strong. Sorry, I'm talking again, aren't I?'

'Right, now,' Jack said, recovering himself. 'Let's see if you can turn your shoulders like that while you're holding the club.'

'I prefer it if it's the man holding the club,' Karen said. 'You know, me Tarzan, you Jane.'

'Yes, well in this game, both the men and the women hold the clubs. Now, let's see you hit the ball.'

Karen tried to swing by turning her shoulders, but she was all over the place and she missed the ball completely.

'I was all right before,' she said, looking cross. 'You've mucked me up, now, Jack Peters. All that turning my shoulders and stuff.'

'No, I haven't,' Jack said. 'Now, listen, Karen. You've got a good grip. You're posture is good. Great, in fact. There's no reason why you can't hit the ball well, if you just concentrate.'

Karen was still frowning.

'After all,' Jack went on, 'in golf, at least the ball is standing still. It's not moving about like it is in other sports. You don't have to go chasing after it.'

Karen looked up at Jack and smiled.

'Maybe that's the trouble. Some girls like to do the chasing.'

Karen had come in to the shop earlier in the week. But, then, Jack hadn't been alone. She had bought golf shoes and a range of clothing so that, as Makrides had asked, she would look the part.

And, look the part, she certainly did, in her pale blue trousers and her white polo shirt and her matching short-sleeved pullover. To complete her ensemble, Karen wore white golf shoes and a white golf glove on her left hand. She looked pretty and immensely desirable which, Jack thought, was precisely what she intended.

With a heroic effort, Jack managed to get both his and Karen's attention back on to the lesson.

When she does concentrate, she's quite a good mover, he reflected. A beautiful mover, in fact.

After a while, Karen was hitting quite a high percentage of the balls a reasonable distance down the range. Every now and then she would mis-hit a ball and, to begin with, this would result in club-throwing histrionics. As she started to get the hang of it, however, Karen's confidence improved and she began to concentrate and swing with growing determination.

'I'm getting to like this, Jack,' she said. 'I never thought I could enjoy hitting a ball so much. You're such a good teacher.'

'And, you're a quick learner, Karen,' Jack replied. Inwardly, he was most impressed with his beautiful pupil. So much so that, for a while at least, he was able to concentrate on her golf swing rather than her body.

'It just goes to show, doesn't it?'

'What goes to show, Karen?'

'How good things can be when you work at something together,' Karen replied. 'Can we stop, now, Jack. Or else we won't have any time to talk.'

'All right,' Jack agreed, with a sigh. 'As long as you promise to come and practice.'

'I promise. I'll come as often as you want me to,' Karen said, with a wicked grin.

'Good,' Jack said, striving to remain the teacher. 'Now, what do you want to talk about?'

Karen leaned the golf club up against the wall.

'Oh, nothing much, really. I just wanted to know what you've been up to since we left school. That sort of thing.'

'I told you. I've been working here, the whole time.'

'And, what about girl friends. Have you had many girls, Jack?'

'A few. But you don't meet that many girls when you work in a place like this six and a half days a week,' Jack explained. 'Why do you ask?'

'Just interested.' Then, suddenly, she grasped Jack's forearm with both hands and looked up into his face. 'I have missed you, Jack.'

'No, you haven't, Karen. You forgot all about me after we left school.'

'All right,' Karen said. 'But, I have thought about you.'

208

'Oh, yeah? When have you thought about me?' Jack demanded, laughing.

'Well, since last week, for a start. I'd forgotten how nice you were.'

'But, Karen,' Jack said. 'Now, you're married to Spiros. You've got a nice house, nice clothes, and a Mercedes of your own. What more could a girl want?'

Karen reached up and kissed him on the cheek.

'You don't know anything, do you Jack Peters? See you next week,' she said, and she walked away down the range.

Hole	Name	Yards	Par	Score
12	A Winter's Tale	511	5	

1

The winter league was approaching an interesting stage. The main purpose of this competition was to keep the members playing, and therefore the bar takings coming in, during the winter. Branfield Park's winter league had always taken the form of foursomes, played early on Sunday mornings throughout the darker months.

'Foursomes?' David spelt out to one of the newer members one afternoon, after he'd put up the entry sheet on the notice board. 'Foursomes is a type of competition in which each pair of golfers has only one ball between them. The players in each team take it in turns to hit their ball until it goes into the hole.'

'Or,' Giles interjected with a laugh, 'until the other side concedes the putt because they think that not even you could miss that one!'

'So you don't get to play with your own ball?' the new member asked.

'No. That is, you have to share it with your partner,' David explained. The man looked disappointed and moved away in the direction of the bar.

'It's funny,' Giles said. 'A lot of golfers don't like foursomes. Most of them prefer to develop a relationship, even a short-lived one, with their own ball. You'll find that only really devoted and hardy, or foolhardy, souls will turn up rain or shine at the Club at eight o'clock on a Sunday morning in winter.'

David knew what it was to be a devoted and hardy golfer. In the past, he had been only too happy to get up at the crack of dawn for the sake of his golf.

210

For most Branfield golfers, winter league was a sociable way of keeping their hand in over the winter. Foursomes don't tend to last too long and golfers could usually complete their rounds, have a drink and still be home in plenty of time to wash the car before Sunday lunch.

But for some, winter league was a serious business. For the stags it was another opportunity to test themselves against each other and, especially, against any young bucks who might think of challenging them. For the stags, golf was definitely about cocks!

A David Attenborough, concealed on a Sunday morning in the beech hedge surrounding the putting green, might, in a hushed voice, have described the scene to camera, thus:

"Often larger than average, the stags wear tight trousers and large jumpers with roll-neck collars to accentuate their size. Stags nearly always carry their bags of clubs. They strike the ball colossal distances down the fairway, pick up their bags and stride off. Sometimes, they will helpfully point as they pass to their opponent's ball, lying in the light rough, fully fifty yards short of their own. This ritual serves to remind lesser players of their place in the scheme of things."

'In contrast, many of the other members of the herd are smaller. The thick clothing they wear as protection against the winter cold, makes them appear more diminutive and vulnerable. Their golf bags, however, are large since they must carry extra clothing and plenty of spare balls. Consequently, they have to pull their bags around on trolleys, which of course makes them slower and leaves them trailing in the wake of the stags."

Branfield's winter league was organised in two stages. First there was the group stage, during which each pair played every other pair in their group. This was followed by the knock-out stage, during which the top pairs from each group locked antlers through a number of rounds until the final. For the stags, the group stage was an irritating diversion. They expected, and usually did, win their groups. Once through to the knockout stage, their aim was to reach the final and to win it; to see their names in gold letters on a wooden plaque on the clubhouse wall.

The Brigadier always played in the winter league, and he played to win it. Indeed, he had won it many times. He invariably topped his group and was usually there or thereabouts as the knockout stage reached it climax, when the other members of the herd were burrowing into their warm beds on a Sunday morning.

This year, however, the Brigadier had had a couple of close matches against some young pretenders and, for a change, he was not at the top of his group. As this was the last Sunday of the group stage, he and his partner, Tony Hockley, had to win their match to be sure of progress to the knock-out stage.

But the Brigadier wasn't worried. The golfing gods had provided, as opponents, just the sort of minnows that stags ate for breakfast. Jimmy McGrath and Mike Newman were at the bottom of their group – no wins and two draws so far; high-handicap players who rarely won and didn't really expect to. They enjoyed getting out in the fresh air and they relished their post-match drink but, equally, they were looking forward to the following Sunday when they would not have to get up so early.

2

The Brigadier and Tony were waiting on the first tee, impatiently pacing backwards and forwards, not exactly pawing the ground but swishing their drivers in anticipation of the coming slaughter.

'Morning Brigadier! Lovely day!'

Although he'd lived in the south for over thirty years, Jimmy had never made any effort to lose his Scottish accent. A former miner, he enjoyed showing off his roots.

Mike, on the other hand, was a local boy, Branfield born and bred, a carpenter who was very good at his trade.

Tony managed a polite smile and a handshake. As a country member, who lived more than fifty miles from the Club, he'd had to get up much earlier than most.

The Brigadier nodded curtly in the direction of his two opponents and offered his hand. Twenty years after retiring from Her Majesty's forces, he had still to adjust to the idea of playing with people from the 'other ranks'. In truth, the two 'specimens' with whom fate had paired him that morning were just the sort of people he could not bear in the Club. Indeed, under the old regime, which he hoped would soon be restored to power, they would never have been admitted to membership. Sound fellows, he was sure, but nonetheless tradesmen who belonged at the tradesmen's entrance.

'Good morning,' the Brigadier said. 'I believe we have to give you ten strokes.'

In foursomes matches, better players must 'give' strokes to their opponents. Each pair adds their handicaps together and the combined totals are then subtracted.

'I make it eleven, Brigadier,' Jimmy replied, cheerfully. 'You two both play off five, I gather. Mike here has a handicap of eighteen and I play off twenty. So, the difference is twenty-eight. Three-eighths of that is ten point five, which rounds up to eleven.'

'Oh, very well' the Brigadier conceded with mixed feelings. On the one hand, having to give so many strokes to his opponents demonstrated that he and Tony were by far the better golfers. And the system is, after all, biased in favour of the superior player. On the other hand, he would rather not have had to give away quite so many strokes in a match he simply had to win. No matter, he did not anticipate much resistance from these two.

The Brigadier teed off and the first hole set the pattern for those to come. Mike's tee shot only just made it to the fairway, Jimmy mis-hit their second and Mike put their third into a bunker. Their opponents did not even need to putt to win the hole.

On the second tee, it was Jimmy and Tony to tee off. Their partners could, therefore, walk down the fairway and wait for the balls to arrive. It is this that makes foursomes such a speedy format. The Brigadier set off but hesitated when Mike made no move to join him.

'Shall we wait down the fairway for them to tee off?' he asked.

His tone suggested that, perhaps, Mike didn't know that this was how these things were done and needed the guidance of a more experienced player.

'Better not!' Mike replied. 'Never sure where Jimmy's ball will go, especially when it's his first tee shot.'

'Oh, very well,' the Brigadier smirked. This was to be an even easier game than he had thought.

And, it was. In spite of having strokes on more than half the holes, Mike and Jimmy were just not in the match. They managed to halve a few but, after twelve holes, they were five holes down with only six left to play.

Initially tense, even the Brigadier began to relax. Over the first few holes, Jimmy's attempts at conversation were curtly rebuffed. The Brigadier answered every question with a single word reply – a model of concentration and efficiency. Tony was a little more forthcoming. He explained that he had once lived locally but moved some distance away. He would have preferred to play nearer his home, but the Brigadier had made it very clear that he expected his continuing support on Sunday mornings.

As the inevitability of their victory became clear however Tony and the Brigadier even began to share the odd joke with their opponents.

No point being too stand-offish when one is about to win so comprehensively, the Brigadier said to himself.

214

He would relax and enjoy earning the two points that would ensure progress through to the next round and, hopefully, towards yet another final. As he relaxed, the Brigadier felt his concentration begin to waver but, no matter, victory was assured.

'We're stuffed, mate!' Mike muttered, as he and Jimmy heaved their trolleys towards the thirteenth tee.

'No way,' Jimmy replied. 'I'm going to have these bastards, you'll see!'

'I don't see how?'

'Well,' Jimmy whispered. 'Lets see just how good the high and mighty fucking Brigadier's concentration is!'

As they reached the tee, Jimmy began to ferret in his bag. From within the cavernous side pocket he produced a Tesco's carrier bag and, with it, a large thermos flask.

'I've got some rolls here,' Jimmy announced. 'Can I tempt you to one, Brigadier?'

'Well…' the Brigadier hesitated. He didn't normally worry about appearing rude. Indeed, it is doubtful if he was ever aware of being rude. All the same, they were about to beat these two characters quite comprehensively. It would surely do no harm to let those from the barracks know that officers too have a human side.

'Thank you, just one please.'

'Corned beef with a hint of Piccalilli,' Jimmy prattled on. 'Made them myself at six o'clock this morning.'

Corned beef with a hint of Piccalilli was not a dish the Brigadier normally consumed at ten o'clock on a Sunday morning. However, he felt he could hardly show disdain for Jimmy's offering.

'Coffee?' Jimmy asked.

Tony and the Brigadier were tucking in to their rolls but the latter was becoming anxious. The players putting out on the twelfth green would, in a few moments, begin walking towards the thirteenth tee.

'Oh, very well.' The Brigadier was becoming irritated, but tried not to show bad grace. 'It is a cold day, after all.'

He swallowed the coffee quickly, noticing, as he did so, how unusual it tasted.

'Nothing like the feel of something warm inside you, is there, Brigadier?'

When Jimmy saw that his suggestiveness had passed over the Brigadier's head, he continued.

'I always add a wee drop of whisky to the coffee. It helps the circulation on a cold day like this.'

The Brigadier handed his mug back to Jimmy and stepped on to the tee, a six iron in his hand. As he did so, the following foursome arrived and began asking Jimmy and Mike how their match was going.

3

It could have been the whisky. Perhaps, it was a sudden increase in blood sugar as a result of the ham rolls and the hot, sweet coffee. Maybe, it was the presence of an audience. The Brigadier usually played so swiftly that those behind rarely caught up and he did not often have to tee off in front of others.

Probably, it was his concentration. Just for a moment his mind was full of so many things – the food, the drink, his opponents, his audience and, fatally, the next round. Whatever it was, he swung the club far too fast. He swayed slightly and hit the ground just before the ball. The small white projectile shot off a few inches above the ground but very soon came to rest some twenty yards away in a clump of long wet grass.

'Oh bad luck, Brigadier!' Jimmy shouted. *Got you, you wee bastard!*

On such occasions, the second player to tee off can often make the same mistake as the first, so eager is he to take advantage of the other's misfortune.

Jimmy held his breath as Mike stepped up on to the tee, but this time his partner produced the goods when they were needed. His ball landed on the apron just in front of the green. The Brigadier was knee deep in wet hay, a hundred and fifty yards behind.

Tony and the Brigadier walked over to the wet grass. Coming in so fast, the ball had burrowed deep into the thatch and Tony decided that the best plan was to hit it out sideways. Unfortunately, the ball was quite happy where it was and refused to emerge. The Brigadier only made matters worse and, after one more try, Tony suggested they concede the hole. Those waiting on the tee were beginning to make impatient noises.

'Can we play through, Brigadier?' shouted one.

'I'd really like to wash the car before lunch!' another called out.

The Brigadier had never endured such disrespect before and it was beginning to bite.

'Come along, Tony,' he barked. 'Let's get on to the next tee. We're still four up with five to play. Just concentrate now and let's get the job done.'

But, as they walked towards the fourteenth tee, it was the Brigadier's concentration that remained fragile. It wasn't just losing the last hole. It was the manner of it. And, the way in which the riff-raff had barracked him. Such a humiliation, if reported in the bar, would be heard by some of the other stags. Before long, his invincibility might be questioned.

'Concentrate,' he said to himself. 'Concentrate!' A victory by five and four would surely secure his reputation.

Tony's drive at the fourteenth was long and straight as usual. Jimmy's was short and sliced but just on the fairway. Mike hit their second shot to a spot thirty yards short of the green.

As Jimmy and the Brigadier walked down the fairway together, Jimmy maintained a barrage of inane chatter to which the Brigadier, drawn in, felt obliged to respond.

'We haven't played very well today,' Jimmy explained. 'It's this bag, I think maybe that's the trouble.'

'I beg your pardon?'

'This bag. It's the first time I've played with this bag. I'm not really used to it yet, d'you see?'

'I'm sorry, I don't understand,' the Brigadier was perplexed. 'How on earth can your bag affect the way you play?'

'Oh, but it can, Brigadier. My golf bag is part of my equipment. If you're not confident with you're equipment, you canna perform well.'

This nonsense was really beginning to get to the Brigadier. Tony's drive had travelled about two hundred and thirty yards, leaving a simple shot of about a hundred and forty yards. The Brigadier approached the ball determined to put it in the middle of the green, a few yards from the flag, and thus close out the match. Jimmy and Mike received a stroke at this hole but their second shot had landed well short of the green.

'After all, Brigadier,' Jimmy continued. 'Your bag is clearly an important part of your equipment. You would nae want to lug my great big thing about on your shoulder...'

'No, quite,' the Brigadier replied.

He stood his bag on the ground and took out an eight iron.

'This is a shot I hate,' Jimmy went on. 'That bunker on the left always catches me out. Either that, or those trees at the back of the green.'

'I can assure you that they are nowhere near where I intend to play,' the Brigadier smirked.

'Aye, they're nowhere near where I intend to play,' Jimmy replied. 'But, I seem to find 'em, just the same!'

'Yes, quite,' the Brigadier hissed. Time to shut you up, my friend, he said to himself as he addressed the ball.

Damned idiot! he thought, as he began his backswing. Those trees are simply not a consideration. Still, better not hit too hard, just to be on the safe side. So, as he swung down towards the ball, he began to put the brakes on, to decelerate. Too late, the Brigadier realised his error and he tried to speed up. However, instead of the satisfying connection he was used to, he caught the ball with the front edge of the club. It skidded along the turf at high speed and buried itself in the vertical face of the bunker.

'Oh, dear,' Jimmy said, softly. 'I know just how you must feel, Brigadier. I end up in that self-same bunker myself, more often than not.'

But, the ball wasn't just 'in' the bunker. Most good players can get a ball out of sand. And, when the ball is lying in the sand at the bottom of a bunker, players of Tony and the Brigadier's calibre can usually land it pretty close to the hole. However, this ball was buried deep in wet sand, half way up the bunker's face. Only a small part of it could be seen. Gary Player at his very best would have been glad to get this ball out.

Jimmy approached their ball on the fairway.

'What are you planning to do?' Mike asked.

'Putt it,' Jimmy muttered.

'What? On this wet grass?'

'Yeah! We don't want to end up in the bunker along with the Brigadier, do we? I'll putt it as hard as I can. Anywhere on the green will do.'

Jimmy's ball skidded across the heavy dew, slowing down all the time, but it reached the edge of the green with just enough kinetic energy to continue rolling until it came to rest about ten yards from the flag.

'Just right,' Jimmy grinned.

Mike and Jimmy had now taken three, or 'net two'. If they could get their ball into the hole with only two putts then, in order to halve the hole, Tony would have to extricate his ball and leave it close enough for the Brigadier to sink his putt. Somehow, that didn't seem likely.

In fact, Mike didn't even need to take his putt. Tony climbed into the sand and swung as hard as he could at the small target, but he succeeded only in causing an avalanche. The ball was now completely buried.

The rules allow careful removal of sand until the ball can be identified. Jimmy and Mike watched as Tony and the Brigadier gently scraped away at the sand until they found their ball. The Brigadier took his sand wedge and swung with all his might. He was a big man and a huge shower of sand was launched skywards. Out with it came the ball but, instead of landing near the flag, it flew over the green and into the plantation of fir trees on the far side.

'That's exactly what I was talking about,' Jimmy said, looking sadly wise. 'If the sand does nae get you, the trees surely will.'

Jimmy and Mike had taken three shots and were only ten yards from the flag. The Brigadier and Tony had taken four and were in the trees. Realising the hopelessness of their position, they conceded the hole and picked up their ball.

'For God's sake, Tony! We're still three up with four to play,' the Brigadier whispered. 'Let's just win this hole and get back to the bar.' His tone, however, was now more desperate than confident.

The next hole, the fifteenth, was fairly straightforward. Both sides teed off and, as usual, Jimmy and Mike were a long way behind the Brigadier and his partner. In fact, Mike only hit their ball a hundred and fifty yards. Even a good second shot from Jimmy left them a long way from the green. The Brigadier's drive was long and straight and left Tony with a shot of about a hundred and forty yards to the flag.

'Let's get this over with,' muttered the old soldier as Tony stood over the ball with an eight iron.

Tony hit the ball perfectly. Indeed, he hit the ball so perfectly that, as it soared into the cold winter sky and arched down towards the flag, those watching thought it must surely fly straight into the hole. Instead, the ball struck the side of the flag-stick, from where it ricocheted at an angle off the back of the green.

'Pity,' the Brigadier muttered. However, he remained confident that victory was imminent. The worst he and Tony could score would be a five. The best the tradesmen could probably hope for was also a five. The hole would be halved and they would be three up with three to play. Dormie.

Even when Mike hit his side's third shot way beyond his ability to only four feet from the hole, the Brigadier's confidence did not waver. There was no way he would concede a putt as important as that. He had seen those missed often enough when it mattered!

The Brigadier's confidence began to evaporate, however, when he and Tony found their ball. After striking the flag-stick a glancing blow, the ball had settled into a depression on some rough ground behind the green. It was not easy to see how the Brigadier could hit it out because, if he swung normally, the club head would be likely to hit the edge of the depression. He practised swinging in a number of ways but the ball was very difficult to reach.

Eventually, with Tony, Jimmy and Mike looking on, the Brigadier took a swing at the ball and, much to his horror, he missed it completely.

The 'air shot' is probably the most undignified of all golf shots. The topped ball, the slice, the shank and the hook, all are bad enough in their own way. But, at least the club has made contact with the ball! With an air shot, however, the play misses the ball altogether and, because the ball is missed, none of the swing's energy is absorbed. So, the club continues on its way, sometimes almost lifting the player off his feet.

All the time, the ball sits there, defiant, daring the humiliated golfer to strike it again. And, that is just what most people do. When the ball has been missed, all most golfers can think about is to try and hit it a second time; to drive out the memory of the previous failure.

And, that is exactly what Brigadier Tufnell did. Before anyone could shout, "Oh, bad luck, old boy!" he had swung his club again. This time, he managed to extricate the ball from its depression and it scuttled across the green, coming to rest some six feet from the flag.

'Oh, well done, Brigadier!' Tony shouted. 'Great shot! We can still get a half out of this hole!'

'I don't think so,' Jimmy said, quietly.

'What on earth do you mean?' the Brigadier demanded.

'What I mean, Brigadier,' Jimmy explained, 'is that we win the hole.'

'But, you haven't sunk your putt yet!'

The Brigadier was confused.

'We don't need to,' Jimmy replied. 'We're playing foursomes, are we not, Brigadier? That means each player hits the ball alternately, does it not? You attempted to strike your ball and you missed it. That was your shot. Tony here should have hit the next shot, but I'm afraid you played out of turn.'

Jimmy held out his tattered copy of the *Rules of Golf*.

'You can check it yourself if you like, Brigadier,' Jimmy went on, opening the book at the appropriate page. 'Rule 29.2 is quite clear. If you play when your partner should have played, you lose the hole.'

'*But, but, that's ridiculous!*' the Brigadier spluttered. If there was one thing he could not stand, it was barrack-room lawyers.

'It may be ridiculous, but it is the rule,' Tony conceded. 'Come on, Brigadier, let's play the next hole.'

They were now two holes up with three to play.

'I don't believe it, Jimmy,' muttered Mike, as they walked together along the sixteenth fairway, the Brigadier and Tony striding out far ahead.

'We haven't finished yet, Mike,' Jimmy confided. 'We're going to beat these bastards.'

'It's only the Brigadier who's a bastard,' said Mike. 'That Tony's all right.'

'What d'ye mean, all right?' Jimmy queried, grinning broadly. 'Why, even the Brigadier said he's a cunt, remember?'

'A country member, you idiot!' Mike laughed.

'Oh, sorry,' Jimmy grinned. 'Listen, Mike, if we can beat these arrogant buggers, it'll be better than sex, will it not?'

'Better than a blow-job, I should think!' Mike chuckled.

He and Jimmy were still laughing when they joined their opponents down the fairway.

'That's right, isn't it Brigadier?' Jimmy called across. 'Winning at golf can be better than sex? Better even than a blow-job!'

The Brigadier wasn't sure what to say. He wasn't used to comparing golf with sex. He certainly wasn't used to discussing his sex life with the 'other ranks' although, privately, he might have conceded that winning at golf, even playing golf, was possibly better than any sex he had experienced for some considerable time.

'Yes, quite,' the Brigadier muttered, and he turned away to hide his reddening face.

But, Jimmy sensed blood.

'I mean, it depends on the blow-job, of course,' he went on. 'But, if a woman swallows, then it can make a big difference. Would you not you agree, Mike?'

'Oh, absolutely!' Mike said, joining in the fun.

'What do you think, Brigadier?' Jimmy said, going for the jugular.

223

'I'm afraid I really have no opinion on that,' the Brigadier said sharply, desperate now to change the subject and force his attention back on to the shot he was preparing to hit.

He did have an opinion on it, of course, but that opinion was no concern of anyone else. So many thoughts were flowing through his head at that moment – his own sexual experience, his feelings of humiliation, his outrage that such an important match should be sullied in this way. It was really no wonder he made something of a mess of hitting the ball. It wasn't a total disaster, both sides scored a five but, because they had to give Jimmy and Mike a stroke on this hole, Tony and the Brigadier lost it. They were now one hole up with two to play.

It was the Brigadier's turn to tee off at the seventeenth. A short hole, but a long drop down into the gorge. And, he was determined to make a good job of it; to finally show these blighters just who was in charge.

'Good luck, old chap,' Tony said to his partner.

'Aye, good luck, Henry,' Jimmy muttered, as the Brigadier passed him on his way to the tee.

'Thank you,' the Brigadier said, trying to appear calm when he was feeling anything but. It wasn't the shot across the water; the narrow trout stream hadn't even entered his thoughts. It wasn't the closeness of the score. After all, victory was surely still certain? No, it was the "Henry". No member of the other ranks had ever addressed him by his first name. He wasn't aware that they even knew his first name. Damned cheek!

Suddenly, all the fears he'd experienced since the new Secretary arrived and the membership had been opened up to a wider social range began to coalesce. Damn them! Damn them all! He would remind them who he was and whom they should respect!

He took an eight iron out of his bag. This shot usually called for an eight iron and the Brigadier didn't give his club selection a moment's thought. In his agitated state, he didn't notice the breeze in his face or the fact that the tee was further back than usual. All he could think about was "Henry" and how he was going to wipe the smile off the face of this nasty little tradesman.

It is never a good idea to swing a golf club when one is angry. Co-ordination is never at its best when anger has taken over. The golf ball should be swept smoothly towards its intended target; not thrashed as if it is to be punished for some misdemeanour. A ball hit in this way will, more often than not, run away and hide.

The Brigadier's ball almost made it across the stream, but then the pain was too great and it dived head-first into the cold water.

'Damn!' the Brigadier shouted as he stormed off the tee.

In this situation, a penalty shot must be taken. Tony hit their third shot on to the green but it wasn't good enough to save the hole. The match was now all square.

4

And so, as they stood on the final tee, Brigadier Henry Tufnell was a broken man. He had had the game and his progress to another winter league final within his grasp. It had been wrenched away by a pair of wretched little artisans who, in his view, should not even be members of the Club.

And, they wouldn't be much longer, not if he had his way. It was high time he made Southern and the rest of the Committee sit up and take notice. If this sort of riff-raff could use such tactics to beat a player of his ability, it would not be long before they too suffered similar indignities. The mob would rule and all the standards of behaviour he had known would be swept away.

Given his partner's anxiety, Tony's tee shot was quite respectable. So, too, was Jimmy's, and Mike was thrilled when he hit their second on to the green to about eight yards from the flag. They were firing on all cylinders now.

The Brigadier hit their ball a little less than was needed and left Tony a putt of about fifteen yards. To win the match, Tony had to get his putt very close and hope that their opponents took three putts.

Normally, Tony's putting was one of the strongest aspects of his game and he would expect to get a fifteen-yard putt to within a couple of feet. Perhaps, close enough for their opponents to concede it. He and his partner would then have scored four.

At that point, the pressure would switch to Jimmy and Mike who would have to get down in two to avoid losing the hole and the match. The Brigadier was still confident of victory, therefore, as Tony lined up his putt.

But, the eighteenth green was wet with dew and Tony misjudged its pace. His putt died on the slope and the damp grass, finishing some four feet short of the hole.

Jimmy hit his putt close to the hole.

'Take it away,' Tony said, conceding the putt. 'Well played.'

Jimmy and Mike had scored a four, their only par of the day.

Now, it was the Brigadier's putt and he had to sink it to halve the match. On his day, a four-foot uphill putt would have presented little problem, but he wasn't the man he'd been. The past hour had reduced his brain and his muscles to jelly. He had no feel for the shot any more.

The Brigadier's putt rolled slowly up the slope and came to a halt some eighteen inches short of the hole.

Faced with this feeble effort, Jimmy couldn't help himself.

'Oh, nice putt, Alice! Does your husband play, Brigadier?'

Jimmy and Mike had won the hole with a four and, with it, the match.

The Brigadier flushed and turned away. He knew, of course, that the match was lost. But, it wasn't just the match. All was lost. The story of this debacle would circulate in the bars and bazaars. Before long, every young buck would know that the Brigadier was there to be beaten and the stag would be dragged down to the level of the herd.

5

'I tell you, ladies and gentlemen,' the Brigadier declared. 'The barbarian is at the gate. Indeed, he has breached our defences and is, even now, among us.'

Brigadier Tufnell had been describing to the Committee, his experience of playing against, and losing to, Jimmy and Mike.

'The sort of behaviour to which my playing partner and I were subjected is precisely the kind of uncouth and unsporting conduct of which I have been warning.'

The Brigadier sensed the opportunity to use his debacle to his advantage. He would exploit the nature of his defeat to win a more important battle. Perhaps, even, the war.

'Ever since the new Secretary was appointed, and ever since the Committee agreed to allow more members to join the Club, the danger has been there that those uneducated in golfing etiquette would bring with them a general decline in normal standards of behaviour.'

The Brigadier had told his tale well and he detected a degree of sympathy from some of those in the room.

'Ladies and gentlemen of the Committee, this decline must be halted. The advance of the barbarian must be reversed, or all will be lost. I appeal to you now to vote in favour of accepting Toby Kelham's most generous offer of a loan. His kindness will allow us to repay the bank's overdraft and thus remove the threat to the Club. It will then be possible to return to the membership policy existing hitherto.'

He sat down, satisfied that his words had had the desired effect on any waverers around the table.

'Oh, come on, Brigadier,' said Giles. 'Don't you think you are being a touch over-dramatic? You lost a golf match. We can understand your disappointment, but we have only your word for it that these chaps behaved badly.'

The Brigadier looked deeply offended, but Giles continued.

'I spoke to Tony Hockley in the bar afterwards and he conceded it was your own fault. He seems to think you both rather threw it away.'

'And, surely we can't be expected to decide something that could affect the whole future of the Club on the basis of one match?' Simon Cornwell asked.

'But, don't you see?' the Brigadier retorted. 'This match symbolised everything that has gone wrong with Branfield Park ever since Crowley here became Secretary.'

'Oh, come on, Brigadier!' said Bill Ellery.

'No, I mean it, Bill, really,' the Brigadier continued. 'Tony Hockley and I were forced to play a match against people we did not know; people against whom we would never have chosen to play. Our opponents, shabby little fellows with the most uncultured of golf swings, departed from every accepted standard of behaviour in order to defeat us. The threat to the Club must be apparent to all who are willing to listen.'

'Here, here!' Toby Kelham chimed in.

All eyes turned towards the landowner. He, in turn, met their gaze.

'Ladies and gentlemen, I have been privileged to be a member of Branfield Park for some years. Like you, I have treasured its wonderful environs. But, more, I have felt honoured to be able to share my golf with people for whom the spirit of the game and impeccable behaviour are equally important. It is to preserve that spirit and to safeguard this haven for that behaviour, that I made my offer of a loan. I had no other motive and I trust my offer will be accepted in the spirit in which it was made.'

'I'm sure we are all most grateful for your offer, Toby,' Giles replied. 'But, before we take a vote on it, I should like to invite David to give us his views. David.'

Giles motioned David to stand up.

'Ladies and gentlemen,' David began. 'I am unable to comment on the Brigadier's match last week. I do know that there have been one or two difficulties with new members in recent months. Dress codes have sometimes been ignored. Behaviour on the course and in the clubhouse has, occasionally, been a problem.'

'However, these hiccups have been few and far between. On the other hand, the benefits of having so many more visitors and some new members have been considerable. The Club is now operating at a profit, albeit a small one. Reducing the overdraft will take much longer, I'm afraid. But, with the support of the bank, which I have every reason to believe will be forthcoming, I am confident the Club will eventually achieve a sound position through better management. Mr Kelham's loan is, therefore, not only unnecessary but, I believe, it is dangerous.'

'Dangerous? What damned nonsense!' The Brigadier interrupted. 'Mr Chairman, surely we've heard enough from Crowley in the past. Admin wallahs will always defend their admin, we all know that. But, we have to think about the future of the Club...'

'Yes, indeed,' David pressed on, ignoring the Brigadier's interruption. 'I believe that it is dangerous for the Club to owe money to one member, as is proposed, here. Mr Kelham has attached two conditions to his loan. One, that the membership and visitor policy should revert to what it was. If that happens, then the Club will cease to make a profit, or to break even.'

'The second condition allows Mr Kelham to demand repayment at any time. If, at some future date, Mr Kelham were to ask the Club to repay his loan, it would be necessary to ask the bank for help. But, the bank would hardly be willing to advance money to a Club that is making such a loss. It is likely, therefore, that receivers would be called in and the Club would have to be sold.'

'Mr Chairman,' the Brigadier interrupted. 'This is alarmist speculation on the Secretary's part. After all, Toby Kelham is one of us.'

'Ladies and Gentlemen,' said Kelham. 'I can assure you…'

'You assurances would mean nothing if you wanted your money back, Toby.'

It was Kate.

'Friends, you all know how much David has done for this Club. Sure, some of the people who have played as visitors and one or two new members aren't my cup of tea. But, that is a small price to pay for having a thriving Club again.'

'Most of the people we have seen in the bar or on the course have been courteous and well-dressed. More than anything, they clearly love their golf as much as anyone in this room.'

'David has worked tirelessly, often seven days a week, to regenerate this Club. Jack now has plenty of customers for his shop and students for his lessons. Mrs Hall is rushed off her feet in the kitchen. There is a real buzz about the place. And, it is all thanks to our new Secretary. I don't want to put any of this at risk and, for that reason, I shall vote to reject Toby's offer.'

A murmur went round the table.

'Well, ladies and gentlemen. I think we have heard all the arguments and now it is time to take a vote. Would all those in favour of accepting Toby Kelham's offer of a loan, please raise their hands?'

'Slowly, hands went up around the room. The Brigadier. Kelham himself, then Frank Partidge. Slowly, a fourth, then a fifth hand joined them.'

'Five in favour,' Giles declared. 'All those against?'

Kate put up her hand. Alongside her, Pat Taylor raised hers. Then, Simon Cornwell and Bill Ellery raised theirs. Finally, Giles raised his hand.

'Five against,' Giles reported. 'The Committee is evenly divided. As chairman, I have a casting vote, and I shall use it to vote against. The proposal is therefore defeated.'

'Mr Chairman, I must object!' said Kelham, loudly. 'On a matter of this importance...'

'Actually, Toby, on a matter of this importance, in which you have a vested interest, I believe you should have withdrawn while the vote was taken.'

Kelham spluttered.

'I see you agree. I therefore intend to record that there were only four votes in favour and five against. In which case, I do not need to use my casting vote. Either way, the proposal is defeated.'

'*This is preposterous!*' the Brigadier roared. 'The Committee has been offered the opportunity to act in the interests of the Club and has signally failed to do so. I am quite certain that, when the members hear about this, as I shall ensure they do, they will wish to consider very carefully who they elect to their Committee at the annual general meeting.'

The Brigadier rose to his feet and looked menacingly at Giles.

'This is not the end of the matter, sir. You may be assured of that! Good night!'

Hole	Name	Yards	Par	Score
13	The Folly	164	3	

1

'This is great fun, isn't Jack?'

'Yeah. You're really beginning to get the hang of it now, aren't you? Don't forget, Karen. Check your alignment.'

'What do you mean, my alignment? Are you being rude or something?'

'No! I've told you before. You can't hit the ball straight if you're lined up wrong. Your body is pointing towards the right, so either you'll hit the ball that way, or your body will get in the way and you'll cut across the ball to the left.'

'I really don't know what you're talking about, Jack Peters. Why do you have to make it all sound so complicated.'

'It's not, really. Look, I'll show you.'

Jack lay a club on the ground with its shaft touching Karen's toes. Then, he asked her to move round and look along the line of the shaft.

'I see what you mean, now,' Karen laughed. 'Oh dear, I never did have much of a sense of direction!'

She stood over the ball again, but this time pointing away to the left. Jack moved behind her and gently pushed her hips and shoulders into position. Karen pushed her body back against his hands. She turned her head and looked into his eyes.

'You do have lovely strong hands, Jack.'

'Now, don't start that again Karen! You promised you'd concentrate today.'

'Sorry, Jack. Mind, I only promised to concentrate during the lesson.'

Jack was trying his best to concentrate, too. Karen had arrived for her second lesson dressed in a short pink skirt, white golf shoes and ankle socks and a scooped, white tee-shirt. Whenever she leaned forward to address the ball, Jack felt himself falling into an abyss of desire.

'How do I look, Jack?'

'Great, Karen,' Jack said. Bloody incredible! he thought.

'So, what have you been doing this week, then?' Karen asked.

'Not a lot. Concentrate, now. Let's see you hit the ball again. Remember, try to keep a smooth rhythm.'

'Ooh, Jack. I go all funny when you talk about rhythm,' Karen teased.

'Karen! Remember, you promised.'

'Oh, all right. Spoilsport.'

She swung the golf club smoothly back and through and hit the ball about a hundred yards down the range. For all her butterfly mind and suggestive prattle, Jack had to admit that Karen was a natural. Halfway through her second lesson, she was already showing a grace of movement that many golfers strive for years to achieve. It was a pleasure to watch. God, was she a pleasure to watch!

'You're making great progress, Karen,' Jack said. 'I don't think you're going to need many more lessons.'

'Oh, don't say that, Jack. I reckon there's lots you can still teach me,' Karen grinned. 'When are we going to play?'

'We can go out on the course next week. Play a few holes, if you'd like that.'

'I didn't mean that sort of play, stupid.'

Jack ignored Karen's remark.

'Yes. I think that would be a good idea. Get you out on the course.'

'So, Jack, have you been seeing any nice young ladies this week?'

'I told you, Karen. I don't have a girlfriend. Not at the moment.'

233

'That's a pity, Jack. A big, healthy boy, like you. How do you manage?'

'I manage, thanks, Karen.'

Jack looked at his watch.

'Well, that's about all we can do for this lesson. Next time, we'll go over to the practice green. Practise some chipping and putting. Then, we'll go out on the course and play a few holes.'

Karen looked disappointed.

'Oh, all right,' she moaned. 'S'pose you've got another lesson, have you?'

As Karen had deliberately booked the last session of the day, she already knew the answer to that question.

'No, I don't. But, I do have some things to do.'

Karen picked up her jumper. She ran her fingers along Jack's forearm and, standing on tip-toe, kissed him on the cheek.

'OK then, Jack. Thanks. See you next time.'

Jack smiled and watched her delectable bottom for a moment as she walked away. Then, he heaved a sigh of relief, turned and walked through into the cabin behind the teaching bay.

She's hard work, Jack thought. Very tasty, but bloody hard work.

Jack liked teaching. Although he was a very good golfer, he had discovered that he was an even better teacher. He particularly enjoyed teaching women golfers, perhaps because most were so keen to learn and would put in the necessary practice. It was rewarding to watch them progress from beginners, swinging in an ungainly fashion at the golf ball between their feet, into players who could enjoy a round of golf with their friends.

He enjoyed, too, the respect and admiration, sometimes adulation, he received from these women. Jack was a big, good-looking boy and he knew that many of his students thought him rather dishy. He was aware of course that, were he not a golf professional, many of them would not have given him the time of day, so he was careful to nurture them without taking advantage.

Karen was different. Jack had known Karen since they were at school and, even then, he'd fancied her. Blond and slim, with a terrific body and an even greater smile, Karen had been the focus of many an adolescent fantasy. Boys thought about her in bed at night and Jack had not been immune. He'd tried to get her to go out with him when they were fifteen or sixteen, but Karen had had so much choice. He hadn't been at all surprised to discover that she'd had done pretty well for herself, marrying Spiros Makrides, living in a big house and driving around the village in her silver Mercedes sports car.

Jack filled a large basket with golf balls that had just been collected from the driving range. The room behind the teaching bay housed the golf ball vending machine. When a golfer on the other side of the wall inserted a token this device, which was about the size of three large washing machines, would fill baskets with practice balls for use on the range. Once hit, the balls became wet and muddy, and so freshly collected balls were tipped into a hopper to be washed before moving on into the machine proper.

As Jack lifted the basket and began pouring the balls into the hopper, he heard the door close. Suddenly, the room became much darker and he turned to find Karen standing very close behind him.

'Do you want me, Jack?'

'Karen! What? What are you doing in here?'

'You do, don't you, Jack? Your mind wasn't on the lesson today, any more than mine was.'

'Look, Karen, I find you very... I mean, I'm a golf teacher and you're the wife of a member. It's not really a good idea for us to...'

But, Karen wasn't listening. Instead, she was fumbling with the buckle of Jack's belt.

'Oh, fuck that, Jack. No, fuck me. You do want me, don't you?'

She pulled down the zip and slid her hand inside his trousers.

'I find you very attractive, of course, but...'

Her hands found him, warm and firm and becoming ever firmer as she caressed him.

'Jesus, Karen! Lock the door at least, for crying out loud. Anybody could come in!'

'I already have, silly.'

She continued stroking him, and she kissed him, opening his mouth with her tongue.

'You're the only one who's going to come in here,' she murmured.

Her closeness and the knowledge that their privacy was secure combined to demolish Jack's remaining self-control. He pulled her to him, enveloping her in his arms. She was so much smaller than he was and this served only to increase his arousal.

As she stroked him more vigorously, he couldn't have stopped if he'd wanted to – and Jack no longer wanted to. He ran his hands over her back and round on to her breasts. Her hands began to move so feverishly that he almost hurt.

'*Jesus, Karen. Go easy!*'

Jack's hands slid down her back and on to her buttocks. She held him close and pushed her loins against him.

'Fuck me, Jack,' she breathed into his mouth, '*Fuck me, please!*'

He found the hem of her skirt and pulled it up as high as he could. When he slid his hand between her thighs, Jack wasn't surprised to discover that Karen wasn't wearing any knickers. He'd noticed during the lesson that her skirt revealed no panty line, and the thought that she might be wearing a thong had further distracted him as he struggled to continue with the lesson. Now, he knew the reason and he felt her gasp as he found her.

Jack was much taller than Karen so, firmly, he turned and lifted her so that she was sitting against the ball washer. He lifted her skirt further and pushed her legs apart. His trousers fell around his ankles and he pushed himself towards her. She pulled at him, her nails digging into the cheeks of his behind. Now, he could reach her and Karen pushed herself towards him, pleading between breaths.

'Oh, Jack! Fuck me, you bastard! Fuck me!'

And, so he did. Jack drove himself into her and Karen bit into his shoulder. Her hands slid up under his shirt, across his broad back and down over his buttocks. Again and again they moved together until, as his thrusting became more and more frantic, Jack could feel his excitement beginning to reach a peak. Then, just when it seemed that satisfaction might elude her, Karen's left hand dropped to her side and came to rest on the ball washer's operating button. In her excitement, she pressed the button and the machine came to life, tumbling and churning the balls beneath her seat. The noisy vibration was the final stimulation needed for Karen's passion to reach its climax.

Aware that there might be golfers only feet away on the other side of the wall, Jack was ready to stifle any sound with his mouth. To his relief, Karen's cries were drowned out by the rumbling of the machine. In his excitement at Karen's pleasure, however, Jack's lingering control finally abandoned him.

They stayed where they were for some time. She pressed herself against him and he enveloped her as he shrank and withdrew. She smiled up at him.

'That was really lovely, Jack. I was hoping when I left home that we'd do it today, but I didn't expect it to be like that. I've never come like that before.'

'It was the ballwasher,' Jack smiled. 'It made all the difference. You should get one installed in your bedroom.'

'It certainly took me by surprise,' Karen laughed. 'But it was you – and this – that did the trick.' She caressed his softening member. 'I wouldn't mind installing that in my bedroom!'

She pulled back and straightened her skirt, tucking in her shirt. He pulled up his pants and trousers.

'We shall have to do that again, and soon,' Karen said, with a smile.

He held her to him and looked into her face.

'Look, Karen. You're right. It was great. Bloody fantastic, actually. But, we've got to be careful. We can't do it again. Just think of what might happen if Spiros found out. And, there's my job…'

'We shall be careful, Jack, don't you worry. But, we will do it again, believe me.'

She smiled and kissed him quickly on the lips before disappearing through the back door of the cabin and out into the darkening car park.

Jack stood looking at the closed door for a few minutes, reliving in his mind the pleasure of the past few moments. He had wanted her, all right, but he hadn't really expected anything to happen. He smiled as he thought again of Karen's passion, and his own.

Then, he began to think of what might happen next and the smile faded from his face.

2

'It was a very close thing, wasn't it?' Kate said.

'Yes, and I don't think that's the end of it,' David agreed. 'Kelham and the Brigadier know they only need a couple more votes to reverse the Committee's decision. I'm sure they'll be working away between now and the annual general meeting to get more of their supporters on to the Committee.'

'Well, all you can do is to keep improving things and hope that people will see things are best left the way they are,' Kate smiled. 'You're doing a great job, David. Everybody knows that!'

'So, why do the Brigadier and his friends think things would be better if the Club took Kelham's shilling?'

'God knows. I wish we knew what they were up to.'

'Whatever, it is,' David said. 'I can't see me being around very long if they succeed.'

Kate looked alarmed.

'Don't say that, David. The Club needs you. We all need you.'

'Be realistic, Kate! If Kelham and the Brigadier regain control of the Club, they're hardly likely to want me around. I'm sure I'll be given my marching orders, pretty sharpish. Anyway, I don't think I would want to stay under those circumstances.'

'Well, let's hope that situation doesn't arise,' Kate replied. 'People will see sense, I'm sure.'

At Kate's suggestion, she and David had met for lunch at *The Black Horse*. The lunch had been excellent, although the portions weren't quite on Mrs Hall's scale. At a secluded corner table, David was feeling more and more relaxed in Kate's company.

'Anyway, enough about the Club. When you rang, you said you had something you wanted to tell me about.'

'Oh, yes, that's right,' said Kate. 'I'm going away, tomorrow.'

'You're going away? Where? And, for how long?' David said, struggling not to reveal the concern in his voice.

Seeing his reaction, Kate smiled and touched his hand.

'Only for a holiday, silly! I'm off to Africa for two weeks. I'm going to meet up with Sarah in Uganda, first. Then, I shall be staying with some friends in Nairobi.'

'Oh, I see,' David relaxed.

'Yes, I only decided the other day. This is the best time of year for me to get away. The only time, really. Before the growing season.' Kate grinned. 'I'll give everybody's plants a good watering and hope they survive 'till I get back.'

'I'm sure they'll miss you,' David said. 'I certainly shall.'

Kate touched his hand again.

'It won't be long. I'm so looking forward to seeing Sarah. She's feeling rather homesick, so I expect we'll have a good old mum-and-daughter heart-to-heart. Which reminds me, have you and Ben had a chance to have a talk about Tess, yet?'

'No, but I'll be seeing him next week. Maybe, I'll try and bring the subject up then.'

'Try and bring the subject up!' Kate laughed. 'Honestly, David, you make it all sound so formal. No wonder the poor boy finds it hard to talk about his feelings.'

'Well, us boys don't find it as easy to talk about our feelings as you girls,' David smiled.

'You have to start somewhere,' said Kate. 'So, do bring the subject up, at least.'

'I promise, I'll try,' David said, rather anxious to change the subject. 'Would you like some coffee?'

'Mm, yes please. But, I must just pop to the ladies, first.'

David sat back in his seat, feeling very relaxed. He and Kate had been more open with each other over lunch and he felt they were becoming much closer. He was already looking forward to her return from Africa.

When Kate came back to her seat, she was looking very furtive

'Guess who I've just seen,' she said, whispering unnecessarily. 'Toby Kelham, and that big Greek chap?'

'Spiros Makrides?'

'Yes. Makrides. They're sitting in a corner of the other bar, looking at some papers on a table.'

240

'Are they, indeed? said David 'I wonder what they're up to? It's probably nothing to do with the Club, of course, but I just can't work out what sort of business those two would have in common.'

They got up to go.

'Perhaps, we could get together again, when you're back. I'd love to hear all about Africa. Could we have dinner somewhere, perhaps?'

'Yes, I'd like that. And, you can bring me up to date on the Branfield saga.'

She took David's hand and kissed him gently on the cheek.

'I've really enjoyed today, David. After the business with James, I've not been good at letting people get close to me. But, I'm getting better, I think.'

'As you say,' David smiled. 'You have to start somewhere.'

3

As David approached his office on Wednesday morning, he was feeling, if not actually buoyant, at least not filled with the foreboding that had seemed to come with the job for the past few months. The Committee had supported him against Kelham and the Brigadier over the loan. The car park through which he had just walked was buzzing with visitors. Best of all, he was beginning to see the possibility of a relationship with Kate.

'Good Morning, Margaret!'

David realised he actually sounded cheerful as he passed through the outer office.

Although Margaret's response was rather muted, David continued into his office, took off his coat and hung it up. Then, he walked to his computer and switched it on. It was a long-time habit, part of his morning ritual. Even though

241

he didn't need the computer right away, he felt more business-like once it was humming away in the corner.

A few moments later, Margaret came into the office carrying two cups of coffee. She closed the door quietly and, as she placed his cup before him on his desk, he looked up and smiled. He saw that she had been crying.

'Can I talk to you for a minute, David? Before you get started?'

She was clearly upset and he indicated the chair alongside his desk.

Margaret sat down and took a sip from her coffee cup. She handed him a letter. David took it and read it quickly. Margaret had written her resignation. He was reading it again, trying to decide how he should respond, when she spoke once more.

'My Tom says I have to stop working here.'

Her voice began to break and she wiped her cheek with the back of her hand.

David felt an urge to brush away her tears but he restrained himself.

'Why? What's happened, Margaret? Has he said anything about... about you and me?'

'God, no! He doesn't know anything about that. Never will. No, he just says he needs me at home. Says, we don't need the money and he can't see why I'm working here when he needs me there.'

'But what's changed? He's never objected to you working before, has he?'

'No. But, now he's retired, he doesn't like being in the house all day on his own. He's bored with his own company and he wants me there, that's all.'

'I can understand that but, surely, he can see how much you enjoy coming to work.'

'Oh, David. You're a very nice man, but you don't understand other men much, do you? You know I enjoy coming to work and especially how much I like working

242

with you. But, Tom doesn't think like that. Never has done. To him, me working is just a silly thing I do to bring in a bit of pin money. As far as he's concerned, my real job is at home, looking after him, warming his bed. If I start talking about enjoying my work, needing to work, anything like that, Tom just tells me not to be so daft.'

'It's not daft to want to do something you find interesting. And, it's not daft to enjoy doing something other people find valuable. You're an important part of things here. I'm sure if Tom understood that, he wouldn't want you to pack it up, just like that.'

'Tom doesn't care if I find it interesting or valuable. As far as he's concerned, the only thing I should find interesting or valuable is what I do at home. Anything else, he don't want to know.'

'Would it help if I talked to him?'

'God, no! Please, don't!' Margaret looked horrified. 'He's not the sort to appreciate another man giving him advice.' She smiled wanly. 'I can just imagine what he'd say if you started telling him what he should or shouldn't let his wife do.'

'Well, is there anything we can do?'

David had already realised there was little to be done to change the situation. Nevertheless, for Margaret's sake, he felt he should continue to express concern.

'No, nothing. Once his mind's made up, that's it. If I don't want a thick ear or a black eye, then I'll just have to do what he wants.'

David was genuinely shocked. He had suspected that, occasionally, Margaret received some rough handling from her husband. Once, she had appeared for work with a black eye caused, she said, by "a cupboard door swinging open." On another occasion, he had remarked about a hand-shaped bruise on her arm, which Margaret had laughed off, saying, "We were having a game." But, he had never before heard her speak openly about violence at home.

243

'Tell me, Margaret. Does Tom hit you?'

'Only when I don't do as I'm told. Or, sometimes when I wind him up. I can be a right bugger at times, and then it's my own fault, I suppose.'

Yes, David could imagine that she could be quite wilful on occasions and that that might infuriate a man like Tom.

'Nobody deserves to be hit, Margaret. And, certainly not by their partner.'

'Oh, sometimes I can be pretty stubborn, you know.'

'I'm sure you can,' David said, smiling. 'But…'

'It'll be all right. Once I'm at home all day, then, he'll stop moaning. In fact, it wouldn't surprise me if he doesn't get fed up with me being around all day after a bit. Send me out to get another job. Silly old bugger!'

'Why do you stay with him, Margaret?'

'Don't have any choice really. The house is in his name and I don't have any money. So, where would I go? Anyway, it's not all his fault.'

'But, surely if you went to a solicitor, got some advice…'

'If I left him, he'd turn my boys against me. Probably never see them again. And I'd end up on my own in some bed-sit. No, thanks, David, it may not be perfect, but it's all there is. There's nothing to be done about it. I'm sorry, but I'll just have to stay at home like Tom says.'

'Do you love him, Margaret?' David asked.

'Oh, we get along all right, most of the time.'

'That's not what I asked. Do you love him?'

'There's bits of him I quite like, I suppose.' Then, after a pause, she went on. 'I was pregnant when we got married. I never knew my Dad and Tom is much older than I am. So, I thought he was lovely at the time. You know, really manly. I needed security and he gave it to me. And, he still does make me feel very secure, I will say that. It's only when I try to do things he doesn't like, that there are problems.'

244

'But, do you love him?' David persisted.

David felt perhaps that he should leave it. It wasn't his problem after all. But, his relationship with Margaret was not just professional. She had helped him in ways that were unconnected with the job during the past few months. A part of him sensed that Margaret leaving now would draw a line under those activities, just when he felt a need to move on. On the other hand, there was a butterfly trapped here and he felt an urge to do what he could to release it.

'No, I don't suppose I do! Not in the way you mean. In fact, sometimes I really hate him. But, married people do feel like that sometimes, don't they?'

Margaret's voice trembled a little and she wiped the back of her hand across her cheek.

'Look, David, I appreciate what you're saying but, you and I, we come from different worlds. When you think of being married, you think of loving somebody and caring for them and being happy together. I think it's lovely the way you talk about you and your wife. She must have been a wonderful person. For me, it was different. My mum had her boyfriends and I wasn't really welcome at home, once I'd left school. Tom took me in and gave me all the things I needed. I know it's not the same sort of marriage you had, but it's all I've got, so I'll just have to put up with it.'

'Well, I'm very sorry,' David said. 'I shall be quite lost here, without you, after all we've done together over the past months.'

'You'll soon find someone else to do the office work,' Margaret smiled. 'And, as for the other, well it's time you found someone else for that, too.'

'Oh, come on!' But David knew she was right and his protest was feeble.

'You're a lovely man, David. You deserve more than just a quick one on the office floor every now and then. You need a lady to do things with, to give you some love.

245

We've done some nice things and we've both enjoyed them, but that's not what you really want. You know that.'

He did know that. In fact, pleasurable as they had been, his brief encounters with Margaret had only served to make him feel the need for more in his life.

'Yes. Well, we'll have to see,' David said. 'There's not much prospect at the moment...'

'Now, who's talking daft?' Margaret replied. 'What about that Kate? She's likes you and it's time you did something about it. If you don't make a move soon, she could get fed up waiting.'

'She is nice,' David conceded. *Very nice*, he thought.

'But, I'm a bit out of practice. I'm not sure I know how to go about it any more.'

David felt rather insensitive, talking about his love life with Margaret. She had freely given him all she had. Now, she was being forced to leave and he was already discussing another woman.

'Anyway,' he smiled. 'You know that. After all, it was you who took the initiative with us.'

'With us it was different, David. We had some pleasure and it was great. Course it was. But, it was never more than that. You know that. With that Kate, it could be different. I've seen the way you sit and talk together. I've noticed the way she smiles at you and I've seen how you look at her. Ask her out or invite her round to dinner. I'm sorry, I shouldn't be telling you what to do!'

'No. Really, I appreciate it. I'll give it some thought, honestly I will,' David said, anxious to change the subject.

'Well, make sure you do,' Margaret smiled, picking up the coffee cups.

'When will you leave?' David asked.

'I have to give a month's notice,' Margaret replied. 'But, I'm owed three weeks holiday. So, Tom wants me to finish at the end of next week, if that's all right with you. He wants to book a fortnight in the sun. Says he needs it after all this rain.'

'Next week! That's very sudden.'

David hadn't expected Margaret to leave quite so soon but, in his mind, he was already working out how he might manage.

'Well, if you can concentrate on finishing this month's payroll, that would be very helpful. I can manage it, but I'd rather tackle it next month, when I've had a bit more notice.'

'I'll do it,' Margaret replied. 'And, I'll get all the books up to date. I should be able to get all that done by next Friday. But, don't worry, if it takes a few more days, Tom will just have to put up with it, won't he?'

She stood up and walked to the door. Then, she smiled, although David sensed she was not finding it easy to do so.

'Don't forget what I said about that Kate. A woman can only wait so long. And, she's no different from anybody else.'

She turned and went out.

David sat back and hugged his coffee cup. He was glad of the opportunity to be alone.

He felt very sorry about Margaret, of course. She was a warm and likeable woman and she'd been very loyal to him during their months together. She had very quickly learned to operate the computer and was willing, almost eager, to take on any new challenge.

And, there was the sex. Margaret had reawakened in him something that he thought had died along with Tess. Her casual attitude towards intimacy had surprised, even shocked him, at first. She had taken the initiative and had given him pleasure simply because she wanted to and because she got pleasure herself. There had been no suggestion of a relationship or of any demands being made, quite the reverse, in fact. After each occasion, she had been at pains to stress that nothing more would be expected or given.

But, when he thought of Kate, David felt some relief at the morning's news. Margaret's attitude towards sex may have been very casual but David knew he would be less than comfortable, should Kate come to see him, if the outer office was manned by someone with whom he had been intimate.

And, he was sure Kate would come to see him. He hadn't really needed Margaret's encouragement. He was already beginning to see Kate as someone with whom he might share a future.

The office door opened again.

'I've had an idea,' Margaret said.

David put down his cup and smiled.

'Well, I hope it's a better idea than the one you came in with last time.'

'How about old Phil?'

'Sorry? Old Phil?'

'Yes. To help you out. Till you find somebody permanent. After all he knows how everything works around here.'

'Oh, I don't know, Margaret. I'm sure Flight Lieutenant Oakley wouldn't want to come back here to work.'

David wasn't sure he wanted the Brigadier's right hand man back, either.

'Not full time, he wouldn't. But, he might be willing to help out part-time. Even, just answering the phone. Otherwise, you're going to be on your own.'

David knew that Margaret was right. Trying to run things without any help at all could be very difficult, a recipe for the kind of stress he now sought to avoid. And again, David thought, having Phil Oakley manning the front desk might reassure the Brigadier and some of the other members that not everything at Branfield Park was changing.

'Well,' David said, slowly. 'I'd have to talk it over with Giles Southern, of course. Make sure he has no objections. Then, there's Phil himself. We don't know if he'd even be interested in coming back.'

'Don't worry about that,' Margaret smiled as she opened the door to leave. 'I've already had a word with him.'

Hole	Name	Yards	Par	Score
14	Return	385	4	

1

David looked down at the steaming cup on his desk.

'Margaret said you needed coffee every hour, at least,' Flight Lieutenant Phil Oakley explained as he stood beside the desk in his tired grey suit.

'Oh, er, thanks, Phil. Thanks, very much.'

The older man smiled nervously.

'I've put today's post there for you, as well. Margaret told me you like it on your desk at the beginning of the day.'

When the door was closed, David sat down at his desk and picked up his coffee.

He hadn't been looking forward to this morning, his first without Margaret to assist him.

Phil Oakley had turned out to be a very pleasant man, exactly as Margaret had suggested. They had spoken briefly on Friday, during the farewell drinks and presentation David had arranged for Margaret. All the staff, and a dozen or so members, had been there in the bar and a few tears had been shed.

Now, he had to go on alone.

He looked at the neat pile of opened mail.

Margaret had organised everything he needed. She had arranged for Phil Oakley to come in each morning after she'd left, until David found a replacement. She had told Phil that David needed coffee first thing and then hourly. Margaret had also instructed Phil that David liked the day's mail open on his desk when he arrived. What else had Margaret said he needed, for God's sake? He suddenly imagined Phil Oakley sidling quietly into the office and offering some more intimate service.

A little hand relief, sir?

David burst out laughing, got to his feet and went to the door.

'Phil, could you come in here for a moment, please?'

Phil looked anxious as he followed David into the room.

'Take a seat, will you.'

The older man sat next to the desk.

'I'm very grateful to you for coming in to help like this,' David began.

'Not at all,' Phil smiled. 'To tell you the truth, I was getting rather bored at home.'

'The thing is, Phil, I don't think there's any point you coming in here and pretending to be Margaret.'

Phil looked puzzled.

'As I explained on Friday, I've put an advert for a clerical assistant in next week's *Herald*. Margaret was a rare jewel, Phil, I'm sure you'd agree. I must say, I'm not optimistic that we shall find anyone good enough to replace her. But, in the meantime, we must muddle along as best we can.'

David took a sip of coffee.

'Neither you – nor I – are Margaret, Phil. It's no use pretending we are. So, I think it would be rather silly for you to be sitting out there waiting for me to dictate letters, that sort of thing; as if you were a clerical assistant.'

Phil still looked puzzled.

'So, what would you like me to do, David?'

'You know this place backwards, Phil. So, what I suggest is that we have a chat each morning about what's happening and decide between us how we'll deal with things. You handle the phone and I'll type any letters needed on my computer. The rest, we'll sort out as we go along. How does that sound?'

'That sounds fine to me,' Phil smiled, clearly relieved.

'Good, er, one thing, before we start. No more coffee, please. Margaret brought me so much coffee that I could hardly sleep at night. From now on, I'll get a drink up in the bar, when I want one. OK?'

'OK,' Phil laughed. 'No more coffee!'

The two men sat by the fire and David explained to Phil all the developments at the Club since the latter had retired: the finances; the bank's ultimatum; the new members; the visitors; Kelham's offer of a loan and the Committee's rejection of it. Most of it, it seemed, Phil had already learned from Margaret. Again and again, the figure of the Brigadier would reappear, looming over their discussion like a dark thundercloud.

'He can be very obstinate when he wants to be, the Brigadier,' Phil said.

'And the rest!' David exclaimed. 'He's been a pain in the backside for me since Day One. I gather he gave you a pretty tough time too, over the years.'

'He did indeed,' Phil agreed. 'He treated me in a very high-handed manner. As if I were an NCO.'

Phil looked thoughtful for a moment. Then, he smiled.

'But, I'm here to work for you, now, David. To help you in any way I can. And, if that involves telling the Brigadier where he can go, that's fine by me.'

'You won't mind saying "No" to him, then?'

'Nothing would give me more pleasure,' Phil smiled.

2

'This is very nice, Jack. Very cosy.'

'The flat? Yeah, I think it's great. I moved in about a year ago, now. The place I had before was crap. Over the other side of town, as well, so it meant a much longer drive to work.'

'So, do you bring all your young ladies here, Jack?'

'Chance would be a fine thing,' Jack laughed. 'Do you want sugar in your coffee?'

'No, thanks.'

Karen took the coffee and sipped it.

'Mm. That's great.'

Then, without warning, the simmering desire that had brought her to Jack's flat took control.

She took his mug from him and kissed him. A long, lingering kiss. Even before the kiss was over, they were clawing at each other's clothes. Shirts, trousers, underwear, all were discarded in the frantic escalation of their passion.

Karen pulled Jack through into the bedroom. There, their remaining garments were cast off before their lust was exhausted across Jack's double divan.

Dripping and self-conscious, Jack fetched the still-hot coffee from the kitchen and, together beneath the duvet, they sipped, hugged and kissed until, once again, desire arose between them.

This time, their coupling was more considered and Jack endured much longer. This time, he took control, beginning his thrusts slowly, then gradually increasing their intensity until, at last, Karen arrived at the destination she had been seeking when she rang the bell to Jack's flat.

'God, Jack. That was fantastic. Absolutely fantastic! How did you do that?'

She kissed him softly on his chest.

Jack smiled the smile of a man who was pretty impressed with himself.

'Oh, I had a word with the ball washing machine. Got a few tips. That's all.'

'Don't joke,' Karen said. 'I'm serious.'

Then, they both burst out laughing and snuggled down under the quilt.

'So, what are you here for, Karen?' Jack asked.

'I would have thought that was obvious,' Karen laughed, and she slid her hand across his belly and gently caressed him.

'No. I don't mean that,' Jack said. 'What I mean is, why here? Why with me? What about Spiros? Isn't he doing the business?'

'Spiros? He does too much business! Oh, Spiros is all right. He's just a great big bear, really. He gives me anything I want. But, he spends all day, every day, either in the gym or doing deals. When he does come in, it's usually late at night. After his *kleftiko*, he's usually too knackered for anything else.'

'All that business sounds pretty boring, to me.'

'Not to him, its not. He loves it. But, I'm bored, Jack. Bored and frustrated. When Spiros brought me into the shop the other week, I saw you there and I knew just what I'd been missing.'

'And, what was that?'

'Passion. Love. I don't know,' Karen replied. Somebody to do something with; to give something to. Spiros doesn't need anything from me, except an occasional fuck and me looking pretty. It's not enough, Jack.'

'What more is there?' Jack said, with a grin.

Karen punched him gently in the side.

'Don't mock, Jack, I'm serious! I'm not stupid, you know. I like looking pretty. Course I do. But, I like doing things, as well. Like the golf. I've really enjoyed doing that. I never thought I could be good at sport or anything.'

'You're a natural, Karen. I've been really impressed.'

'Yeah? Well, when I told Spiros about it, was he interested? Was he fuck? All he wanted to know was, had I bought the best clubs, and did my bag look smart?'

'So, what are you going to do about it, Karen,' Jack asked, hugging her to him.

'Oh, I don't know. Nothing, I suppose. Spiros didn't listen when I told him about my golf lesson. He's hardly likely to pay much attention if I say I'm bored, or I want to do something else with my life, is he?'

'No, I suppose not.'

'Course,' Karen grinned. 'You could always go and have a word with him for me, Jack. Tell him you know how I feel, what I need, that sort of thing.'

'I can just imagine Spiros loving that. I'm sure he and his mate Dinos would give me a very sympathetic hearing.'

'Oh, go on Jack. For me,' Karen said, laughing.

'Sorry, Karen. You'll just have to put up with driving around in your Mercedes for a bit longer.'

'Oh, well,' she grinned. 'Let's see if I can talk you into it.'

Karen burrowed head-first under the warm bedclothes and his whole body quivered as she found him.

The street lights were coming on as they went down the stairs together. They shared a last, lingering kiss before Jack opened the door.

'Can I come again, Jack.'

'Course you can. Any time.'

Karen slipped out into the street and turned as she climbed into her Mercedes.

They were both too busy waving to notice the black BMW parked down the road.

3

'Now, look here, Oakley. Let me see those applications!'

'I'm sorry, Brigadier. I have my instructions from Mr Crowley. Membership applications are confidential. Only he and Mr Southern…'

'But, dammit man. You know full well that I always go through the membership applications on a Monday morning.'

'I know you vetted them in the past, Brigadier, of course I do. But, as I understand it, Mr Crowley and Mr Southern are responsible for that now.'

The Brigadier was perplexed. Flight Lieutenant Oakley had always been so compliant. He tried another tack.

'Look, Oakley, er, Phil, old chap,' the Brigadier began again, sitting down. 'You and I have worked together for a long time, haven't we? You, of all people, know how important it is that only the right sort of people are admitted to the Club.'

'I know you think that's important, Brigadier.'

'And, you know it, too, old boy! This club has always been a very special place, Phil. And, you and I, between us, have made it special. We did that by making sure that only the right sort of people were invited to join, and that only a few, select visitors were permitted to play.'

'And, I wasn't one of them, I gather,' Oakley said, calmly.

'I don't understand, man. What are you talking about?'

'What I'm talking about, Brigadier, is your precious members. Those people, who you say are the 'right sort'. The select few. Lovely people, as you say. They thought I was lovely, too, when I worked six or seven days a week to run their precious golf club for them, didn't they?'

'I really don't know what you're getting at? Everyone here greatly appreciated the work you did for the Club over the years.'

'But, not enough to let me play golf on their beloved course, apparently?'

'Now, look, Oakley…'

'Oh, its Oakley again now, is it, Brigadier?'

The worm had turned, and there now was no turning it back.

'I worked my socks off for you, Brigadier. Over the years, I did everything I could for you and your darling club. On your behalf, I wrote letters to some of the nicest people telling them they weren't good enough to mix with the members of this club…'

'Damn it, man. Sometimes, we all have to do things that are difficult. Standards have to be maintained…'

'Standards! Do you know what, Brigadier? When I retired, the members of this club; that elite group who set the standards by which others are measured; those special people who must be kept apart from ordinary folk; the members of this Club wouldn't even let me play here as a visitor. I could understand they might not want me as a member; they might find it difficult mixing with the servants, and all that. But, would it have hurt them to let me come and play now and then?'

'Look here, Oakley. Everybody appreciated what you did enormously. It's just that it was felt that…'

'It was felt, Brigadier? By whom was it felt? You forget, Brigadier, I know how such decisions are arrived at. I know that there is only one person here who decides who can and who cannot be a member, who may or who may not play as a visitor.'

'Yes, well…' The Brigadier shifted uncomfortably.

'Yes, Brigadier. It was you who decided that I wasn't good enough to play here, wasn't it?'

'Come now, Oakley. Sometimes painful decisions have to be taken. That's what leadership is about. Dammit, man, you know that.'

'I know that there is a different leadership here, now, Brigadier. One that is trying to open the place up, let some air in, and undo the damage that you and I did over the years. You, by keeping out perfectly good people who could have brought some life to the Club. And me, because I colluded with you and because I made such a mess of running the finances.'

The Brigadier sat, open-mouthed.

'I failed in my job, Brigadier, because I never stood up to you. Never told you what I thought. Well, I'm doing it now. I'm sorry, but you can't have those applications. So, if there's nothing else…'

The Brigadier stood up. He wasn't sure what to say. This was outside his experience. In the army, this kind of insubordination could be dealt with by putting a man on a charge, by court martial, even. But, this wasn't the army. Here, there was no redress. He knew that. And, deep inside, he knew, too, that there was truth in what Oakley had said.

The Brigadier muttered.

'Very well. Good day, sir.'

And, quietly, he walked from the office and out into the hallway.

4

'I've never driven one of these things before. They're quite fun, aren't they.'

Roger Yates, the local council's planning officer was enjoying himself. He'd come to make a final inspection of the new bunker alongside the fifth green. As he explained to David, his only real concern was that the work should not be visible from the footpath that ran across the course.

'Let's drive out there in a buggy,' David had suggested.

Then, seeing the look on the other man's face, he'd offered him the wheel. All men are boys, really, and most men love to get behind the wheel of a golf buggy. Not that they are able to go all that fast. A governor on the motor prevents any real turn of speed. But, along a narrow path, through the trees or beside the gorge, it can sometimes feel as if you are flying.

Driving over the old stone bridge, David looked around and saw brightly clad golfers behind, ahead and to either side. Not a high density compared with many courses, but enough to make the place feel alive. How things had changed, he thought, since the first time he'd driven this way.

'Let's stop here,' David suggested, when they reached the fifth tee. 'We can walk down the fairway and along the footpath.'

Roger looked back at the buggy.

'Don't worry,' said David. 'We'll take the long way back. You'll get another chance to drive!'

Roger grinned and the two men walked across to where a small white signpost marked the point at which the public footpath crossed the course boundary.

'This is a very ancient path,' Roger explained. 'That's why the local ramblers were so keen to keep it looking much the same.'

They walked side by side along the path and stopped where it came out on to the fairway. Everywhere around them, the first signs of spring were visible. Buds were swelling, shoots were emerging and, here and there, birds would swoop past carrying pieces of nest building material in their beaks.

'Fabulous spot, isn't it?' Roger remarked.

'Very special,' David agreed. 'My job is to keep it that way and get more people playing on it at the same time.'

'Well, you've made a good start, at least,' Roger said. 'I can see no sign of the bunker from here.'

The two men followed the line of the footpath across the fairway and into the undergrowth on the other side. From no point on their traverse were they able to see any part of the new bunker. Bob Morgan and his boys had done an excellent job.

'That's fine. Can we just go and look at the bunker itself. Check that it's been built according to the plans. Then, I can sign it off.'

They were about two hundred yards from the fifth green and the walk up the fairway took a few minutes. Standing beside it, David thought how insignificant the new bunker looked, considering all the problems it had caused.

'Didn't you have some trouble about the position of this bunker?'

'Yes, we did,' David replied. 'One of our members, Brigadier Tufnell, wanted it sited over there, at the front of the green.'

'That's right,' Roger said. 'I remember, now. One of your people kept coming in to the office and trying to persuade us to allow it to be built over that side.'

'That will be Flight Lieutenant Oakley. He's retired now, although he's come back part-time to help for a while, until we can appoint a new assistant.'

Roger walked on to the green itself.

'Amazing stuff this, isn't it?'

'What, the grass?'

'Yes, it doesn't look like grass at all, does it?' Roger smiled. 'I mean, the stuff my lawn's made of at home, that's grass. Full of moss and weeds, it is. This stuff? Well, it's more like velvet!'

They walked back along the length of the fifth fairway towards the tee. On the way, David stopped to talk to a couple of golfers who were preparing to hit their shots into the green.

'That makes a change,' he said, as they moved out of earshot. 'They're not vicars.'

'Sorry?'

'Oh, nothing,' David smiled, as they climbed into the buggy.

With David as navigator, Roger drove slowly around the front nine until they stopped alongside the eighth tee.

'What a view!' Roger exclaimed. 'I mean, I'm no golfer but even I can see that this is a great tee shot.'

'Yes, it is, isn't it?'

'Mind you, I suppose the landscape will look a little different around here if these houses get the go-ahead.'

'Sorry?'

'I mean, they'll be hidden in the trees, for the most part. But, in the winter, when the trees lose their leaves, they could still be visible. I wonder, while I'm here, if I could just have a quick look round?'

'A look round?'

'Yes, just a quick look. As you know, the developers haven't made a formal application for outline planning permission, yet. But, they've asked us to give them some idea of how we might respond, if and when they do.'

David was puzzled. He had no idea what Roger Yates was talking about.

'Well, I suppose it's only sensible,' David said, slowly. 'Drawing up plans costs a lot of money. I can understand them not wanting to go too far down that road before they know whether or not they'll be able to proceed.'

'Oh, they've drawn up some plans,' Roger replied, indicating a folder in his briefcase. 'But, as you know, we're only talking about an outline proposal at this stage.'

He keeps saying, "as you know", David thought. What am I supposed to know? He decided to play along.

'Can I just have a look at that drawing, Roger? See if it's the same as the one I have in the office?'

'Yes, sorry,' Roger said, reaching into the red folder. He withdrew a large sheet of paper and unfolded it across the steering wheel.

David was staggered.

Printed across the A2 sheet that Roger was holding was a drawing of golf course. Each fairway and green was outlined and, around and between them, cross-hatched shading indicated areas of woodland. And, in that woodland, were black blocks. Houses. Dozens of them!

'Ah, yes,' David said, anxious that Roger should not close up the plan before he'd had time to look at it. 'Let's see, where are we, now?'

Slowly, he ran his forefinger along a few fairways until he came to rest on the eighth tee. As he did so, he absorbed as much as he could of the proposed building site.

'Here we are,' David pointed. 'On this hillside, here.'

'Ah, so, this house here,' Roger said, indicating the plan, 'will be in that wood over there.' He pointed across the valley.

261

'This is a good vantage point, isn't it?' David said. 'You can see that these three houses are just over there in that dip.'

He pointed to the right.

'Look, Roger. As you like driving our little buggy so much, why don't we drive around the course and you can work out where each house is as we go.'

'Can I?' Roger smiled. 'That would be great. Save me a lot of time, too.'

So, with David as map-reader, Roger steered the buggy along fairway after fairway, up woodland tracks and down gravel paths. Eventually, having circumnavigated the entire course, they arrived back at the clubhouse.

'Do you think there will be any problem with planning permission?' David asked casually at one point.

'Well, I expect there'll be plenty of objections. There always are. But, the county plan requires us to build a certain number of new houses, so if it's well-designed to fit in with the landscape, I can't see why there should be too much difficulty.'

'Good,' David smiled.

'I suppose there are always people who will object to building new houses in the countryside, just on political grounds,' David said, a little further on.

'Yes, I suppose so. There are bound to be some people who won't like the idea of a mini-Wentworth Estate in the heart of this area, especially as we've been selling off so many council houses.'

'Why do you say that – a mini-Wentworth Estate?'

'Well, a private estate with its own golf course. It's a similar concept really, isn't it? Just on a smaller scale,' Roger explained.

Its own golf course? David thought. *Branfield Golf Course!*

They had finally parked in front of the clubhouse.

'Great bit of driving, Roger!' David said. 'Let me treat you to a cup of coffee.'

Roger looked at his watch.

'I ought to be getting off, really…'

'Nonsense. You've been working all morning. You deserve a cuppa and I could certainly do with one. Come on, let's go up to the bar. You've not seen the inside of the clubhouse, have you?'

Sensing Roger's reluctance, David took the planning officer's arm and steered him into the office.

'Well, all right. A quick cuppa wouldn't go amiss,' Roger smiled and looked again at his watch. 'But, I mustn't be more than ten minutes. I'm due at a site meeting at twelve o'clock.'

'Ah, Phil!' David said, as they entered the outer office. 'We're just going up to have a quick cup of coffee. Care to join us?

Phil could detect, from David's expression, that his attendance was not voluntary. He put down his pen and stood up.

'That's great. You can leave your coat and briefcase here, if you like, Roger,' David said, taking the young man's anorak and leather case from him before he could raise any objections. 'It's very warm in the bar.'

Phil led the way out of the office and across the hallway.

'This is all very grand,' Roger said, looking around.

'Yes,' Phil agreed. 'It was the vaulted hall of the original farmhouse, I believe.'

As they reached the foot of the stairs, David stopped.

'Look, I'm sorry. You'll have to excuse me for just a moment. I've just remembered an urgent phone call I must return. Phil, you go ahead with Roger and I'll join you in just a moment.'

David waited until the two men had reached the top of the stairs and disappeared into the bar. Then, walking as

263

quickly as he could, he returned to the office and closed the door.

The briefcase was on Phil's chair and David made a mental note of how it was lying. Opening it quickly, he pulled out the red folder and, from that, the large drawing.

Glancing at the door, he moved quickly to the photocopier.

Damn! It was switched off. David pressed the switch and waited. The machine's heating cycle seemed to take an eternity.

David looked at his watch. Three minutes gone.

The drawing was folded down into A4 size. David placed the first side face down on the copier and pressed the green button. Nothing happened.

'*Bugger!*' he cried, as he saw that the "PAPER EMPTY" lamp was flashing.

David almost flew across the room to the stationery cupboard. He grabbed a new pack of A4, frantically tore open the packaging and pulled out a stack of paper. He thrust it into the copier paper tray and slammed it shut.

He listened for any footsteps outside the door. Six minutes gone!

Again, he pressed the green button and, this time, the machine burst into life and the silence of the office was shattered by a cacophony of rumbling and light.

Even before the first sheet had emerged from the copier, David had opened the cover, refolded the plan and pressed the green button once more. Then, he did it again. And, again. Just to be on the safe-side, to ensure that he hadn't missed anything of the original, David made copies across the folds in the drawing. At last, when he was satisfied he had copied the entire drawing, albeit in pieces, he refolded it, put it back into the red folder, pushed the folder back into the briefcase and arranged the briefcase on Phil's chair just as he had found it.

Nine minutes!

Quickly, David gathered up the contents of the photocopier out-tray, slid the sheets of paper into his desk drawer and went back into the outer office. Hearing voices approaching, he grabbed the telephone on Phil's desk.

'Yes, OK. Thank you for telling me. I'll look forward to hearing from you in the near future,' David was speaking loudly into the purring phone as the door opened.

'Bank manager!' he explained as he replaced the handset. 'So sorry about that, Roger. I hope Phil's been looking after you all right.'

David helped the young local government officer into his coat, handed him his briefcase and led him to the door.

'So, you'll let us have a piece of paper, to say the bunker's all right?'

'Yes, it'll be out to you in the next couple of weeks,' Roger smiled. Then he looked again at his watch. 'I'm sorry, I must be going or I'll be late for my next meeting.'

'Do you have far to go?'

'No, only over to Browndean Farm.'

He shook David's hand.

'Thank you very much for the coffee, and for all your help earlier.'

David shook his hand vigorously. Almost too vigorously.

'Thank you, Roger. You've been most helpful.'

'What was all that about?' Phil asked, as David closed the door.

'What was all what about?' David replied casually, as he walked through into his own office.

'Oh, come on, David. I may be an obsolete model, but my radar is still operating. You were up to something, weren't you? While we were out of the room?'

'Whatever gave you that idea?' David asked, innocently.

'It could be the fact that the bank manager hasn't telephoned us, so you didn't need to answer his call. I handle the phone calls, remember?'

'Ah, yes,' David said. 'He rang, er, while you were upstairs.'

'That's funny. I could have sworn I switched this phone through to the bar before we went upstairs,' Phil smiled.

David grinned at the older man.

'All right, gov, you've got me bang to rights! I was up to something and, if you swear not to tell anyone, I'll show you what it was. But, first, I do need a cup of coffee.'

While Phil fetched the coffee, David retrieved the copied plans from his drawer. He turned the key in the office door and the two men sat side by side at the refectory table.

David spread out the sheets of paper on the table. The photocopying had been done so hurriedly that several of them were skewed.

Eventually, David had arranged the copies in what, he considered, was a fairly accurate representation of the original drawing.

'This is the golf course,' he explained to Phil.

'I can see that,' Phil said, thoughtfully. 'So what are all those black things round the edge – in the woods, as far as I can see?'

'No wonder the enemy ran for cover when you were in your bomber, Phil! You don't miss a thing do you?' David's respect for the old Flight Lieutenant was growing.

'They're houses,' David explained. 'At least, they're proposed houses. Young Roger brought out the original drawing while we were driving round the golf course. He thought I knew all about it. I played along with him and let him drive me around and show me where all the houses are to be built.'

'Then, you stole the drawing while we were having coffee and photocopied it?' Phil said, with a grin.

'That's a very serious charge, Phil. I hope you've got some evidence to back it up.'

'How about: I'd just used the last of the paper in the photocopier and switched it off before we went upstairs. And, now it's switched on and full of paper?'

'Got me, again!' David laughed. 'So, somebody is sounding out the local planning office about building houses on our golf course and turning the whole place into a mini-Wentworth Estate. But, who?'

'I should have thought that was obvious,' Phil replied. 'The houses, or most of them, are sited around the golf course, all right. But, the access road to them runs right round the course, and it's mostly on Browndean Farm land, which is owned by Toby Kelham.'

'So it is!' David gasped.

'Perhaps he's doing all this on behalf of the golf club,' Phil suggested. 'Maybe, he intends to apply for outline planning permission, then come to the Committee and say, here's a way out of your financial problems.'

'Do you really think so?' David asked.

'Not for a moment!' Phil laughed. 'I imagine once the Club has accepted his loan, he'll wait a few months, then call it in. The Club won't be able to pay and will have to go bust. Kelham, or rather Kelham and whoever's he's working with, will buy it from the receiver and then they'll start work on creating their private estate, complete with its own exclusive golf course.'

'Wow!' David exclaimed. 'But what makes you think that Kelham has anyone working with him, Phil?'

'He's a landowner, David. A farmer. I should have thought he'd need to work with a builder or a property developer to carry this plan through.'

'No prizes for guessing who that might be,' David said. 'Kate saw Kelham and Makrides poring over some paperwork when we were in the *Black Horse* last week.'

'Kate? Kate Earnshaw? The plot thickens,' Phil grinned.

'Anyway, if it is Makrides,' David went on. 'That might explain why Kelham was so keen to get him into the golf Club.'

'Yes,' Phil agreed. 'That way, they could both wander around the course without attracting too much attention.'

David pointed to the corner of the drawing. The copy was rather blurred around the edges, but a feint stamp could be discerned.

'MK Developments, I think,' Phil muttered, his old eyes an inch from the paper.

'Yes, I think you're right,' David agreed. Then, he sat up.

'Look, Phil. This is all pretty fantastic. The AGM is in two week's time and the members are going to elect a new committee. If the Brigadier has his way, they will put in place a committee that will accept Kelham's loan. If they do, they're stuffed...'

'Do you think the Brigadier knows about this?' Phil interrupted.

'I don't know,' David said. 'I would doubt it, personally. My guess is, they're just using the old devil. Anyway, I want to present this drawing at the AGM. So, not a word to anybody until then, OK?'

'OK,' Phil smiled. 'And, if you like, in the meantime I could do a bit of research. See if I can find out just who owns MK Developments.'

'That would be great,' David replied.

'There's only one other thing that puzzles me about this whole thing,' Phil said, thoughtfully.

'Oh, what's that?'

'It's this,' Phil replied, with a broad grin. 'Just what were you doing in the *The Black Horse* with Kate Earnshaw?'

Hole	Name	Yards	Par	Score
15	Hard Lesson	**401**	**4**	

1

'I find it so difficult to remember everything, every time, Jack. Do you think, perhaps, I should try a different game?'

'No, not at all, Mary. OK, you're not going to be joining the European Tour. But, there's no reason why you shouldn't be able to swing a golf club well enough to enjoy a round with your friends or your husband.'

'If you say so, Jack.' His middle-aged pupil looked doubtful.

'I do. Remember, we've been talking about posture and grip. Just try to spend some time this week bending at the hips and not at the waist. Work on moving your left hand round the club a little more. You can do that without playing golf and, if you do, by next week it should feel more natural. Then, we'll work on chipping and pitching around the green.'

'I must say, you make it sound very easy, Jack.'

'It is, Mary, believe me,' Jack smiled. 'See you next week.'

Mary picked up her clubs, said goodbye and walked across to her car. The sun had just dipped below the horizon and, compared with the brightly lit teaching bay, the car park appeared almost dark.

Jack began to close up. He'd been teaching since nine o'clock in the morning and he was feeling tired. Teaching needed a good deal of concentration but he had, nevertheless, enjoyed his day. It had come upon him unexpectedly, this facility for teaching. Most of his youth had been spent out on the golf course, developing his own skills and playing for himself. He had been really surprised to discover that he could impart those skills to other people, and that he felt almost as much satisfaction when he helped

269

others to improve as he did from his own game. His teachers at school, if they remembered him at all, would have been quite amazed.

Jack switched off the floodlights, leaving only the overhead bulbs burning. He took the bucket of balls and the clubs he'd used for demonstrating through into the room behind the bay – the room where Karen had first surprised him. That first time had certainly been the most unexpected and exciting.

Jack and Karen had had sex on several occasions since. She'd stopped him while he was driving home and they'd parked in a field. They had done it late one evening in the car park at *The White Hart*. And, a week ago Karen had turned up at his flat. To begin with, she had appeared to ignore him if they passed each other in the clubhouse. Gradually, however, Karen had become more open in the way she approached him and had made a point of talking to him, even touching him. It was almost as if she wanted people, Spiros even, to know.

The last time – yesterday – had been particularly reckless. Jack had stopped in the village to pick up some groceries, when Karen drove by. They talked and she'd persuaded him to get into her car. They'd kissed and, before he could object, she had driven off at high speed towards her house. Apparently, Spiros was away on business and wouldn't be back until tomorrow. She'd grabbed Jack's hand, taken him inside, up the stairs and begun undressing him and then herself. Whatever reservations Jack might have felt about screwing Spiros' wife in Spiros' bed were quickly dispelled when Karen removed her underwear and pulled him into bed with her.

Jack almost became aroused when he thought about it. But, he was also beginning to worry about his position at the Club – a job he really liked and was good at. Karen might be beautiful, and she might be brilliant in bed, but

270

there was almost certainly no future, and possibly a lot of danger, in their relationship.

Stupid to risk your future for a fuck, Jack thought, even if it was a good one.

'*Hello, Jack!*'

Jack was startled. It was almost dark in the store-room and, as he turned round, the two men in the doorway were no more than vague, black shapes. As his eyes adjusted, he could see that one was young, about his own age, while the other appeared much older, more wizened.

'I'm just closing up,' Jack explained. 'Are you after lessons, or equipment, or something?'

'It's you we're after, Jack,' the older one said.

'Me?'

Suddenly, Jack sensed that this was not a business call.

'Yes, Jack. We've come with a message for you from Mr Makrides.'

'Mr Makrides? Spiros?'

'The same, Jack. It seems you've been helping yourself to some of his property. And, Mr Makrides? Well, he's not very happy about it.'

'Not very happy, at all,' the younger visitor chimed in.

'His property? I don't understand.'

'Yes, Jack.'

Older visitor picked up one of Jack's clubs and made a pretend swing with it.

'It seems you've been playing on fairways you've no business playing on. Putting your ball into somebody else's hole, so to speak. I might even say sticking your club into somebody else's bag, if you get my meaning, Jack.'

'I don't, not really,' Jack replied, although he was beginning to get the drift.

'Let me explain, Jack. Now, Mr Makrides has a young and beautiful wife...'

'Karen?'

'The same, Jack. Mr Makrides asked you, paid you, to give her golf lessons. But, it seems you've been giving her more than lessons. It appears, in fact, that you've been giving her one. Indeed, it seems that you have been giving her more than one. Isn't that right, Jack?'

'That's really between me and Karen, don't you think?'

Jack thought he would try to argue his way out of what was clearly not going to be a pleasant chat.

'It's what went on between you and Karen that Mr Makrides is unhappy about, Jack.'

'Most unhappy,' younger visitor added.

'How, how did he find out?'

Jack's voice was beginning to quake and he suddenly remembered that he'd wanted to go to the toilet for some time.

'Let's just say that me and my colleague here are Mr Makrides' security advisers. Ever heard of CCTV, Jack?'

'CCTV? Closed circuit television? Yes, of course. We have it here at the Club. In fact, the cameras have probably recorded you arriving,' Jack said.

'When you're a security adviser, you learn how to avoid appearing on other people's CCTV, Jack. Pity you didn't think about that before you paid a visit to Mr Makrides' house, yesterday.'

'Yesterday? I didn't see any cameras.'

Jack was pretty sure now that this meeting was not going to end amicably and, for a moment, he thought of pushing past the two thugs and making a run for it. Unfortunately, they looked as if they would offer more resistance than the wall alongside them. They might also be armed.

'Hidden,' younger thug said. 'Even Karen, er, Mrs Makrides, didn't know they were there.'

'Does now, though, silly bitch,' older thug smirked. 'The thing is, Jack, Mr Makrides has asked us to give you a message.'

'I think I've got the message, all right,' Jack said. 'You can tell Spiros that I won't be going anywhere near Karen again. In fact, I'd already made up my mind not to see her any more.'

'I don't think you need worry about that, Jack.'

'Oh, good.' For a moment, Jack began to feel that that was all there was to it.

'No, Mr Makrides has already made it very clear to Mrs Makrides that you won't be seeing her again.'

'Or she, you.' Jack had begun to realise that the younger man was not as stupid as he looked. He had moved so that Jack could no longer look at both his visitors at once.

'But, Mr Makrides wanted his message to take a more memorable form than just words, Jack.'

Before he could move, the younger thug had grabbed both of Jack's arms from behind.

The older villain withdrew a golf club from Jack's bag.

'What do you call this club, Jack?'

'That? It's er, a driver.'

'And, this thing?' the older man asked.

'That's a clubhead cover,' Jack explained. 'It stops the clubhead from being damaged.'

'Well, lets put it on, shall we? Don't want to cause any more damage than necessary.'

The older thug slid the padded cover over the head of the driver. He held the club in both hands and began to swing it backwards and forwards, slowly at first but then faster and faster until it swished menacingly through the air. It was obvious to Jack that the man had held a golf club before. Quite a good grip, actually. A bit too strong, maybe. Probably end up hooking the ball hard to the left, but...

THUMP!!

Even though he was half expecting it, the blow to his stomach winded Jack and made him double up in agony. For a moment, he could barely breathe and, almost as soon as he could, another blow hit him, again in the stomach.

The older man slid the driver back into the golf bag and Jack thought for a moment that the attack was over, that the message had been delivered.

Then, his assailant took another club from the bag.

'And what's this club called, Jack?'

Jack didn't answer. Jack couldn't answer. He had only enough time to brace himself before the five iron smashed into his ribs. Without speaking, the man replaced the club in its bag and selected another. Again, the pain was terrible as a different club struck him in the side.

Further blows, each with a different club, landed in Jack's stomach, on his arms and on his legs. Finally, having exhausted the club selection, his assailant grasped the shaft of one of the clubs. He brought the rubber grip down twice on Jack's head with just enough force to leave him dazed. As warm blood trickled down his face, the younger thug released his grip and Jack slid to the floor.

'I do hope you've understood Mr Makrides's message, Jack. We wouldn't want to have to come back for another round with your clubs.'

'And, you won't mention any on this to the police or anybody, will you?'

Younger thug tapped Jack's head with the side of his foot.

'Or, somebody will certainly be round to finish the job.'

The two visitors turned but, by the door, the older man spotted another golf club leaning against the wall.

'Oh, Jack,' he sneered. 'We haven't used this one, have we? It's a putter, isn't it?'

He turned to where Jack was lying and swung the Ping putter hard into Jack's crotch. The pain in his left testicle was unbelievable. Jack curled up to protect himself, fearing the man might take two, or even three putts.

'Won't be putting that anywhere for a bit,' older smirked to younger.

'Bye, Jack!' said younger.

And, with that, they were gone, leaving Jack groaning on the cold concrete floor of the storeroom.

2

David switched off the lights and set the alarm. He'd been working late and it was now quite dark outside. The high-pitched tone of the alarm was still sounding as he turned away and walked towards his car.

'*Damn!* Somebody's left the range lights on.'

The driving range was covered by the same alarm system. This wasn't the first time the lights had been left on at night. It was easily done, especially if the last person to leave the professional's shop had done so while it was still daylight.

Unfortunately, David would now have to go and turn the lights off, then struggle along the path in the dark back to the main building to reset the burglar alarm. He cursed as he put his briefcase in the car and started across the car park.

His irritation increased when, as he entered the deserted driving range, he saw that, at the far end, the door behind the teaching bay was still wide open.

'Oh, for God's sake!' David muttered.

Now, he would have to open up the shop, find the keys and lock the door before he could switch off the lights and re-set the alarm.

'This is ridiculous. How could Jack go off and leave everything wide open?'

It had been a long day and David felt the weight of unwanted responsibility. How many times, when leaving his school late at night, had he spotted a light still burning or a window left open in a downstairs classroom? Then, as now, he would have to sort out a problem of someone else's making, just when he was tired and ready to go home.

As he approached the open door, David heard a sound from inside the room. He stopped and listened. For a moment, he could hear nothing, but he felt his heart thumping heavily in his chest.

Then, again, a sound. A groaning sound.

'Who's there?'

David tried to sound authoritative.

'Is anybody there?'

This time the noise was louder, and definitely human.

David stood in the doorway and peered into the darkened room. Blinded by the overhead lights, he could see nothing. But, the noise was clearer now.

'Who is it? What are you doing in there?'

'*Ooh! God Almighty! Ow! Jesus! Bloody bastards!*'

David relaxed as he recognised the voice.

'Jack? Is that you? What's the matter with you?'

'Course it's me! Switch the fucking light on, for Christ's sake!'

David's eyes had adjusted now and he could see the switch to his right. Stepping across, he turned on the storeroom lights.

Jack was lying on his back against the far wall. There was congealed blood on the top of his head and down the side of his face. David crouched beside him.

'What's happened to you, Jack? Have you had an accident or something?'

Jack was trying to sit up, but every time he put any weight on his arm he would wince and slump down again.

'Here, let me help you.'

David took hold of Jack's arm and tried to lift him.

'*Owww! Leggo! Jesus Christ!* I think my arm's broken. In fact, I think everything's broken, Boss. Just leave me here and fetch the undertaker. He can lift me straight into a coffin. It won't hurt so much, that way...'

'Don't talk rubbish, Jack. I'm not a doctor, but even I can see that you need an ambulance, not an undertaker!'

'No! No ambulance!' Jack snapped. 'No ambulance, Boss. And, definitely, no police. OK?'

'No police? Who suggested the police?'

Until now, David had assumed that Jack had simply had an accident.

'What's been going on, Jack? How on earth did you get into this state?'

'Just an accident, that's all. If you can help me up, I'll get off home and I'll be fine in the morning.'

Jack struggled to a sitting position and leaned back against the wall.

'What sort of accident?'

David looked around the room.

'There isn't anything in here except the ball washing machine, and a couple of golf clubs.'

'Yeah, that's right,' Jack said. 'The ball washer jammed and I tried to free it with a golf club. Must have caught hold of my arm and thrown me across here. I'll have to see my solicitor about it; sue the club for damages. Now, Boss, if you could just give me a hand to get up…'

David had walked over to the machine. It certainly didn't look damaged and there was no golf club near it. To his right, the mains isolating switch was in the 'OFF' position.

'It was very sensible of you to get up and switch the power off after you were thrown across the room, Jack. Wouldn't want anyone else to go the same way, would we?'

David smiled down at the young man.

'What? Er, yeah. I thought it best to…'

'Stop talking nonsense, Jack! Come on. You can hardly move. You certainly couldn't get up and switch off the power to that machine. And, what's all this stuff about "No police?" Why would the police be interested in an accident with a ball-washing machine?'

277

I may not be a headmaster, any more, David thought. But, I can still tell when a boy is lying to me.

'It's a private matter, Boss. Nothing to do with anybody else, honest. Just help me get up and I'll be off home.'

Jack winced as he stretched out his arm.

'Those injuries don't look much like a private matter to me, Jack. But, if you say so, I'll just switch off the lights and go home. It's going to get pretty cold tonight, by the look of that clear sky.'

'Oh, all right,' Jack groaned as he tried again to get to his feet. He seemed to hurt everywhere. 'But promise me, you won't involve the police.'

'Not unless I have to,' David agreed. 'Come on, let's get you inside and have a look at those injuries.'

With a great deal of effort and a lot of groaning, David managed to help Jack to his feet. Wherever he tried to support the younger man, the result was the same. A cry, a wince, a shudder, or a gasp. Jack seemed to have injuries all over his body and David could think of only one thing that could cause that much damage.

'Somebody's given you a beating, haven't they, Jack?'

'Just a warning, I think, Boss.'

Jack gasped as he leaned against David's arm.

'Not one you should ignore, by the look of it,' David said. 'Come on, let's get you over to the changing room.'

Together, the two men made slow and often agonising progress along the driving range and across the car park to the clubhouse.

David unlocked the front door, turned off the alarm and switched on the lights. He led Jack through into the men's changing rooms.

'Sit down, Jack. We need to get your jumper and shirt off.'

Jack made a feeble attempt to protest, but he was happy to be in the warm after lying out on that concrete floor. Gingerly, he raised his arms so that David could ease his

278

jumper over his head. The shirt was easier and, when he'd removed it, David crouched down to inspect the young man's body.

'Well, they certainly knew what they were doing, Jack. Your arms and body are covered in bruises, but it doesn't look as if you have any broken bones.'

'They knew what they were doing, all right. Professionals, if you ask me.'

Jack looked down at his bruised trunk and winced.

'What about your legs? Come on Jack, let's get those trousers off.'

Ignoring his protests, David helped Jack to his feet and unzipped his trousers. They dropped to the floor to reveal a similar picture. Multi-coloured bruises were spreading over the surface of each thigh.

The head wound, too, was more impressive than serious although David felt it might need stitches.

'The best thing for you is to have a hot shower. Wash off all that blood and dirt. Warm up your muscles, too. Then, we can get you dressed and you can tell me all about it.'

David ran the shower until it was hot. He turned to see that Jack had removed his underpants. The left side of his groin area appeared to be one large bruise.

'You're not going to be doing much with that for a while,' David chuckled.

'Funny, that's just what they said!'

Jack tried to share the joke, but it hurt too much to laugh.

While he was in the shower, David checked Jack's clothes for size and went across to the professional's shop for some replacements.

A good idea of Margaret's that, he thought with a smile.

Half an hour later, the two men were sitting in front of the gas fire in David's office. Jack was slowly sipping coffee and his injuries were hidden beneath his new clothes. The head wound didn't look too bad, either, now that his hair was brushed over it.

David leaned forward.

'So, Jack, what's been going on?'

'As I say, it was just a warning.' Jack gazed into the fire.

'From whom? Who would want to give you a warning?'

'Somebody who didn't like me giving his wife lessons.'

'Or, what you were teaching her, more like.' David was beginning to understand.

'Something like that,' Jack smiled. 'Obviously thought that was his job.'

'And, who might the aggrieved husband be? No, wait a minute! Not Spiros Makrides? Jack, don't tell me you been having an affair with Karen Makrides.'

Now, David understood. Not many people would be happy to discover that somebody else was bedding their partner. He could see that Spiros Makrides would be upset, to say the least, if he found out that someone was screwing his wife, the beautiful Karen. The difference, however, was that Spiros Makrides had the means to do something about it. He had a small army of tough-looking characters who manned the doors of his nightclub, sorted out any trouble and generally did his bidding. One of them, Dinos, even carried his clubs for him when he played golf. They were professionals, all right. Jack was lucky. If they'd meant to do him real harm, they could certainly have done so. This was, as Jack had said, a warning.

'Not an affair, exactly. I just got my leg over a few times, that's all. It wasn't even my idea although I'm not saying I put up much resistance,' Jack smiled. 'But, Karen was gagging for it, Boss, honest.'

'I'm not sure Mr Makrides would want to hear you say that, Jack. The thing is, what are we going to do about it?'

'Nothing! Nothing at all. If we go to the police, he'll deny it and send his men back later to finish the job. No, thanks! I'll just take my medicine and keep my head down from now on, thanks.'

David didn't like the idea of doing nothing but he couldn't fault Jack's logic. He remembered the poor widow who had her head cut off in *Zorba the Greek*. These Greeks obviously took matrimonial matters pretty seriously.

'Well, you're not going to be in any fit state to work for a while, that's for sure. I'll drive you home and you can phone in in the morning. Say you aren't well, or something. OK?'

'OK,' Jack readily agreed. He was feeling very tired now and the warmth from the fire was making him sleepy. He really didn't want to move again.

David went outside, switched off the driving range lights and locked up. When he came back, Jack was almost asleep and he was sorry to rouse the young man. Eventually, he got him into the car, did up his seat belt, and started the engine. It was almost ten o'clock by the time David had delivered Jack to his flat and driven to his own home. He let himself into the dark, empty house, slumped into a chair and poured himself a drink.

3

'Mr Makrides is here asking to see you, David.'

Phil had put his head round the office door. 'I said you were busy, but he is pretty insistent.'

'Oh, he is, is he? Well, I'd quite like a word with Mr Makrides, myself.'

David got to his feet and followed Phil into the outer office. Makrides was sitting by the door, dressed in a very sharp suit and looking intently at his heavy gold wristwatch. He looked up as the two men came in.

'Ah, the boss! Just the man I want to see.' He stood up smiling and offered his hand. David shook it briefly and turned away towards his office.

'Come on in, Mr Makrides. I think I can guess why you are here.'

'Spiros, please. You know why I am here?' Makrides sounded surprised.

'Sit down, er, Spiros, please.' David thought it best to sound reasonable.

'I said, I think I know why you are here. But, why don't you tell me?'

'OK, I come straight to the point, Mr Crowley. The boy, Jack, he has been, er, playing around with my wife, Karen. He has seduced 'er.'

'As I understand it, Mr Makrides, Spiros, Karen and Jack have been playing around with each other.'

'You know about this? Is worse than I thought! How many people know about this?'

'Only me and Jack at present, as far as I know. And, I only know about it because, last night, I found Jack out on the driving range. He had been badly beaten up and I had to clean him up and take him home.'

'And, he told you I did this?'

'He's under the impression that the people who did it were acting on your behalf.'

'I know nothing of this. What do you think I am, an animal?'

'Well, I have no proof, of course, and Jack isn't about to go to the police. Nevertheless…'

'Nevertheless, nothing! You say I did this. To anybody! You will be sorry. Do I make myself clear?'

'Perfectly clear. What is it you want, Mr Makrides?'

Why on earth had the Brigadier agreed to this character joining the Club? David thought.

'The boy. Jack. He must go. Fired! I don't want him here. If people know he fuck my wife, everybody laugh at me.'

'I'm sure he's not going to go around telling everybody about it, Mr Makrides.'

'He done that already! He already told you.'

'Yes, but…'

'No buts. He got to go. I want him out!'

'Look here, Mr Makrides, Jack is a young man who is liked and respected by most of the people in this club. Your wife is a beautiful young woman. The two of them were attracted to each other and they've both made a mistake. Jack has realised that and I'm sure Karen has, too…'

David thought he sounded like a headmaster dealing with a difficult parent.

'She done that, all right. She's gone to stay with my mother in Cyprus. When she come back, I want that boy out of the way.'

'As I say,' David went on. 'Jack realises his mistake and I am sure there will be no repetition. On the other hand, I must say I take a rather dim view of people who go around, making threats and beating up people they don't like. If there is any repetition of that sort of behaviour, then I'm afraid the Club may wish to reconsider your membership.'

'You're not listening to me, are you, Mr Crowley? This boy, he has dishonoured me. I am not asking. I am telling you. Either he goes or you and your club will be very sorry.'

'Now, you listen to me, Mr Makrides.' David raised his voice while still trying to sound firm but reasonable. 'This is a golf club and, as I see it, golf is a game of honour. When we play golf, we play according to a set of rules and a standard of etiquette. We don't threaten our opponents. We don't cheat our opponents because, if we do, we cheat ourselves. If we have differences, then they must be dealt with in a reasonable way.'

He's not buying this, David thought.

'*Enough of this bollocks!*' Makrides got to his feet. 'You talk of honour. I fuck your honour. You talk about rules and, that other thing you said. Fuck them! This boy; he is a professional golfer and he has not acted with honour. Now, he must pay for his actions. You get rid of the boy or there will be trouble.'

He turned and walked out, slamming the door behind him.

Oh dear, David said to himself, leaning back in his chair. I must be losing my touch.

In the old days, he had been renowned for his ability to pacify the most indignant of parents. Makrides, however, was not an indignant parent and his threats had to be taken seriously. Jack could testify to that.

'Problem?'

David hadn't heard Phil come in.

'Just a little one. Makrides has demanded that I get rid of Jack.'

'Jack? What's he got against Jack?' Phil looked puzzled. 'I mean, I know Jack gave him golf lessons; not that you'd know it. But, it's not Jack's fault if Makrides never bothers to practice.'

'It's not because he's useless at golf,' David smiled. 'I can't tell you why he wants Jack sacked. But, he says, if I don't fire him, it will be the worse for us.'

'A word of advice, David,' Phil looked serious. 'Makrides may be a hopeless golfer, but he's a far from useless businessman. And, as I understand it, he's also got some pretty nasty thugs on his payroll. My granddaughter asked me to drop her and some friends off at his nightclub the other week. I certainly wouldn't want to cross any of those characters he's got manning the door. Don't treat his threats too lightly.'

'Oh, I won't. But, I think he's just angry at the moment. I'll give him a few days to calm down. Maybe he'll be more reasonable after the weekend.'

4

'Oh, I shouldn't worry too much about Makrides. He sounds like a typical bully to me. You stood up to him and that's the one thing bullies don't like.'

Kate smiled at David. 'I wouldn't be surprised if you never hear from him again.'

David found Kate's confidence infectious and before their lunch had arrived he was feeling much more cheerful.

Kate had returned from Africa looking tanned and, David thought, even more attractive. She had invited him to lunch at *The Black Horse* because, she said, she had something important to discuss with him and the dining room at the Club was not private enough. David was intrigued and, although he hadn't intended to talk about Jack, Karen and Makrides, before long he'd found himself taking Kate into his confidence.

'The thing is, the poor guy has a point. Makrides arranged for Jack to give his wife lessons and she ended up getting rather more than he'd paid for. Jack has acted quite unprofessionally. He abused the relationship between a teacher and his student. If one of my teachers had had sex with a student at my school, I would have had to take disciplinary action and I'm not sure he would have kept his job.'

'But that's quite different, surely? Your teachers were adults and the students were still children. Even if some of them didn't exactly look like it, or behave like it,' Kate grinned. 'Jack and Karen are the same age. They're both adults. Jack's a healthy young man. I don't think you can entirely blame him if Karen goes after him like a bitch on heat.'

'No, I suppose not. The Professional Golfers Association would probably take a pretty dim view of it, though. I hope Makrides doesn't try involving them, or Jack could find he won't be working here, or anywhere else for that matter.'

'I'm sure Makrides won't do that. He doesn't sound to me like the sort to go through official channels.'

Then, quite unexpectedly, she placed her hand on David's arm and looked into his face.

'Look David, I'm sorry about poor Jack's beating, but this is really his problem. I don't want you putting yourself in danger just to protect him. Promise me, you won't take any risks.'

David was about to reassure Kate that the last thing he felt like doing was standing up to Spiros Makrides, when he was interrupted by the arrival of their lunch. They were sitting at a corner table and David felt more relaxed now that he'd shared the problem with Kate. Her expression of concern for his safety had suddenly made him feel quite confident.

'Anyway, enough about Jack,' Kate said brightly. 'I've asked you here to talk about something much more important than that.'

'Oh?' David looked puzzled.

'Yes. You know that in six weeks' time, the Club is holding its annual charity golf day.'

'Of course I do,' David said. 'I'm the one who has to organise it, remember?'

'Oh, yes, sorry,' Kate smiled. 'Well, I was sort of wondering if you would consider playing as my partner for the day?'

David was stunned. Ever since Kate's phone call, he had been wondering what it was she wanted to talk about. He hadn't for a moment imagined that this was what she had in mind.

'Oh, that's quite out of the question, I'm afraid. You know I don't play golf any more.'

David ran through his usual polite rebuffs.

'I'm sorry, Kate. I'm sure we can find you someone else to play with that day.'

Kate listened, obviously unimpressed.

'I don't want someone else to play with, David. I want to play with you. I know you say you don't play any more and I also know why. I just want you to hear me out and then to think about it. OK?'

'All right, I'll listen.' Deep down, David felt a small crack open up in his defences. 'I'll listen, although I can't promise I'll change my mind.'

Kate took a sip of wine.

'Look, David. I know that, after your wife died, you stopped playing golf. You say you felt guilty because you carried on playing during her illness and you believe you neglected her.'

'That's about it,' David said. 'I feel I let her down. I wasn't there when she needed me. I was just being a selfish bastard.'

'Were you? You don't strike me as a selfish bastard,' Kate went on. 'I went through it myself, remember? If I'm honest, there were times when I found it so hard to see James suffering and gradually getting weaker that I couldn't cope. I would run away; take the dogs for a walk; go to my sister; anything. You see, I wasn't always there for him because I needed to look after myself.'

'I see,' David said quietly. 'And, don't you ever feel guilty?'

'Of course I bloody do! Hardly a day goes by when I don't think of poor James lying there alone while I was out somewhere. Sometimes, I get angry with him for dying; then I feel guilty for feeling angry. But, I had to go on. I had to survive. I had Sarah to worry about, and my mother, at the time.'

'I see,' David said. 'But, I was just thinking about myself. I couldn't cope, seeing Tess so ill, day after day. I just ran away from it all.'

'Exactly. You weren't off playing golf because you didn't care about Tess. You carried on playing precisely because you did care so much about her.'

'But, I wasn't there with her. I ran away.'

'I don't believe that. You weren't out all the time. And, anyway, you were under great strain, just as I was. You can't be blamed. You mustn't go on blaming yourself, just

287

because you didn't behave as heroically as you would have liked. Coping with the death of a loved one is never easy, but one thing I've learned is that it doesn't make it any easier if you insist on blaming yourself.'

'I'd agree there. I've been putting myself in the dock and finding me guilty for the past three years. It's become something of a habit, I'm afraid.'

'Well, it's time to break that habit,' Kate smiled. 'Do you really think that Tess would want you to be sitting at home moping, depriving yourself of playing golf, cutting yourself off from other people?'

'I hadn't really thought about it.'

'Well, think about it! You loved Tess. Tess loved you. When you love somebody, you want them to be happy. I never met her, but I'm sure Tess would want you to be happy; not behaving like some miserable creature, slinking in the shadows.'

'I'm hardly that,' David protested, although, he had to admit, Kate's description wasn't that far from the mark.

'Sorry. I didn't mean to be unkind, but I don't want to see you unhappy either.'

Again, Kate reached across and touched David's arm.

'David, you can't have become as good as you were at golf if it didn't mean a great deal to you. You must have got a lot of pleasure from playing and you deserve to experience that pleasure again.'

'Maybe,' David said. 'Perhaps you're right. I'm just not sure I'm ready yet.'

'Listen, David, this charity golf day is in aid of cancer research. What better reason could you have for coming out of retirement than to help raise money for that? If you like, you can think of playing as a tribute to Tess.'

'I hadn't realised it was to raise money for cancer research.'

'Well, it is, so why don't you think it over? If it helps, talk with Tess about it. Give it some thought and, when you're ready, let me know your decision.'

The lunch was over and they walked outside to the car park. Kate leaned over and kissed David on the cheek.

'Just make sure you decide to play, that's all.' She grinned, then climbed into her little van and waved as she drove away.

Hole	Name	Yards	Par	Score
16	Homeward	**380**	**4**	

1

'*Course you've got to play, Dad!*'

'There's no course about it, Ben. I'm still trying to make up my mind.'

'But, what is there to decide?' Ben said, with a grin. 'A nice looking woman asks you to play with her...'

'Play *golf* with her,' his father corrected.

'Same thing! She's clearly got fed up with waiting for you to ask her, so she's making a move. It's obvious, Dad.'

'It's not obvious to me.'

'Because you're too slow to catch cold! That's why she's had to do something about it.'

'OK,' David conceded. 'Let's just say that you're right. I'm not saying I think you are, but let's just say that Kate is interested in, well, having a relationship with me...'

'No doubt about it, if you ask me,' Ben smiled.

'If that is the case,' David went on. 'And, I were to, let's say, get involved with her. That wouldn't worry you? At all?'

'No! Why should it? For Christ's sake, Dad, it would be a relief! For one thing, I could stop worrying about you being on your own all the time. And,' Ben grinned, 'I wouldn't have to keep trying to convince my mates that you're not gay.'

They both laughed.

David had driven over to Ben's college and they were enjoying Sunday lunch in a pub alongside the Thames. It was a beautiful spring day and drifts of daffodils flowed along the opposite bank. Mid-way through the meal, however, father and son both agreed that the day was not as warm as they'd first thought. They had picked up their plates and were now sitting inside at a table near the fire.

'So, you worry about me being on my own?' David asked.

'Yeah, of course I do,' Ben said. Then he made a joke of it. 'I don't want you turning into a stubbly old recluse. Could frighten my girlfriends away, when I bring them home.'

'*If* you ever bring them home, don't you mean?' David laughed. 'But, seriously, it doesn't bother you to think I might go out with, even sleep with, somebody else. Somebody other than your mother?'

Ben looked serious, for the first time.

'Dad, don't be daft. Of course, it doesn't bother me. Mum's been dead for four years. You turning into a celibate old man is not going to bring her back.'

'We haven't talked about her much, have we, Ben? Since she died, I mean.'

'Well, there's not much to talk about, really, is there?'

'Do you miss her, Ben?'

'What sort of question is that, for Christ's sake? Of course, I miss her!' Ben said.

'What do you miss about her?'

'What is this, twenty questions? Look, I miss her, OK?'

Ben was beginning to feel uncomfortable.

'I know you miss her,' David persisted. 'I just want to know what it is about your Mum that you miss. Or miss most.'

Ben sighed, as if irritated. Then, he spoke quietly.

'All right. I miss her being there to ask about things. To show things to when I want an opinion. I miss that warm feeling I had whenever I walked through the front door.'

'Yes, that was a special ability of hers, wasn't it?' David said. 'The minute I got out of the car, I used to feel glad to be home. I couldn't wait to go indoors and tell her about all the things I'd been doing.'

291

'Mind you,' Ben smiled. 'I'm not saying I miss Mum making me get up early at weekends. Or, tidy my room. Or, do my homework when there was football on the telly.'

Then, he thought for a minute.

'Actually, I wouldn't mind her doing any of that again. Not one bit. God, I wish she was still here, Dad.'

For a moment, David thought that Ben was about to cry. He felt his own tears begin to flow. Not just for himself, for missing Tess. But, for his son, even though the boy was bigger than he was.

'So do I, Ben,' David said. 'So do I.' And the two men, father and son, hugged for a moment.

'I'm sorry, Ben.'

'What for?'

'Oh, I don't know,' David said. 'I'm sorry if I haven't been there to talk to since your Mum died; if I've been too wrapped up in my own problems, at school and so forth. I'm sorry if I wasn't there enough for you when your Mum was ill.'

'Dad! For Christ's sake, stop saying sorry, will you?' Ben said. 'You've been great. If we haven't talked about Mum, it's as much my fault as yours. And, when will you stop apologising for playing golf when Mum was ill. I was off out with my mates most of the time, so if anybody was selfish, I was.'

'So, you don't think I shouldn't play golf, then?'

'Dad, I've been telling you for ages. You didn't neglect Mum by playing golf. And, even if you did a bit, you can't change that now. If you want my opinion, you've neglected me far more by not playing with me since she died. I'm the one who's lost out!'

Ben suddenly grinned.

'What do you mean?'

'Well, I used to enjoy taking the money off you every week. Supplemented my income on a regular basis that did.

It's been a real struggle since you stopped playing, I don't mind telling you!'

'*You cheeky blighter!*' David said. 'You only won because I was too generous with your handicap. I bet I could beat you easily, if we played off level.'

'You think so?' Ben laughed. 'Come on, then. We'll go back to the college and see if you're still as cocky when I've thrashed you. Let's see you put your money where your mouth is.'

'But, I don't have any clubs,' David pleaded.

'You can use my mate Mike's. Or, are you going to use that as an excuse to chicken out?'

'Certainly not! It's time you were cut down to size, my boy.'

David paid the barman and the two men left the pub, laughing.

Of course, it was no contest. David wasn't really in the match. He hadn't hit a ball in anger in over three years, although one or two shots suggested that his game was still there inside, somewhere. While he struggled to rediscover it, David marvelled at the effortless way Ben hit the ball and the accuracy of his approach shots.

'It's these clubs,' David complained at one point. 'I don't know the course as well as you do,' he groaned, a little later.

David lost by three and two over only nine holes. But, he was happy to be beaten. Happy, indeed, to be playing after so long. It was a beautiful day, made even more beautiful because he was playing golf again with his son.

'It's a pleasure,' Ben grinned, as he extracted the five pound note from his father's grasp.

'Next time,' David smiled. 'You wait until next time.'

They walked towards the car.

'I've really enjoyed myself today, Ben.'

'So have I, Dad. I'm glad we had a talk about Mum.'

'Me too,' David said. 'Let's make sure we talk again.'

293

2

David knew there was a problem as soon as he got out of the car.

In front of the clubhouse, a small group of greenkeepers had gathered. When he was a headmaster, teachers would often wait outside his office in the morning to accost him the moment he arrived. They only ever seemed to bring him a problem or bad news and, from the look on Bob Morgan's face, David suspected that nothing much had changed.

'Morning, David!' Bob said. 'Got a problem, I'm afraid. Somebody broke into the buggy store last night and took out several of the buggies.'

'They stole them, you mean?' David asked.

'No, it's worse than that, I'm afraid. They drove six of the buggies out around the course, churned up several greens and then dumped them in the lake.'

'Good God!' David muttered. 'Which greens have they damaged?'

'As far as I can see, they had a go at five of them, although only the tenth and the seventeenth are really bad.'

'Any idea who it was?' David asked. It was just something to say, really. There was no way Bob could know who had perpetrated this act of vandalism.

'Drunken local youths, I expect. I wish I could get hold of 'em right now.'

'Let's go and have a look, shall we?' David suggested.

He joined Bob and two of his men in the Land Rover. As they drove out around the course, David could see the tracks made in the grass by the buggies. It was clear that, whoever had driven them, had done so in such a way that they churned up the course as much as possible.

'It looks bad, but we can soon put most of that right,' Bob shouted over the noise of the engine. 'The greens will take more time, though.'

To David, the first green they arrived at didn't look too bad. Wheel tracks arced several times across the turf, but Bob explained that the damage was mostly superficial.

'We'll have this one back in action in a couple of weeks,' Bob said.

The picture at the tenth green, however, was quite different.

'It looks as if they had a race, round and round the green,' David suggested. 'There's hardly any grass left.'

'It seems that way,' Bob agreed. 'They probably spent longer here because it's so far from the road. Nobody would have heard them. Same with the seventeenth, I should imagine.'

They drove slowly across the course, passing two more slightly damaged greens. Eventually, they arrived at the seventeenth green.

David stared aghast at the destruction the vandals had caused. Only a few days before he had passed this point on his way to speak to Bob about a chemical order. He remembered thinking then, in the morning sunshine, that the seventeenth green was the finest corner of the course. Perhaps the finest spot on any course. The surrounding banks and trees made it a natural amphitheatre, a fitting venue for a match approaching its climax.

Now, tyre tracks had been gouged deep into the surface of the green. David was not a green-keeper but even he could tell that weeks, perhaps months, of work would be required to repair the damage these senseless idiots had done in a few minutes.

'The buggies are up there,' Bob pointed.

He steered the Land Rover up the path towards the seventeenth tee and, from there, in the direction of the lake. The buggy tracks led the way, down the bank and into the water. On the bank, two men stood beside a tractor.

'The lake', as it was called, was really a large man-made pond, created to store irrigation water near the highest point on the course. During the day, water was pumped into the lake. Then, during the hot summer nights, its contents were sprayed over the greens and fairways.

The two men had attached a cable from the tractor winch to something in the water. One of them revved the tractor engine and the other guided the cable as it tightened under its load. Very slowly, the roof of a buggy emerged from the water. Disguised, under a layer of weed and leaves and mud, the buggy was barely recognisable.

'Are they ruined?' David asked, fearing the worst.

'Difficult to say,' Bob replied. 'We've got two out so far and they don't look too bad. Of course, we shan't know until we've hosed them down and dried out the engines. I can't imagine they'll just burst into life, though!'

'No, nor can I.'

David was already thinking of the cost of replacements. If the club had owned the buggies, it wouldn't be so bad. The members would have had to walk for a while, but they could get used to that. Unfortunately, the buggies were leased and the leasing company would want its pound of flesh. The insurance might cover it, as long as nobody had left the store open or the buggy keys in the ignition.

'Well, do what you can,' David said. ' Keep me posted. I'm going back to the office now.'

'OK,' Bob said. 'The boys are out now, moving the flags on to winter greens. Can you put up a notice in the clubhouse, explaining what's happened.'

Winter greens, or temporary greens, are closely mown circles on the fairway that are used as the putting surface when the proper greens are frozen or waterlogged. The members hate using them, even in the winter, and David could already imagine the groans and moans. Still, there was nothing to be done. He left the group by the lake and set out to hike down the eighteenth fairway towards the clubhouse. David enjoyed walking in the fresh air and, after what he had just seen, he felt the need for some quiet thinking time.

As he reached the clubhouse, the Brigadier was waiting for him.

'Bad business, this Crowley. Bad business. Like to horse-whip the lot of 'em. Damned vandals!'

'Me, too, Brigadier. Me, too!'

For once, David found himself wholly in agreement with the Brigadier.

'Anything I can do to help?' the old soldier asked.

For a moment, David was at a loss for words. The Brigadier had never before offered real help with anything. He looked up and saw that the old soldier was genuinely upset.

'I remember standing beside my father when they were building that seventeenth green. He said then that it was one of the finest greens we'd ever see and I don't think I've come across better. Now look what they've done to it, the bastards!'

'Bob and his boys will put it back the way it was, Brigadier. You can be sure of that.'

'I hope so, Crowley. I hope so.'

The Brigadier looked thoroughly dejected.

'In the meantime, it would help if you could explain the situation to anyone you meet. Let them know we're doing everything we can to get the course back to normal as soon as possible.'

'Will do!' the Brigadier said, suddenly looking more cheerful. He walked away, his spirits apparently lifted by his newly allocated responsibility.

David went through into his office. It was at times like these that he missed the quiet presence of Margaret in the outer office and the cup of coffee that appeared almost as soon as he had sat down at his desk.

The chirp of the telephone broke into his thoughts.

'Good morning, Mr Crowley.'

It was Spiros Makrides.

'Good morning, Mr Makrides. What can I do for you?'

'The boy, Jack, you have fired him. Yes?'

'Well, no, actually I haven't. As you know, Jack is not employed by the Club, and I'm not really sure I have grounds for terminating our contract with him,' David bluffed.

'Really, Mr Crowley, you disappoint me.'

'I'm sorry, Mr Makrides. I'm not sure I can help you at the...'

'You were late in this morning, were you not, Mr Crowley?'

'Yes, I've been dealing with some vandalism; damage to several of the greens, I'm afraid.'

'That's terrible, terrible,' Makrides said. 'What people will do these days, eh? Let's hope that they don't have to come back and do any more.'

Suddenly, David felt very cold.

'I don't understand, Mr Makrides. Why should they have to come back and do any more damage?'

'Let me make it simple, Mr Crowley. The boy, Jack. Some of my friends are very unhappy that the motherfucker is still at the Club. I try to explain to them what you say. That you have to have grounds for dismissal, that you have your procedures, but my friends, they don't understand. They say to me, "Spiros, you have been dishonoured. We must defend your honour." They tell me, if that boy is not fired today, they will have to finish the job. I try to tell them not to do any more damage to the beautiful golf course, but you know what friends are, don't you, Mr Crowley?'

David put the phone down slowly and slumped in his chair.

So, this wasn't mindless vandalism, after all. Makrides' men, it was, who had churned up the greens and dumped the buggies in the lake. And, if Jack didn't leave, they would be back to do even more damage in the future.

The Club couldn't take it. Already, he would have to cancel several societies booked in for golf days. That meant a loss of valuable income. And, it would be impossible to attract new members with half the course out of action. He could go to the police, of course. He should probably have done so already. But, these characters were clever and they were hardly likely to leave clues lying around. There was no way round it.

David picked up the phone.

'Ah, Jack, is that you? How are you feeling? Good. Listen, Jack, I need to have an urgent chat with you, I'm afraid. Can I pop out to see you sometime this morning? About 11 o'clock? OK, I'll see you then.'

David replaced the handset.

Sorry, Jack. But, there's no other way.

3

'The bloody bastards!'

Jack became very angry when David described the damage to the course.

'Bastards, all right,' David agreed. 'Makrides' men made it look to anyone else like senseless vandalism. Then, he made sure I knew who and what was behind it.'

'Have you told the police?' Jack asked.

'I will, but I can't really see them finding anything. These are professionals. They'll have made sure they weren't seen and, if they were, that they can't be identified. There's nothing on our CCTV tape. I had a quick look through that before I came out.'

'How long do you think it will take to get the course back into action?'

'Most of it will be OK by the weekend, Bob reckons. We'll have to use some temporary greens for a month or two, of course.'

'So, why the visit, Boss? You could have told me all this over the phone?'

David sat back, sipped his coffee and looked at Jack. The recuperative powers of the young are amazing, he thought. A week ago, Jack could barely stand and his body was a mass of bruises. No doubt, beneath his baggy sweatshirt, some injuries remained, but the young man who now sat beside him was a picture of masculine health and vigour.

'We have a problem, Jack,' David began. 'The Club has a problem and you have a problem and, between us, we have to sort it out.'

'Yeah, I can see that,' Jack said. 'You think he's going to go on hitting the Club until you get rid of me, right?'

'Right!' David was relieved that he hadn't had to spell out the predicament.

'Look, Jack,' David said. 'First, you're beaten up. Now this. The physical damage to the course itself will cost quite a bit to put right. It's already cost us a tidy sum. We've had to cancel several society golf days. Those societies bring in a lot to the restaurant and the bar. If Makrides' boys do any more damage, word will start to get around and people who might have thought of joining could go elsewhere. That will cost us even more. The Club is only just beginning to get back on its feet ...'

'So, you want me to quit to save the Club, right?'

'Believe me, Jack,' David said. 'If Makrides doesn't stop, there won't be a club in six months' time. Then, none of us will have a job!'

'It's as bad as that, is it?'

'Worse, I'd say. As I told you, the bank gave us six months to turn things around. We're now trading in the black, just, and Mark Essam is making encouraging noises.

But, if we don't keep increasing our income, if we start going backwards again, I think the bank might call it a day.'

'What would happen then?'

'If the bank calls in its overdraft, the Club will go bust. Receivers will then be brought in and the course and clubhouse sold to the highest bidder. I suspect that's just what Makrides and his friend Kelham want. If that happens, I don't suppose the new owners will be too bothered about people being from the right class. The membership fees will probably be huge but, as long as you can pay them, you'll be able to join.'

'So, all the Brigadier's efforts to keep the Club exclusive will have been a waste of time?'

'Not just a waste of time,' David agreed. 'The Brigadier's misguided efforts have created the Club's problems, and the result will be the exact opposite of what he intended.'

'The silly old bugger!' Jack said. 'The thing is, you know, he's a bloody good golfer. If he'd just stick to playing golf, there wouldn't have been a problem at all.'

'Maybe, but it's not only the Club that has a problem here, Jack. Your little liaison with Karen has only added to our difficulties. Not that I approve of his methods, but Makrides does have a point, Jack. You bedded his wife when he was paying you to give her golf lessons. Who knows what he might do next? Your own career could be in jeopardy.'

David smiled.

'I only hope she was worth it, that's all.'

'She was, actually,' Jack grinned. 'Karen's not as stupid as she makes out. And, she was getting really interested in golf when we were, you might say, distracted.'

'But, I guess you're right. I suppose I'll have to leave the Club. I can cope with that. But, it does grieve me to see Big

Mak and his mates getting away with murder. Well, not murder exactly, but violence and intimidation.'

'I know. I feel the same. It's infuriating, but I don't see any other way,' David said.

Then, he thought for a moment.

'I tell you what, Jack. If I tell Makrides that you've gone,' David said. 'Can you disappear for a few weeks? Go on holiday, or something? That should get him off our backs, for a while at least. Then, depending on how things turn out at next week's annual general meeting, we'll make a decision about if and when you can come back. OK?'

'Fine by me,' Jack replied. 'I could certainly do with a bit of sunshine, right now. Get some warmth into my muscles.'

'That's great,' David said, getting to his feet. Then, he smiled. 'Although, if I remember rightly, it was you getting too much warmth into your muscles that got us into this mess in the first place!'

They walked down the stairs to the front door.

'I've just had an idea myself,' Jack said. 'Makrides isn't the only one around here with friends.'

'Now, Jack,' David said, climbing into his car. 'You won't do anything stupid, will you?'

'Me? I'm not going to be here, am I? I shall be away soaking up the sun, somewhere.'

'That's all right then,' David said. 'Any idea where you might go?'

'Dunno,' Jack shrugged. Then, he grinned. 'I've heard that Cyprus is very nice at this time of year.'

As David pulled away, he looked in the mirror and saw Jack smiling.

Cyprus? he thought. *Cyprus!* Suddenly, as the car accelerated, he began to rock with laughter.

4

'You're a bloody idiot, Phil! Fancy putting yourself at risk like that? Look what they did to poor Jack. And, he's twice your size.'

'You underestimate me, my dear boy,' Phil laughed. 'I might appear weak and insignificant. But, don't forget, I spent my career preparing to bomb the living daylights out of helpless civilians from thirty thousand feet.'

The two men were sitting in front of the gas fire and both were in good spirits. Phil had been reporting to David on the fruits of his research into MK Developments.

'My grand-daughter tried to help me, to start with. Very clever girl, Becky. She sat me down in front of her computer and we went on to the internet. Wonderful system, isn't it? Anyway, we found the website for Companies House. Unfortunately, although that gave some details about the company, it didn't say who the directors were. However, what it did tell us was the address of their registered office.'

'So, you called round to see them, did you? Just like that.'

'Not immediately. That's where the clever bit comes in,' Phil replied, tapping the side of his nose. 'First, I went over to Mayfield Press. They're on the Business Park on the Stratfield Road. Their main activity is producing business directories. They were always ringing up here at one time, trying to get us to advertise with them. Anyway, I hope you don't mind, but I explained that we were thinking of taking out an advertisement in their next edition.'

'Oh, no!' David groaned. 'Now, they'll keep calling me, asking when we want to place our order.'

'Perhaps. Anyway, the chap I spoke to kindly gave me his business card. A very obliging fellow.'

303

'And, don't tell me,' David laughed, assuming a look of mock horror. 'You used his card when you went to call on MK Developments.'

'I only flashed it about,' Phil explained, with a grin. 'I didn't actually pretend to be anybody I wasn't.'

'I'll believe you! Anyway, go on with the story. I'm enjoying this,' David said.

'Well,' Phil continued. 'I thought I'd better go in mufti. I put on my old raincoat so that I should look as seedy as I could. The people from these firms often seem to look like that, don't they? It was a bit of a search but, eventually, I found their offices, upstairs behind the shopping centre. The girl on the desk would make our Alison look like a candidate for Mensa. I gave her my spiel about them placing an advert in the directory. Not surprisingly, she said I would have to speak to one of the directors.'

'And don't tell me. They are...'

'Precisely. Mr Spiros Makrides and Mr Toby Kelham.'

'So, that's what MK stands for?' David said.

'You would have thought so, wouldn't you?' Phil replied. 'But, in fact, it stands for Makrides Kyprianou. Perhaps, Makrides started the company when he came over from Cyprus, and Kelham came on board afterwards, I don't know.

'Anyway, in keeping with my scruffy appearance, I had quite forgotten any paper, and my pen wouldn't work. So, the dear lady kindly gave me a piece of the company's headed notepaper. Actually, I think I looked so seedy, she just wanted to get me out of the office.'

Phil flourished a sheet of cream paper.

'Exhibit A,' he said. 'Ladies and gentlemen of the jury. You will note that there, along the bottom of this piece of paper are the names of the directors of the company in question. I rest my case.'

'*Brilliant!*' David cried. 'Absolutely bloody brilliant.'

'It was pretty good, wasn't it?' Phil agreed. 'I haven't enjoyed myself so much for a long time.'

'Right,' David said. 'Now, we've got their plan – I went and had it copied on to one sheet this morning – and, thanks to you, we have written proof that Kelham and Makrides are the people behind it.'

'I must say, I can't wait for the meeting.'

'No, nor can I,' David said, getting to his feet. 'Come on, Phil, I'll buy you lunch. You deserve it. Not a word to anybody about this before the meeting, though. Remember, *"Careless Talk Costs Lives!"'*

When David returned to his office after lunch, he had a visitor.

'Well, I must say, Crowley,' the Brigadier began. 'I'm very pleased. It is such good news!'

'Good news, Brigadier?'

'Yes, indeed. Excellent news! Kathryn was so excited when she told Martha and me that you have agreed to be her partner on the charity golf day. I haven't seen her smiling like that for many a year, I can tell you.'

'I'm very pleased, too, Brigadier.'

'I should think so, my boy. I should think so. There is always much rejoicing in heaven for a sinner that repenteth, what?'

'I'm not sure if giving up golf counts as a sin, Brigadier,' David smiled. 'And, I can't promise Kate, or anyone else, that I'll play as well as I once did.'

'Not important, my boy! Not important. You're playing again, that's what matters. Only an active golfer can understand what golf means to someone, inside. Wouldn't you agree, Crowley?'

'Did you come in for anything special, Brigadier? Only, I did want to get some papers ready for the tomorrow's AGM.'

'No. It's just that. Well...'

305

It wasn't like the Brigadier to hesitate, David thought.

'Look here, Crowley,' the Brigadier said. 'It's the AGM I wanted to have a word about.'

'The AGM, Brigadier?'

'Yes. As you know, a number of people have been nominated for the Committee. New people. And, to put it bluntly, Crowley, many of them are, like me, persuaded that the Club will be better off if it accepts Toby Kelham's loan.'

'And, you think they will form a majority of the Committee, Brigadier?'

'Almost certainly, my boy. Almost certainly. The point I'm making is this. If that happens, if the Committee agrees to accept Toby's kind offer, well, then things will begin to return to normal around here.'

'What exactly do you mean by normal, Brigadier?'

'Why, memberships and visitors back under control, of course, dear boy!' the old man replied.

'And, you think that will be in the best interests of the Club, do you, Brigadier?' David asked.

'Of course it will, man! Of course it will. Anyway, when things return to normal around here, I hope we – that is, you and I – can work together for the good of the Club. What do you say, Crowley?'

'Oh, I don't think anything is certain, Brigadier,' said David. 'As I understand it, the voting may go either way. The members will hear both sides of the argument. When they have done so, the present Committee may be re-elected. But, if the result goes the other way, I should obviously have to consider my position.'

'We shall see, Crowley. We shall see,' the Brigadier said. 'I am very confident that sense will prevail.'

'And, so am I, Brigadier. So am I.'

David sometimes thought that these meetings might be shorter if he and the Brigadier said things only once.

The Brigadier stood up and walked to the door. Then, he hesitated.

'There is just one other thing, Crowley. If you and Kathryn are going to play together on the charity golf day, then I should like to challenge you both to a match.'

'You, Brigadier?'

'Yes. That is, Martha and me. Mixed Foursomes. Against you and Kathryn. What do you say?'

'You're on, Brigadier,' David said, smiling. *'You're on!'*

Hole	Name	Yards	Par	Score
17	The Fall	145	3	

1

'I don't think this need take very long, Mr Chairman,' the Brigadier began, getting to his feet.

'Ladies and gentlemen, the case in favour of accepting Toby Kelham's generous offer of a loan is so overwhelming that little discussion is needed.'

Approximately two hundred members had turned up for the Annual General Meeting of the Club and the bar was packed. Even with all the chairs from the restaurant and the offices, there were not enough seats, and people were perched on tables, leaning on radiators and squatting on the floor.

From his place at the top table alongside the retiring Captain, David scanned the audience. The Brigadier had certainly worked hard at getting out his supporters. His confidence in the result – a Committee elected to do his bidding – appeared well founded.

'This loan,' the Brigadier went on, 'will enable the Club to pay off its overdraft at the bank. Freed from the need to trade – such a dreadful word, that – at a profit, the Club will be able to restore the former membership criteria and restrict the number of visitors. Branfield Park will thus return to the conditions that have prevailed for so many years; conditions that served us so well and that made this club unique.'

'It goes without saying that Branfield has always had a very special place in my heart. My father helped create the course and I grew up with it. Perhaps, that is why golf has become such an important part of my life.'

'What is it that is so special about golf, you may ask? Ladies and gentlemen, I will tell you.'

308

'Work hard at it and it will reward you, but only to a degree. For, there will be ups and downs, unexpected setbacks and undeserved strokes of good fortune. And, just when you think you have mastered it, the game will punish you for your arrogance and remind you of your frailty.'

'Now, you may say to me, "but, that is life". And, I will reply to you that golf is life, ladies and gentlemen, golf is life! In my opinion, golf is life in a way that is reflected in no other game or sport.'

'I believe that golf, as we have known it at Branfield Park, encapsulates all the finest qualities of peace and tranquility, sporting challenge, good manners and good companionship. And, only by maintaining the exclusivity of the Club, can we hope to retain those qualities.'

'The new Secretary has lately recruited a large number of additional members to the Club and has also allowed a substantial number of visitors to play on the course. His well-meaning attempts to remedy the effects of earlier financial mismanagement have already had deleterious effects. These changes must be stopped and, if at all possible, reversed if the unique atmosphere at Branfield is not to suffer permanent damage.'

'I urge you therefore to vote on to the Committee those candidates who support the proposal to accept the loan from Toby Kelham.'

The Brigadier sat down to substantial applause. He beamed and modestly raised his hands. He sensed that victory would not be long delayed.

'Thank you, Brigadier,' Giles said. 'Does anyone wish to comment on what Brigadier Tufnell has said?'

A number of hands were raised and Giles pointed to Mark Essam.

'Thank you, Chairman.' Mark Essam moved to the front of the room.

'As a member of this Club, I fully appreciate all those qualities about Branfield that the Brigadier has so rightly praised. This is indeed a very special place and, if accepting the loan on offer could really preserve the Club in its present form, I would certainly be in favour.'

'But, I am also the Club's bank manager, and I must say that I do not see how such an outcome is possible. When your new Secretary arrived, he and I agreed that an increase in income was essential to the Club's survival. That will still be the case if this loan is used to pay off the overdraft at the bank. Otherwise, a further loan will be needed, and so on. If Mr Kelham decides, at some point, that he wants his loan repaid, how will this be achieved? I must tell you now that, if the Club returns to its former, foolish ways, when expenditure greatly exceeded income, it will be no use crying all the way to the bank.'

Essam returned to his seat in an almost frosty silence. A forest of hands rose around him, and Giles motioned Toby Kelham to respond. He drew himself up to his full height and moved centre stage.

'Ladies and gentlemen, Chairman,' Kelham began, with a gracious smile. 'One is, of course, accustomed to the negative sentiments of bank managers.'

A titter ran round the room.

'But, I can assure Mr Essam, and I can guarantee all of you here, that such concerns are quite unfounded. I have, over the years, come to love Branfield and those qualities about it that Brigadier Tufnell so eloquently described. My only motivation in offering this loan is to ensure that those qualities are preserved far into the future. Nothing more; nothing less. Mr Essam's suggestion that the Club will be more vulnerable is really quite unfair. It is, after all, because money is owed to his bank that the fine traditions of Branfield Park are now being compromised. I can promise you all that no such threat will exist if the Club accepts my offer of a loan.'

Kelham smiled as he resumed his seat to applause only slightly less enthusiastic than that which had greeted the Brigadier's speech.

David smiled at Phil.

'Thank you, Toby,' Giles said. 'It seems fairly clear where the feeling of the meeting is leading us. Before I ask David Crowley to speak, does anyone else have anything to add?'

'Yes, Mr Chairman, I should like to say a few words.'

It was Kate.

'Well, ladies and gentlemen,' she began. 'It's been an interesting year as Ladies Captain. Early on, the Committee received a report from the auditors explaining the dreadful state of our finances and, last August, I helped appoint our new Secretary. Since then, I've seen him bring about the most amazing changes in this Club. Whereas before the atmosphere was insular and moribund, now the whole place is buzzing with life.'

'Yes, life! You've heard Henry say that golf is life. Or, at least it is like life. As some of you know, I spend my days working with plants and one thing that has taught me is that life is about growth, fresh air and an input of energy. Without those things, life drains away.'

Kate paused.

'Like it drained away from my husband,' she said, quietly.

'When James died, the members of this club were all so kind and helpful. I've never had the chance to thank you publicly. That is why I am now saddened that people whom I respect and like should be so ready to stifle the growth and energy that David has brought to the Club. I hope you will think carefully before you decide to do so.'

Kate's face was flushed as she sat down. Sporadic clapping broke out but quickly died.

'Thank you, Kate,' Giles said. 'I very much agree with what you have said and I should like to express my

311

appreciation for what David has done over the past months.'

'Point of Order, Mr Chairman!' the Brigadier was clearly annoyed. 'Surely, it is wholly inappropriate for you to express your opinion at this juncture? Is not the chairman required to be neutral in any discussion?'

'Henry,' Giles responded, firmly. 'I shall be Captain of the Club for only another few minutes. If you and the meeting don't like me expressing my opinion, then you will not have long to lump it.'

Giles turned away. 'Does anyone else have anything to add?'

'Yes, I should like to express my support for the Secretary.' Simon Cornwell had some difficulty getting to his feet, and he held on to his chair as he turned to address the gathering. In his other hand he held the meeting agenda and the papers shook slightly as he spoke.

'I was one of those, with Kate, with Giles and the Brigadier who interviewed our new Secretary last year,' Simon went on. 'I recognised then that he was a man of considerable ability who had the knowledge and skills we needed, and still need, at Branfield Park. But, I sensed, too, that David had been through some rather difficult times and that he needed a new challenge in his life.'

'I hope David won't mind when I say that, in some ways, they were alike, he and Branfield. Both had enormous merits but both had rather lost their way. And, both needed a new direction, if they were to thrive.'

Simon looked across at David who returned his smile.

'I had no idea,' the old doctor went on, 'what a transformation would occur when we brought the two together. Over the past nine months, David has worked enormously hard for this Club. He has reformed our finances and completely revolutionised the atmosphere in the clubhouse and on the course.'

'If I may use a golfing analogy, he has been the driver in the Club's golf bag. With his energy and skill, he has driven us as far as he could down the fairway. And, here we sit, in an excellent position now to move forward. I am confident that, if we give him our support, David will be the right club to take us further down the course.'

'What sensible golfer, therefore, standing in the middle of the fairway and with the right club in his hand, would turn round and hit his ball back towards the tee, towards uncertainty and danger?'

Simon turned towards Kelham and the Brigadier.

'And yet, that is just what Henry and Toby and their chums want us to do. As sensible golfers, I am sure you will choose the sensible course.'

As Simon resumed his seat to quiet applause, David noticed a number of people turn to one another, smile and nod.

The Brigadier raised his hand.

'You've already had your opportunity to address the meeting, Henry,' Giles pointed out, and he turned towards the audience.

But the Brigadier was not about to be constrained by such procedural niceties. Getting quickly to his feet, he raised his voice to command the attention to which, over the years, he had become accustomed.

'Ladies and gentlemen!' he began. 'Dr Cornwell speaks most poetically, does he not? However, when he compares the Secretary to the driver, surely he misses the point? Branfield Park is a members' club and it is for the members to decide how they wish to play the course; in which direction they will aim their Club. It is not the Secretary's role to be the biggest club in the bag, driving us forward. He is merely a paid employee and it is his job it is to take the members where they wish to go, not where he decides to lead them.'

'Here, here!' Kelham barked.

However, Simon Cornwell's words had had an impact on the mood of the meeting and there was no repeat of the earlier standing ovation. The Brigadier resumed his seat in almost complete silence.

'I think we've exhausted the golfing analogy, now,' Giles said, determined to regain control. 'If there are no new points that people wish to raise, I shall ask David to give us his views.'

Toby Kelham raised his hand.

'Surely, Chairman, as Brigadier Tufnell has just pointed out, the Secretary is an employee of the Club? All we need from him is information. We're all aware of his views. Is it not the views of the members that should be heard here?'

'Quite right!' the Brigadier murmured, and one or two others muttered assent.

They're trying to stifle me! David thought.

'You're absolutely right, Toby. David is an employee. We employed him to manage our finances. As far as I can see, and in the opinion of our bank manager, he has done that very well indeed. It would therefore be negligent of us not to ask his views on the question of your proposed loan to the Club'

He motioned to David.

2

'Thank you, Chairman,' David smiled as he stood up. 'Actually, it is information rather than my views that I am going to give you this afternoon. I trust that, when I've finished, Mr Kelham will be satisfied.'

David went on to explain the state in which he had found the Club's finances, the steps he had taken to improve the cash flow and financial management. He concluded with a summary of the present position and an optimistic forecast for the coming year.

'Very impressive,' Kelham interrupted, acidly. 'However, if the members vote to accept my loan, as I am confident they will, none of what you have told us will be at all relevant.'

'Perhaps not,' David said, turning to the audience. 'However, it may be that, when you've heard what I have to say, some of you will feel differently about taking Mr Kelham's money.'

'Objection, Mr Chairman!' Kelham interrupted, again. 'The damned feller's got no right...'

'Oh, do be quiet, Toby!' Giles retorted. 'Carry on, please, David.'

'Before I continue,' David said. 'I should like to ask Mr Kelham one or two questions regarding his loan.'

Kelham looked surprised and uneasy.

'Mr Kelham, could you tell us again what it was that motivated you to offer this money to the Club?'

Kelham looked exasperated.

'Really, Mr Chairman. This is ridiculous...'

'Bear with us, Toby,' Giles replied. 'David simply wishes to clarify matters for the members.'

'Oh, very well,' Kelham sighed. 'As I have already made perfectly clear, I offered the loan so that the Club should be freed from the constraints imposed by the bank. Satisfying the bank manager's demand that the Club increase its income to meet expenditure has resulted in all these new members and visitors. In short, I offered the loan, sir, so that we could reverse the damaging effects of your management!'

Kelham was becoming angry, but David remained calm.

'So, Mr Kelham, you are willing to lend the Club one hundred and seventy five thousand pounds at commercial rates, is that correct?'

Kelham nodded.

'The interest on such a loan will amount to about fourteen thousand pounds a year, is that correct?'

'If you say so,' Kelham replied. 'Really, Mr Chairman, is all this necessary?'

'So,' David turned again to the meeting. 'The Club already makes a loss of about forty thousand pounds a year. To that, we must add the interest on your loan. Let's say, for convenience, that by next year we have run up another fifty thousand pounds of debt. What would happen then, Mr Kelham?'

'Well, I presume I should make a further loan.' The landowner was beginning to look distinctly unhappy at David's line of questioning.

'A further loan, Mr Kelham? Are you telling us that you are willing to go on bailing the Club out far into the future?'

'Mr Chairman!' the Brigadier boomed. 'This is quite monstrous! The Secretary is behaving as if this were a court of law and Mr Kelham were in the dock. I insist that you end this cross-examination, immediately.'

'Objection over-ruled, Henry! Now, please sit down and be quiet.'

The Brigadier had never before been spoken to in this manner and certainly not in front of a general meeting of the Club. He became quite puce and opened his mouth to speak. Before he could utter a sound, however, David went on.

'So, the Club becomes more and more indebted to one of its own members, one of the largest landowners in the area. That's a very generous commitment for you to take on, Mr Kelham?' David smiled.

'As I have said, I am a very wealthy man.' Kelham smiled benignly at the audience. 'Ladies and gentlemen, I have been very fortunate and I wish to share some of my good fortune with others, before it is too late...'

'If it is not impertinent, Mr Kelham, how did you become such a wealthy man?'

'It is impertinent, sir. Damned impertinent!'

316

'I'm sorry,' David looked abashed. 'However, can we assume that it was not by lending money to insolvent companies?'

'Of course not!' Kelham was becoming angry again. 'But, this is quite a different matter. My purpose here is not to make money out of the Club but to help it in its hour of need.'

'A very commendable motive, if I may say so,' David smiled and Kelham relaxed.

'Other than a return to the old restrictions on members and visitors, the only condition you have attached to your offer is that the loan is repayable on demand, is that correct, Mr Kelham?'

'That is correct. I did not wish to impose any unnecessary impediments to the acceptance of my offer. It is perfectly normal business practice to require that a loan be repaid on demand.'

'But, you would accept that, were you to demand that the Club repay the loan, it would have no way of doing so?'

'That is quite irrelevant. As I have said, my intention is to relieve the Club's debt problems, not to add to them,' Kelham smiled modestly at the front row.

'So, to sum up, Mr Kelham,' David said. 'You are willing to make this very substantial loan to the Club, and the only conditions are that the Brigadier here controls the intake and that the loan is repayable upon demand? That is indeed a very generous gesture.'

'*Hallelujah!*' the Brigadier exhaled. 'Mr Chairman, now that the Secretary has at last recognised what has been clear to everyone else in the room for some time, may we proceed with the election of a new Committee?'

David ignored the old soldier.

'A very generous offer, indeed, Mr Kelham,' he went on. 'And, do we have your word that your only intention in making this offer is to help preserve the Club in its present form?'

317

'Of course you do! Mr Chairman, I am becoming very tired of all this. I must say, I did not expect such a grudging reaction to my generosity…'

David interrupted the landowner and raised his voice to address the audience.

'Ladies and gentlemen, if I could have your attention for a little longer!'

He stood up and unfolded The Drawing, now enlarged to A1 size, and turning, he pinned it up on the notice board behind the platform.

'A short while ago, this drawing came into my possession,' David explained.

All around the room, heads craned to read the plan and puzzled looks were exchanged.

'I hope you can all see,' David went on. 'That this drawing shows Branfield Park Golf Club and the land immediately surrounding it.'

'If you look closely, you will see that, in the woods all around the course,' David pointed. 'Here, here and here, and over here, proposed houses are shown. Large, five and six bedroom houses with double garages, it would appear from the drawing.'

The room was silent now as everyone tried to make out what was on the drawing.

'Each house is linked to a perimeter road that runs right round the course, at some points on land owned by the Club, but mostly over land belonging to Browndean Farm Estate, which is, of course, owned by Mr Toby Kelham.'

A gasp went round the room.

'Where the hell did you get that drawing?' Kelham demanded. 'Mr Chairman, the Secretary is in possession of private property. That drawing contains confidential, commercially-sensitive information. I really must object…'

'Be quiet, Toby,' Giles snapped. 'Where David obtained the drawing from is surely less important than what is on it? David, continue, please.'

'What is envisaged here is a private estate of houses enclosing its own exclusive golf course. Something along the lines of Wentworth Estate, although on a smaller scale. You will note that the drawing also proposes a considerable enlargement of the Clubhouse and the construction of a hotel.'

'This is extraordinary,' the Brigadier exclaimed, staring at the drawing. 'Quite extraordinary!'

'I'm sure you will agree,' David said, 'that such proposals have little to do with preserving the existing character of the Club. Indeed, were they to receive planning permission and be carried through, these developments would change the face of Branfield Park beyond recognition.'

'But, who is behind these plans?' the Brigadier demanded.

'The plans include substantial development on Mr Kelham's land. It is difficult to imagine that he is unaware of what is on the drawing. In fact, I suspect he is more than just aware. I believe that it is he who is behind the proposals.'

'That is a very serious allegation, sir!' Kelham stood up and turned to the audience. 'Ladies and gentlemen, believe me. I have only the best interests of the Club at heart...'

'You will see that here,' David continued, raising his voice above that of the landowner. 'In the corner, the drawing is stamped "MK DEVELOPMENTS". Some excellent detective work by Phil Oakley has revealed that MK Developments is a local property company...'

David held up the sheet of cream headed notepaper.

'...And that that company has only two directors – Mr Toby Kelham and Mr Spiros Makrides.'

A hubbub began and grew steadily louder. David had to raise his voice even more in order to be heard.

'I believe that Mr Kelham and Mr Makrides have been working together to gain control of Branfield Park Golf

Club with the intention of building a large number of very expensive houses which, no doubt, would be sold at a considerable profit.'

'This is ridiculous, Chairman!' Kelham cried. 'How long are you going to let this employee make allegations about a member of the Committee? How could we conspire to take over the Club, as the Secretary suggests?'

'By strongly supporting Brigadier Tufnell in his attempts to keep out visitors and new members,' David went on, almost shouting, now. 'Mr Kelham knows full well that that strategy will lead the Club into financial disaster.'

David turned to the members.

'Ladies and gentlemen, so far, I have given you information. Now, for my views. The loan you are about to accept from Toby Kelham will mean the end of this Club. The changes I have brought in to keep the bank manager happy may be unpalatable. However, they are nothing compared with the development envisaged in this plan.'

'If you accept his loan, Mr Kelham will, at his convenience, demand that it be repaid. The Club will be unable to pay and will be forced into receivership. MK Developments will then seek to buy the land and begin their development. When the Club goes under, all existing memberships will cease. I should be surprised if their plans include re-admitting many of you to what will be an even more exclusive set-up.'

At this, angry murmuring began to roll around the assembled members.

'This is disgraceful!' roared the Brigadier over the din. 'Absolutely disgraceful! Toby, how could you even think of such a plan? Why, it would destroy the Club!'

'Oh, shut up, Henry!' Kelham sneered. 'You silly old fool! Don't you see, the Secretary is right. It's not me but you and your stupid ideas that have destroyed the Club. You, with your ludicrous military title! I happen to know that the nearest you ever got to any fighting was watching it

320

on Pathe News – you're pathetic! It's your elitist delusions that have kept people out of this Club. And, as a result, there wasn't enough money to pay the bills. That's what's done the damage! All we did was to spot a failing business and come up with proposals to rescue it.'

Kelham turned to Makrides.

'Come on, Spiros, bring that drawing and let's get out of here.'

Makrides got to his feet and moved towards David. As he did so, Kate stepped forward and barred his way.

'Get out of my way, you silly bitch!' Makrides shouted, and he pushed her roughly to the ground.

Stepping over Kate, Makrides attempted to grab the drawing. Before he could do so, however, the Brigadier reached behind him and pulled "The Captain's Driver" from its brackets on the wall. This old club, in fact an ancient brassie had, for many years, resided above the mantelpiece. Originally, new captains of the Club had used it to mark their inauguration by driving a ball down the first fairway, but it had not been used in anger for years. Now, it had all the force of the Brigadier's rage as, holding it near its head, he brought the shaft down on Makrides' arm.

'*You motherfucking bastard!*' Makrides shouted. He seized hold of the club and, with his other hand, pushed the Brigadier backwards. The old man fell heavily against the wall.

David stepped forward to help Kate and Makrides raised his fist.

'I think you'd better leave, don't you, Mr Makrides?' David said calmly, as he put his arm around Kate's shoulders.

'Come on, Spiros. Let's get out of this place!' Kelham shouted.

Makrides hesitated. For a moment, he looked David directly in the eye. Then, he took hold of the old club in both hands and snapped its ancient hickory shaft over his knee. The audience let out a collective gasp.

'Is a stupid fucking game, anyway,' Makrides sneered. He threw down the pieces of the club and turned away.

When the scuffle began, everyone in the room had stood up.

Now, like the waters of the Red Sea, the congregation parted to allow the co-conspirators to leave. In total silence, the two men ran a gauntlet of staring eyes and silent glares as they made their way to the door.

3

'A visitor for you, Henry, dear.'

The Brigadier sat in his armchair by the fire. He didn't look up. He did not even acknowledge his wife's announcement.

'Sit down, David, and I'll bring some tea.'

Martha Tufnell was indeed a warm and handsome woman. She plumped up the cushions behind her husband's head before departing for the kitchen.

David took a seat opposite the old man. And, he did look an old man. David hadn't previously thought of the Brigadier as old. Suddenly, though, he had aged and he was visibly more elderly than he had seemed only a week or so earlier.

'Good morning, Brigadier!' David offered his hand but the Brigadier made no move to shake it. Indeed, he seemed quite unaware of David or his hand.

'It's good to see you up and about,' David said, cheerily. Still, there was no response.

After the ferment at the Annual General Meeting, the Brigadier had seemed elated. He had talked excitedly to anyone who would listen about the events of the afternoon.

322

Later, that evening, however, he had suddenly collapsed into melancholy. The doctor had been called, but he was at a loss.

'These episodes can last for days or weeks,' he had assured Martha. 'But, they do eventually pass.'

Martha knew that the young doctor had no idea what he was talking about, but she decided not to hurt his feelings.

And so, the Brigadier had taken to his bed. He appeared quite ready to lie there forever, but his devoted wife would not permit it. With great patience, and no small expenditure of energy, she hauled him from his bed each morning, dressed him and guided him downstairs to the fireside. And, there he remained, staring but unseeing.

'Preparations for the charity golf day are well underway,' David went on. 'I must say, I'm really looking forward to our match.'

Martha Tufnell brought a tray of tea. There were three cups. Even though she knew her husband would not partake, she poured him a cup and placed it at his right hand.

'Have you been practising, David?' she asked.

'Yes, I have,' David admitted. 'I'm very rusty. I don't want to make a fool of myself, certainly not in front of Kate.'

'I'm sure Kate isn't bothered how well you play golf,' the Brigadier's wife said, with a kind smile.

David blushed.

'It's not just that,' he smiled. 'I need to be at my best to take on the Brigadier here.'

Then, turning to the Brigadier, David explained.

'We have forty teams, now, Brigadier. The day should raise quite a sum. And, there'll be a raffle. We've had some excellent prizes. I'm beginning to wish I hadn't invented that rule about the Secretary not being allowed to buy tickets.'

David looked at Martha Tufnell and she smiled in gratitude.

'It was kind of you to come,' she said. 'Please don't feel you have to stay for very long.'

After a while, David did feel he had exhausted all the openings he could think of. None had elicited any response from the Brigadier and he rose to go.

'David's going now, dear,' Martha said. 'Say goodbye.'

No response.

David picked up his briefcase, walked to the door and opened it.

Just as he did so, he heard a quiet voice.

'Bloody fool.'

David turned and looked at the Brigadier.

'Sorry, Brigadier. Did you say something?'

'Bloody fool. *Been a bloody old fool!*'

Quietly, David returned to the fireside and sat down opposite the old soldier. Martha Tufnell held her breath.

'Who's been a bloody fool, Brigadier?' David thought that perhaps Henry Tufnell was accusing him of some misdemeanour. That, at least, would suggest a return to normality.

'I have. Been an absolute bloody fool.'

'Why do you think that, Brigadier?'

'Been a bloody fool. Been a bloody fool for years.'

Steady on now, Brigadier, David thought. Confession may be good for the soul, but let's not overdo things!

'In what way have you been a fool?' David asked.

'Stubborn old fool. Resisted change at every turn. Look where it got me. Nearly destroyed the Club. Been a bloody silly fool!'

'That's all in the past, now, Brigadier,' David said, quietly. Now that he had started, he was anxious to keep the old boy talking.

'So am I, Crowley. So am I. I was living in the past. And, that's where I belong. Silly bloody old fool!'

'Come now, Brigadier. You're punishing yourself too much. You weren't responsible for what Kelham and Makrides were trying to do.'

'But, Kelham was right, don't you see.'

The Brigadier leaned forward, anxious to get his point across.

'By keeping people out, I only made the Club's problems worse. That's why we were in the mess we were in. And, that's why Kelham and that spiv feller were able to try and take over. I kept everybody else out and then I let in a damned Trojan Horse.'

'But, as I say, that's all over, now, Brigadier. We've got to get you out of that chair and back on to the golf course.'

'No, that's all in the past, now, Crowley. I've failed the Club, don't you see? No place for me there, any more. No. I shan't play again.'

David was becoming alarmed. He'd heard of people giving up, turning their faces to the wall and just dying. But, he hadn't come across people giving up and refusing to play golf. That was taking things to extremes, he thought.

Then, David realised, that was just what he had done. He leaned forward and took the old man's hand.

'Listen, Brigadier. I thought like that myself after my wife died. I felt I'd let her down and that led me to pack up playing golf. Different people tried to persuade me to start again. You were one of them. Kate, er, Kathryn was another. In the end, I realised that, even if I had been in the wrong – and I'm no longer even sure about that – my not playing wouldn't put anything right. The only person I was hurting was myself.'

'But, don't you see what an idiot I've been?'

'Maybe you have, Brigadier. But, don't punish yourself for it.'

David got up and went to the door.

'It took me over three years to realise I was wrong, Brigadier. Don't let it take that long with you.'

When David had gone, the Brigadier sat for a while staring at the floor. Then, he turned to his wife.

'This tea's cold, dear. Do you think I might have another cup?'

When Martha returned with the tray a few minutes later, she was feeling more buoyant than she had for some time.

'This must be a special day, dear. You've another visitor. Come in Mr McGrath.'

The Brigadier looked up at Jimmy.

'Morning Brigadier!' Jimmy said, brightly. 'I was sorry to hear you haven't been well.'

Jimmy sat down opposite the Brigadier.

'Everybody's been missing you at the Club these past couple of weeks, Brigadier. I said I'd come and find out when you're going to play again.'

'Oh, I don't know, Mr McGrath. It's kind of you to inquire, but I think my playing days are probably over. After all that's happened.'

'After what happened, Brigadier?'

'Well, you know. I was the one who caused the Club's problems with my stupid restrictions. Then, I supported those characters because I thought they'd help me keep the Club the way I wanted it. And, all the time they were out to destroy it. I don't deserve to play again, not at Branfield.'

'Stuff and nonsense, man!' Jimmy exclaimed. 'You were only doing what you thought was right, Brigadier. We've all done that at some time in our lives, only to discover we were completely wrong. Isn't that true, Mrs Tufnell?'

Martha smiled warmly at Jimmy.

'Yes, of course.'

'There you are, Brigadier. You're outvoted, two to one, so you must be mistaken!'

The Brigadier looked puzzled then, slowly, he began to smile.

326

'Would you care for a drink, Mr McGrath?'

Jimmy looked hesitant.

'I've a drink here, Brigadier,' he said, indicating his teacup.

'*Not tea, man!* A proper drink. Martha, bring in the whisky, would you, dear? Mr McGrath, you do drink whisky, I believe?'

'Aye. I'm not known as James the thirst of Scotland for nothing, Brigadier!'

'Splendid!' the Brigadier exclaimed, and he took the bottle and poured out two generous measures.

'Here's to you, Jimmy,' the Brigadier said, raising his glass

'And, here's to you, Brigadier.'

'Ah,' the Brigadier said. 'I've been thinking about that. Kelham was right when he said that my stupidity had brought the Club to the brink of ruin.'

'That's all in the past now, Brigadier,' Jimmy said.

'And, he was right, too,' the Brigadier continued, 'when he made fun of me for using my military rank. It is, after all, more than thirty years since I served in the army. I think perhaps it's time I stopped asking people to call me Brigadier, don't you, Jimmy?'

'Aye, I do, Henry,' Jimmy said. 'So, when are we going to have that game?'

Out on the driving range, David was on his fourth basket of practice balls and he was beginning to feel tired. It had been a long day but he nevertheless felt obliged to practice. He had a new titanium driver and he wanted to get his swing back into shape. The Charity Golf Day was less than a week away and, now that the Brigadier was back in action, David felt an urgent need to polish up his game.

'Can't let the old boy beat me,' David muttered to himself as he adjusted his grip slightly. The plane of his swing was still too flat, but he was getting nearer to his old action. Moreover, he was getting the old taste back.

But, it wasn't just the Brigadier who was on his mind. David was excited that Kate would be his partner on the day. Now that his future at the Club was more settled, David's thoughts were turning increasingly towards Kate. They had been meeting regularly for lunch and for coffee, but he'd hesitated about asking her out. He sensed that she too was wary of where their relationship might lead.

The charity golf day would decide more than who wins a golf match, David determined.

Riot Puts Future of Nightclub under Cloud

By Sam Jones, *The Herald's* Chief Crime Reporter

A mass invasion of the Crystal Rooms on Saturday night by local youths has put the future of the town's favourite night-spot in doubt.

Police say that, at about 11.30pm on Saturday evening, around one hundred young men arrived at the Club in Bank Street. The youths charged the main entrance, overwhelming the door-keepers.

Smashed

Once inside, the mob embarked on an orgy of destruction. Chairs, tables, lighting and disco equipment were all destroyed. One witness, who did not wish to be named, said, 'It was terrifying. Everything that could be smashed, was smashed.'

While most witnesses attributed the trouble to excess alcohol, some onlookers suggested that it was more organised. 'They went upstairs and broke the water pipes,' said one customer. 'The whole place was flooded before anybody could do anything. All the decoration and carpets are ruined.'

Another eyewitness said that the young men concerned were from the Oakmount district of the town. 'A lot of them are Oakmount School kids and some are members of Oakmount Rugby Club,' she alleged.

The crowd dispersed before police arrived. There have been a number of complaints to police that the nightclub's doormen used excessive force in ejecting the youths. Several young men later visited the Mayflower Hospital A&E Department with cuts and severe bruising.

Assault

A police spokeswoman said that the Club would not be able to re-open for some time because of the damage. She added that several complaints against the Club's doormen had been received, alleging assault.

'When police arrived at the Club, they found various substances and these are being analysed. In view of this and the allegations of assault, we shall be asking magistrates to suspend the Club's license.'

The *Crystal Rooms Nightclub* is owned by Mr Spiros Makrides. He was not available for comment. A barman at the club said that Mr Makrides is believed to be in Cyprus.

Hole	Name	Yards	Par	Score
18	Almost There	**392**	**4**	

1

'I wouldn't dare eat a breakfast like this every day,' Giles said, holding his waist and laughing. 'No wonder John Hall is so huge!'

'Nor me,' David agreed. 'But, I thought we could make an exception today.'

As it was the charity golf day, David and Giles had agreed to meet early for bacon and eggs.

And, the rest! Mrs Hall had augmented their order and the two men had also ploughed their way through sausages, mushrooms, tomatoes and fried potatoes. Not, that either was complaining

'We both have a big day ahead of us, so I think we're entitled to indulge a bit,' Giles said. 'I must say, David, I'm really looking forward to today. Our charity days have always been such low-key affairs in the past. The place has been buzzing all week and I gather that twice as many people as usual have formed teams. Your match with the Brigadier is the talking point of the Club.'

'Yes, I must admit I'm looking forward to it myself, especially as I'll be playing with Kate. Mind you, I can't say I'm sorry the old boy's not at his best. I gather he could be pretty formidable on his day.'

'Yes he was. But, he hasn't been he same since Jimmy McGrath defeated him in the winter league. And, then there was the AGM fracas, of course. Mind you, I think he's taking today pretty seriously. I've seen him on the driving range several times this week.'

'Which, suggests that you are too,' David grinned. 'Otherwise, how would you just happen to have seen him?'

'It's a fair cop!' Giles laughed. 'But, my practice was strictly in the interests of the Club. You forget, I have to hit the first drive of the day. We wouldn't want everybody to be embarrassed if I fluffed it, would we?'

'Certainly not,' David mocked. 'Such devotion to duty is truly admirable.'

'Damn,' Giles said, smiling. 'Now that I've reminded myself about hitting the opening drive, I'm getting anxious again. If you'll excuse me, David, I'll just go and hit a few more practice balls.'

The charity golf day at Branfield was intended to mark the start of the new golfing year. Normally, the new captain played host. However, following the trouble at the AGM, after which the meeting was suspended, Giles had been asked to remain at the helm until a new captain could be chosen.

The pair walked together to the professional's shop where Giles bought a couple of driving range tokens.

'Alison here has done a great job of keeping the shop going while Jack's been away,' David said.

Alison beamed. Receiving praise was not something at which she'd had much practice.

'Thanks, Mr Crowley. Mind you, I won't half be glad when he gets back!'

'I think we all will, Alison,' Giles smiled.

David walked over to the equipment sheds where he found Bob and three of his boys sitting on a bench in the corner, drinking tea.

'The course is looking great, Bob. The damage is hardly visible, now.'

'Thanks, David,' Bob said. 'The boys have worked very hard these past few weeks. They're all looking forward to having a game themselves, I think.'

None of the young greenkeepers had ever been allowed to play on the golf course. Bob himself had been favoured occasionally by the Brigadier, but even that had not happened for some time. In recognition of their work, therefore, David had suggested and the Committee had agreed that, on the Sunday following the charity golf day, the greenkeepers and their families would have free use of the course.

The course was indeed looking great, David reflected, as he approached the first tee. There, inside a small marquee, he found Jimmy McGrath and Mike Newman, seated behind a trestle table. Mike and Jimmy were but two of a small army of volunteers who had given up their time. Elsewhere, around the course, others would carry out a range of unseen but important functions.

'All ready, boys?' he asked. David had never quite stopped speaking like a headmaster.

'Aye, we're ready, David,' Jimmy replied. He and Mike were there to hand out scorecards to the teams. Later, they would man the scoreboard in the bar and record the results as the teams returned. In theory, the result was unimportant as the aim of the day was to raise as much money as possible for charity. However, to a golfer, the result is always relevant and the scoreboard would become the subject of much anxious attention towards the end of the day.

David returned to his office to find Phil Oakley putting golf balls across the carpet.

'That won't do you much good,' David laughed.

'No, I know,' Phil agreed. 'None of the greens out there are anywhere near as flat as this. But it does help steady the nerves.'

The *Herald* advertisement had born fruit and Phil's stint as part-time clerical assistant had come to an end the previous Friday. However, he would, as he said, still be coming in a great deal. In recognition of his services to the Club, his life membership had now been confirmed.

'So, if there's anything I can do to help, I won't be far away,' Phil smiled.

'Thanks,' David said. 'I'll remember that, the next time we need a private investigator.'

Their conversation was interrupted by a knock on the door. Mark Essam, dressed all in red with matching trousers and jumper, smiled self-consciously as he came in.

'Good Lord!' Phil exclaimed. 'This must be the only time you'll ever see a bank manager in the red.'

He left to continue his putting.

'Well, David, I wanted to be the one to tell you. The bank has agreed to extend the Club's overdraft, as you requested. There are one or two conditions but, generally, the people at area office are pretty impressed with the way you've turned this place around.'

'What sort of conditions?' David asked, warily.

'Oh, nothing much,' Mark grinned. 'There was a slight suggestion that a few special memberships – you know, half price for the Club's bank manager, that sort of thing – might help them make up their minds.'

'Get away,' David laughed. 'That's how we got into this mess in the first place!'

The two men walked out to the first tee where a small crowd was gathering to support the Captain as he drove off. Some of those watching had several hours to wait before their tee-off times and many of their opening drives would, therefore, be alcohol-assisted.

'On the tee,' Jimmy announced, over the loudspeaker. 'The retiring Captain, Giles Southern!'

Giles addressed the ball and swept it smoothly, about two hundred yards down the fairway. All the money invested in baskets of practice balls had paid off and, smiling with relief, he went over to join his wife.

'On the tee, another auld Scotsman, and the sports editor of *The Herald* newspaper, Mr Iverach McKay!'

McKay had somehow convinced his editor that it was perfectly possible to cover the event for the newspaper and, at the same time, play in it. He walked on to the tee, took

333

out his driver and swept his ball away. It came to rest about ten yards beyond Giles' ball.

A few people clapped and McKay, too, looked relieved. He smiled at his wife, Flora, and the two couples set off together down the first fairway.

As he watched them go, David felt a touch on his sleeve. He turned to find Kate smiling up at him. Her smile was infectious and David thought how attractive she looked in her cream shorts, white shirt and navy jumper. It won't be easy, he thought, to concentrate on beating the Brigadier today.

'Kate, you look marvellous!'

He kissed her on the cheek and she hugged him warmly.

'I'm so looking forward to today,' Kate said in his ear.

Then, she stood back and looked him up and down. David was wearing his all-black outfit.

"You look just like Gary Player, Dad," Ben had said, when he'd worn it for their game the previous week.

"What do you mean, the matching black ensemble?"

"No, because you look as if you're old enough to play for the seniors!" his son had said, laughing.

David had enjoyed beating the boy that day.

'This is the first time I've seen you looking like a proper golfer,' Kate smiled. 'Mm, pretty impressive!'

'You wait till I actually play,' David laughed. 'Then, you'll be impressed!'

David and Kate watched the next match tee off and then walked together towards the clubhouse. The area was crowded with golfers and well-wishers preparing for the day. They stopped here and there to talk with some or to share a joke with others.

'This is what a golf club should be like,' Kate said. 'Not that stuffy old place you inherited.'

'Yes, it is great isn't it,' David agreed.

'It is, and you're the one who's made it great.' Kate turned to him. 'Oh, David, I'm so glad you came along.'

334

Before David could reply, the nearby crowd parted and there stood the Brigadier, tall and impressive with both hands resting on his driver like a Saxon king with his sword.

'Ah, David!' the Brigadier cried. 'Good to see you. Good morning, Kathryn,' he added, inclining his head slightly.

'Ready to do battle, Brigadier?' David asked.

'I can't wait,' the Brigadier replied.

'He hasn't slept a wink, thinking about it,' Martha said, smiling as she came up to them.

'Well, that should give us a chance,' David replied. 'With a bit of luck, he'll nod off before we're half way round.'

'No chance of that, my boy. I'm far too excited. There's nothing I like more than winning a close match.'

'Oh, Henry,' Kate said, hugging his arm. 'You're like a little boy. David doesn't mind who wins, do you, David?'

'Well, I wouldn't go quite that far,' David grinned. 'Actually, I'm pretty keyed up for it myself.'

'Honestly, you men!' Martha laughed. 'I can see we'll have to keep them from each other's throats, today, Kate.'

'David looked at his watch. 'We're off in about forty minutes, aren't we. So, if you'll excuse me, I'll just have a little walk round, see that everything is all right. Then, we'll let battle commence.'

2

The matches on Branfield Park charity golf days were always mixed foursomes, each team comprising a man and a woman, sharing one ball. Kate especially liked this format because she and David would spend the match working closely together.

David and the Brigadier elected to drive off on the odd holes; one, three, five and seven, and so on. Kate and

Martha would tee off on the even holes. The ladies had the advantage of teeing off from the ladies' tees, which could be level with the men's tee, or anything up to fifty yards further forward. Once they had teed off, players on each side would hit the ball alternately until it was in the hole.

'On the tee, Henry Tufnell!' Jimmy announced.

Like most people in the Club, David had yet to feel comfortable using the Brigadier's first name. He smiled at the announcer. Without Jimmy's intervention, the old soldier would still be 'the Brigadier'. And, probably, he wouldn't be here today.

Henry Tufnell teed up his ball, swung smoothly and swept it about two hundred and thirty yards down the first fairway.

He reached down and picked up his tee. As he walked past David, he smiled as if to say, 'Match that, laddie.'

David felt rather nervous as he lined up his shot. Most of his practice had been aimed at re-establishing a smooth rhythm and he tried to focus on that now.

He looked up and caught Kate's eye and she smiled at him. Then, he swung his driver and sent the ball soaring down the left side of the fairway. The ball came to rest five yards from the Brigadier's.

'Game on, Henry,' David said.

'Game on, dear boy. Game on!'

The two couples walked together down the fairway. To begin with, the Brigadier strode ahead in his usual manner. Until, that is, Martha called to him.

'Henry, dear. We're playing with David and Kate, today. Do you think you might walk with us.'

The Brigadier immediately slowed up.

How does she do that? David thought. And, he watched as his wife's kindly handling transformed the old Brigadier, often feared and sometimes disliked around the Club, into charming old Henry.

336

Martha hit her ball into the green with a swing as smooth as silk. Kate followed suit with an equally impressive rhythm. Both had clearly been well coached, David thought. Women may not hit the ball as far, he reflected, but they can be difficult to beat because, unlike men, who strive for distance, members of the fairer sex are usually content with accuracy.

Two putts each side and the hole was halved.

But, on the second, Kate sliced her drive to the right and, at the fourth, she put her ball in the stream. Martha and her husband went two up.

'I'm so sorry, David!' Kate said, as they walked up the long path through the trees towards the fifth tee. 'I'm not playing very well, am I?'

The Brigadier and Martha had turned the bend a little way ahead. David put down his bag and stopped.

'Listen, Kate. Stop apologising. You're doing fine, really! But, even if you weren't playing well, it wouldn't matter to me. I am just so pleased to be out here on this beautiful course, playing golf with you as my partner.'

Kate let go of her trolley and gave David a hug.

'That's exactly how I feel, too,' she said, quietly.

She began to pull her trolley again, then she stopped and grinned.

'So, let's get up there and give these two a proper match, shall we?'

At the fifth hole, Martha sliced her approach shot into the new bunker and, ironically, her husband was unable to extricate himself from the very trap he had set for others.

The old soldier and his wife were still one hole up at the turn where, alongside the tenth tee, Jimmy and Mike were waiting with crates of beer and soft drinks.

'Perhaps, I'd better not offer you a drink, Henry,' Jimmy grinned. 'After what happened in the winter league?'

337

'Another world, Jimmy,' the Brigadier replied, helping himself to a bottle of *Black Label*. 'That was quite another world.'

Another world, maybe, but the lager, nevertheless, found its mark. After his wife had set him up with an excellent drive, Henry Tufnell overhit his approach to the tenth and his ball was lost in the woods.

The match was now all square.

'David's very nice, isn't he?' Martha said as she and Kate walked together down the winding path towards the eleventh tee.

'Very,' Kate said, and she gave the older woman a warm smile.

'Kathryn's a damn fine woman, y'know, David,' the Brigadier said quietly as he and David walked the same path, some fifty yards behind their partners.

'I know, Henry,' David said, and he too smiled.

He had more to smile about a few moments later when his tee shot to the eleventh hit the front edge of the green and rolled up to three feet from the flag.

In reply, the Brigadier pushed his ball to the right, leaving his wife an almost impossible shot. They took a four, while David and Kate got their two and were now one up.

As Kate prepared to drive from the fourteenth tee, David stopped her.

'Old McKay suggested that this hole could be played by driving to the right of the lake. It's a shorter route although more risky. I would have to hit my approach to the green over the water.'

'You want me to drive over on to the fifteenth fairway?' Kate asked.

'What do you think?' David asked.

Kate smiled up at him.

'We have nothing to lose but our balls, David!'

338

Her smooth, graceful swing sent the ball arcing out away from the fairway and it came to rest a few yards from the water, only a hundred and fifty yards from the green. Between ball and flag, however, lay the lake.

Martha took her husband's advice, played safe and drove down the middle of the fairway. From where her ball landed, the Brigadier hit a majestic four iron into the middle of the green. He looked across the water to where David was standing. He might be out of earshot, but his triumphant expression was clear.

Now, David was under pressure. He took out an eight iron; felt a slight breeze in his face and changed to a seven. He addressed the ball, but then had more second thoughts and changed back to an eight iron.

His indecision proved fatal. The ball was well struck but it found the water a few yards short of the far shore.

'Damn!' David said, looking dejected. 'I am sorry, Kate. I've messed this hole up, haven't I?'

'Don't be silly!' Kate replied. 'We're playing a game. Together and that's what matters! So, stop apologising, remember.'

The Match was back to all square.

The fifteenth and sixteenth holes were halved and it was late afternoon as the foursome rounded the bend and walked out on to the seventeenth tee. There was no wind and the sun warmed their backs. No other golfers were in sight as David looked down into the gorge; down at the green far below. The gurgling trout stream emerged from the woods, sparkled and returned from whence it came amongst the trees.

'This must be heaven,' he said to Kate.

'Yes, it is, isn't it?'

'I wasn't just thinking of the golf.'

'No. Nor was I,' she smiled.

Having never played the seventeenth before, David had no idea how hard to hit his ball. But, he watched the

Brigadier carefully and both men landed safely on the recently restored putting surface. Two putts each and the hole was halved in three.

They climbed the long path up the other side of the gorge to the eighteenth tee. It was the final hole and the match remained all-square.

'Whatever happens, David. It's been a great match!' the Brigadier said.

From the ladies tee, Martha Tufnell drove her ball smoothly down the middle of the fairway. Position A1.

Kate, on the other hand, sliced her ball a long way to the right.

'Oh, dear,' she said. 'I'm so sor…'

'No apologising, remember,' David laughed. 'All I have to do now is hit the shot of a lifetime to halve the match!'

It was no exaggeration. The green lay nearly two hundred yards away. David knew he could make the distance with a three wood. However, the ball would have to carry about a hundred and seventy yards to clear the pond. The Brigadier, in the middle of the fairway, was only about a hundred and fifty yards from the flag.

'I could play safe,' David suggested. 'Hit it over towards the front of the green. We could hope Henry and Martha mess it up.'

'The way they're playing, I don't think there's much hope of that,' Kate suggested. 'Anyway, what's stopping you hitting it towards the flag?'

'I'm not that confident I can clear the water,' David replied.

'Well, you've got lots of balls, haven't you?' Kate said, with a grin.

'In my bag, maybe,' David laughed.

He looked at the shot again.

'OK, I'll give it a go!'

David took a few practice swings, trying to imprint the feeling of rhythm into his muscles and into his brain. Then, he addressed the ball and swung the club as smoothly as he could.

At first, David thought he hadn't hit the ball hard enough. Just for a moment, it seemed it would sink into the waters of the pond. But, it didn't. Instead, it landed on the top edge of the far bank, checked and came to rest on the green, some ten yards from the flag.

Suddenly, Kate was jumping up and down, hugging him and kissing his cheeks.

'That was fantastic, David! Absolutely fantastic,' she kept repeating. 'This has been such a wonderful day!'

'It's not over yet,' David said. He was thinking that the Brigadier might yet hit his approach shot close to the flag and win the hole, and the match.

'No, you're right,' she replied, quietly. 'The day isn't over, yet.'

The Brigadier wasn't able to produce any magic and he left his wife with a twelve-yard uphill putt to the flag.

With the match still evenly balanced, the four walked together up the fairway. As they did so, people began to emerge from the clubhouse and, by the time they had reached the green, quite a gallery had assembled.

The buzz of the crowd died as Martha Tufnell stood over her ball. Her putting action was as smooth as her golf swing.

Maybe the grass had grown a little since the morning, or perhaps there was dew on the turf late in the day. Whatever the reason, she didn't hit her putt hard enough and the ball came to a standstill some four feet short of the hole.

Martha Tufnell looked dejected as, her part in the proceedings over, she walked across to her trolley and replaced her putter.

'Not to worry, dear,' her husband said. 'I'll soon pop that in.'

The Brigadier placed a marker behind his ball, then picked it up and put it in his pocket.

Kate walked over to their ball. Between it and the hole, the green sloped steeply from right to left. She crouched down to get a better idea of the correct line and, as she did so, David stood beside her and placed his hand on her shoulder.

'I should aim about three feet out to the right.'

'OK,' she smiled up at him.

Kate struck the ball perfectly and its arcing trajectory brought it to a halt only six inches from the hole. So close, indeed, that a gasp ran through the encircling spectators.

The Brigadier conceded Kate and David's putt. They had scored a four and he now had to sink his putt to halve the match. He replaced his ball and removed his marker.

'That's OK, Henry,' David called out. 'Take it away!'

For a moment, the Brigadier hesitated. Then he realised; David had conceded his four-foot putt. The hole, and the match, were halved.

Most of the other competitors were by now around the green and they broke into spontaneous applause as the final four players shook hands, left the green and walked towards them. David had his arm around Kate's shoulder and she was smiling.

Some way behind them, the Brigadier said to his wife, over the noise. 'A great match, dear.'

'Yes, dear,' Martha replied. 'I think they are!'

3

The bar was crowded and noisy. More noisy than the Brigadier could ever remember, although he didn't seem concerned. He returned from the bar and handed round the drinks.

'Well, cheers, everybody,' he said, raising his glass. 'That was a very fine gesture, David.'

'What was that, Brigadier, er, Henry?'

'Conceding that four-foot putt on the last. It was quite a tester, I don't mind telling you.'

'We'd had a great match, Henry,' David replied. 'The lead changed hands three times. It would have been a shame for it to be lost with a missed putt on the eighteenth.'

'It was a wonderful match but, nevertheless, it was a very generous gimme,' the Brigadier repeated.

He took a sip from his tankard.

'That's what I don't understand about you, David.'

'What's that, Henry?'

'Well, you're an excellent golfer. And, a gesture like that shows that you're also a very fine sportsman.'

'Kind of you to say so, Brigadier.'

'So, why were you so keen to abandon all tradition, to change everything about the Club?

The Brigadier looked thoughtful. Then he went on.

'I mean, don't get me wrong. I accept now that everything you've done has been for the benefit of the Club. You've made an enormous impact, here.' He waved his arm at the room. 'The place is clearly thriving. But, I just wonder... I just wonder if it was so necessary to throw out all the tradition to achieve it.'

'But, I didn't, Henry,' David replied. 'And, conceding that putt just proves my point.'

He took a sip of his beer and thought for a moment.

'Golf is a great game, Henry. To you and me, perhaps, it's the greatest game. But, it's the game that is great, not all the stuff that has come to be associated with it. The exclusivity, the elitism and the snobbishness. Those things have nothing to do with golf itself, don't you see?'

'Perhaps,' the Brigadier conceded.

'When I came here, I found a wonderful golf course and a group of people who just wanted to keep it to themselves. Whereas, when I drove round the course, I just wanted every golfer to have the chance to play on it. Of course, I

343

know they can't all play here. But, a lot now can, and I believe the Club is better for it.'

'I think perhaps I see what you're getting at,' the Brigadier said, thoughtfully.

'What I'm getting at, Henry, is this. The people at this Club thought they were civilised and that, beyond the boundary fence, civilised standards disappeared. I hope the business with Kelham and Makrides helped dispel that myth.'

'Yes, quite,' Henry muttered.

'You see, Henry,' David went on. 'I believe it is not that civilised people play golf, but that golf civilises those who play it. The nature of the game, its rules and its etiquette, together these things encourage people to behave towards each other in a more civilised manner. We've already seen that with some of the newer members of the Club, wouldn't you agree?'

The old man sighed.

'I suppose you're right, David, but it's difficult to change long-cherished ideas when you get to my age.'

'Oh, I don't know,' David grinned. 'I gather you and Jimmy McGrath have a regular game these days?'

'Yes,' the Brigadier smiled. 'But, when you've been so involved in the affairs of the Club for so long, it is difficult simply to take a back seat and be an old golfer.'

'I can understand that,' David said. 'And so, I've had an idea. We're getting a lot of junior members in the Club now, as you know. Jack will teach them to play, that's not a problem. But, they need someone to get them organised, to arrange competitions, matches, that sort of thing.'

David grinned.

'Someone who, at the same time, can introduce them to all the civilising standards we've been talking about. I wondered if you would be willing to take it on?'

'Me?' the Brigadier looked astonished. 'Oh, I don't think the youngsters would want an old duffer like me around, really I don't.'

'I think you would do it very well. Honestly, I do. Why don't you have a think about it and talk it over with Jack, when he gets back next week?'

'What are you two talking about so earnestly?' Martha Tufnell asked as she sat down next to her husband. Kate took the seat next to David.

'We've just been looking at the scoreboard,' Martha explained. 'There's a lot of excitement about the final results.'

'It's been a wonderful day,' Kate said, smiling. 'I was wondering if you would all like to come back to the house for supper?'

'Oh, that's very kind of you, Kathryn...' the Brigadier began.

'But, we've got to get home, haven't we, Henry?' Martha interrupted. 'Come along, dear, we'd better be going.'

With much shaking of hands and kissing of cheeks, Martha and Henry Tufnell departed.

'What about you, David,' Kate said. 'Will you come back for supper?'

'I'd love to,' David replied. 'I've got to sort out some things here, first. Lock the money away, and so on. That'll take me about an hour, I should think.'

'OK,' Kate smiled. 'I'll go ahead and get things ready and you come over as soon as you can.'

4

There wasn't that much to do, really. It was just the ingrained feeling of responsibility, a relic of his days as a headmaster. Jimmy and Mike had the scoreboard organised and John Hall was looking after the money from the raffle.

345

David chatted for a few moments with various people in the bar. He laughed as he was obliged to hand over five pounds to Iverach McKay after the old reporter proudly explained how he'd hit his shot from the fifteenth fairway on to the fourteenth green.

Then, he went down to his office. David sat for a few minutes, the ticking clock keeping him company, and thought about all the changes of the past few months. The job, Margaret, his relationship with Ben, golf again.

And, Kate.

He closed his eyes and, for the first time, David felt that he wasn't any more an ex-headmaster or a bereaved husband. He wasn't a former anything. Instead, he was a golf club secretary and, perhaps, someone with a future.

After a while, he got up and went into the deserted changing rooms. The shower was warm and inviting and, when he was dry, he put on his favourite soft white cotton shirt and light chinos. It was only when he reached the car that he realised he didn't actually know where Kate lived. Returning to the office, he opened the filing cabinet and looked up her address in the membership file.

The cottage was large and rambling and stood alone in a country lane about two miles from the Club. As the car came to a halt on the gravel drive, Kate appeared at the front door. She, too, had changed and looked very inviting in her cotton summer dress.

'Hello,' she smiled, and she hugged him. 'Come on through.'

They sat for a while on the terrace and watched as the last of the sun sank below the trees.

'This is a lovely garden,' David said. As far as he could see from where he sat, the lawns ran to at least half an acre. Thick hedges and bushes enclosed them on all sides. Shrubs, bushes and trees gave the whole the feeling of a private park.

'I love it,' Kate replied. 'Come on, let's go for a walk.'

They picked up their wine glasses and walked round the garden. They ambled slowly, talking about many things. Their lives, their likes and dislikes, their hopes and fears.

Suddenly, Kate stopped.

'I must say,' she said. 'I was a bit miffed that you didn't tell me before the AGM about Kelham's plans. Phil Oakley and Giles knew, but I didn't. It was quite a surprise.'

'I am sorry, Kate,' David grinned. 'I just thought it would be safer if you didn't know. That way, if you were captured by the enemy and tortured, you wouldn't be able to give anything away.'

Kate punched him gently in the ribs.

'Oh, I see. It wouldn't matter if I were taken prisoner and tortured, only if I revealed all about your precious golf club!'

Actually, David had wanted it to be a surprise, for Kate as much as for everyone. Now, though, he wished he'd told her.

She took his hand.

'Seriously, David, there must be no secrets between us. After the business with James, I couldn't bear that.'

'Yes, I know,' he said. 'I promise. No more secrets.'

It was a beautiful summer's evening and they strolled on together in the garden for about half an hour. Kate explained the different plants and why or when she'd planted them. David pointed out plants he knew, but couldn't name.

After a while, she put her arm in his and they went on close together over the soft grass, past the conifers and the silver birches.

'It's getting a bit chilly,' Kate said. 'Time for another drink, I think. Let's go back to the house.'

She took his hand and led the way across the lawns, through the French windows and into the lounge.

Kate walked over to the cabinet and began to refill their glasses.

David came up behind her to watch and, as he did so, he put his hands round her waist and looked over her shoulder. In response, Kate pressed herself back against him and tipped her head to the side. David gently kissed the side of her neck.

'Mm, I wondered when you were going to get around to that,' Kate said, quietly.

David kissed her again and ran his hands up and over her body. She turned and looked up into his eyes.

'There's only one way a day like today can end, David.'

She kissed him softly on the lips and, as she pressed against him, Kate could feel that he was becoming aroused.

'I'm glad to see you've brought your clubs with you,' she whispered.

'Only my driver, I'm afraid!'

Together, they laughed. Then, she took his hand and led him out into the hall and across to the stairs.